IMPROBABLE FORTUNES

IMPROBABLE FORTUNES

a novel by

JEFFREY PRICE

ARCHER
New York ⟿ Los Angeles

A GENUINE ARCHER BOOK

ARCHER/RARE BIRD

601 West 26th Street · Suite 325 · New York · NY 10001
archerlit.com

FIRST HARDCOVER EDITION

Set in Minion
Printed in the United States

10 9 8 7 6 5 4 3 2 1

Publisher's Cataloging-in-Publication data

Names: Price, Jeffrey.
Title: Improbable fortunes: a novel / Jeffrey Price.
Description: First Hardcover edition | Los Angeles [California] ; New York [New York] : Archer/Rare Bird Books, 2016.
Identifiers: ISBN 978-1-941729-08-3.
Subjects: LCSH: Cowboys—Fiction | Mining—Fiction | Colorado—Fiction | BISAC: LITERARY/Fiction.
Classification: LCC PS3616.R5261 2016 | DDC 813.6—dc23.

For Jennie

PROLOGUE

BY MORNING, SEVERAL THEORIES would circulate Vanadium as to why their town had been destroyed. Vanadium's First Church of Thessalonians would put forth the notion that the Almighty had finally gotten around to clearing off His cluttered desk only to discover a stack of neglected outrages, perpetrated in these environs, so great as to demand His immediate retribution. Some of the standouts were the Spanish Conquistadors' introduction of Vanadium's first native inhabitants to slavery, small pox, and syphilis; the Mormons' massacre of the Utes; the range wars of the 1870s; the many murders over water, women, and the receipt for the uranium mined—not two miles from Vanadium's Main Street, that was expedited to Japan via the Enola Gay. The pagans in town believed their misfortune was caused by the Curse of the Utes—a hex put upon this land by shamans and trotted out whenever anything went wrong. But in the cold light of day, when everyone had settled down, they would come to the consensus that what had befallen them was simply because Marvin Mallomar, one of the richest men in the United States, had moved there from New York City and formed an unlikely friendship with a dim-witted local cowboy by the name of Buster McCaffrey.

It had been raining for seven days straight, and on this auspicious night, most of Vanadium's regulars would decide to "drink in" rather than venture into the wet. It was now 1:30. The neon light of the High Grade Bar switched off. The Busy Bees, the area's anarchistic motorcycle gang and Lame Horse County's largest manufacturers of methamphetamine, saddled up their Harleys and pulled out of the parking lot. Although business this evening was slow, the Busy Bees were up 9.5 percent for the second quarter. Their success was no accident, for Cookie Dominguez, the gang's leader, had modeled his sales and distribution system on an organization he much admired, that being the Mary Kay Cosmetics Company.

Here they came now, grim-faced and rain-slickered, throttling down Main Street heading back to their secure compound twenty miles to the west, giving the town one last defiant crankpin exhaust blast as they passed the town's proudly misspelled welcome sign suggesting that everyone: "Quit Your Damn Bellyachin' Your in Vanadium." As the Geiger Motel sign, with its neon Geiger counter needle that twitched from "vacancy" to "radioactive" shut off, the town was officially closed.

Two bug-encrusted sodium lights illuminating Main Street's convexly-graded stretch of black asphalt created the image of the back of a giant sperm whale skimming krill near the surface. Water, from gutters and downspouts, poured down both sides of the whale's spine—flushing its skin clean of cigarette butts, candy wrappers, dead cats, flattened blue jays, snuff spittle, and horse manure. This sluice was then hurried into Vanadium's storm drains and sent westerly into the San Miguel River. There, it descended two thousand feet into the valley where it took the Dolores' hand in muddy matrimony and poured through the slickrock canyons of Escalante—rolling like a marble along the linoleum floor of the Great Basin through Utah, Arizona, and Nevada, and out kitchen faucets where Vanadium's fulsome appellation was unwittingly quaffed by people in Los Angeles. At least, that's how people in Vanadium liked to think of it. Vanadians were, by way of geography and the fact that most of them were direct descendants of Butch Cassidy's Hole-in-the-Wall Gang, a naturally xenophobic and suspicious lot. This original outlaw breeding stock was attracted to the canyon in the 1890s for its remoteness and defensibility. Vanadium was miles from the railroad, the transportation of choice for Pinkerton agents—who were, by and large, city boys out of their depth chasing bandits in the backcountry on horseback. If Pinkertons, or any other kind of lawmen, were foolish enough to attempt a sortie on Vanadium, they would find themselves riding the gauntlet of its one steep road into town. The slow-climbing pace the incline demanded offered countless opportunities for boulders to be pushed from above and the children of outlaws to hone their marksmanship skills on live targets. The reputation of Vanadium as a dangerous and hard-to-get-to place stuck. For those living outside the law, Vanadium became the perfect place to raise a family—especially if the breadwinner was away most of the year robbing banks in the neighboring states or stealing cattle across the border in Old Mexico.

Generation after generation had struggled to live on this land—parts of it, beautiful. One might say this community existed much like its native bristlecone pine, which during long periods of drought, allowed itself to mostly die in order to keep alive a small, tiny ember of life until better circumstances presented themselves. For Vanadium and greater Lame Horse County, desiccated and exhausted from years of poor land management and cattle ranching, toxic from reckless mineral mining, that life-saving ember came to them in the form of the atomic bomb. Uranium was everywhere in the hills surrounding Vanadium, and the US government along with its proxy, the Atomic Mines Corporation, wanted as much of it as they could get. And so began Vanadium's "go-go" years starting with the US Atomic

Energy Act of 1946. One need only visit the town's salvage yard to identify Vanadium's outlandish prosperity in those years: impractical DeSotos, Cadillac Eldorados, Studebaker Hawks, Buick "Deuce-and-a-Quarters," stacked one atop each other. And these were only the ones that escaped the bank. Old timers would say it was the one-two punch of the 1982 Start Treaty followed by the accident at Three Mile Island that turned off the bubble machine forcing Atomic Mines to shutter its facility. Vanadium let itself slowly die for twenty years. Then, Marvin Mallomar came to town.

The mud-filled clocks, retrieved in the aftermath of the flood, were in general agreement that it was 2:34 when all hell broke loose. It started with an explosion above the town, muffled by the rain and lightning. A few moments later, there was the horrible sound of trees cracking and boulders thundering as a giant wave of red mud and rocks came crashing down Piñon Street, taking a hard left onto Main. The lava went in and out of escrow at the town's newly installed Vanadium Premier Properties—smashing its contrived western storefront. It flattened Nature's Grains Whole Foods, which, until Mallomar came here, had been the Feed and Saddle Shop. It pushed his Einstein's News and Books off its slab and sent it hydroplaning westerly down the street toward Utah—where some of Professor Einstein's ideas were first tested underground. It pushed the meat freezers from Lugar's Prime Meats out the front of the store and sent them careening through Boho Coffee and Poet's Corner—which used to be El Cid's Guns before Mallomar arrived—scouring all the books containing the answers to how the planet might be saved, while grabbing hundreds of pounds of gourmet roasted coffee beans, kneading and folding them into the moving brown meringue that already contained similar-looking deer and elk feces. All of Main Street was suddenly moving. A parked car, obediently waiting for its owner to consummate his assignation at the Geiger Motel, was carried away. A dead horse, with its legs up in the air, was swept past the Rodeo Arena—where perhaps it had seen better days. And then a man came moving by. Fighting the muddy undertow, he held an arm up in the air as if calling for help from a lifeguard on a beach in the Hamptons. Then, he too, was gone.

The Vanadium Volunteer Fire Department had been the First Responders. Most of the men were either drunk or hungover when they climbed aboard the two old fire engines that sallied forth into town. By the time Sheriff Shep Dudival showed up, the wheels of social order were already coming off. There was much shouting, obscenity tossing, and blaming. The sheriff stood tight-lipped as he witnessed two volunteer firemen fighting over a five-thousand-dollar Rancilio Epoca Italian espresso maker that they had salvaged from the mud. It was the sheriff's experience that men often became unglued in the face of an overwhelming task. The cleanup would certainly qualify as that. Authority needed to be established quickly. He let the men see him as he walked to the edge of the mud field and lit a generic cigarette. He wanted to provide the two looters an opportunity to relinquish the espresso maker and regain their self-respect.

Down Main Street, the sheriff could see the hooves of the dead, upside-down horse heading west toward Egnar. A pickup truck was stopping for a naked hitchhiker covered with mud. *Lucky sonofabitch,* the sheriff mused to himself, *some drunk that just missed being swept away.* He turned his attention back to the looting firemen who, disappointingly, were not deterred by his presence. They were still squabbling over the booty. The sheriff walked calmly to the first man and kneed him in the vastus lateralis—the "Charlie Horse" muscle as it's called in schoolyards. He slapped the other man in the Adam's apple. Both men doubled over in pain and quickly relinquished the espresso machine—letting it drop into the arms of the moving mud.

There was some muttering under breath, but nobody had the guts to take it further.

Despite Main Street being a complete disaster, there would be no help from FEMA. There would be no help from the governor in the form of road crews, nor the National Guard, or building loans. There would be no speeches from the president about how all our thoughts and prayers were with the people of Vanadium. The shuttering of Vanadium's once strategic industry, the Atomic Mine, had reduced them to the invisible status of any small western town with a population of three hundred and sixty-seven. But then, Vanadians would never want the damn government, anyway.

The sheriff would probably be calling the high school principal later in the morning asking if he needed any dirt for the new ball field. The larger ranchers could be called upon for heavy equipment. Vanadium could supply the dump trucks. A full day—maybe two—and the road would be open to traffic. But where exactly had the mud come from? That was the plate of beans in front of the sheriff now. As he peered through the rain, he coolly reverse-engineered the mud's path. His eyes tracked up Main Street to Piñon to the top of Lame Horse Mesa. He thought for a moment, then flipped his cigarette into the mud. Some men had just arrived with a Caterpillar D9. "Hey, can you fellas get me up to the Mallomar place?"

It was dawn by the time they cleared the road well enough for a rescue team to get to Mallomar's Big Dog Ranch. The rain, at this higher elevation, was coming down as stinging cornsnow. The sheriff let it gather on his eyebrows as he squinted at the jumble of aged Montana logs, glass, steel, and broken furniture that had once been the forty-thousand-square-foot residence of Mr. and Mrs. Marvin Mallomar. It was just last April that it had been on the cover of *Architectural Digest*. Mallomar's French architect boasted that there were more steel I-beams used in the construction of this house than the new American Embassy that he had recently completed in Dubai. And yet, the mud had gone through the reinforced Adirondack/Frank Lloyd Wright-style edifice as easily as a black bear going through a screen door. The once magnificent lodge now looked ridiculous—its massive Corten roof having accordioned down on itself like a clown's top hat.

One hundred yards away, a late model Audi Q7 and a black Mercedes AMG could be seen standing nose down in the mud, their rear ends sticking up in the air like ducks feeding on a pond. When the sheriff ran the plates, he came up with what he already knew. The cars belonged to Dana and Marvin Mallomar. Mallomar was often out of town on business. When he was, Dana, his young and beautiful wife, was left at the ranch with the twenty-one-year-old foreman, Buster McCaffrey. There had been rumors in town about their relationship, but gossip held no interest for the sheriff unless it helped him solve a crime. Right now, he was hoping no one had been at home when this happened. An ambulance was ordered anyway. Sheriff Dudival hiked up the hill following the mudslide. On a flat bench above the house was an emptied reservoir. Everyone in town had made fun of Buster McCaffrey for bringing a douser to the property to find water to fill a reservoir above the house, but dammit if he hadn't done it. Unfortunately, for some reason, the levee had failed and let loose twenty acres of water on the residence and the town below. Several hours later, with the help of two bulldozers and a Bobcat, they uncovered the wrought iron front door. It was pinched shut from the weight bearing on it. Four men put their shoulders to it, but it wouldn't budge. A bulldozer was suggested, but they didn't want to do any more violence to the house for fear of further cave in. One of the men eagerly suggested using his acetylene torch that he had brought with him in the back of his truck. Another man suggested placing hydraulic jacks on either side of the door to take the pressure off the jams. The sheriff considered both ideas and went with the hydraulic jacks. This caused the acetylene torch man to throw his shovel and stomp off in a fit of pique. People in this part of the country typically carried odd things in the backs of their trucks for years in the hope of one day using them in a heroic and manly fashion. So, one can only understand the man's frustration, being so close to finally using his equipment—only to be edged out at the finish line.

The jacks were installed and everyone eagerly gathered around the door for the big question: were there any dead people inside? The sheriff was well aware of the Volunteer Workers' Dark Little Secret: in exchange for having to get up in the middle of the night to ride on the back of the fire engine or drive the Emergency Medical Technician Ambulance two hours to Grand Junction, they got to witness only what doctors, police, and priests were allowed to see. The Burned Beyond Recognition, The Head That Went Through the Windshield and Rolled a Hundred Yards Down the Road, The Blue Teenagers' Bodies Pulled From the Frozen Pond, and The Surprised Expression on The Man's Face Whose Wife Spotted His Car in the Parking Lot of the Geiger Motel and Shot Him With His Own Elk Rifle. The sheriff always figured that voyeurism had something to do with this volunteer business. That's why he never prevented the men from having a good eyeful before body-bagging the victims.

The sheriff nodded to one of the two young men standing by the door to go ahead and open it. Cautiously, he turned the handle. The door swung open surprisingly easy. So far, so good. Then suddenly a three-year-old Galloway steer, wide-eyed with fear, mucous blowing from its nostrils, came charging through the doorway, trampling the men.

"Shit!"

"Jesus Christ!"

"Goddammit!"

And again, another "Shit!"

After the initial astonishment had passed, the men, of course, said "shit" and "goddammit" a few more times then laughed to relieve the tension and embarrassment of being frightened in front of one another. Finally recomposed, they turned on their Petzl headlamps and tentatively entered the breech once more. No sooner did they take their first step into the darkened shaft that another steer bolted out at them. And then another, and another, until forty-nine by the sheriff's count had blasted past them—shitting themselves with fear.

There's a detail for the journal, the sheriff thought to himself.

Now, no one seemed quite so eager to go back into the house. Who wanted to risk having their ribs broken by a six-hundred-pound animal trapped in the dark? There was a metallic clanking of Zippos as they lit up cigarettes to mull this over. Suddenly there was a voice behind them.

"Howdy, boys."

Everyone slowly turned to see a tall, skinny cowboy squinting into the daylight from the doorway. The buckle of his belt was missing, and his pants were half undone. In his arms was a semi-conscious woman in her thirties, raven-haired and as beautiful as a movie star.

"Well, goddamn…it's Buster."

"Crap," said the sheriff as he threw his latest generic cigarette down into the mud.

Buster McCaffrey smiled sheepishly, and even a half a smile was something to behold. Tall and thin as a stretch of barbed wire, his teeth were as big as a horse's—big enough to accommodate Eskimo scrimshaw of Whale Hunting in the Bering Sea—and freckles formed a saddle over the bridge of his wad-of-bubblegum nose. His hair was reddish and fanned around his small jug ears like twists of dried hay. Above each eye was a brow bent like a piece of angle iron in permanent amazement. Taken separately, his characteristics would seem odd, one might even say freakish. And yet, gathered all together, his appearance, for some reason, comforted people. If you asked them why this was so, no one could ever say. But whether they realized it or not, Buster subconsciously reminded people of Howdy Doody.

"Hey, uh…some mess, huh?"

The men turned their attention to the woman in his arms. She was wearing black satin cargo pants and a somewhat soiled white top that provided a gauzy view of her nipples. Clutched in her hand was a piece of black metal.

"What's that there she got, Buster?"

Buster looked down to see what the fellow was referring to.

"Ah b'lieve that's a burner from that ol' Vikin' stove top. She was diggin' in the mud with it."

"Mrs. Mallomar?" said the sheriff.

Mrs. Mallomar just looked at him blankly. Buster jiggled her to get her to respond.

"Uh, you r'member the sheriff, doncha, ma'am?"

When she still didn't speak, Buster winked to the head Emergency Medical Technician on the job. "Ah think she's gonna need some *seein'* to." The EMT nodded with tacit understanding. It would actually take the better part of four months before anybody understood the half of what had transpired in this house.

The EMTs came forward to relieve Buster of Mrs. Mallomar, but she clung even tighter to his neck.

"No, I'm staying with him!"

Everyone looked back to Buster. He visibly blushed, knowing that none of Mrs. Mallomar's antics were being lost on the sheriff. Buster, trying his best to avoid the sheriff's eyes, turned to Mrs. Mallomar, cajoling.

"They're jes' gonna take ya down to the clinic and check ya out, ma'am. Ain't that right, fellers?"

"That's right, ma'am," one of them said to Mrs. Mallomar's bosom.

Now came the hard part. Buster pried Mrs. Mallomar's fingers from his neck and tried to pass her over to the EMTs, who, by this time, had a stretcher with restraining straps waiting. Mrs. Mallomar, obviously disoriented by the ordeal of the last six hours, resisted their help with punches and kicks as well as a jazz-scat stream of profanity—the verbal thrust of which dealt mostly with different forms of sodomy.

Buster waited out her solo and then said, "It's all right, ma'am. They'll be nice to you down there. We're jes' gonna put this back, ma'am," and gently pulled her fingers from the stovetop burner. "We're done with our diggin' fer now."

"No, please!"

"Ma'am, it's for the best."

"Ow, my god! What was that?"

A female EMT had surreptitiously brought a syringe from the vehicle and plunged fifteen milligrams of Versed into Mrs. Mallomar's exposed left buttock as the others wrestled her onto the gurney.

"It's just a little something to help you relax."

"But you didn't even ask me if I was allergic to anything!"

"*Are* you allergic to anything?" the EMT said, a little late in the game.

"Why don't we just see if I go into cardiac arrest, you stupid bitch?" Even in her weakened state, Mrs. Mallomar was formidable. Buster tried to be helpful.

"Uh, did ah mention…she ain't allowed to have nuthin' with wheat in it," Buster said.

It seemed like an eternity—with the sheriff staring a hole in him—before Mrs. Mallomar was stowed into the ambulance. Buster shook his head and blew a low whistle.

"Jiminy, look at that house!" Buster said. The sheriff was still silent. "I guess you're pretty disserpointed with me right now, ain'tcha?"

"Buster..." The sheriff began to say something, but stopped when he noticed two of his deputies eavesdropping.

"Don't you have something to investigate?" the sheriff barked. They snorted insolently and sauntered away.

"What's there to investigate? The house jes'...done fell down," Buster said nervously. The sheriff sighed like the last of the air from a flat tire.

"Buster, I'm gonna have to ask you a few questions."

Buster scraped the helix of his right ear with his little finger and scrutinized what had accumulated under his fingernail.

"Shoot."

"Where's the mister?"

"Uh, ain't he with you?"

"No, he is not."

"Maybe he drove hisself away."

"His car's still here."

"It is?"

"It is."

The sheriff studied Buster's face as it momentarily clouded with that new piece of information.

"Is he in that house somewhere?"

"Ah don't rightly think so. Ah b'lieve he left the house."

"You'd tell me if anything had happened to Mr. Mallomar..."

"Ah know what yor thinkin', Sheriff. All's ah can tell you is he was fine last time ah seen him."

"And when was that?"

"Las' night."

"Last night. He came home last night and you were here in the house with his missus?" Buster squirmed at the implication.

"Well, sir. Ah *were* in the house tryin' to get them cattle out." This, to Buster, was the big news of the evening—that a herd of cattle had actually been inside a house. "Did y'all see 'em?"

"Musta been 'bout fifty head in there," one of the rescue men answered convivially, but slunk away when the sheriff glowered at him.

One of the deputies emerged from the house, wiggle-waggling something above his head.

"Mr. Mallomar's wallet!"

The rescue workers were now watching the sheriff's reactions. As far as they were concerned, there was enough evidence to hang the foreman.

"Do you know why Mr. Mallomar would leave the house without his wallet or his car?" Buster scratched his head, cogitating on that.

"It's a booger, Sheriff."

"Yes, it certainly is a booger."

The sheriff led Buster further away from the others.

"Remember what we always said about lying?"

"Yes, sir."

"Were you having sexual relations with Mrs. Mallomar?"

Even Buster, who had never read a newspaper in his life, knew how much trouble a former president of the United States had gotten into with this question, and how better off the president would have been by just telling the truth. But now, when it came time to his turn at bat, he, also, looked for the same nuance of language to hide behind. Unfortunately, he lacked the language skills to pull it off.

"Ah ain't at liberty to say," he offered weakly.

"Why not?"

Another man came through the doorway holding a rope that had been fashioned into a noose. Once again, the sheriff turned to Buster.

"What's this?"

Buster looked at it every which way—as if seeing a rope for the first time in his life.

"Lord, if ah know. It's got kinda a loop on the end of it."

"It's called a *noose*!" Buster flinched. "Why would they have a noose just laying around the house?"

Buster took a deep breath.

"Ah ain't at liberty to say."

"You ain't at liberty to say? Where'd you get this kind of talk?"

"That's what Mr. Mallomar used to say when he dint wanna tell somebody somethin'," Buster said glumly.

"*Used* to say?"

"Says. That's what he says all the time and ah guess ah took it up."

"I'm sure Mr. Mallomar is gratified with the results of his mentorship. That is, if he's not laying dead under that heap of a house over there." The men were all waiting for this conversation to conclude in the only way it could.

"Buster, I got no choice but to take you in."

"Aw, but Sheriff, ah ain't killed nobody…"

"That's what he always says," someone muttered.

"Turn around. I'll have to cuff you." Buster almost burst out in tears, but complied docilely. As the sheriff escorted him to the back of his cruiser, Buster called out to the diggers.

"Hey, fellers, keep an eye out for my ro-day-oh buckle, will ya?"

Sheriff Dudival pushed his head down to fold him into the back seat.

"Buster, that's the least of your damn problems."

ஐ

DOWN AT BOOKING, THE corrections officers gave Buster a more thorough pat down. Then they fingerprinted him, photographed him, and collected his personal effects. He surrendered a bag of Bugler with some rolling papers, the keys to his Chevy Apache truck, his lucky Ute arrowhead, and his Colorado State Fair wallet with four dollars in it. The corrections officer looked up and smirked when he found a dried buttercup pressed between his social security card and an unpaid parking ticket. He was told to unstring the shoelaces from his manure-covered White's Packers so they couldn't be used to commit suicide. They took his hat. They gave him an orange county uniform and a towel, and then led him to lockup.

Someone, probably the sheriff, had sent down orders that Buster be put in the "suicide watch" cell. It was brightly lit with a big porthole-like window that faced the correction officer's desk so he could keep a constant eye on him. Buster sat on his bunk and looked around his new digs. The toilet was a one-piece stainless steel job, as was the sink. There was no mirror and, worse, no window. Was it possible for someone who had spent his entire life outside to survive the rest of it inside? He could already feel his strength ebbing. He would surely die if he couldn't be out under the sky. That is, if they didn't execute him first.

Buster sighed and looked at his hands. They were as big as Rawlins baseball gloves and just as broken in. What made him think he could make his way in the world with his brain instead of these? Probably Mr. Mallomar. He was always overvaluing, pumping things up. Maybe his friends had been right when they'd told him not to get mixed up with people like the Mallomars. There was going to be plenty of time for regret. He wasn't going anywhere. In his mind, he began to flip through the stupid events leading up to this—as if they were the embarrassing red-eyed snapshots the sober person always takes of the drunks at a party.

Dudival stormed past Janet Poult, his secretary, who'd already heard what had happened at the Mallomar ranch on the police scanner, and slammed his office door behind him without even a "howdy-do."

He sat at his desk and rubbed his face with tedium and aggravation. Under the harsh florescent light, his face was a craggy composite of avalanche chutes, scree slopes, and deeply cut drainages, the result of forty years of wearing a badge in Lame Horse County. When he opened his eyes he saw that his lunch had been brought in—a paper plate of beef taquitos that Mrs. Tejera, the cook at the High Grade, had made especially for him. White fat had begun to congeal at its borders—the chalk outline of a murder victim on a sidewalk. Dudival knew that she was an illegal but left her alone. Vanadium couldn't afford to have their best Mexican cook sent back to Chihuahua. She made chicken mole from scratch, and he would be damned if he'd send her packing. As the highest ranking elected official in the county, it was the privilege of the sheriff's office—a precedent set by his predecessor Sheriff Morgan—to adjudicate most matters himself, without the help of judges or outsiders. But what he could do for Buster?

Having no appetite, he threw his lunch in the trash and unlocked the top drawer of his desk removing his private journal. He opened it from the beginning and read in his own faded handwriting the narrative that he began recording over twenty years ago.

PART ONE

CHAPTER ONE

Native Son

According to town lore, Buster McCaffrey was born on New Year's Day. His mother, a slight nineteen-year-old Mormon girl from Monticello, Utah, left her folks to run off with a Jack Mormon—one who had lapsed in his faith and broken from the church. McCaffrey *père* was said to have worked for the Atomic Mines Corporation. This was 1987 and by then the mine was over forty-five years old—requiring the miners to go down two thousand feet to work a seam. Sheriff Dudival was never able to gather a complete picture of the man. Some said he claimed to have worked at the famous Eldorado uranium mine in Canada. Because of this experience, management put him on a jackleg percussion drill. A co-worker vaguely remembered a guy named Tom McCaffrey as a complainer, that he hadn't been on the job more than a week before he started saying the mine tunnels were narrower than what he was used to up in Canada—and the place was giving him claustrophobia. One of the muckers—the people assigned to slushing the blasted rock and ore from the stopes and bringing them up the chutes to the main haulage-way—remembered a new guy, he believed his name was McCaffrey, being assigned to a miniature diesel bulldozer—six feet long and four feet wide. The muckers were paid less than drillers, but on the bright side, they got to sit on their asses all day. One of the old timers said he recalled a story about a guy—was it McCaffrey?—asleep on his dozer, not fifty feet from where the blasting crew put a charge of Tovex in the hole. After the blast, this fellow, McCaffrey, had the brass to tell the supervisor that fumes from his diesel had stultified him. He blamed the Atomic Mines Corporation's lack of proper ventilation, once again citing the Eldorado Mine in Canada as the paragon of mining procedure. Management asked Sheriff Dudival to run a background check on him. When it came back, Sheriff Dudival said that McCaffrey wasn't who he said he was. There had never been a McCaffrey on the payroll at the Eldorado Mine in Canada and his Social didn't match. Concerned that he might be a troublemaker or a rank malingerer angling for a free ride on Workmen's Comp, the Atomic Mines people instructed Sheriff Dudival to escort him off the property.

Dudival recorded in his journal that he waited for him at the main gate the next morning, but McCaffrey never turned up for work. He learned that McCaffrey and his wife had bought a little piece of land up on Lame Horse Mesa—this was when you could still get it for cow pies—and headed over there to tell him he was fired for falsifying his application.

He found the McCaffreys living in an abandoned sheepherder's wagon. Sheriff Dudival knocked on the tiny, rickety door. This missus came out and said McCaffrey was gone.

"Where did he go?"

"Didn't they tell you?" she said, tearing up.

According to Sheriff Dudival, Mrs. McCaffrey broke down and said that her husband had come home from work the day before with bad news. There had been an accident at the mine. He had been exposed to a deadly level of radiation.

She said the doctor at the mine gave her husband one week to live. Even worse, he said there was a 90-percent chance he would contaminate their unborn child if he were to stay with them—in as close quarters as theirs. She suggested that they move, and get a second doctor's opinion, but he wouldn't hear of it. There was no time, or money. No, the only thing for him to do, in everyone's best interest, was to leave. Were any of the other men exposed as he was? No, he said. But then, none of the other men had stood up to the Corporation and complained about the unsafe mining conditions, either. Had management tried to kill him? Who knows? I'm dead anyway, he answered. He asked that she put a change of his clothes in his rucksack and hand it to him through the window with some of the money from the coffee can. With much hand wringing and tears, off he went to die at the Miners' Hospice in Grand Junction.

After telling the tragedy to Sheriff Dudival, she apologized for not offering him a cup of tea or coffee and asked why he had driven all the way out there. Dudival was momentarily flummoxed. There was no use, at this point, telling her that her husband had been fired. He excused himself saying that there was something in the patrol car that Atomic had asked that he give her. Sheriff Dudival had just been to the First Bank of Vanadium exchanging parking meter coins for paper money. He put the bills in a plain envelope and wrote "Atomic Mine—McCaffrey" on the front of it.

"He left without collecting this," he said. "Good luck to you, little lady."

He handed over the money and left.

The night the baby came, the Mormon girl was alone. Even if there had been a phone in the creaky sheepherder's wagon, there was no one she knew to call.

Confident from her experience as midwife to countless kittens and cattle born on her parents' Utah farm, she went into labor at four in the afternoon. Calmly, she boiled some water and prepared clean rags for swaddling. Things went smoothly at first. She dilated. Buster's head began to appear, albeit painfully. From the mother's perspective, the baby's skull was as large as a Hopi dancing gourd, and his shoulders were as broad as the front quarters of a spring lamb. She bore down. She squatted. She used imagery—pretending he was a stubborn piece of sourdough that needed rolling out with a rolling pin. Dithered, she even tried pulling him out by his ears. But he was just too big—a "buster," as it were. Six long hours later, labor ground to a halt, with the baby hanging halfway out. To complicate matters, a storm had moved in and had blown four-foot snowdrifts across the mesa. Buster's mother decided to go for help. She put on her overcoat and headed for the highway walking bow-legged through the snow, with Buster hanging upside-down from her body, swinging between her legs like the clapper of a church bell.

Fortunately, Buster's mother was young and strong enough to plow through the snow and climb three barbed-wire fences. There had been much conjecture in later years as to whether this had a bearing on Buster's lagging mental development. Being introduced to the world upside down for such an extended amount of time must have had an adverse effect on him, everyone said—not least because of the life-long scar that ran along the medial section of his skull, from when mama didn't quite clear that last barbed wire fence at the highway.

It was the cowboy, Jimmy Bayles Morgan, the only one in town sober on New Year's Eve, who stopped to help her. Vanadium's sole doctor had recently had his medical license revoked. The closest hospital was one hundred and twenty miles away. The mother had lost too much blood already, and there was no time to be delicate about it. Jimmy was forced to make a decision that even a doctor would have been reluctant to make. In the back of his pickup were chains for delivering breach-birthed colts. And so, Buster McCaffrey was yanked roughly into this world, and his mother left it less than an hour later. That's how the sheriff recorded it in his journal. Jimmy, not knowing what else to do with this gigantic baby, wrapped him in a horse blanket and drove him and the body of the dead mother to the only place that was open that night, the sheriff's office.

Sheriff Dudival called Janet Poult and told her to get down to the jail immediately to do some emergency nursing. She had just had her fourth child. Her breasts were huge and still filled with milk. So much did she lactate that the sheriff's Half 'n' Half and Dr. Peppers were forced off the shelves of the office refrigerator and replaced with Ball jars filled with her breast-pumped over-production. Before long, Dudival was able to track down Buster's mother's family but they'd wanted no part of him. His mother had been shunned. To her kin, she no longer existed; therefore, Buster didn't exist, either. That's how the sheriff recorded it. The only thing left was to give the girl a proper burial. The county paid for the service and named Buster a ward of the court.

Jimmy Bayles Morgan wanted to keep him for his own, but the Women's League of Vanadium would not hear of it. Buster was no stray calf, dog, or crippled chipmunk that had limped into cow camp. He was a human being, they said, and more importantly a Christian—despite his dubious pedigree. Besides, Jimmy Bayles Morgan was a rough character and a blasphemer to boot. And so, the town set out to find Buster a good Christian home.

CHAPTER TWO

Adopted by the Dominguez Family

BUSTER'S MOTHER WAS BURIED on a sunny January day at the Lone Cone Cemetery. The storm that caused her death was long gone. In fact, all the roadside snow had already melted, and it now looked as if the storm had never happened. Mrs. Poult brought Buster to say a final goodbye before showing him off to local prospects for adoption. Serving as Official Breast Feeder was beginning to show its wear and tear on poor Mrs. Poult. It was virtually impossible to get Buster to give up a sore nipple once he had clamped on. Mrs. Poult would be forced to pinch Buster's nostrils together making him gag for air while she switched him off to the auxiliary. Once, when she had fallen asleep while nursing, she awoke to discover the breast that Buster had been suckling had been reduced to the size of a zucchini, while the other one was still the size of a 4-H winning eggplant.

After the last shovelful of dirt had been thrown on his mother's coffin, Buster was passed around to interested parties. Everyone agreed that he was a nicely behaved baby of sanguine temperament. Jimmy Morgan looked on grumpily as Edita Dominguez held Buster over her head and jiggled him until a long strand of drool ran from his mouth down onto the head of her eldest son, ten-year-old Cookie. From the expression on his face, one could gather that he was none too happy to acquire a new brother, although perhaps it was too soon—it had been only three months since his last baby brother suffocated mysteriously in his crib. Mrs. Dominguez, on the other hand, was thrilled to tears as she hugged Buster and looked entreatingly to the Vanadium Women's League for approval. They gave it.

Mrs. Dominguez was a Cantante. The Cantantes were a famous Hispanic family who, some people said, lived in Vanadium before the Indians used the area as a respite from the brain-cooking heat of Sleeping Ute Mountain. When the whites came, the Cantantes were able to coexist peaceably with them because they had nothing the whites wanted. The Cantantes did not compete with them for grazing land, for they raised no cattle. Nor were they involved in the early contretemps between the cattlemen and the sheep men, for they herded no sheep. They already had a trade—one that had been passed down through generations. They were tile makers. Their work could still be found on every countertop and in every restroom in Vanadium. They manufactured their products at their ten-acre homestead and were particularly famous in tile circles for their "Negrita," a small black octagon which received its distinctive lustrous ebony patina by way of a long-held family secret: the tiles were kilned under layers of sheep manure.

The Cantantes were the first Vanadians to keep books and have a bank account. During the Great Depression, they were the first to supply food and clothes to the needy, even to the Indians. The

Cantantes were the first to use a lawyer instead of arson and firearms to resolve a business conflict, the first to suggest a tax to provide schooling for Vanadian children, and the first to suggest having a lawman who was responsible for keeping the peace in the town.

Edita Cantante was the first woman to be elected President of the Vanadian Rotary. She was also the head of the PTA and the Library Association. To their faces, the Cantantes were respected. But to their backs, Vanadians distrusted them. They were suspicious of their success and their ability to handle money. Some people said the Cantantes were Maranos—secret Jews hiding from the Spanish Inquisition—in spite of the fact that they wore conspicuous crucifixes and attended Catholic mass three times a week. That's why the family always felt they had to try a little harder. They drew the line, however, with the first serious man to court their eldest daughter, Edita Theresa, Buster's new mother.

Carlito Dominguez had been a drifter and a small town Romeo when he met the zaftig and serious-minded Edita. He was quick to size up her family's influence in the area. Likewise, her father, Jorge and his brother, Guillermo, were quick to size him up as a loser devalued further by the mestizo cast to his features. Needless to say, they disapproved of the match.

"Edita," they said. "You don't have to marry the first man you meet."

"Why not?"

Why not, indeed? After all, who was she to meet in this county of Anglos and Indians? Dominguez was the first Hispanic to come to Vanadium in a long time. There was no telling when the next one would breeze through in an emerald AMC Gremlin. In the end, her family would be worn down by her mopiness and her silence around the dinner table. They agreed to let them marry. Despite their nagging reservations, they took Dominguez in and taught him the family business. Then he was found, soon after the nuptials, drunk at the High Grade, Vanadium's only café and bar, bragging about how much money his new family had. Guillermo Cantante, Edita's uncle, dosed Dominguez' tequila with a maggot he had harvested from a two week-old road kill. That night, Dominguez ran a fever of one hundred and seven degrees and dry-vomited and shat for eleven hours straight. When the concerned Edita stepped out of the room to empty his chamber pot, Carlito was given some friendly advice. He was told he was never to drink and talk about the family's money again. After that, he didn't. And when Carlito was found having an affair at the Geiger Motel with a divorcée who worked at the cooling and heating store, once again, Uncle Guillermo stepped in. A large and powerfully built man, he grabbed Dominguez through the window of his truck before he could pull out of the parking lot and drove him to a far out location on Lame Horse Mesa. There, Guillermo staked him five feet from a red ants' nest and painted his genitalia with clover honey. When Guillermo returned three hours later after meeting friends in town for coffee, Dominguez's bitten member had already swollen to the size and color of a Chinese Emperor's coy. Once again, Uncle Guillermo gave him some friendly advice. Don't be unfaithful to Edita. After that, he wasn't. Years passed, and the old Cantantes eventually died off leaving Dominguez as head of the family. His ascension to the tile throne was soured by a daily reminder of his treatment at the hands of the Cantantes. His son Cookie, by some cruel genetic twist of fate, had grown into the spitting image of his old nemesis, Guillermo Cantante.

Enter Buster. He went from being an orphan to the center of attention with his three brothers and two sisters. Cookie, the eldest, did not take part in the joy of having a new baby in the family. Instead, he observed from the shadows. While technically still a child, Cookie already had the personality of a dyspeptic adult soured on the world. He was scary-looking to begin with. Even before he got diabetes, even before he was on his own and became bloated and puffy from alcohol, cheese sticks, and TV trays of Banquet fried chicken, his eyes—two malevolent drips of Bosco—looked swollen shut in a wince of unspeakable pain; pain that, when the time was right, Cookie Dominguez would make sure the world came up with the balance due.

One day, completely out of the blue, Cookie asked sweetly if he could feed the baby. Edita was heartened by his, request—pleased that Cookie had finally accepted his new little brother. Patiently, she instructed Cookie on how to lift Buster into his high chair, how to tie the bib around his neck, and make up his little food tray with a little dab of mashed peas, apple sauce, and pureed carrots, and how much food he should put on the spoon. Then she put the spoon in Cookie's hand and stood back with her hands on her hips waiting for Cookie to begin. He put the spoon down.

"What's wrong?" She said.

"I want to feed him by myself."

"Can't I stand here and watch, *bollito*?"

"No."

"Why not?"

"I want to be alone with him."

Edita hesitated. Her initial reflex was to say no, the loss of her last baby still haunting her.

"Well, what's it gonna be?" Cookie said, "I don't have all day."

But then, she thought, perhaps it was time to lay her fears to rest.

"All right, Cookie. If you think you can do it by yourself. I'll be in the next room."

He waited with his hands at his sides until she left. Edita stood and listened before setting to work at the ironing board where a three-foot pile of Dominguez's shirts awaited. She turned off the iron's steam function to better hear. It was quiet in the next room, so she began to iron. A few minutes had passed when she thought she heard a choking sound. Or was it a baby chortling? She stopped and cocked an ear. No, that was choking! She threw the iron down and ran to the kitchen where she saw Buster, red-faced and desperate, trying to put his fingers in his mouth to clear his throat. His brother, meanwhile, sat impassively across from him, doing nothing. Edita pushed Cookie out of the way and quickly yanked Buster from his highchair, laid his stomach across her knees and began pounding his back. No good. She sat him up and performed what she could remember of the Heimlich maneuver that she had seen in a restaurant. Two violent contractions of her fists in Buster's solar plexus sent the obstruction flying from his windpipe across the room where it smacked against the wall. Now being able to breathe, Buster managed a laugh and playfully reached lovingly for his brother's face, but Edita held him tightly to her hip. At first glance, the object that Edita found near the wall, looked to be a Hershey's Kiss. In that scenario, Cookie, out of affection for his brother, imprudently gave him a piece of hard-to-swallow candy. On closer examination, however, the object in question turned out to be a moving piece from the family's popular board game.

"*Sorry*," Cookie taunted as if playing the game.

"How did he get this?" Edita demanded.

"How the fuck should I know?"

Edita, slapped him so hard she turned his face sideways like a movie stuntman's.

"Can I give him a bath?"

"Go to your room!"

How was it possible? All of her children were raised the same way, given the same amount of attention and yet, while the others were thoughtful and obedient, helpful around the house—even talking about the colleges they wanted to attend some day—Cookie was pen pals with a man by the name of Richard Ramirez—who, Edita later learned, was a serial killer on San Quentin's death row.

She expressed her misgivings regarding Cookie's moral turpitude to her husband, since he spent more time alone with Cookie than anyone else.

"*Entender algo.* I am not his father. His father is the Devil."

It was clear that Buster's security would rest solely on Edita's shoulders. To her husband's growing frustration, she moved the baby's crib into their bedroom where it stayed for four years. During the day, while she cooked, did the laundry and the vacuuming, Edita carried Buster in a sling on her back. She bore him in this fashion until he weighed nearly sixty pounds—it having the welcome side effect of correcting her congenital scoliosis a doctor in Denver told her would never improve without surgery.

When Buster was finally placed on the ground, he was only allowed to play with his sisters. They fussed over him—cornrowing his red hair and dressing him in their clothes. This went on until he was eight—despite a constant barrage of sissy name calling by Cookie. Buster's sequestration with his sisters came to an end when he was ten and already a foot taller than Cookie—who was a paddle-footed, squat and corpulent nineteen. Still somewhat fearful, Edita felt Buster was now physically capable of protecting himself.

"I'm thinking of letting you play with your brothers."

"O-kay!!!"

"But you have to be very careful around your brother, Cookie."

"Why, Mommy?"

"Something is wrong with him…up here," she said, tapping her temple with a finger.

"Ah'm awful sorry."

"Don't be sorry. Just careful."

Her warning delivered, Buster was released into the company of his brothers. The younger ones were delighted. Maybe they would no longer be on the receiving end of the games Cookie invented for them to play. In those games, the younger boys played the role of Hapless Law Enforcement to Cookie's Sadistic Criminal Mastermind. No matter how hard Hapless Law Enforcement tried, they always wound up crying.

"You know how to play DEA Man?" Cookie inquired of Buster.

"Nope, ah shor don't."

"Well, you're gonna be the DEA Man. He's the man with the badge."

"Gosh, thanks!"

In the game of DEA Man, Cookie and his younger brothers had to move several five-pound bags of tile glaze around the compound and keep it hidden from Buster who was the green agent sent to the West from Washington, DC. There wasn't much more to the game than that. The fun part for Cookie was when Buster discovered the drug cache. He would then jump him or descend from a rope somewhere and employ different faux martial arts moves. Unfortunately, the bullets in Buster's imaginary government-issued sidearm had no effect on Cookie. Buster endured being karate chopped and flipped on his head too many times to count, but he never complained nor tattled on him.

When Fridays rolled around, the Dominguezes would load all the kids into the back of the truck for a drive into town. Buster liked to sit above the rear fender of the pickup with his nose in the wind like a dog. All the kids had a few bucks in their pockets from chores and an idea of how they wanted to spend it—even though it always came down to the same things, candy for the boys, teen fashion magazines for the girls.

Vanadium's Main Street had resisted paving for over one hundred years—almost as if the town was holding out for the return of horse-drawn carriages. People passing through on their way to Utah drove slowly, not to enjoy Vanadium's down-on-its-heels Victorian architecture, or raised wooden sidewalks, but rather to avoid potholes that were deep enough to conceal a man on horseback wearing a stovepipe hat.

Dominguez guided his Dodge Power Wagon into an empty space in front of the Buttered Roll, the town's only restaurant without a bar. In those days, before Mr. Mallomar came to town, Vanadium hadn't any need for more than one restaurant. The prevailing attitude was that paying for a meal outside the home was a useless extravagance. Buster could see Sheriff Dudival in the window booth having a cup of coffee and a cigarette with a crusty-looking cowboy. They both took notice of him. In fact, they seemed to be talking about him.

"Have your asses back here in forty-five minutes," Dominguez said.

The kids all jumped off the truck and left on their predetermined missions. Cookie lumbered out the back with the difficulty of a fat kid. It didn't help that he insisted on wearing a big woolen overcoat whenever he went to town—even in the broiling heat of summer. No one talked about it, assuming it was his sad way of concealing his weight problem.

The pockets of Cookie's coat were slit on the inside to allow his hands to reach all the way through. To the proprietor of a shop, it looked like he was just standing by the merchandise with his coat open, but inside the coat, his hands were grabbing whatever he desired. Cookie, alone, was responsible for 75 percent of Vanadium's retail "shrinkage."

It was time to get going. He only had forty-five minutes. His parents insisted they be back at the house on Fridays by sunset. He started walking off by himself, then noticed Buster.

"Hey, fuckwad. Come with me."

Happy to be included, Buster followed his brother into the hardware store. Cookie made a cursory inspection of plumbing supplies, power sanders, fuse boxes, rattraps, and poison. He was not really interested in any of that. He knew the owner of the store was watching him and that diddling around long enough would tax the proprietor's attention span. When he saw him go back to reading his paper, Cookie headed to the real object of his desire—a pyramid of .22 caliber ammunition in the gun department. Dominguez had, ill advisedly, given Cookie a single shot J. C. Higgins rifle without ever bothering to ask why it seemed he always had an unlimited supply of ammo for it. Cookie opened his coat and slipped a few boxes into his shirt, then hissed at Buster.

"Get over here, moron."

Buster came over and stood next to him.

"Unbutton your shirt."

"Gosh, why?"

"Just do it, numbnuts."

Cookie stuffed two more boxes of .22s into Buster's shirt.

"Okay, follow me. Not too fast. Stop and look at some shit like you're shoppin'." Buster took him literally, and on the way out, stopped to stare at some bags of steer manure. Cookie looked at him sangfroid. "*¡Si no eres el idiota más idiota que he conocido!*"

When the forty-five minutes were up, everyone returned to the truck that was already loaded with groceries. On the way out of town, a truck that had the logo of a contractor's company on the door panel, pulled up beside the Dominguez's. The person on the passenger side of the moving truck rolled down his window.

"Hey, Dominguez, the boss wants to redo the floor of the Vanadium Hotel lobby."

"Tell them to call you at the office," Edita said nervously. She didn't like this kind of communicating on the highway. Dominguez ignored her.

"How many square feet?" He yelled back to the men, further aggravating her.

While this mobile business meeting was being conducted, in the back of the truck, Cookie cornered Buster.

"Let's have 'em."

"Have what?"

"The shells we boosted, gringo."

"Ah put 'em back."

"You what?"

"If ah'da kep'm that woulda been stealin'."

Cookie wanted to throw him off the truck, but he knew he couldn't lift him. Instead, he grabbed Buster's cowboy hat from his head and angrily Frisbeed it into the back of the truck conducting the business conference at forty miles an hour alongside them.

"Hey…!"

His other brothers pretended not to see it, but Buster's sisters immediately came to his defense.

"That was mean!" they both said.

"Mommy gave me that hat for cleanin' the house."

"So go get it, if you want it so fuckin' bad!"

Buster looked at his hat fluttering around in the back of the adjacent pick up truck.

"Better get it now while you still have a chance," Cookie taunted. "Chickie, chickie, bruck-bruck!"

Buster's brow furrowed. Feebly, he tried to calculate the physics of this. Could he do it? Could he jump from the back of one moving truck to another?

"Don't do it!" his sisters pleaded.

"Shut up, you little cunts! If he wants it so bad, let him jump for it!"

Buster did not want to see his hat ride away. He put one foot on the side of the truck and braced one hand on the top of the cab—where inside his foster parents sat, unaware.

"All right," the passenger of the other truck said to Dominguez. "See you tomorrow at ten-thirty." The contractor's truck started to accelerate away.

"Don't do it!" Buster's sisters screamed.

Buster had already waited too long when he jumped. He missed the side of the passing truck, but managed to get his hands on the tailgate. Unfortunately, his long legs reached the road—the tips of his cowboy boots burning from the friction.

Inside the Dominguezes' truck, Edita and Dominguez were too busy arguing to notice Buster being dragged past them.

"Do you have any idea how dangerous that was—what you just did? There is such a thing as a telephone, you know."

"Shut up."

"You have children in the truck," she said, wanting to have the last word.

Now smoke began to billow into their windshield from the truck in front of them.

"I think he blew his rings. I better catch up and tell him."

Dominguez sped up and as they drove through the smoke, he and Edita were able to see Buster hanging by his fingertips, his boots on fire.

"How the hell…?"

"*¡Dios mío!*" Edita cried.

Dominguez sped up and began honking his horn. In the meantime, Buster's higher mammalian instinct for self-preservation overcame his fool's insubordination and commanded all the strength of his tall, skinny frame to pull himself up. Slowly, his feet came off the pavement where the friction had already erased the points on his cowboy boots and the tips of his socks. Shaking and trembling at every juncture of muscle and tendon, Buster managed to get himself up on the rear bumper. He waited a moment to catch his breath then flipped himself over the back tailgate. Gone from view momentarily, he suddenly sprang to his feet—triumphantly waving his hat. All of this took place without the knowledge of the driver and passenger of Buster's current vehicle—loudly singing along with Reba McEntire's "Is There Life Out There?" on the radio.

After they recovered their wayward passenger, Dominguez pulled over and interrogated the children in the back of the truck.

"Who let him do that?"

Dominguez stood waiting for an answer. Cookie remained silent. The younger brothers cast their eyes to their laps. Finally, Dominguez looked to his little daughters. Surreptitiously, one of them pointed a teensy-weensy finger in the direction of Cookie.

"You little coc—" Dominguez said to Cookie, cutting off the obscenity.

Cookie just smirked at him. There it was—the dismissive expression of Guillermo Cantante. Dominguez balled his fist. He wanted to slam it into that insolent, fat face of his, but he could wait.

This being the Sabbath, Mrs. Dominguez prepared fish balls, boiled chicken, beef brisket served with little potato pancakes, and crepes filled with ricotta cheese and topped with applesauce. Dominguez, at his wife's direction, was not allowed to kiln tiles on the Sabbath. In fact, the Cantantes had inculcated him with the notion that he was not to lift a finger until Sunday morning.

There were other strict observances in the Dominguez household—the most draconian being no television. Mrs. Dominguez, trying to identify the causes of Cookie's nascent criminal pathology, had determined that television inspired violence and took the Emerson down to be sold at the This 'n' That Shop. Instead, the children spent their typical evenings cleaning the house, reading, and doing their homework. When those tasks were completed, they were expected to work on their respective art projects.

Buster's project had been the creation of frescoes made on the bedroom wall next to his bunk. There was no denying Buster's eye for anatomy and composition. His subjects, always horses and cowboys, were applied to the wall in a classic seven-layer Flemish style. The problem, to Mrs. Dominguez's chagrin, was that Buster used boogers and not paints to create these naïve masterpieces. The removal of this dried and hardened medium was impossible to achieve without the removal of the underlying paint as well. Patiently, Mrs. Dominguez redirected Buster's artistic talent to the age-old Kasbah art form—where awl and ball peen hammer were employed to tap intricate bas-reliefs on metal plates—in Buster's case, discarded pie tins from the Buttered Roll.

After dinner, Cookie was busy in the tool room where he had constructed a Red Grooms–like model of the Vanadium jail to the smallest detail—fabricating the steel bars for the cells from a shopping cart he boosted from the grocery store.

"Cookie Dominguez!"

It was his father bellowing. It was time to pay the piper for encouraging Buster's truck hopping. Cookie turned off the soldering gun and stoically walked outside. His father was already standing there. He silently gestured to the kiln room, which was, in the Dominguez family, akin to "the woodshed."

Cookie stepped into the outbuilding. Along the sides of the room were racks supporting sheets of tiles ready for boxing. But the centerpiece was the propane-fired, fifty-three-cubic-foot, front-loading Delphi kiln—the largest in the state of Colorado—capable of 2,350 degrees Fahrenheit. Without speaking, for they had been through this routine before, Dominguez gestured for Cookie to bend over a stack of boxes.

ꟾ

It was now Labor Day and the annual Vanadium Rodeo. The rodeo was a big deal in town. Everyone participated in some way. The girls, who weren't riding in an event, baked pies and made lemonade for the refreshment booth, which donated its proceeds to 4H and Future Ranchers of Tomorrow. All the boys, if they didn't want to be teased, competed in the junior rodeo events.

If there was one thing in Cookie's life that he could point to with pride, it was his collection of blue ribbons for saddle bronc riding. He had been champion in the kids' division five years running. While the other boys rode sheep in the kiddy events, Cookie rode the real thing—wild-eyed broncos. This year, however, he faced an unlikely competitor in his adopted brother. Buster, by the end of the summer, had reached the preternatural height of six-one, and while no one had ever shown him how to ride a horse, there was some innate quality in his undocumented DNA that gave him what they call in cowboy parlance "a leg up." There was no other way to explain his aptitude—other than what life had taught him so far—to hang on.

In the saddle bronc riding event, Cookie drew the horse The Hell You Say. The Hell's gimmick was to put his nose down as soon as he cleared the gate and kick his back legs straight up over his head. Most riders slid off this steep incline in the first second, but Cookie dug his spurs in hard above the horse's shoulder and made it easily past the eight-second buzzer. Sheriff Dudival, who volunteered every year as a rodeo clown, helped him off and shooed the aggravated horse away. The Judges scored Cookie the full twenty-five points on the animal, twenty-one on the rider's performance and a combined forty-nine other points, bringing his total to a hard-to-beat ninety-five out of one hundred. Jared Yankapeed, an older cowboy, offered Cookie a congratulatory pull of Crazy Crow bourbon—which Cookie promptly drained as he glowered in the direction of his competition.

Cookie, ever the good sportsman, had only moments before, found a bumblebee and shoved it up the rectum of his adopted brother's horse.

"Next up, from Vanadium, Colorado…let's hear it for the orphan, Buster McCaffrey!"

Buster climbed into the chute and eased himself into the saddle of Never Inoculated. He got a good grip of the single rein attached to the halter, then nodded to the official that he was ready. The gate flew open. Suddenly Never Inoculated's eyes widened, and his cheeks puffed out like Dizzy Gillespie doing *Caravan*. He sprung out on all four hooves like a deer—three spine-jarring times toward the center of the arena, then sat down and dragged his ass like a dog with worms. Then, bee-bitten, he launched straight up in the air, then came down hard on his front legs and kicked with everything he had. Buster started to lose his seat. Never recoiled off his back legs to his front, cracking Buster's nose into his mane. Buster, nose gushing blood and on the verge of passing out, lay back on the horse's rump. Never Inoculated recoiled off his back legs and spanked Buster on his way out of the saddle—propelling him ten feet, fifteen feet, twenty feet. Some people who were there that day insist that Buster was sent fifty feet into the air! High above the arena, Buster could see all the way to Lone Cone peak. He took a deep breath and savored the smell of Vanadium—the manure of the feedlot all the way to the diesel and oil of the salvage yard on the other side of town. And just over there was his cinder-blocked school, the First Church of Thessalonians, the back of Main Street's Victorian façade—above that, Lame Horse Mesa. In that moment, he loved this town. The crowd gazed up at him, incredulous. There were his sisters standing by their post at the lemonade stand—afraid for him. And there was a pretty girl, about his age, all decked out in fringed rodeo regalia with blonde Annie Oakley pigtails. Why, if that wasn't the prettiest girl he'd ever seen!

I'm going marry that gal, he thought.

But then he suddenly realized he was on his way down. Where was that horse, anyway? Oh, there he was, down there. Buster scrambled with his legs to regain his balance, adjusted his feet just so—and then to everyone's utter astonishment, landed squarely on Never Inoculated's saddle. The horse was so shocked, looking back at the bloody-nosed Buster, that he just stood there and peed. Then the eight-second buzzer went off.

The Judges took a good fifteen minutes to figure out exactly how to score this rodeo miracle. Had the horse done his best to vanquish the rider? Yes, since the horse actually tried to kill the rider. Did the time the rider was out of the saddle count against the clock? Yes, since the rider's feet never touched the ground. The Judges therefore concluded that since a maneuver like Buster's had never been done before, he was to be awarded a ninety-nine. They held back a perfect score on principle. Everyone in the Dominguez family was delighted when the blue ribbon was presented—except Cookie, of course. He would have received a second place ribbon but was disqualified for bad sportsmanship when the winners were announced. He had been seen making a defiant humping motion behind an unwitting sheep, which the judges didn't appreciate—this being a family event. Dominguez was even more unappreciative. The ride home from the rodeo was quiet and tense.

The Dominguez boys were asleep when Dominguez came to the bunkhouse and shook Cookie awake, then left for the kiln house. Cookie sat on the edge of the bed for a long time before he stuck his feet into his slippers and went outside. Buster, pretending to be asleep, went to the window and watched as Cookie walked the seventy-five yards to the kiln house, slid open the heavy steel door and went inside—momentarily lit by the red glow of the kiln's ignition button. After that, he couldn't see what happened. After half an hour, Cookie returned to his bed. Buster leaned over his bunk to see him, but Cookie had the covers pulled over his head, even though it had been a very hot night. Buster thought he heard Cookie crying.

ꟹ

THAT WAS HOW SUMMER ended. The sheepherders were now taking their flocks to lower elevations for winter in the Dolores Canyon, and Dominguez needed to bank enough manure for his black tiles until spring. He rented a large dump truck and set off with the whole family for a Sheep Shit Round-up. They collected sheep droppings at three of the largest outfits on Lame Horse Mesa—the Pusters', the Stumplehorsts', and the rim rock acres of the Morgan property, in exchange for a meager royalty for manure rights. One by one, Dominguez dropped off each of the children to shovel dung into mounds from the different sections. At the end of the day, the old man stopped by each pile, which they uploaded to the truck.

Buster's area was defined by the Lame Horse Escarpment on one side and the Hail Mary, a defunct silver mine that had been boarded up for almost twenty years, on the other. Buster shoveled until his hands were raw with blisters. By sunset, he had gathered a dung pile ten feet high. Exhausted, he walked to the canyon rim where an outcropping of rocks formed the entrance to the Hail Mary. Ordinarily, he would have jumped at the chance to squeeze through the wooden slats of the boarded-up mine entrance and explore, but he was too tired. He laid down, instead, on the red rock mine tailings—which still held their warmth from a day in the sun. In the canyon below, the Dolores River shimmered like a hot ribbon of solder. The wind was picking up, and aromas of sage and juniper brought welcome therapy to Buster's senses. He sat and stared at a stand of hundred-year-old firs that had somehow escaped the lumberman's axe. In the middle of them, a dead pine leaned against a healthy young tree—perhaps its own progeny.

How long, Buster wondered, would the young tree have to hold his deceased ancestor before the wind or rot set him free? Suddenly Buster heard someone whispering behind him. It was coming from the mine.

"Who's there?" Buster said.

Now nervous to be out there by himself, he got to his feet and warily looked around, but his investigation was interrupted by the sound of a horse's hooves approaching. A cowboy, on a paint horse, was riding his way—faster than he'd ever seen, over rocks and marmot holes, spewing curse words all the way. Just when Buster was sure he was going to be trampled, the rider yanked the reins and put the horse into a skid—its front legs rearing up and pawing the air inches from his head. Then the cowboy jumped off and, with spurs clanking, stomped towards him.

"What the fuckin' hell you doin' up here?"

"Nuthin," Buster said.

"You high-gradin' my mine?"

"No, sir, ah ain't," Buster said, his mouth dry. The cowboy stared at him dubiously.

"Don't fuck with me, boy."

"Ah'm jes out here workin'. "

The cowboy took a bag of tobacco out of his pocket and some rolling papers.

"Ah serpose yor one of them Messican shit shovelers."

"Yes, sir."

"Don't be so fuckin' proud 'bout it! You jes' wanna throw in the sponge and shovel shit all yer lahf?"

"Uh, uh, uh…" Buster stammered.

"Well, shoot, Luke or give up the gun!"

"No sir. Ah ain't gonna shovel shit all mah lahf!"

"That raht? Then what're you fixin' to do?"

"Ah'm a fixin' to, uh..." Buster's voice trailed off, realizing that he really didn't know. The other Dominguez children, with the exception of Cookie, would quickly say that they were considering law and medicine. Buster had no such aspirations—only that he wanted no job that required staying indoors. His foster mother told him not to worry—that one day his calling would come to him. Here, standing cocky and bowlegged before him, armored in sage-lashed leather chaps, a rope, and a sweat-stained four-ply beaver hat, with a powerful, loyal beast saddled at his side impatiently pawing the ground wanting to get going—anywhere—was what he suddenly decided was all he ever wanted.

"Ah'm fixin' to be lahk you...a cowboy."

"That's very interestin'. Very interestin', indeed. Pay ain't ver' good 'n yood be kickin' 'round in the comp'ny of scum mostly."

"Heck, ah'd be havin' my own place here."

"And jes' how do you plan pullin' that off?"

"Sheriff says anythin's posserble if a feller puts a mind to it."

"Oh, he said that, did he? Anythin's posserbull. You jes..." The cowboy snapped his fingers. "And ya got yorself a ranch!" The cowboy laughed and laughed then bent over coughing until he expectorated a wad of yellow phlegm on the ground that was variegated with blood like the yolk of a quail's egg.

Buster almost gagged. "Well, ah'm sure it aint gonna be that easy..."

"No, pard," the cowboy said, wiping his mouth. "It ain't goner be easy. Some folks out here kilt for their land. But anythin's fuckin' posserble! 'Fact jes last year, ah seen a heifer born with two heads!" The cowboy pulled at his crotch making an adjustment. "Quirley?"

"Uh, sure." Buster said, not knowing that he was agreeing to a hand-rolled cigarette.

He looked on with horror as the cowboy tapped the tobacco into the rolling paper, licked the gummed end, then put the whole thing in his mouth to wet it. Buster didn't want it anymore, but didn't want to incite him. He could see the notched grip of a Colt peeking out from a shoulder rig under his coat.

"There you go, *cowboy*." He lit it for him and lit another one for himself. "You lahk it out here?"

"Yes, sir, ah do."

"It ain't fer ever'body," he said, casting his squint around the mesa. "Takes a lot of seein' to." The real meaning of that understatement would not become clear to Buster for another ten years.

Buster went over and rubbed his horse's nose.

"What's his name?" Buster said puffing his first cigarette.

"Name's Nicker," the cowboy said disingenuously, not quite pronouncing it that way.

"That ain't a very nice name," Buster said.

The cowboy's eyes flashed and he snatched the butt from Buster's hand, pitched the ember and stuck it back behind his own ear.

"Nicker's the sound a horse makes, for yor goddamn infermashun! Do you know who the hell yor speakin' to?"

"No sir, ah don't."

"Ah'm Jimmy Bayles Morgan!" he said angrily. "Don't you go to the school?"

"Yes, sir!"

"Don't they teach ya who the goddamn founders of this town was?"

"Ah thought the people who found it were the Indians."

"No! The folks who *kep'* it."

"Kep' it from what?"

"From the socialists with the labor unions and what not, you nitwit!"

"Ah don't know nothin' 'bout all that."

"Are you a cretin or a moron?"

Buster only knew what a moron was.

"Ah'm a cretin, sir."

"Bro-ther, you take the fuckin' cake!" The cowboy laughed, shaking his head. "All right, jes tell me one fuckin' thing you *do* know with all the damn taxes ah pay in this damn county to ed-u-cate you."

"January fifteenth is Martin Luther King Day."

That caused another spell of coughing from the cowboy.

"Are you fuckin' with me? That's what they teach you in school…about a goddamn womanizin' communist? What grade you in…fourth?"

"Seventh."

"Christ Almighty, seventh grade!" The cowboy turned and looked down into the valley, seeming to focus on the Vanadium Elementary School. "Ah got a good mind to ride down there Monday mornin' and pay that school a visit!"

"Please don't do that!" Buster blurted.

The cowboy narrowed his eyes and slowly approached Buster until they were nose to nose and he could see the dark brown nicotine stains on the cowboy's teeth and the smell of his consumptive breath.

"Why the hell shoont ah?"

Buster had no idea who Jimmy Bayles Morgan was, but one thing was certain, he would say anything right then to keep this character from embarrassing him at school.

"Because we're fixin' to learn 'bout the town founders in the eighth grade."

"About how my granddaddy, Sheriff Morgan, saved this damn town from damn Swedes and wop anarchists?"

"Yessir. We're gonna be gettin' that."

Jimmy Bayles Morgan studied his face for a moment longer and spit. "You ain't really, are ya?" Buster's eyes started to fill with tears. "You just didn't want ol' Jimmy ridin' down there raisin' sand. Ain't that the truth of it?"

"Yes, sir."

"Lemme tell you somethin', *bub*," he said, jabbing Buster in the chest with a crooked, rheumatoid finger. "Ah don't abide with a lahr." Fortunately, the pair was interrupted by the sound of Dominguez's dump truck. The cowboy turned and regarded its broad form breaking the horizon.

"That the big bug?"

"That'd be Mr. Dominguez, my foster daddy."

"Uh huh… What's that greezy frijole like?"

"He's all right, ah guess."

"Nothin'…*funny* 'bout him?"

"He ain't funny at all."

"Is that raht?"

Jimmy Bayles Morgan hocked up another goober and spit. Buster's heart sank. He wasn't intending to leave. Dominguez climbed down from the truck.

"Morgan."

"Do-ming-gez," Jimmy greeted him, accenting his ethnicity.

"My boy causing you trouble?"

"Trouble?" Morgan looked at Buster coolly. "How could he give me trouble? He's jes' b'tween hay and grass. Why, matter a fact, sir… Ah'd say, from all the shit ah seen shoveled, you got yerself a mighty fine worker here."

Dominguez stepped up from behind Buster, put his hands on his shoulders, massaging and sort of pinching the muscles running up to his neck.

"He ain't my own, but he's a good boy."

Jimmy Bayles took in the Walmart Studio portrait and nodded appreciatively.

"Ah'm a big believer in family, mahself."

Dominguez did not extend the repartee. They stood there in silence. Finally…

"You got my check?"

"Yes, indeedy, ah did."

"Okay then."

"Ah reckon ah best be puttin' a wiggle on."

And with that, Morgan sauntered back to his horse and made a clicking sound. The horse dropped his front legs on command and Morgan just stepped on without even having to put a boot in the stirrup. The horse then stood up on all fours—horse and rider casually loping down a game trail into the canyon. Jimmy Bayles stopped for a moment and looked back at Buster, then continued out of sight.

"What the hell was that about?"

"Ah really coont tell ya," Buster said.

Dominguez let it go, turning attention to more important things.

"That's a nice pile of guano you got there. Biggest one in the family." He motioned for the other children to get out of the truck and help load it.

"We'll use this load for the firing tonight," said Dominguez. "Maybe I'll even show you our family secret—that is, if you're interested."

"Sure," Buster said, taking Dominguez's offer as a sign of commendation. Cookie, overhearing the compliment from the truck, took it with a sigh of relief.

After dinner had been eaten, the plates washed, the carpet vacuumed, and the kitchen floor had been mopped with Spic 'n' Span, the children were bid to bed. As the boys walked to the bunkhouse, Cookie Dominguez was suspiciously friendly to Buster. It wasn't that he had stopped hating him, he still hated him. It was just that now he pitied him. He knew better than anyone what Buster was in for.

It was around 11:30 when Dominguez opened the door to the bunkhouse. He came and shook Buster awake.

"I'm doing a run of black octagonals. Come on."

"Be raht there," Buster said.

Dominguez left him to rub the sleep from his eyes. Ever so carefully, he shimmied down the side of the bunk bed so as not to wake his temperamental brother, but Cookie was only pretending to be asleep. He watched Buster go out the door and cross the garden, thankful that it wasn't him that was being shown the family secret tonight. A few moments later, a huge explosion blew the windows out of the bunkhouse.

Sheriff Dudival arrived at the scene with a fire truck. The heat from the explosion of the giant propane tank turned the cinder block building into a pile of white ash—still pulsating with enough heat to melt the windshield of Dominguez's truck. The children were huddled around their mother who was, understandably, in shock. Cookie was now the psychotic head man of the family. His first act was to keep Buster away from the real Dominguezes. Somehow, Buster got the feeling that he was being blamed for this.

Dudival approached the family.

"Mrs. Dominguez, I'm very sorry about your loss."

Mrs. Dominguez burst into tears and held her children coveyed up around her.

"Anybody have an idea how this happened?" The Dominguez family responded en masse in the direction of Buster who was sitting alone in singed pajamas on the other side of the yard.

"Why don't you ask *him*?" Cookie spat. "He was the last one to see him alive."

Sheriff Dudival nodded that he'd take that under advisement and approached Buster. Dudival sat down next to him. Together they watched the hook-and-ladder boys ratchet a good forty-five feet up the front yard's cottonwood tree to retrieve Carlito Dominguez's smoldering right haunch.

The sheriff lit a cigarette.

"Hurt?"

"Don't think so."

"What happened?"

"What do you think fuckin' happened?" Cookie shrieked, eavesdropping. "He killed him!" Sheriff Dudival looked back at Cookie, his face puffy from crying and made a mental note for his journal that, despite his gigantism, Cookie was something of an emotional weakling. Mrs. Dominguez put a gentle hand over her son's mouth to quiet him.

"You get along with him…Cookie, is it?"

"He don't cotton to me fer some reason only he knows hissef."

"Okay, let's leave that for a moment. Were you out here when the explosion happened?"

"Yes, sir."

"What were you doing out here at this hour?"

"Mr. Dominguez wanted to show me somethin'."

"Show you what?"

"How he makes them black tiles a his."

"Uh huh," said the sheriff. He'd heard the rumors about Dominguez and Cookie, but Social Services was never called in, so he wrote it off as racially inspired gossip.

"But ah couldn't get the door open."

"Why was that?"

"Ah guess it were locked."

"And then what happened?

"All hell broke loose."

"You ever have any bad feelings with Mr. Dominguez? Like maybe he wasn't treating you as well as his real kids, something of that nature?"

"No, sir. Ah lahked him."

"You liked him."

"Yes, sir."

Dudival just looked at him. "Will you excuse me for a moment? I'm going to have a look around."

"Sure thang."

Dudival got out his flashlight and began to pace the debris field. He stooped to look at something stuck on a sagebrush, then fumbled around in his shirt pocket for his reading glasses. It was a little scrap of paper with the letter V printed on it. He held it up to his nose and sniffed it, then put it in his pocket and kept walking. Something else had caught the beam of his flashlight. On the ground, one hundred yards directly in front of the kiln, was the cylinder from the workings of a lock. It was still hot to the touch. Dudival figured that it was from the kiln door. Someone had hammered a brad into the keyhole preventing the handle from being turned. Dudival put that in a Ziploc snack bag, then stood up, brushed the dirt off his pants and looked at Buster who quickly pulled his finger out of his nose. The two of them stared at each other for a moment, then Dudival turned and walked away.

Dudival would enter the evening's events in his journal this way: *The death of Carlito Dominguez was due to a faulty exchange valve in his kiln that prevented the build-up of kiln gas from being released thus resulting in a lethal explosion.*

When Dudival got back to his cruiser he immediately gagged. The inside of the car was filled with the smell of Dominguez's burning flesh. He managed to suppress the urge to vomit—grabbing an

Ol' Piney car deodorizer from his glove compartment and holding it to his nose. He drove with it held there, all the way home.

Three blocks above Main was Hemlock, which led to his trailer subdivision. Hemlock was a workingman's street with its lawn displays of defunct clothes washers, hot water heaters, rusted manual lawn mowers, and blown car engines. Dudival, now approaching his own place, turned off his headlights, slowed to a crawl and pulled over to the curb. He was very proud of his house. It was as old as the others, but looked brand new. Two years ago, he freshened the exterior with a coat of "Regimental" from the "Sea and Sky" paint collection at Home Depot. He also sprayed gallons of Round Up on the perimeter to abate the weeds threatening the civilization of his crushed green gravel lawn. But he wasn't studying his house to admire his industry. He was looking for a sign that someone was waiting inside to kill him. As benign a force to serve and protect that Dudival was, his predecessor, Sheriff Morgan, employed a style of law enforcement that inspired revenge—so he couldn't be too careful.

Dudival zigzagged from tree to tree until he was next to the house. He would take nothing for granted—no matter how silly this may have seen to his onlooking neighbor, Mrs. Doser, who'd gotten up in the middle of the night to take her anti-seizure medicine. Her husband, Mr. Doser, believed, when he was alive, that the uranium market would one day rebound and high-graded (stole) chunks of yellowcake from the mine in his Jetsons lunchbox. By the time Atomic Mines closed its operations, Mr. Doser had accumulated three hundred pounds of the stuff, which he kept for thirty years in barrels in the spare room next to where he and his wife slept. Back in the day, the mine officials actually extolled the health benefits associated with radiation. That's why it came as a total surprise to the Dosers when the mister came down with leukemia. And even though Mrs. Doser had to have her bladder and 80 percent of lower bowel removed a few years later, she was still spry and nosy. She took a chair to her window and watched Sheriff Dudival, pistol drawn, crouched for action, sneaking up to his own house—like he always did—and wondered how a person could live like that.

Dudival stood at the right side of his living room window and peeked in. He was looking for the telltale glow of a cigarette, the clearing of a throat, or the sniffling of a tweaker's runny nose. Then, he unlocked the door and crept inside using a combat position to "cut the pie" at every doorway. When he was finally satisfied no one was lurking, he closed the curtains and turned on one small lamp that he'd redeemed with coupons from the generic brand of cigarettes that he smoked. As for his house, it was obvious at first glance that it belonged to a bachelor. Dudival's stock answer when the subject of marriage came up was that he never got around to it, like a forgotten item on a grocery list. When pressed, he would tell people he never found the right girl, but they would have to be from out-of-town to believe that. Folks from Vanadium knew that, long ago, he had actually found the right girl—the most unlikely of girls. To everyone's understanding, but Shep Dudival's, the romance was doomed from the start. But that didn't stop him from trying—just as newcomers to Vanadium find it hard to accept that tomatoes don't grow well at this altitude.

The décor of the house was neat in a military way—no dirty clothes strewn about, no piles of magazines and newspapers, no TV dinners left out, or filled ashtrays—the detritus typical of a man living alone. Instead, a bed made as tightly as the envelope of a Hallmark card, a small Pledge-polished fold-leaf oak table with a tin tray from the fifties that extolled the beauty of the Rockies as a travel destination, and a La-Z-Boy recliner with a TV tray positioned in front of a black and white Zenith with rabbit ears. There was an area shag rug that was the color and texture of Chef Boyardi spaghetti, a gun safe, an old-fashioned percolator, and a framed black and white picture of a young boy standing next to a hard-looking peace officer with a brush mustache and campaign hat at the gun range in the quarry.

Sheriff Dudival took off his duty belt, his flack vest, his uniform, and carefully hung them up. He went to the bathroom, peed, and flossed his teeth. The cylinder lock, which he had collected earlier in the evening in an evidence bag, now went into his safe. He changed into ironed, cotton pajamas, got into bed and opened his copy of Mrs. Humphry's *Manners For Men.* "Gentleness and moral strength combined must be the salient characteristics of the gentleman..." When Dudival's eyelids began to dunk like catfish bobbers, he turned off the light.

CHAPTER THREE

The Svendergards' Inhibitions

AT DOMINGUEZ'S FUNERAL, THE family—whose minds had been poisoned by Cookie—made it clear that they were no longer interested in keeping Buster. Buster's availability was passed along to the various friends and Lookie-Lous who were there for the free food served at the wake by the Buttered Roll restaurant. The Women's League of Vanadium—in emergency session—had decided on the Svendergards, a middle-aged couple who were childless and had missed out on adopting Buster in the first draft round. Mr. Svendergard owned six hundred and forty acres on Lame Horse Mesa, but was neither a farmer nor a rancher. He owned the Svendergard Cement Company, which sold gravel and concrete. Svendergard had been responsible for blasting over a hundred gravel pits, leaving the once beautiful ridgeline—as their neighbor, Jimmy Bayles Morgan was heard to grouse—"as pockmarked as Uncle Joe Stalin's goddamned face." Rumor had it that breathing all of the dusty particulate had a sclerotic effect on Mr. Svendergard's vas deferens, preventing the proper expulsion of reproductive fluids. That's what people in Vanadium said, anyway. On first meeting Gil and Zella Svendergard, one was struck by how fat and pink they were. Coupled with their blonde eyelashes and eyebrows, they bore an uncanny resemblance to Yorkshire swine. But despite the fact that the Svendergards were hale, corpulent, and jolly people, they never mixed well in Vanadian society. Some felt it was because they lacked a normal interest in horses, fishing, and guns. There was plenty of gossip about them in Vanadium, but nothing, please pardon the pun, concrete. Sheriff Dudival's background check only showed a Chapter Seven filed in 1993, which was not deemed serious enough to hinder the adoption. As Buster took his things from the Dominguezes truck and carried them to the Svendergard's, Cookie Dominguez suddenly jumped out from between the two trucks. He grabbed Buster by the hair and, as a gesture of fond farewell, punched him in the mouth.

"I'm gonna kill you someday," Cookie said.

"That's not a very nice thing to say," Mr. Svendergard said as he and his wife stumbled onto the scene.

Cookie took a fake jab at Mr. Svendergard's face, making him flinch. Content with having intimidated a grown man, Cookie smirked and returned to his grieving family.

"What's got into him?" Mrs. Svendergard asked.

"He thinks ah kilt his daddy," replied Buster.

The mister helped Buster to his feet. Mrs. Svendergard gave him a Kleenex to blot his bloody mouth. As the Svendergards climbed into their cement truck—which advertised the family company on its door panel—they couldn't help wondering if they had made a serious mistake.

ꟷ

It was Mr. Svendergard who first discovered deposits of sand and gravel in Vanadium. He was a big believer in concrete, and the Svendergard compound was a showcase for his concrete artistry. Every structure on the property was made from the stuff—the domicile, floors, walls, countertops, showers, baths, and sleeping platforms. "Buster, they haven't come up with anything better than concrete since the Egyptians," Mr. Svendergard said. "Concrete is made from a filler and a binder. That binder is usually cement paste. We use normal size aggregates to make a heavy-duty product. Aggregates are the stones we quarry then wash. Am I going too fast for you?"

"No, sir," Buster said, not understanding one thing he'd said.

"Wanna see the gravel loft?"

The gravel loft was the biggest building in the complex. Six cement trucks sat side-by-side, ready to be loaded with washed gravel from a large chute that was connected to a silo. He showed Buster a red handle that was connected to a large chain that went all the way up to the ceiling.

"Go ahead and pull it." Buster was reluctant, but Mr. Svendergard encouraged him. Buster gave it a yank. When he did, gravel spewed out of the chute and emptied directly into the rolling tank of a cement truck.

"You just dropped a ton of gravel."

"Cool," said Buster.

"I designed this set-up myself," said Mr. Svendergard. Believing that he had finally found a concrete acolyte, Mr. Svendergard's next act was to take Buster out of school. He had decided—taking into consideration Buster's prodigious food intake, and the clothes and boots that he quickly outgrew—that the free full-time labor that

Buster offered could push concrete production 12.5 percent, which could cover Buster's overhead. Buster became the only ten-year-old boy who was allowed to drive a cement truck, operate heavy machinery, and use dynamite. That, alone, would have given Buster considerable prestige among the boys his age, but Buster was not enrolled in school.His absence prompted a visit from Sheriff Dudival.

"Is there some problem, Sheriff?" Mr. Svendergard asked.

"No problem. I just came out to see how things were going with the boy."

"He's fine," Mrs. Svendergard was quick to say.

"I was just wondering why you haven't enrolled him in school."

"The kids in school call him a murderer."

"There's worse things."

"What would that be?" challenged Mrs. Svendergard.

Sheriff Dudival just looked at her blankly. Possibly in his experience, there were worse things than to be called than a murderer, but he didn't say.

"Is the boy around?"

"Sure, he's around."

"May I talk to him, please?"

Mr. Svendergard turned to his wife.

"I'll go get him," she said.

"How's the cement business?" the sheriff asked Mr. Svendergard while waiting.

"I can't even get enough Portland to keep up with demand."

The sheriff assumed that that was good thing and nodded appreciatively.

Now Buster entered the room with Mrs. Svendergard.

"'Lo, Sheriff."

"Hello, Buster."

The sheriff noticed that everyone's eyes darted back and forth to each other as if there was something funny he was not being let in on.

"How's it goin'?"

"Good," Buster said.

The four of them just stood there awkwardly.

"Mind if I talk to the boy alone for a moment?"

"Sure," said Mr. Svendergard. "I've got a truck goin' out, anyway."

The sheriff then looked at Mrs. Svendergard and smiled curtly. She got the message and followed her husband out of the room. Maybe it was a small thing, but Dudival noticed that her blouse had been put on inside out.

"I brought you something," Sheriff Dudival said, presenting Buster with a book that had been gift-wrapped with an FBI Most Wanted flyer.

"Mrs. Humphrey's *Manners for Men*. I've read it many times myself. Thought it might be…" He pulled up short. "Are they treating you all right here?"

"Yes, sir."

"Anything you want to tell me about?"

"Not much to say."

The sheriff noticed something behind Buster on the Svendergard's breakfront. He stepped forward to examine a tin pie plate that had—with ballpeen and awl—been hammered into a portrait of someone.

"Ah made that," Buster said proudly.

"He looks familiar. Do I know him?"

"You shor do. That there's the late Mr. Dominguez."

"I see." The sheriff handed the plate back to Buster. "I think you nicely captured him."

"Thanks, Sheriff." Then Buster whispered entre nous, "Ah'm workin' on one a Mr. Svenergard. Gonna surprise him."

"Well, I'm sure he'll appreciate that."

They stood there for a moment. Buster was to offer nothing more.

"Okay, then. I guess I'll be going. I've written my phone number on the inside of that book cover just in case you ever need it."

"Okey doke," Buster said.

Buster had not been exactly forthcoming with the sheriff about his living conditions. The Svendergards, as it turned out, weren't just about cement. On a warm day a few weeks after moving in, Mr. Svendergard purchased several bales of hay and had instructed Buster to stack them one on top of the other by the gravel silo. Zella cheerfully rolled out a large archery target.

"Ever shot a bow and arrow before?" said Mrs. Svendergard.

"Nope."

Then Mr. and Mrs. Svendergard disappeared giggling into the maintenance barn. When Buster was finished hoisting the target up onto the hay bales, he turned around to find Gil and Zella reappear from the barn completely naked except for the hawk feathers in their Indian headdresses.

"Oh gosh…" Buster guffawed and covered his eyes.

"It's okay, Buster. You can look at us." Buster peeked between the crack in his fingers. So much for the pinkness of the Svendergards' skin.

"Jiminy Christmas, Mrs. Svendergard," Buster said.

"Buster, take your hand away from your eyes. There's nothing to be embarrassed about," Mrs. Svendergard said. "Look, *I'm* not embarrassed."

"Everybody's got the same equipment, son."

"Buster, it's *clothes* that are the problem. They hide us from our real selves."

"Mind if ah keep mine on, for the heck of it?"

"Of course not. We just thought it was time for you to know who *we* were. And that you should never be ashamed of your own body. Buster, no matter what they've taught you at Sunday school, just know this—the human race enters the world in an innocent state," said the uncircumcized Mr. Svendergard.

"Uh huh."

"The system corrupts us," the mister continued—his wagging finger seeming to power the metronome of his wagging scrotum. "They turn us into vessels filled at the altar of consumerism!" Buster tried to digest that. A vessel was a boat. That's as far as he got before Mrs. Svendergards' breasts caught his attention. For a chunky woman, her bosom was firm and aerodynamic as the chromed nosecone of a '53 Studebaker Champion. And then there was her pubic hair. It was the same color as her eyelashes, and a copse of it climbed out between her legs and encroached her belly button like summer vines over a window. "That's why, when we take off our clothes, we're making a statement. And do you know what that statement is, Buster?" And Mrs. Svendergard's rear end was pink and plump and swaybacked into a perfect dimpled hollow where a fellow could lay his head—if he so desired—while taking a nap under a shade tree.

"I said, do you know what that statement is?"

All Buster knew was that he was the luckiest boy in town. And then he fainted—because in the last seventy-five seconds he had forgotten to breathe. After the initial shock, Buster accepted their enthusiasm as second nature and joined them—in the water-filled quarries where they bathed naked, riding their Shetland ponies in the buff, jumping on the trampoline and playing naked hangman at the basketball hoop. Nudity, and the adoration of the Great Aten, the Egyptian Sun God, had long ago replaced the Svendergard's regular churchgoing.

"Hail Aten, thou Lord of beams of light, when thou shinest, all faces live. Hail Aten!"

"Hail Aten!" Buster repeated, arms outstretched, palms facing the sun. That's how Buster and Mr. Svendergard began each day at the concrete company.

The earth circled Aten three times and as the equinox began, the Svendergards were visited once again by Sheriff Dudival.

"Good afternoon, ma'am."

"Good afternoon, Sheriff," Mrs. Svendergard said, quickly fidgeting with the last button of her blouse.

"I hate to bother you, but I was by the school this morning and Buster's name came up. He hasn't been enrolled for the fall term."

"Sheriff, with all due respect, our position on this hasn't changed. We don't want to send him to a place where he's going to be bullied."

"Ma'am, any kid who remembers Buster allegedly killing anybody would be in high school by now."

"He's getting a good education here."

"Then if you don't mind, someone from the school will be by to test him to see how he's getting on."

The next day, a social worker and a school administrator came by to give Buster a test to see how well he understood the basic principals of grade school math and English."We think this young man should be back in school," they said, packing up their pencils and papers. "He's sorely lacking in multiplication skills and has no understanding of punctuation."

"He's learning to run a business! Can you teach him *that* in school?" Mrs. Svendergard said, showing them the door—and for some reason, spelling out her defense in the air with her finger. "No, you don't! Exclamation mark. Do you? Question mark."

As for school, it started, once again, without him. Things went back to normal if one could call it that. Then one night, Mr. Svendergard didn't turn up for supper. Buster and Mrs. Svendergard searched the entire compound, but Mr. Svendergard was nowhere to be found. Buster used his special phone number to call Sheriff Dudival. Thirty-six hours later, the naked body of Gil Svendergard was finally discovered. He had been standing on the famed steel scaffolding of his own design, rinsing off a gyrating cement truck with a high-pressure hose. Somehow the loading gate of the gravel chute had opened behind him, pushing him off the platform and inside the barrel of the truck, where he was mixed and tumbled with a fresh load of concrete intended for a condo project in Telluride.

"Any idea how that happened, Buster?" asked the sheriff, interviewing him in the Svendergard's living room.

"Nope," said Buster.

"No idea who pulled that gravel chute up there?"

Buster thought about that for a moment.

"Welp, there ain't but the three of us here. The missus never go up there…"

"But *you* do, right?"

"Yep. Ah do a considerbull 'mount a work up there."

"And you never saw anybody else around here…on the property?"

"Nope."

"And if you happened to pull that cord on the chute by mistake, you'd own up to it, because mistakes *do* happen in life."

"Yessir, they shor do."

The sheriff waited for him to say something.

"So…did you make a mistake?"

"Ah don't b'lieve ah did."

"And you and the mister never had any harsh words or other contretemps?"

"You mean like him not lettin' me go to school?" The sheriff thought he was finally getting somewhere.

"That's right. Like that."

"Truth is, sir…ah dint wanna go."

The sheriff's eyes fell, once again, on the Svendergards' breakfront where he noticed that there was a second pie plate on the shelf. This one was of Gil Svendergard. The sheriff put a hand on Buster's shoulder and pulled him closer to him so he could speak in a low voice.

"Now look here, Buster, I'm going to give you fifteen seconds to admit that you might have had a hand in this. If you did, I'll figure something out. I swear nothing bad will happen to you. I'll just get you some help. Understand?"

"Yessir."

The sheriff stood back and just looked at Buster's blank face for fifteen seconds waiting for an answer. None came. Once again, Sheriff Dudival, in his capacity as sheriff and Coroner, reported it in his journal this way: *Gil Svendergard suffered an accidental death due to a contraption of his own devise for loading and cleaning cement trucks that never passed a safety test by OSHA or a certified engineering company. He was unclothed.*

There was a big turnout of women for Mr. Svendergard's funeral, despite the fact that none of them had ever been friends with the missus. Word had gotten out that Mary Boyle, owner and cook at the Buttered Roll, had prepared marinated flank steak with roasted peppers on freshly baked rolls for the wake.

Buster had liked Mr. Svendergard and had enjoyed living there for the past two years, so he didn't have to force himself to cry when the hearse drove up from Crippner's Funeral Home. Buster, in all the time he had lived with the Svendergards, had never cut his red hair, nor did he shave—since it was the order of day at the Svendergards to go *au natural* in all things. Wearing one of Mr. Svendergard's dark suits, his white shirt sleeves stuck out a good six inches, the gestalt was that of an orangutan in cowboy boots. Sheriff Dudival gently guided the boy to the back of the hearse where he, Skylar Stumplehorst—one of the biggest ranchers on the mesa—and two contractors, who were still owed concrete jobs, lined up behind the back door of the open hearse. Mr. Svendergard had requested that he be buried in a simple pine box—convinced that his worldly remains would quickly be carried off by Isis to begin its long journey home to the sun. This turned out to be a big mistake. To begin with, when the man from Crippner's Funeral Home rolled the coffin out the back of the hearse into the waiting hands of the pallbearers, the weight practically tore each man's arms out of their sockets. The people at Crippner's had had little success in removing Mr. Svendergard from the cement chunk that he was originally delivered in. Their chief embalmer wasn't trying to be ironic when he said that it would take a better man than he—Michelangelo's hammer and chisel perhaps—to free Gil Svendergard from the chunk of cement that enslaved him. His first half-baked attempt ghoulishly separated a foot with the shoe still on it from the corpse, so Crippner's decided to quit while they were ahead, or at least while the body still had a head.

The pallbearers took half a dozen wobbly steps under the weight of what surely was four hundred pounds, when Mr. Svendergard's body suddenly broke through the bottom of the pine boards and fell to the ground. The gravediggers, it turned out, had gone for a drink. With the limited manpower on hand, the pallbearers had to resort to flopping the cement-encrusted corpse end over end. Mrs. Svendergard gasped and wailed with each flop, until, like craps, seven was the lucky number and the conglomerate that was Mr. Svendergard fell into the grave, head down.

Buster shoveled a spade of dirt over his second adopted father, hoping that, after a short period of mourning, everything would return to normal. Would Mrs. Svendergard still read Robert Louis Stevenson's *Kidnapped* to him while cleaning his ears in her naked lap? He certainly hoped so. Mrs. Svendergard cornered Sheriff Dudival before he could close the door of his patrol cruiser.

"I don't think I can keep Buster."

"Why not?" Sheriff Dudival asked.

"I don't... I don't feel comfortable being alone with him."

"Do you believe Buster was responsible for your husband's death?"

"I don't know."

"Then what is it?"

"I think he'd be better off in a family with a male role model."

Mrs. Svendergard was not just thinking of Buster when she made that suggestion. She had received an unexpected phone call that morning from a golf properties consortium in Coral Gables, Florida. A famous golf course architect, Gordon McClain III, had flown over her property in an UltraLight airplane on the way to Phoenix and was taken with the eccentricity of her topography. This was his specialty in golf course architecture—finding the challenging sites in what he called the "American vernacular." Mrs. Svendergard wasn't interested in the vernacular side of things as much as she was in the price per acre. He said that his consortium would not be willing to go over four thousand per. They would spread the payment over ten years. Mrs. Svendergard said that would be fine with her and gently put the phone down in the cradle. She quickly scribbled the figures on the back of a nudist magazine called *Svenska Exposures* that was by the phone. She ciphered 640 times 4,000 divided by 10. She looked at it again. Could this be right—256,000 a year? Zella and Gil only lived on forty thousand, and they had spent like Romans! The way she figured it, she could live for thirty or forty more years and never have to lift a finger! She could leave narrow-minded Vanadium with its freezing winters and live her dream: the Brisa Suave assisted living nudist commune in Costa Rica. Mrs. Svendergard broke down and cried. Buster, who was in the kitchen cleaning up the breakfast dishes, assumed she was on the phone talking to a relative who was offering condolences and came to put a comforting hand on her shoulder. Mrs. Svendergard looked up and blubbered at him.

"My God, I can't believe this has happened to me."

"Ah'm sorry, Mommy."

Buster was going to be a problem. There was no way she could take him to the most famous nudist colony in the world. Buster would be an embarrassment to her. Time and time again, she tried to explain to Buster that looking at someone naked and sexual stimulation were two different things. But despite her patient pedagogy, Buster stubbornly insisted on parading around the house with an erection. If this was her chance to finally get out of Vanadium, she wasn't going to miss it because of him."I'll send somebody up for his clothes," said the sheriff.

"They're in the car," Mrs. Svendergard said.

Sheriff Dudival looked around at the people at the funeral heading for the parking lot. There was the quiet Mary Boyle from the Buttered Roll. Mary was a good person in her early thirties married to Bob Boyle, a one-time star on the rodeo circuit. The sheriff put in an emergency call to the Vanadium Women's League.

CHAPTER FOUR

Learning the Ropes at the Boyles'

MARY BOYLE WAS IN the back of the Buttered Roll stuffing tarragon tuna fish into beefsteak tomatoes when the little bell rang on the door. It was Sheriff Dudival acting as emissary for the Women's League of Vanadium.

"Hello, Mary, may I speak with you for a moment?"

She wiped her hands on her apron and came out, a look of dread on her face.

"Certainly, Sheriff. Anything wrong?"

"No, no. I just wanted to know how things were going for you at home."

"You mean, since Bob…?" She didn't complete the sentence, which would have been: "…beat the living crap out of me and I dialed nine-one-one convinced that he was really going to kill me this time but then I begged you to not arrest him because it would've only made life more difficult for me than it was worth and you didn't?"

"Yes, since then."

"Things are great," she said. "Thanks for asking."

Yes, the sheriff had not arrested Bob, even though the law said it was mandatory. This was but another of the laws that Sheriff Dudival felt better left to his discretion. Mary refused to go to a women's shelter and she had three young children that she would have had to take care of herself—no daycare being available in Vanadium in those days.

"Happy to help," he said. "But, uh…" He tilted his hat back to scratch his head. "I was wondering if you might do a little something for me."

The Boyles lived behind the Buttered Roll, the restaurant Mrs. Boyle had bought before she married Bob, a rodeo star who'd been a regular customer. Like most newlyweds, they'd had big dreams. Theirs was to buy the defunct Victorian Vanadium Hotel on Main Street. It had been built in the forties to house the mining executives who then frequented the town, but when the mine closed, the place had gone to seed. The asking price was $140,000. Mary thought that they could refurbish the place to its former glory. With pencil and paper, Mary and Bob sat down every night and worked out a financial plan. They would support themselves on the Buttered Roll income and bank Bob's rodeo winnings.

The Boyles' savings plan went into effect and was working well—even after they had their first child. Mary was still able to run the restaurant and manage the baby. It became a little more difficult after the second child, one year later. At that point, she had to close the restaurant for dinner and serve breakfast and lunch only. Her third child was born autistic. The Vanadium school wouldn't let him stay in kindergarten. They said he disrupted the class. So, Mary had no other choice but to home school. The Buttered Roll was now only open for breakfast.

In the meantime, Bob's career had taken an unfortunate turn. A Brahma bull, by the name of Insult to Injury, threw him fifty feet in the air—after nearly amputating his right hand when it wouldn't come free of the harness rope. Insult charged as he scrambled for safety. He hooked Bob through his shirt and threw him down on the ground and then proceeded to stomp on his groin with such force that his scrotum was forever crimped around the edges like one of Mary's sage and butter raviolis. Bob rarely finished in the money after that. He told Mary that their family problems were a distraction and he couldn't maintain focus, but the truth was the incident with Insult caused him to lose his nerve. He became unstable—the slightest incident would set him off. If the kid at the Dairy Queen told him that they'd run out of butterscotch dip, he'd storm out looking for someone's head to rip off. He'd show up at the High Grade just to pick a fight. But after the news spread about his flattened testicles, no one took him seriously as a brawler. So, he took the fight home.

If you'd asked him, Bob would have told you that he loved Mary more than words could say—and he meant it. But deep down he suspected that she considered him a loser. Sometimes he would go to stroke her hair or caress her face, and find himself hitting her. When his autistic son acted up, Bob would try to hug him into stopping, but wound up shaking him until foamy spittle flew from his mouth. When his daughters protested, he whipped them with his champion rodeo buckle.

After Sheriff Dudival came to the house the night of the 911 call—and acquiesced to Mary's request that he not be arrested—he nevertheless made it clear to Bob that if he ever saw Mary in town with a bruise or a black eye, he would personally drive him to Canon City State Prison. Bob knew that Sheriff Dudival meant business, so after that he made sure he wore Mary's quilted oven mittens when smacking her.

As for Buster, Bob beat him up in the guise of giving him boxing lessons, but Buster considered himself fortunate that a male role model was actually taking the time for him. In appreciation, Buster tapped out a pie plate portrait of Bob depicting him astride a rip-snorting bucking bull. Bob regarded his tribute gimlet-eyed.

"Who the hell is that supposed to be?"

"Why heck, Pop…it's you."

"I meant, the *bull*."

"The bull?"

Bob, in his post-traumatic state, believed the bull to be Insult to Injury and further, that Buster had rendered him aboard his old nemesis to have a laugh at his expense. He grabbed Buster by the hair and pulled him down, sideways to his height.

"Friend, you done woke up the wrong passenger!"

"Ow, Pop! The bull don't have a name. He's jes' 'Bull!'"

Bob's eyelids fluttered a few times as if a hypnotist had just snapped his fingers and told him he could stop being a chicken. He took a deep breath and let go of Buster's hair.

"Sorry, kid. One of these days, I oughta go git my head examined."

"Ah'll git rid of this plate direkly, so yool never have to think about it, Pop."

Buster started to walk to the trashcan, but Bob stopped him.

"The hell, you say! What you done there is special… It's like I'm on my own damn coin!" He looked at it again, this time admiringly. "I'll tell you somethin' I'll never tell her. I wish you were my son—instead a that re-tard, Bob Jr,." he said, gesturing back to the house.

"Aw, he's all right, Pop. He's jes a lil techy."

"Crime of it is, I was hopin' to pass down everthang I knew about cowboyin', but there you damn have it!"

Buster swallowed hard and dared to speak.

"Uh…ya think you could teach *me*?"

Bob may not have known how to send an email or chip a golf ball with a fifty-six degree wedge to make it hop twice then stop dead six inches from the flag, but before he lost his confidence, he could throw a rope around the engine of a moving train and rope a steer and tie its legs together in nine seconds flat.

"Why the hell not?"

They started off with a thirty-foot extra-soft rope. Bob taught him how to lay it out, to coil it, make a spoke and swing it. Bob taught him how to throw a Figure Eight that could catch the head of a steer and his front legs. He taught him the Roll Over to catch all four legs. He taught him how to throw a loop standing, and he taught him how to throw one on a moving horse. And when Bob was sure Buster had the fundamentals, he taught him the surefire stuff to impress the girls. In a few weeks time, Buster was able to do the Slow-motion Roll across his back, the Tiny Loop Scoot along the ground like he was walking a dog, and the crowd pleasing Texas Skip with two ropes—alternating jumps between each one without taking off his hat.

As for riding, Buster had already proven in the Vanadium Labor Day Rodeo that he could stay on a horse. Bob had actually been in the crowd that day—marveling along with everyone else. But as Bob now pointed out, *staying on* a horse was not exactly the same as *riding* a horse.

By way of illustration, Bob led his bay mare into the corral. He grabbed her mane while holding the reins and then, in one smooth motion, swung himself up in the saddle. His posture was upright; his knees lightly making contact with the rib cage of the horse, but from the knees down his legs flared out, his boots in stirrups—the weight on the balls of his feet, heels down. He let the reins drop. The bay waited for the light to change. Then, Bob gently touched her left underflank with the back of his spur and she moved her hips to the right. He tapped under her right side and she sashayed to the left. Now, Bob leaned slightly forward in the saddle and the horse began to trot. He put pressure on her with both legs and she began a slow, graceful lope in a circle. Bob's ass never left the saddle; his pelvis rocking back and forward with her movement—all the while with an odd look of bliss on his face that Buster had never seen when Bob was inside the house.

Teaching Buster, in the weeks and months ahead, produced in Bob unexpected vigor. He began to love cowboying again as Buster's unalloyed enthusiasm recorded over his own fear. So when he saw the ad for the Copenhagen Rompin' Stompin' Show in *Ranch World* magazine, he threw caution to the wind and mailed in his entrance fee.

Before Bob left for the arena in Cheyenne, Wyoming, he gave Buster, as a gesture of gratitude, a lariat—which he had braided himself some twenty years ago—when cowboys still used Plymouth Yacht Linen. He jury-rigged a surrogate roping critter with real bull's horns so Buster could practice throwing the lariat while he was away. All of this may have been small potatoes to recommend Bob as a member of the human race, but it was something. In fact, the minister even mentioned it at Bob's funeral.

Bob arrived in Cheyenne in the early evening and checked into the Cock Robin Motel. He ate the sandwich that Mary had made for him, did some push-ups and sit ups, then went to bed. That night, he had a dream that he was going to be killed by a bull. The next morning, he tried to brush it off, but when he went to the arena to sign in and get his number, his delicate mental state came under attack.

The more successful cowboys had flown in on their own Cessnas. That was the first thing that irritated Bob; that he had to drive all the way there in a twelve year-old truck with a bad front end. Then there were the obligatory jokes about his crushed testicles. To make matters worse, he didn't draw a very good bull. But he made it to the buzzer and he didn't get hurt, so that smoothed his hackles somewhat. He placed fourth and won $1,500. A rodeo clown, who he used to go drinking with, felt sorry for the ribbing the other cowboys had given him and counted out six white crosses for Bob's ride home. However, Bob didn't take the present in the spirit in which it was given.

"I should have the ten thousand dollars, not this shit!" And that may have been Bob's problem in a nutshell—not to poke fun at Bob's anomalous anatomy. When you've been the best at something, nothing less ever seems good enough.

The 450-mile trip home was a hellish drive in a howling spring snowstorm. It took him thirteen and a half hours to get back to Vanadium. Buster was outside when he saw Bob's truck pull up, still covered in ice and snow. Buster had the presence of mind to make himself scarce when he saw what Bob's glazed eyes looked like. The house was a mess. The kids had runny noses, and everyone was screaming. His autistic son, Bob Jr., was singing the hook to a pop song in a black lady's falsetto—over and over again. Bob started counting to ten. His mouth was dry, and his breath was putrid from the white crosses and the bile of his own bad temperament. He went to the refrigerator and grabbed a beer. Mary was in the kitchen—noisily grinding walnuts for an order of banana cake, which had to be ready by six. Bob tried to stand there nonchalantly like the loose-jointed, laconic cowboy he used to be. At this very moment, he was of two minds. He was either going to call upon all of his strength to act normal, tell his wife he had won a little bit of money, or he was going to take the Hamilton blender and bash her head with it.

Buster was standing on the back of Bob's pickup throwing a lasso at his surrogate roping steer. Over and over again he flung it, tied it off on one of the aluminum cleats on the perimeter of the truck bed, jumped down and wrestled it to the ground and tied its wooden legs. That's when he heard the screams from inside the house. He left his rope tied to the steer and ran inside. The kids were all crying. Mary, a deep purple gash above her right eyebrow, was being dragged from room to room. Buster didn't know what to do. He had never confronted a full-grown man before. He stood there and watched as Bob punched her and kicked her. Suddenly, he found himself flying across the living room in slow motion and into the back of Bob Boyle's legs. Buster threw him down, took a stretch of rope from his belt and quickly cinched it around Bob's ankles. Mary woozily got up and went to the kitchen where she retrieved two ten-inch Calphalon fry pans and clanged Bob's head on both sides until his blood rolled off the catalogue-promised non-stick surface. She was able to get in three more cymbal crashes before Bob worked the ropes off his feet, broke her nose and ran howling like a banshee out of the house.

He started up his truck and hit the gas sending a rooster tail of loose gravel up against the building. His ears were ringing as he tore down Possum heading for Piñon. Bob had no idea that he was dragging the practice steer—still tied to the truck. Up ahead, the Red Hat Produce man was backing up the street to make a delivery. Bob put his foot down on the brake, but his boot went right to the floor. He smacked into the tailgate of the produce truck going fifty miles an hour. He survived the actual collision, but then, the momentum of the surrogate steer sent it flying through the back window of the cab. The bull's sharp horns, which Bob had attached with baling wire, smashed through the glass. One of them pierced the back of his neck, passed through his brain stem and out of his astonished mouth.

Sheriff Dudival arrived on the scene, and, together with Mary and Buster's testimony, worked out the cause of death. Bob was not able to stop the truck because his brake line had been cut.

"Mary says you put up a pretty good fight with Bob. Is that true?"

"Ah don't rightly rem'ber much 'bout it."

"Do you know how the brakes on a vehicle work, son?"

"Yesssir. Ya put yer foot down on the petal and that's what stops 'er."

"Do you have a pocket knife?"

"Yes, sir."

"May I see it please?"

Buster dug around in his jeans and came up with a rusty old pocketknife.

"You didn't cut those brake lines with this pocket knife, did you son?"

"No sir. Ah did not."

The sheriff ran his thumbnail along the blade to see if there was any residue.

"Okay," said the sheriff handing it back to him. "You can go back inside now."

There was an inquiry into Bob's death. The sheriff had noted in his journal that *the brake line on Bob Boyle's vehicle had been chewed through by a marmot...* Marmots, as groundhogs are called in the area, often chewed through the under-hoses of cars left parked outside for a long time. It was possible that a marmot chewed through the brake line of Bob Boyle's truck; however, no one in his or her right mind believed it. Dudival, himself, kept a little piece of the questionable brake line in his evidence safe. *Ultimate cause of death: brain trauma caused by bull's horns.*

Anyone you talked to in Vanadium was now convinced that Buster had not only killed Carlito Dominguez and Gil Svendergard, but Bob Boyle, as well. The question that weighed most heavily was why Sheriff Dudival was protecting him.

Mary had decided that Buster's presence in the house would only be a constant reminder to her children of what had happened to their father. At the inquest over Bob's death, she informed Sheriff Dudival of her decision. As one might imagine, Buster had become difficult adoption material.

As she tearfully left the courtroom, Mary stopped to kiss Buster goodbye. Banged up as she was, Mary was already Looking

Better Without Bob—which should have been the title of a country and western song. She hugged Buster and held him close for an embarrassingly long time.

"You're my hero," she said, and slipped something into his hand. When Buster looked down, he saw that she had given him Bob's championship rodeo buckle.

"Aw, Jiminy, Mrs. Boyle, Ah cain't take somethin' like this… A feller's gotta earn it."

"Believe me," she said, "…you did."

CHAPTER FIVE

The Stumplehorst Outfit

THE WOMEN'S LEAGUE OF Vanadium was quickly running out of good Christian homes for Buster. Sheriff Dudival, who until now had worked behind the scenes on Buster's behalf with no less cunning and resourcefulness than a Vatican cardinal-prefect, begged the League to give him one more chance to place Buster before they sent him off to the county orphanage.

He had one last good idea, the Stumplehorst family. The Sheriff would have to bring to bear all of his powers as a salesman, for this was not an easy sell. What he had in his favor was that it was round-up time, and the Stumplehorst Ranch usually paid for temporary hands. With Buster's adoption, all it would cost them to have another able-bodied wrangler would be room and board. Sheriff Dudival scribbled that thought down on a napkin as he waited to meet Skylar Stumplehorst for breakfast at the High Grade.

"Can he ride a horse?" It was obvious that Stumplehorst knew very little about Buster.

"He's probably the best rider and roper in this county now that Bob's dead."

"We have some strange hands in the bunkhouse, but I don't think there's a killer among 'em."

"No one's been able to prove he's killed anybody."

"I don't want to die. Is that so unreasonable?"

"Stumplehorst, you're not afraid of that boy; you're afraid of what your wife is going to say if you make a decision without consulting her." This was a sore point with Skylar Stumplehorst. Skylar Anderson had been a two-bit cowboy until he impregnated Calvina Stumplehorst in the back of his truck at the conclusion of "Rattlesnake Round-Up." She was from a ranching family that only produced women—which was why her father, Calvin, insisted that Skylar change his surname to Stumplehorst. After Calvina's mother and father passed, Skylar was sitting pretty. Calvina bore him four daughters, who, like their mother, treated him like the uncouth yokel he was.

"I call the shots out there."

"Prove it."

"All right, I'll take him." Stumplehorst regretted that statement immediately, but before he could say another word, Sheriff Dudival threw down three bits for his coffee and walked out.

That afternoon, Sheriff Dudival drove Buster up to the ranch before Skylar could change his mind. Rearing up above the massive timber gates were twin wrought iron rampant colts. They had been copied from the handles of the famous pistols—between them were the letters S-T-U-M-P-L-E-H-O-R-S-T.

"Cain't ah just stay with you at the jail, Sheriff?"

"I'm sure there'll be plenty of time for that later."

As they pulled up the road to the house, Buster could see three of the Stumplehorst daughters hanging laundry in the front yard. Hope, Faith, and Charity were fine examples of sturdy Lame Horse Mesa girls, but it was Destiny Stumplehorst, Buster recognized from the rodeo, who had him in her enthrall. She was in the corral brushing out her mare, Maple, who was named after the syrup and not the tree. Both Maple's and Destiny's ponytails had the same tight braid. Destiny had a constellation of freckles across her face as if she had held the wrong end of a can of Rustoleum. Buster had become, since living with the Svendergards, quite adept at imagining what people looked like without their clothing, and he imagined Destiny might just have the best figure of any girl in town, but there was more to his admiration than merely the physical. He liked the meticulous way she combed out her horse's mane and tail. He liked the way she wore a red bandana in her hair to keep it clean. He liked the way she chewed gum in little inconspicuous movements like she was biting the inside of her cheek thinking about something important. Then, without warning, she turned and looked right at him. Their eyes met, and Buster quickly slumped down in his seat.

"What is wrong with you?" the sheriff said.

"Nothin."

"Come on now. Sit up. This is no way for a gentleman to make a first impression."

At the head of the driveway stood Skylar and Calvina. Calvina's father, Calvin Stumplehorst, was one of the most admired men in Vanadium. At nearly 450 pounds, he had to have extra-large saddles custom made by the Botero Leather Company in Valencia, Spain. In a bar fight, he would use his stomach to knock his opponent to the floor and then lay on them—like the famed Flat Rock in Arches National Park. Calvin Stumplehorst was the one who had put money into the refurbishing of the IOOF, the International Order of Odd

Fellows. He was the one who had organized the building of a rodeo arena. He had three mistresses, one Chinese, one Mexican, and one albino. He had an extensive collection of Red Skelton records that he would listen to in the tack room and laugh and laugh until tears rolled down his florid face. It was said that Calvin Stumplehorst, until he got himself a bellyful of cancer, could eat a whole mule deer by himself in one sitting. After they removed his stomach and reattached it to his small intestine, his oncologist told him that if he ever ate anything larger than a Le Sueur pea, it would be the end of him. He followed his doctor's instructions and lost 250 pounds. No longer the imposing figure that he had once been, he adapted to the person he now was. He took up the writing of poetry and chronicled in verse every aspect of the ranch and the land he loved. Some of his stuff made it into the local newspaper because he owned it. One poem was submitted to *The Paris Review* along with a contribution for $2,500. It was published in the fall edition of 1961. It went like this:

This is my damn house / This is my damn broke-down tractor / This is my damn dog / This is my damn horse / This is my damn rock / This is my damn ranch

But in the end, even being the poet laureate of Vanadium was not satisfying for a man of such Herculean appetites. And so, one Saturday night, he put four pounds of short ribs in his personal crock-pot with a bottle of red wine, a can of tomato paste, three onions, fresh thyme, and two bay leaves from his garden. In the morning, he saddled his favorite swayback pony, took one last ride around his property, and went to International Order of Odd Fellows where he hung an oil painting of himself that he had commissioned. Then he returned home, ate all the short ribs, retired to the tack room, put on a Red Skelton record and, unlike Socrates, died an exquisite death.

As big a life as Calvin lived, his eldest child and inheritor of his lands, Calvina, lived a small one. You could see it in her face, which was pale and indistinct. It was less a face than it was a grave rubbing. When she was a teenager, Calvina had been sent off to Uncle Hebron in Truth or Consequences, New Mexico. He was a General in the Salvation Army. There, she was indoctrinated in the ways of sobriety, piety, and parsimony. She saw firsthand what a profligate lifestyle could lead to—drunkenness, venereal disease, illegitimacy, and hopeless destitution. Now, as the baroness of the Stumplehorst Outfit, many of the Army's principles were embedded in everyday Stumplehorst life. They prayed twice a day in the outbuilding once used to house the Red Skelton collection, now a house of God. No music or television was allowed. The girls were given a dollar a week of spending money. Skylar was given $4.75. Everyone in the family had to carry the traditional Salvation Army Little Black Book—and account for every penny spent. Calvina inspected each and every one for discrepancies on Friday nights before Evensong. And lastly, the children were not sent to the public school. Calvina taught them at home from a curriculum sent by mail from the Thessalonians Home Study Course of Oxford, Mississippi.

The Stumplehorst family had twelve hundred irrigated acres bordered by a worm fence that was laid out by old man Stumplehorst in the 1940s. Four hundred head of Angus meandered across the wavy grass like black holes; quarter horses raised for hobby, neat rows of chicken coops and swine pens, and twenty acres of planted vegetables. Not even the fashion designer Ralph Lauren in Ridgway, Colorado, had a ranch like this. And he had *money.* The Stumplehorsts didn't have money. They had the US Government.

When Calvina's father died, so died his distracted way of managing the ranch. She immediately sought out the government programs that had always been available, but never utilized by her father whose interests, as previously noted, were elsewhere. In short order, she cobbled together a dizzying network of subsidies that increased the

Stumplehorst Ranch's financial wherewithal six-fold. A rancher needs land to graze cattle. By enlisting in the Federal Land Lease Program, she was able to add four thousand acres to the ranch—allowing them to build a bigger herd. And while she was at it, she might as well avail herself of the government's Risk Management Insurance Program that made it possible to hedge volatility in the beef market. She also helped herself to a USDA Rural Development Subsidy, which paid for the irrigation and soil preparation of their new organic squash and lettuce business. Her husband, Skylar, who was no Andrew Mellon, but a reduce-the-size-of-the-government Republican nonetheless, was uneasy with her high finance shenanigans and told her so.

"Tell me something, Skylar," she'd said, when he balked. "If you saw a dollar laying there in the middle of the road, would you, or would you not, pick it up?"

ꙮ

CALVINA STUMPLEHORST TOOK ONE look at the patrol cruiser coming up the driveway and saw the boy in the front seat. It was obvious that Skylar had not told her about his conversation with the sheriff.

"What's this about?"

"It's nothing," Skylar said, trying to cast it off. "It's a kid I said I'd let work here for six months." The tumble of that deviated syntax set off alarm bells for Calvina. Her eyes narrowed. A partial truth, or worse, a lie, was being told.

"Is that Buster McCaffrey, the murderer?"

"Nobody's ever proved that."

"That's what the sheriff told you." Calvina was always one step ahead of him.

"It's just for six months. We can use him for round up."

"You haven't adopted him."

"Of course, not. You think I'm an idiot?"

Buster got out of the police cruiser and took off his hat. Long, tangled, dirty hair spilled out.

"Uh, 'lo, Mommy. 'Lo there, Daddy."

Faith, Hope, Charity, and Destiny Stumplehorst giggled. Mrs. Stumplehorst turned purple and hissed something in her husband's ear and stormed back to the house.

In the barn, Skylar put on his leather sheep shearing chaps and took an electric cutter to Buster's hair. Unbeknownst to Buster, he had an audience peeking in through the workshop window—Destiny Stumplehorst and her three sisters.

"The missus doesn't want you to call her 'Mommy,' unnerstan?"

"Yessir."

"You can call me Pop if you want, though."

"Okay, Pop."

"But don't call me Pop around the missus."

"Whatever you say, Pop."

After Skylar had buzzed Buster all the way down to the scalp, Buster reached up, touched the top of his head and whistled.

"Jiminy Christmas!"

Skylar then instructed Buster to take off his clothes and stand against the cinder block wall. Skylar let him have it with the fire hose. The girls outside watching had to cover their mouths as they squealed with laughter at the sight of their newly adopted naked brother. Destiny had to pull Charity's hair to get her out of the way so she could get a good look. The girls were all dumbstruck by the size of Buster's johnson—which, even under the duress of freezing cold water, gave the impression of a Slinky making its way down a flight of stairs.

Satisfied he'd loosened all the grime and vermin from Buster, Skylar proceeded to burn his clothes, hat, and boots. Buster was given a new pair of Carthart workman's pants, a shirt, two pairs of skivvies, two pairs of socks, and a pair of White's Packers.

"You'll sleep with the other fellers in the bunkhouse."

As they walked outside, the Stumplehorst girls scrambled out of the way.

"People in town tell ya we're rich?"

"The Dominguezes always tole me not to listen to what people said in town."

"Well, we're not rich. So get that outta your head right now."

"Yessir."

"And be don't be goin' around here losin' tools or throwin' em on the ground. And don't take a whole handful of toilet paper when you wipe your ass. It's a waste of money and it clogs up the septic."

"Yessir."

The bunkhouse was a drafty old wooden building that leaned over on its hip as if it had been waiting a long time for a bus. Buster adjusted his clothes in his arms so he could offer his hand to Skylar and say what Sheriff Dudival had told him to say when the time was right.

"Mr. Stumplehorst…wanna say ah 'ppreciate the op-por-too-nit-ty."

Skylar looked at him and didn't know whether to laugh or to cry. He shook his hand without saying anything. It was his wife's idea to put him in the bunkhouse. If it had been up to him, he would have put him in the house. But it wasn't up to him. He just hoped that Buster wasn't going to resent the accommodations.

The men awoke at four thirty in the morning. They washed and dressed in the dark. They were then made to stand outside in the corral and hold hands while Mrs. Stumplehorst administered the Morning Prayer. Anyone who overslept or dodged the prayers was not eligible for breakfast. Every couple of weeks or so, a man from Delta came down and randomly tested their urine. Any man caught playing a musical instrument, drinking, playing cards, reading an X-rated magazine, or talking to her daughters was summarily fired. The men, of course, hated her, but like her own husband, they had no other place to go.

Buster opened the bunkhouse door and stepped inside. There was only one electric light bulb hanging from the apex of the rafters. The board and batten structure was heated by a potbelly stove in the corner. Either everyone was too lazy or too tired to stoke it. There were ten men in their cots, ages twenty-five to forty-five. The air was blue from tobacco smoke and stunk from clothes, body crevices, and feet that may not have been washed in months. The men turned to look at Buster then looked away, disinterested. They were doing a variety of things—one cowboy was stitching a torn bridle, another man was sitting on another's back squeezing a cyst that the other man couldn't reach himself. Some were just laying there with their eyes open looking at nothing. Buster wandered around the room until he found the only bunk available. It was situated next to a cracked window. The bed was unfortunately missing half of its slats. The mattress showed the tale of its long use with pastel splotches of yellows, ochres, and reds. Buster took the bedding that the old man had given him and patiently fixed things up as best as he could.

There was a mandatory lights-out at 9:30. Buster had chewed bits of newspaper into pulp and caulked the cracks in the wall that were blowing a steady stream of chilled air into his left eardrum. He tried to go to sleep, but he was too excited about the prospect of being a real working cowboy. As disjointed as his life had been, he felt that there was a direction, an unseen hand guiding him to where he was now—even if he was sleeping on a putrid mattress. Quietly, he slipped out the side of his bed so the other men couldn't see him and got on his knees and prayed. He prayed for the people who had raised him, living and dead.

That night, Buster had a dream. He was the boss man on a wagon train that was heading out west to start a new life. It was a heavy responsibility—being the boss man. Some of the people he led were folks he knew—like the Dominguezes, Svendergards, and the Boyles. In each valley they came to, he had to judge the soil, the quantity and quality of the water, whether there was enough timber to build homes, churches, and schools. Each place, so far, had fallen short, and they kept moving—a train of twenty prairie schooners creaking across the slickrock and dry soil. Buster opened his eyes. He was awake, but he could still hear the creaking of the prairie schooners. Then he realized that it was the bunk beds in the room that were creaking from the men masturbating.

At four thirty the next morning, the cowboys reported outside for prayers in the corral, then shuffled into the dining hall—heavily, as if their feet were shackled. Single file, they stopped to grab coffee from an urn by the door and sat down at a long wood-planked table. Skylar was already seated at the head with his cup of black coffee. The men all said perfunctory *g'mornin*'s and stared down expectantly at their empty plates. Jared Yankapeed, Stumplehorst's top hand, sat next to him on his left. Mrs. Stumplehorst sat on his right.

Spirits lightened when the Stumplehorst daughters appeared from the kitchen with platters heaped with flapjacks. Mrs. Stumplehorst, always on message, had the girls make Jesus cakes—pancake batter that had been poured in the shape of a crucifix. Destiny Stumplehorst, primly and properly, never once making eye contact with the any of the hired hands, finally made her way to Buster's left and placed his plate in front of him. Unlike the others, his pancake was not in the shape of the cross, but rather, in the shape of a heart. Buster turned and looked at her. Her face was inscrutable. Their eyes met for a brief instant, and then she returned to the kitchen. Destiny, like most teenage girls the same age as boys, was clearly running a furlough ahead of Buster in the sexual education department. He could feel his blood evacuate his extremities and take cover in his cheeks. Suddenly self-conscious, Buster raised his eyes to see if Mrs. Stumplehorst was watching him. Her nostrils dilated slightly as if she was trying to sniff impropriety in the air. Buster took fork to Bisquick and mashed it until it was unrecognizable. There was a quick prayer over the food followed by the distraction of twelve men eating with their mouths open. Buster, on his first day, had so far escaped being fired.

Now the door opened and two new men dressed in old-fashioned khaki workman's clothes entered. It was no coincidence that their entrance had been timed with the completion of prayers. It wasn't as though they didn't believe in a greater power. They just didn't believe that greater power to be Calvina Stumplehorst. Ned Gigglehorn was in his mid-sixties. He was the more squat and muscular of the two. His neck was thick and wide at the shoulders and shaped like the base of a stalk of celery. However, there was no ignoring his most salient characteristic—that being the blackened band of skin around his eyes. He'd been shot directly in the face with snakeshot. This was referred to as a "raccoon face" or in the vernacular of the older locals, a "'coon face." Miraculously, the shot didn't blind him, but the particles, deeply imbedded in his skin, were there for life—a punishment by the local constabulary and Mine Management for a speech he gave in 1969 at the Odd Fellows Hall calling for a wildcat strike. His disfigurement would have made an ordinary man shy from showing his face in public, but not Ned Gigglehorn. He stared at people aggressively—daring people to look at him and see for themselves how capital regarded labor.

The taller man, who sat down opposite Buster, was Doc Solitcz. He and Ned shared a cabin together—separate from the others. He was in his seventies, rail-thin with a shock of white hair that he combed across his forehead like John F. Kennedy. He conveyed a certain curiosity in the twinkle of his eye—a curiosity that cost him his medical license when he thought to remove his own appendix to test the efficacy of the new method of spinal anesthesia. Calvina Stumplehorst gave the de-frocked doctor free room and board in exchange for veterinarian care for their line of quarter horses and cattle and, more importantly, science lessons for their daughter's home school courses—*if* he agreed to feather in creationism. He reconciled his principles by shrugging off religion as nothing more than the Enlightenment's lazy eye—somewhat crossed and out of focus—but not fatal to the patient.

Breakfast would be the only meal the two men deigned to share with the others. Dr. Solitcz looked across the table at Buster, a slightly humored expression at the corners of his mouth.

"You the McCaffrey boy?"

"Yessir."

"We've followed your career with keen interest. Haven't we, Ned?"

"You're the one who killed his foster fathers."

"That ain't true," Buster said, coming to his own defense.

"No?"

"They never proved it!" Skylar Stumplehorst said, repeating what Sheriff Dudival had told him.

"Well, if you're wrong..." Gigglehorn sipped at his coffee, "...you're next."

Some of the other hands at the table laughed, but Gigglehorn wasn't joking. Despite the light-hearted sound of his name, he never went for a joke if there was a throat available.

Mrs. Stumplehorst gave a little snort. 'That would serve him right for bringing this heathen under our roof!"

"Gigglehorn..." Mr. Stumplehorst protested, "...you take the cake! Why would this young man here wanna kill me of all people?"

Gigglehorn calmly tapped a verboten cigarette out of his pack of Luckies, lit it, and blew smoke across the table at Mr. Stumplehorst.

Buster looked to Mrs. Stumplehorst for her reaction, but funnily enough, she said nothing—only stiffening ever so slightly.

"Mr. McCaffrey here is going to kill you because you've exploited him. Plain and simple."

"I will not have you make trouble under my own roof, you big-mouthed bastard!" bellowed Mr. Stumplehorst.

"Mr. Gigglehorn…" Mrs. Stumplehorst said, mildly interceding on behalf of her husband, "…if this young man is to murder my husband, I sincerely doubt he will be motivated by your dusty socialist principles." Calvina nodded with self-satisfaction to her daughters who, except for Destiny, were watching the breakfast debate with slack-jawed disinterest.

"Ma'am, I believe that, in this young man's short time here, he has already been given justification for killing your husband."

"And what would that be, Mr. Molotov?"

Gigglehorn stood to his feet and bellowed at Skylar Stumplehorst.

"You gave the poor sonofabitch a bed that wasn't fit for a *dog*!"

Ned was always monitoring the working conditions at the ranch on behalf of his fellow workers, and a detail like Buster's bed had not escaped his attention. Buster looked nervously to Mrs. Stumplehorst for her reaction. Surprisingly, she seemed unperturbed—more concerned with the sticky handle on the maple syrup pourer than Gigglehorn's outrages.

"Uh, is there a problem with your bed, son?" Mr. Stumplehorst asked, finding himself alone in all of this.

Buster just looked down at his plate.

"What's he gonna say? The kid's only got two gears—Shy and Murder," said Gigglehorn.

"It ain't exactly first rate, truth be tole, sir," Buster said, quietly.

"Well, if that's true, there's nothin' to get homicidal about, son. I'll tell you what…seein' as you're unhappy with the sleeping arrangements from now on you can sleep with the Doc and Foghorn Leghorn here. How's that?"

"That'd be jes fine with me," Buster said turning to Doc and Gigglehorn to see if it was okay with them. Gigglehorn stared at him blankly—his mouth, once again, his undoing.

Stumplehorst, pleased with his Solomonic judgment, got up from the table. "Then we'll have no more talk about this murdering business from now on. Will we, McCaffrey?"

"No, sir."

Then, Mrs. Stumplehorst clapped her hands twice, and the hired hands stood and marched from the table in single file, passing her at the doorway.

"Thank you for breakfast, ma'am," it was compulsory for them to say, as they all shuffled out. Buster wanted to look back at Destiny, but he dared not.

At the corral, the other hands had already saddled up before breakfast. Buster had yet to be assigned a horse.

"That's your cayuse…over there," someone said.

There was a lone, unsaddled stallion in the corner of the corral and he was a sad sight, indeed. He was filthy and hadn't been brushed or seen to all winter. The other fellows were watching Buster's reaction, straight-faced. A joke was being played out on the new guy or possibly Mr. Stumplehorst—if pushing Buster to his limit could lead to his murder. Buster slowly approached him.

"'Lo there, old clomper. How ya doin'?"

"…Name's Stinker," Jared Yankapeed said. "You'll see why any minute now."

Buster stood a few feet away having a reconnoiter. The nag's chest leaned noticeably over his front hooves. Bob Boyle had taught him that when a horse did that, it meant it was trying to get the weight off his caudal hoof, or heel, because it was in pain. Buster lightly touched his side and the hay burner shuddered. He waited, letting the horse get used to him, then smoothed a hand over Stinker's sides. When Stinker relaxed, Buster gently lifted his front leg and placed it between his knees. The sole of his hoof was packed with hardened mud and debris, but the culprit was the hoof wall. It was raised—creating painful pressure against the shoe all the way up to his navicular bone.

"Well, that ain't good…" Buster said quietly. "Any a you fellers know where they keep the far-yers tools 'round here?"

"Stumplehorst's gonna be out here presently. He don't wait on nobody."

"Won't taker but a minute," Buster said.

"Yor funeral…"

Yankapeed gestured to one of the other cowboys. Sourly, he got down from his horse and went into the shed. He brought back a toolbox with the farriers' tools—pincers, hammer, rasp, and hoof knife. He tossed it at Buster's feet then got back on his own horse.

Buster laid the horse's leg across his knee. He pried off the shoe, scraped the inside of the hoof removing all debris and impediments, clipped the hoof wall all the way around with the pincers, drew the rasp across it until it was nice and level, replaced the shoe, hammered in the nails, bending them over then rasping that surface smooth, then dropped the leg back to the ground. He accomplished all of this in one minute and forty-five seconds. Now, having his rhythm, he completed the other three legs in a total time of four minutes and thirty seconds. None of the other cowboys had ever seen anything like it. As for Stinker, he looked ready to tap down a crystal staircase in a Busby Berkeley musical. Buster threw a blanket on his back, then his saddle and bridle and gave him a comforting chuck to the jowls.

The boys in the corral could hear the door slam shut at the house. The old man was coming. Buster calmly walked the toolbox back to the shed. As Mr. Stumplehorst opened the gate, Buster took three great strides—leaping into the air and landing squarely on Stinker's back without ever touching the stirrups. One of the boys, though he would never admit this to Jared Yankapeed, even wrote his mother about it.

"Ever'body ready?" said Mr. Stumplehorst.

"Yep," said Buster eagerly.

No one else answered. Unlike the cattle round up scene in *Red River*, there was no yipping or yahooing, no horse rearing, no hat waving. Such was the apathy at the Stumplehorst ranch, which was understandable. The day's work of a cowboy was often monotonous and mundane and this was going to be another one of those days.

Being the beginning of May, there was grass coming in, but the herd had to be moved several times a day so they didn't wear out any one spot. As soon as they moved the cattle, the Stumplehorst daughters would enter the area with a chicken coop on wheels and let the chickens feed and defecate their particularly nitrogen-rich effluent, stimulating the regrowth of grass. This progressive system, by the way, was another program paid for, on the Stumplehorsts' behalf, by a subsidy from the US Department of Agriculture. In the afternoon, some of the cowboys were released from cattle moving to ditch burning. Buster was given a torch connected to a BBQ-sized propane tank and sent off to burn the irrigation ditches that had clogged with weeds and grass impeding the flow of water to the alfalfa fields. After that, Buster chopped firewood—another job without an end. Each of these tasks Buster took on with unbridled enthusiasm—much to the annoyance of his colleagues. Some people spend their whole lives unhappily searching, while others are fortunate to find the one thing they were born to do. And Buster was the latter.

After ditch burning, Mr. Stumplehorst instructed Buster in the milking of cows. Buster, being the newest hand, would now have the job of rising an hour earlier for that chore.

"Why cain't ah jes milk 'em in the affernoon?"

"Cows're allus milked in the mornin'! It's allus been so. Their teats'd be draggin' on the damn ground if we milked'em in the affernoon! Got any more dumb queshuns?"

"No, sir!"

Next, Buster was assigned to the woodpile. There, he called upon every fiber of being so as not to let his attention slip and chunk the axe into his shin—for the woodpile was next to the house where Destiny and her sisters were hanging laundry and weeding the vegetable garden. At one point, Buster looked up to see Destiny watching him from behind a laundry line of women's undergarments. She puppet-wiggled the hook-end of her mother's brassiere as a gesture of hello. His heart raced as it did when he got a snoot-full of milkweed. Buster wiggled a finger back at her and scrambled through the left side of his brain for something to say.

"Saw your horse get kicked in the corral today," he said.

"Is that right, smooth talker?"

Before Buster could improve his repartee, Mrs. Stumplehorst came outside and gesturing to the sky, issued new orders to her daughters. They immediately took the laundry down from the lines and hurried inside just as it started to rain.

That night, Buster gathered his gear from the bunkhouse and dragged it across the lawn to Doc Solitcz and Gigglehorn's cabin. Calvin Stumplehorst had assembled it himself from a Sears Roebuck catalogue kit in 1943. It had a nice front porch, two bedrooms, and a loft. Buster knocked on the door.

"Who's that?" That was Doc Solitcz's voice.

"Buster."

"Oh, Christ," said Doc Solitcz, followed with a sigh of resignation, "come in."

Buster entered and dropped his kit. The room smelled of tobacco, oil paint and old man's clothes. A seventy-eight of the forties singer Jo Stafford played "Haunted Heart" on the Philco. There was a small fire going. Doc Solitcz ignored him, quietly attending to his hobby. He was an amateur botanist. In the corner of the room was a press where he dried and flattened botanical specimens on archival paper. On the other side of the room, at the foot of Gigglehorn's bed was an easel with an unfinished painting of a little bird. There were over forty more oils hung all the way up to the rafters. Gigglehorn's avian subjects all bore the same distinction of being painted with enraged expressions, even the tiniest bluebirds and sparrows. Buster stood there waiting for the old man to say something.

"Upstairs," Doc Solitcz finally said, examining an oreocarya longiflora through his magnifying glass.

Buster shouldered his gear and ascended a narrow staircase that swayed precariously as he climbed. At the top, the height of the loft was a mere five-foot-five. Buster was unable to stand straight when up there and was forced to walk around bent at the waist—as if receiving a Japanese ambassador for the first time. There was nothing up there except a single bed. Buster sat on it. He wondered what he should do next. He didn't want to intrude and pacing was awkward.

"What are you doing up there?"

"Nothin.'"

"Come down here, then." Doc Solitcz said.

Buster slowly descended the stairs, gradually straightening his frame.

"Look, McCaffrey, I'll be honest with you: if it weren't for my friend's big yap, you wouldn't be here."

"Yes, sir. And don't think ah ain't ah-ap-preesh-yi-atin' him talkin' up fer me."

"Nothing against you, personally, but as you can see, this cabin's less than nine hundred square feet and you're taking up four hundred and fifty of it just standing there."

"Well, sir, ah'm sorry 'bout that. Cain't hep how big ah yam. Ah'll try to stay outta yor way."

"Well I appreciate that. Thank you."

Buster just stood there.

"What is it?"

"Ah don't want you ta think ah'm nosey, but ah were jes wunnerin…"

"*Wunnerin'* what?"

"Ah were jes wunnerin' how Mr. Gigglehorn here's the only one who's allowed to smoke at the breakfast table and talk back at Missus Stumplehorst."

Doc Solitcz chuckled to himself and considered whether to tell him or not.

"Well, I don't suppose I'd be telling tales out of school…" Doc Solitcz pushed a fresh plug of tobacco in his pipe. "Ever been to Nucla?"

"It's 'bout ten miles from here, ain't it?"

"Mr. Gigglehorn grew up out there…in a socialist commune."

"Ah hear tell of it."

"Well, Ned's parents and about a hundred of them belonged to the International Workers of the World, Wobblies, they were called. And he was brought up with this cockeyed notion that it was one's sole duty to promote the cause of the Workers…"

The doctor went on to say that as a grown man, Ned was a famous orator in these parts—always looking for a soapbox to stand on to address a crowd. Some of these speeches had been made at the Atomic Mine before they fired him in 1963. He was a regular speaker at the International Order of Odd Fellows on Main Street, but he wasn't shy to exhort the drunks at the High Grade Bar—even interrupt people's dinners at the Buttered Roll. One might think it would be hard to raise a crowd in an ignorant mining town to hear a speaker extol the virtues of Marx, Engels, and Mao Zedong or to be punished by Ned's off-key rendition of "There is Power in a Union," but Ned could always fill a house. Before cable and satellite made it possible to raise a television signal in Vanadium, going to see Gigglehorn was big entertainment; not to hear him speak, mind you, but to see him fight. The Atomic Mines Corporation, when notified Gigglehorn was holding forth, invariably sent their stooges to shut his trap. When this happened, the town was treated to an epic battle.

Gigglehorn had worked a pick and shovel since childhood. The muscles in his back piled all the way up to his shoulders to the back of his ears leaving little room for his neck. His forearms were as big as fire extinguishers—his fists, hard and knotty as the handles of a shillelagh. When he threw a punch, it wasn't just his angry one hundred and eighty pounds he put behind it, but the power one only possesses from standing on the moral high ground. Sometimes it would take ten men to send him to the hospital—most of them joining him there with broken noses, jaws, ribs, and ruptured spleens. Eventually, Atomic Mines ran out of men who were willing to interfere with his First Amendment Rights and sent Sheriff Morgan.

Morgan carried two WWI-era Officer's revolvers in .455 Eley. The revolver in his right holster was loaded with deadly dumdums. The cylinders in his left were loaded with bespoke cartridges filled with graphite, granite dust, and metal shavings. This was what Sheriff Morgan used on poor Gigglehorn. However, his 'coon face was not enough to deter Gigglehorn from maintaining his speaking schedule. He was only quiet when the sheriff and his deputies escalated the violence and cracked his skull open—putting him in a coma.

Gigglehorn was never "quite right" after he was discharged from the hospital two months later. He could be walking or riding in a pasture when suddenly he would be gripped by—what he would describe as—a magnetic force that wanted to pull his head to the earth. He would be forced to lay there—anywhere from fifteen to thirty minutes—popping and jerking on the ground like a drop of water on a hot oiled pan. During one of these attacks, an associate noticed that Gigglehorn was having a seizure twenty feet from where a hydrology company recently drilled a dry well for the Stumplehorsts.

After someone removed the rag from Gigglehorn's mouth and he could finally speak, he insisted they drill on the very spot where he had fallen. When they did, they hit water twenty feet down, and Ned Gigglehorn started a new career as a Paranormal Douser. That's why Calvina Stumplehorst was compelled to put up with his big mouth—no matter how rude or insulting he was.

"Mrs. Stumplehorst thinks that Ned, even if he doesn't believe it himself, has been touched by the very hand of God. That's why he can do or say anything he likes." Doc Solitcz relit his pipe. "Out here, water's more important than principles."

Suddenly, the door shuddered with the weight of a body slammed against it.

"That will be Mr. Gigglehorn. Clear a path for him. He was speaking tonight at the Grange Hall."

The latch on the door was fumbled with then Gigglehorn stumbled in and fell to his knees. Slowly, he rose back up to his feet and propelled himself on booze fumes across the room to his bed—where he collapsed face down.

"How many showed up, Ned?"

"Two. But two's better than nothing. Who's that other person in the room?" he said, face planted deep into his pillow.

"The kid who killed the foster fathers. He's staying with us."

"Okay," he said and then passed out.

ꟹ

THE OUTFIT SADDLED UP at daybreak. A storm had moved in from the LaSalles putting a few inches of snow on the ground over night. It would burn off by ten, but Stumplehorst wanted to check on the calves, anyway. Buster and his colleagues were told to grab a sinker and a cup of coffee and hit the trail. For a few hours, the boys had searched every nook and cranny looking for strays that had gotten separated from their mothers. Not finding any slowly enervated them. Buster found Jared Yankapeed and a half-dozen hands having a smoke on a south-facing draw while they warmed themselves in the morning sun.

"Any a you fellers been down to the river?"

"No need. All present and 'counted for," said Jared Yankapeed.

"I'm pretty shor ah sawr a mom and her calf come down there from the ridge."

"Well, why don't you jes head on down there? 'In-vestergate the sichee-ashun.'"

Some of the cowboys laughed when he said that. Evidently, his move out of the bunkhouse had not enhanced his popularity. But no matter, Buster was actually working as a cowboy; his horse liked him and the air smelled like grass. As he worked his way down the draw, he came upon two sets of tracks in the mud and dismounted. Poking his finger at them to see how fresh they were, he noticed a lone buttercup, trying to work its way through the ground, had been trampled. Thinking this might be a nice present for Destiny, if he ever gathered the courage to talk to her again, he gently lifted the buttercup from the mud, cleaned it and placed it in his wallet.

Buster continued following the tracks. No more than one hundred yards down the trail, he encountered a lone calf bellowing for his mother. He leaned over and saw another set of tracks continuing on to the river. He rode on, the calf following willingly. The closer he came to the river, the muddier the lowland became. Now he could hear the bellowing of the mama cow and he urged Stinker in that direction. As he came around the bend, he could see the longhorn mother cow half-submerged, lying on her side in a muddy slough.

"Don't you fret, ma'am. Ah'll get you outta there in two shakes."

"Fergit her fat ass, get *me* out of here!"

Now that was something. The voice sounded exactly like Mr. Stumplehorst's. Buster twisted around in his saddle to look for him.

"I'm down here!"

And there he was, indeed. Skylar Stumplehorst was trapped beneath the cow, his head barely visible above the water line.

"Hey, Mr. Stumplehorst…what're you doin' down there?" Buster kind of guffawed at the absurdity of it all, not realizing how this was aggravating the old man.

"What do you think I'm doing, ya da…?" The "damn idiot" part was garbled as the cow moved and Stumplehorst was momentarily pulled under the water. He fought his way back up and gasped for air.

"What was that, Mr. Stumplehorst?" Stumplehorst was going to repeat what he had said, but thought better of it. Was this how Carlito Dominguez, Gil Svendergard, and Bob Boyle saw their last moments on earth—the kid getting them all alone, with no one around as a witness?

"I said, I was trying to get this cow outta here and then she plumb fell over on me."

"Ah can see that now," Buster said, leaning forward in his saddle. Buster gestured a thumb in the direction of the calf.

"Found her calf up yonder."

"Oh did ya?"

"Yep. Where's yor horse?"

"She run off."

"Well, ah s'pect she'll turn up at feedin' time."

"S'pose so." *I'm dead*, Stumplehorst thought to himself. "So, uh… how you likin' yor new bed?" he said, trying to present himself as a caring human being that didn't deserve to die so young.

"Oh, ah'm likin' it real fahn. Those two gennelmen're a coupla characters, ah'll tell you that!"

"That they are. That they are." There was a long pause. Then Stumplehorst couldn't wait any longer. The black water was rising up his nostrils as he and the cow sunk lower into the mud. "Say, son…I was jes wonderin'…" he asked, choking.

"Yes, sir?"

"Could you be so obliged as to throw me a loop?"

"Why, Mr. Stumplehorst…if you needed hep, why dint ya jes say so? Watch this!" Buster proceeded to take his lariat and spin a small loop on one side of his horse, roll it over his shoulders to the other side. "Whatcha thinka that?"

"Em-pressive," Stumplehorst burbled, the water now up to his eyeballs.

"Shucks, that was nuthin'."

Buster widened his loop and spun it over his head until he and Stinker were completely under it, then stood up on the saddle and jumped, skipping the rope beneath his boots—once, twice, three times and then once on one foot. When he checked for Stumplehorst's approval, he was chagrined to find the old man had completely disappeared under the water, missing the big finale! Deflated at having lost his audience, Buster tossed a ham and eggs loop over the cow's horns and sat back down in the saddle. He tied off the lariat and chirked for Stinker to back up.

Stumplehorst weakly held onto the cow's head as it was released from the mud's suction. He was on all fours, coughing up bog water.

Buster jumped from his horse, slung him over his shoulder then placed him in the saddle.

"Where're those other coffee boilers?" Stumplehorst croaked.

"They paddled back to lunch," Buster said, climbing on the back of the horse.

"Oh they did, did they?"

Buster giddy-yapped and Stinker, not thrilled with the extra freight, gave a world-weary moan and began trudging up to the three-mile ridge that splintered in four sections like the food dividers on a camp plate. On the bottom left of the plate was the Puster's ranch, then the Stumplehorst's in the middle, and Jimmy Bayles Morgan's pony outfit on the right, at the top of the plate the pockmarked Gil Svendergard property. Buster slowed to read a sign posted at the Puster gate. It was a notification that the ranch had been taken over by the First National Bank of Vanadium."What's this mean?"

"Ol' man Puster gone and went belly up…" Stumplehorst said.

"Huh?"

"Threw his cards in."

"That's too bad, ain't it?"

"Well, he weren't much of a bidnis man, truth be tole."

"Why don't the folks 'round here give him the money so he can keep the place?" Stumplehorst turned around in the saddle and just looked at him.

"That's a good one."

They rode on. Buster was thinking.

"Think the bank would let a feller like me take it on?"

"And there'd be unicorns…and dear old pappy'd rise from the grave and we'd all go fishin'. No, son, that there would be highly unlikely. A little thang called eco-nomics comes into play. Know what that is?"

"No, sir. What issit?"

Stumplehorst went to answer, but realized when it came right down to it, he didn't know what economics was, either.

"All I can tell ya is this. You could study it yor whole damn life and still not unnerstan it." He could see the perplexed expression on Buster's face. "Look, son, I ain't tryin' to be an asshole. But the way thangs er set up, a hard workin' cowboy like you's *never* next in the chute for a place like this. Never. Ever. That's jes the God's honest truth."

Buster nodded, but didn't believe it. He just figured Mr. Stumplehorst was still rattled from almost being drowned by the cow.

"Mind if I ask you a somethin', since we're still chewin' on this eco-nomics issue?"

"Sure, Pop."

"That Svendergard woman. How much she git for that old place of hers after you…uh, after her old man, uh…how much did she get per acre from that golf course feller?"

"She tole me not to tell nobody."

"Well, I'm your *Pops.* You can tell your Pops anythin'."

"But she was my mama."

"Well, she ain't your mama no more, son. She run off to a nudie camp."

Buster was still reticent.

"Haven't you ever played poker? Kings beat Queens." Buster considered the wisdom of that. He had a point.

"Four thousand an acre."

"Four thousand an acre! Holy Christ Almighty! Four thousand an acre for the ugliest piece of land on Lame Horse Mesa?" The news made Stumplehorst wiggle his legs like a little girl. "Are you sure you didn't hear fourteen *hundred* an acre?"

"Ah heard what ah heard, Pops. Four thousand."

"Hmm," was all Stumplehorst said. He was quiet after that.

ၵ

MRS. STUMPLEHORST AND HER daughters were serving the hands lunch at the outdoor picnic table when Buster rode up with the old man. By now, Stumplehorst had recovered enough to make a grand entrance and got off the horse by himself. Bowleggedly—and with boots still filled with water—he squished his way to the table, giving every man the stink eye and causing each one of their forks to freeze in various proximities to their mouths. His wife looked at him quizzically as he sat soggily next to her. Getting a whiff of him, she grimaced and clasped a hankie over her nose and mouth.

"Gracious, Skylar, why do you smell so?"

"That there is a very good question, mother." He paused to blow some black gunk out of his nose into a napkin and look at it disdainfully. "I SMELL, cause jes one hour ago, I had one foot in the very sulphurs of HELL!" He now pointed to Buster. "And this boy, here, who you were all quick to con-dem, goddamn SAVED me!" He waited for this pronouncement to sink in to everyone at the table.

"Whoop-dee-doodle," his wife finally said. Undeterred, he moved on to Jared Yankapeed, seated on the other side of him. He put his face up to his, LBJ-style. "Question is…where was you, *top hand*?"

"I were…"

"Porch perchin'!" Stumplehorst said, finishing his sentence. "That's where you was!" He then grabbed Yankapeed's plate of food from under his nose and walked it to the end of the table and threw it down. Then he picked up Buster's plate and carried it back with him. "Son, from now on, yor eatin' next to me."

Every eye at the table was on Buster as he made the *Pomp and Circumstance March* to the head of the table. Destiny, pleased as she was with Buster's coup, was smart enough to indicate nothing to her mother and sisters. She watched as Buster sat down next to her father then, poker-faced, served the latecomers their lunch. Buster smiled up at her, smiled at her father. Could it be that in two short days Buster had climbed out of the slough of questionable provenance to be accepted as suitable company for their daughter? Mrs. Stumplehorst, who was watching Buster's moment in the sun, redirected her attention to Destiny—the mother's kestrel's eye detecting a damning blush on her suprasternal notch.

"Keep him away from our daughter," she hissed to her oblivious husband.

Stumplehorst harrumphed. He was alive and not about to let his wife ruin the triumph of his resurrection.

"Take a powder," he said. Then turning to Buster, the new apple of his eye, "How's the beef, son?"

"Top shelf," Buster said, but it was the heap of mashed potatoes that he found more interesting. Beneath, was a folded piece of notebook paper. He was careful to slip the note into his hand without the old lady seeing him read it under the table. It said, *Get them to take you to the Puster Auction.*

CHAPTER SIX

The Puster Auction

Ground Zero: The Puster Auction

PLUMMETING MEAT PRICES AND the payments on a $145,000 tractor he needed like another solar keratosis dealt old man Puster the last bad card on a cattle ranch that had been in his family since 1876. There was a great deal of faux solemnity as everyone from Lame Horse Mesa pawed through the Pusters' possessions. The stock would be sold at below-market prices. The Stumplehorsts had assigned Doc and Ned to look over the Puster quarter horses and cattle, while Skylar and Calvina, the Morgan Stanley of ranch foreclosure, had already anchored down front row seats for the land auction. Skylar was betting that the secret price paid for the Svendergard Cement Company had not yet reached the ears of Vanadium's Main Street. Sure, there might be some ass-scratching neighbors taking a lowball swing at the place, but no one had the resources of the Stumplehorsts. If what Buster had told her husband about the Svendergard property was true, a bid of six hundred and forty thousand could net them five million next year when they flipped it. Calvina was so excited she forgot herself and held her husband's hand.

Buster parted company with Ned and Doc when they went into the barn for the livestock auction. He was on his own mission to find Destiny. He caught a glimpse of her in front of the Puster's house with her sisters looking over the household items. Laid out on several tables were all the pots and pans, cheap crystal glasses for special occasions, used clothes and silly romance novels. Buster could see Mrs. Puster sitting in the window of the house. He smiled and waved to her, but she was too sad to wave back. Buster took a deep breath and approached the girls. Trying to be amusing, he picked up what looked to be a hot water bottle that had a hose attached to the end of it, put the business end of it in his mouth and the bag under his arm and started prancing around in front of Destiny, pretending to play the bagpipes.

"Oh, you take the high road and ah'll take the low road… Areee! Areee!"

Destiny looked at him aghast then doubled over, laughing herself sick. At the end of the table, Jimmy Bayles Morgan, under a wide brimmed Mexican-style cowboy hat, regarded him sour-faced, as he sorted through a bargain bin of household odds and ends, toying with an electronic garage door opener.

"Know what that thing is ya got there?"

"No," Buster admitted.

"That there is a *doose* bag. The part you got in your mouth goes up a woman's dingus." Buster nodded with the new information and let the nozzle fall limply from his mouth.

"A young man makin' an ass of hisself over a flirty little girl… cain't say ah much abide a that," Morgan said. The auctioneer's microphone squawked to life. Jimmy Bayles ambled off to the land auction. Whoever bought this property was going to be important to him—he would have to get permission to take his pony rides across their property from his to the Bureau of Land Management.

The Cowboy Auctioneer was a familiar attraction at all these events. His tuxedo jacket and his black Stetson lent a little class to an event that was not much higher on the social ladder than vultures tearing apart a dead cow.

"All right, folks, we got a six-hunnert and forty acre ranch with a main house and four outbuildins' opening at five-hunnert an acre—do I hear five-hunnert? Five-hunnert, I've got five-hunnert, do we have six, give me six, do I hear six, six-fifty, seven. I've got seven-hunnert do I hear seven-fifty, seven-fifty, seven-fifty, eight. I've got seven-fifty, do I hear eight with four outbuildin's, do I hear eight-fifty?"

Skylar and Calvina Stumplehorst had agreed to hold back until some of the steam had left the bidding. Now was the moment. Skylar raised a finger slightly.

"I've got eight-fifty, eight-fifty, do I hear nine?"

None of the ranchers would go nine. As far as they were concerned, it was already over-priced.

"Nine," someone said from the back.

Everyone, including Skylar and Calvina, turned in their folding chairs to see. It was a little man in a gray suit and cordovan wing tips—the little holes of which were already filled with cow shit. No one had ever seen him before.

"I've got nine, do I hear nine-fifty, nine, do I hear nine-fifty?"

Skylar raised a laconic finger.

"I've got nine-fifty, do I have a thousand?"

The person in the back answered silently this time.

The bidding went back and forth—for what seemed like hours—but only took minutes. Twelve hundred fifty. Thirteen hundred. Skylar thought he'd shaken the man off with a bid of fifteen hundred, but the gray suit's response was "two thousand." Skylar wanted to go higher, but Calvina gripped his finger and held it down in her lap. Now the real estate agents, representing clients on cell phones, wondered whether the man in the gray suit knew something that they didn't know. Coldwell Banker bid twenty-five hundred an acre. Re-Max upped it to three thousand. Sotheby's kicked it up to four thousand. This group batted it back and forth in rapid succession: four thousand five hundred, an acre, five, six, seven… They stopped to catch their breath as if to say seven thousand an acre—what are we thinking? Then the little man in the gray suit raised his hand and said, "Seven-five hundred."

ꟷ

THAT NIGHT SKYLAR STUMPLEHORST was not able to sleep. Seventy-five hundred an acre times six hundred forty Stumplehorst acres was either four point eight million or forty-eight million—depending upon where you thought the decimal point should go. It didn't matter, because either way, it was more money than he'd ever dreamed of getting his hands on. He looked at Calvina asleep on the pillow next to his—her gray skin bunched and folded like refrigerated biscuit dough. It had been years since they'd had sex. It had been even longer since they'd had a laugh. If he sold father-in-law Calvin's damn ranch, they could afford to separate and go their merry ways in style. Living in Las Vegas, thought Skylar, yielded several possibilities besides the obvious Nevada state tax exemption. He didn't know the man in the gray suit—Glasker, they said his name was—but it was obvious he was an intermediary for a man of lucrative hidden purposes. It was only a matter of time, Skylar thought, before developers would come knocking on the Stumplehorst door needing more land for trophy homes and condos. And he, Skylar Stumplehorst, would be ready. He'd say, "Boys, I'm willin' to sell you two hundred and fifty acres at ten grand per—jes to get the ball rollin." *That's right*, thought Skylar, *you've been to the state fair. You don't sell the whole caboodle at once like some damn hick. You give them a little taste then hold back the lion's share for when the prices really go up!* Skylar rolled away from his wife and wondered whether the Wild Heifer Ranch, forty miles north of Las Vegas, still had "Greek style" on their laminated sex menu.

There was someone else at the ranch that night having trouble sleeping—and it wasn't because Doc and Ned were downstairs snoring as loudly as tyrannosauruses in the death throws of extinction. Buster couldn't stop thinking about Destiny Stumplehorst. Even though they'd hardly exchanged two words, Buster had already dreamed of saving her from drowning, saving her from a runaway loco horse, and saving her honor from the untoward advances of terrorists who had snuck over the border to scout Lame Horse Mesa's "soft targets." All of these dreams ended the same way with Buster marrying Destiny in a small ceremony atop a hill with all of his former parents, brothers, and sisters in attendance. How could he turn his dreams to reality? That was the question he tossed and turned with. Buster wasn't feeling sorry for himself, but wondered why his three previous fathers hadn't taken the time to clue him in about love. He squinted at his alarm clock. It was 3:30. No use beating a dead horse. Quietly, he eased out of bed and got himself dressed.

The temperature had dropped into the thirties that night. Buster watched the steamy breath of the horses in the corral for a while, and then decided to look in on the cows. Buster grabbed a shovel and cleaned up the manure that had gathered during the night. He laid down fresh straw and saw to their feed. Once the feed had been put in their troughs, he closed the head gates—holding the cows in place while he went around the other side and pulled up a stool. The cows' teats and udders had to be sponged off with an antiseptic solution before milking.

Buster was performing this task in a gentle and respectful way—cleaning, then pulling and squeezing the cow's teats to release the milk into his pail. He suddenly got a start when he felt warm, soft hands surrounding his. He stopped. Slowly, he bent down and looked under the cow's belly. Destiny Stumplehorst had quietly taken a stool, sitting on the opposite side of the cow. Buster couldn't see her face, but he knew it was her from the *Tom and Jerry* slippers. He didn't say anything, and neither did she. Then she took his hand off the cow's teat and pulled it toward her. She put his hand on her knee, then parting her robe, moved his hand between her thighs to her vagina—which to Buster felt smooth and slippery like the first peel off a spring onion. Buster, in the meantime, had his ear pressed tightly to the cow's flank. His first sexual experience was being chaperoned by a cow. Destiny guided his hand to her clitoris and slowly moved her pelvis, then after a few moments, her whole body seemed to pulsate rapidly like ABS brakes in a skid. Then she made a little noise, stopped, withdrew his hand, got up from the stool, and went back to the house.

For Buster, the rest of the day was a blank. He missed lunch. He let deer flies bite him and mosquitos drink his blood. There had not been a single thought in his head but for Destiny. If life were to offer him nothing else besides her, he would die satisfied. He was going to marry her, that much he was certain. Back at the cabin, after forgetting to eat dinner, Doc Solitcz and Ned Gigglehorn tried talking to him, but he could only see their lips moving.

He excused himself and went to bed where he stayed in his clothes, laying on his side and watching the hands on his alarm clock slowly move until it was four o'clock in the morning and time to milk the cows.

Now back in the barn, he sat down to milk the first cow, his heart galloping. He squeezed and pulled the first cow's teats as if they were the magic lantern that would make Destiny reappear. He milked the cow dry, and Destiny did not appear. He picked up his stool and moved to the next cow. He milked her, as well. Still, no Destiny. Buster continued to milk the next four cows hoping for Destiny to materialize, but she did not.

Later that day, Buster was mending a four-strand barbed wire fence on the back of the property. Fence mending was another never-ending job for a ranch hand. Cattle were always putting their weight against a fence—either to get at the proverbial greener grass or just to test their boundaries. Buster made a loop at the end of the broken strand and ran a piece of barbed wire from his reel through it, wrapped it four times back on itself, took the fence stretcher and proceeded to splice in the graft when he felt the vibration on the ground of a horse approaching. Stinker whinnied and stamped his no-longer-tender feet, so it was probably Maple.

"Were you waiting for me last night?" Buster continued doing what he was doing.

"Cows gotta get milked, one way or 'nother."

"I'm sorry."

"Nuthin to 'pologize for."

"Aren't you gonna look at me?"

Buster shifted around to face Destiny.

"Daddy says this is what you wanna do with the rest of your life."

"What's wrong with livin' on a ranch?"

"It's all right if you're five years old," she said. "After that, you gotta be brain dead to wanna be here."

"That so?"

"I don't belong here, Buster. I look at my mother and father... my sisters doodling pictures of Jesus in their school notebooks like he was some boy they had a crush on…those men at breakfast and I think…this has to be a mistake. Are my real parents still out there somewhere, heartsick, still trying to find me…stapling my picture to a telephone pole?"

By the time she was done, she was crying.

"What're ya talkin' 'bout, fer petesake? They *is* yor parents."

Destiny smiled, wiped her nose on his sleeve.

"You're awful sweet, ya know that? You'll make someone a good ranch husband."

"I shor hope to, all raht."

"You know, my sister, Charity…she thinks you're cute."

"That so?"

Buster stood up. Stinker was making Maple nervous and he thought he better get his hands on her halter before she started kicking him.

"All she wants is to be a rancher's wife and have a bunch of kids."

"Nuthin' wrong with that."

Stinker was trying to nuzzle Maple. She didn't like it and started to move her hind end in position for a headshot.

"That's why I think maybe you and her should get together."

Maple let Stinker have it with a kick in his chops. He stumbled back.

"Well, thank you, ma'am, for thinkin' a me, but ah'm o'ready fixin' t'marry someone else."

"Who's that?"

Buster moved Destiny's boot out of her stirrup and stepped into it from the other side, lifting himself up to her level.

"Ah'm gonna be marryin' you."

She looked at him like he was crazy and laughed. Then she leaned forward and kissed him. Buster wrapped his arms around her and held her tight as Maple suddenly bolted and ran off through the pasture—

with Buster standing in one stirrup. They must have galloped for a mile—with Buster subtly reining her into a circle—before she realized the futility of it and stopped right where she had started—her passengers' lips still pressed together. Then Destiny pushed Buster's foot out of the stirrup, forcing him to drop to the ground. And she galloped back to the house.

By 5:00 a.m. they were back in the barn kissing again. Buster had not slept or eaten in twenty-four hours and was starting to hallucinate. Breaking finally for air, he tried to get his wits back.

"Yor mama, uh Mrs. Stumplehorst, she'll be comin' down here soon and if she sees me..."

"She won't be coming anywhere 'til she has her bowel movement at five-forty-five. She takes her tonic." It was true. Every evening to stave off depression or constipation from drinking the hard well water, Mrs. Stumplehorst mashed to a paste lavender leaves, dandelion root, dogwood bark, apple seeds, coffee grounds, anise seeds, and cayenne pepper, added two cups of cod liver oil as the delivery system, then drank it. Until the inevitable, which was usually around five-forty-five the next morning, she found it wise to stay within twenty feet of a toilet.

With Buster's concern for his termination of adoption/employment out of the way, Destiny resumed kissing him with renewed vigor. To Buster, Destiny's mouth, after having a morning cup of chamomile tea, reminded him of chewing on a fresh piece of alfalfa. She now slid his hand into her opened blouse and placed it on her left breast as if she were showing him the correct way to Foxtrot. Buster solemnly followed her lead. Then, like the other times, as if becoming aware of herself, she suddenly removed his hand and promptly left the barn.

ꟸ

ON SUNDAYS, THE STUMPLEHORSTS went into town for church. In the summertime, the other cowboys rented a leaky houseboat on Groundhog Lake for the purpose of getting drunk, but none of them asked if Buster wanted to come. Despite all of Buster's efforts to be helpful and friendly, the other hands held firm to their belief that he was a suck-up who had killed Bob Boyles—the cowboy Mickey Mantle of Vanadium—and would have nothing to do with him.

Lovesick and lonely, he decided to walk into town. He didn't get more than a quarter mile past the Stumplehorst driveway before a truckload of cowboys stopped when they saw him walking on the shoulder of the road.

"Hey pard, you all right?"

"Yeah, ah'm all right," Buster answered.

"Then what the fuck are you doin' walkin' 'long the road?" They sped off, kicking gravel in Buster's face. Their incomprehension was understandable. Cowboys never walked—the only reason for foot travel was the breakdown of a truck or a horse. After a while, Buster lost heart and turned around to go back. As he reentered the Stumplehorst gate, he heard the sound of tires behind him. It was Sheriff Dudival in his police cruiser—another person not to walk when he could ride. He rolled down his window and drove slowly alongside Buster.

"Good mornin'."

"Mornin', Sheriff."

"Just thought I'd drop by to see what you were up to."

"Not much. Ah can tell you that."

"We pulled a truck out of Miramonte reservoir last spring. It was under the ice for God knows how long, so the frame and body panels stayed in good condition. Nobody ever claimed it. I've kind of made it my own little project."

"Well, that's nice, Sheriff. Real nice."

"Got it over at Fall-Out Salvage. Why don't you come help me? I'm just putting a couple finishing touches on it, then I thought we'd go for a ride."

"Ah don't rahtly know much 'bout cars 'n' sech."

"That's how one learns…by trying new things."

"Welp…okay." The 1961 Chevy Apache truck was hardly what Buster had imagined.

Dudival had cut the bottom out of the cab and replaced it with OEM galvanized floor pans, installed ten-bolt chrome mounts, an Oberhauser intake, an Edelbrock 600 carburetor, an electric igniter, a 420 turbo transmission, a four-speed shift kit, and six coats of crème paint with accented side panels of Indian paintbrush red. A 420-cubic-inch V-8 cadged from a Camaro involved in a vehicular homicide powered what had originally been a six. Fortunately, it had just been a rear-end collision, and the seats were relatively unbloodied and useable. The sheriff's finishing touch was a like-new CD stereo that he had rescued from a Cadillac Escalade. That owner had gone headlong off Vanadium Hill while being fellated by his children's SAT tutor. They fired up the 400 horses and went for a joy ride down Highway 141 singing at the top of their lungs along with the Sons of the Pioneers' "Tumblin' Tumbleweeds."

"*See them tumblin' down,*" bellowed Sheriff Dudival in his Eddie Arnold baritone.

"*Pledgin' their love to the ground,*" answered Buster.

"*Lonely, but free I'll be found…driftin' along with the tumblin' tumble…*" Suddenly the sheriff's voice weakened as if something had caught in his throat, his eyes filling with tears. Dudival took a clean hankie out of his pocket and blew his nose—caught off-guard by yet another bout of sentimentality that seemed to be ambushing him more and more these days. For some reason, he was plagued with this at the most inopportune times. It could come over him hearing an old song or watching a movie. *The Best Years of Our Lives* was a particularly hard movie to watch unless he was by himself and could blubber with abandon.

ௐ

SHERIFF SHEP DUDIVAL HAD been raised in Beecher Island, Colorado, on the eastern slope just a few miles from the Kansas border. Beecher Island wasn't really an island, nor was it much of a town. Its only claim to fame was its war memorial dedicated to Lt. Fred Beecher who died on a clump of trees and gravel in the middle of the Arikaree River in 1868. General Philip Sheridan, fresh from the Civil War, had a new idea concerning the best way to neutralize the Cheyenne Indian forces in the area that were cutting telegraph wires and harassing settlers. He put together a small expeditionary force that could travel fast, attack, and retreat, an early proponent of "guerilla warfare." This was probably lost on Pvt. Shep Dudival when he found himself, one hundred years later, stationed outside Saigon at Cu Chi. He and his brother, Adler, had flipped a coin to see who would stay to work the family farm and who would go to do their duty for God and Country. Shep lost.

Buster attempted to reel him back with the next verse of "Tumblin' Tumbleweeds."

"Ah know..." Buster sang, *"...when night has gone..."*

"...that a new world's born at dawn..." answered Sheriff Dudival hoarsely. *"Deep in my heart is a song... Here on the range ah belong..."*

"Driftin' along with the tumblin' tumble...weeds...!" Tears were streaming down Sheriff Dudival's face. He turned away from Buster.

Unlike the other grunts in his unit, Dudival liked Vietnam. The farmers around the military base reminded him of the hard-working residents of Beecher Island. There was a Vietnamese girl by the name of

Bian Trang who cleaned his hooch and washed his laundry. The other guys extorted sex from their hooch girls, but not Dudival. He took the American mission to win hearts and minds seriously and therefore treated Bian with respect. Over time, he developed deep feelings for her, and she for him. Her family, the Trangs, lived nearby. Dudival would often ride his Honda 50 to their farm—loaded with presents from the PX, food, gym shoes—Prell shampoo being a particular hit with them. Her father, Mr. Trang, could fix just about anything with a screwdriver and baling wire. His daughter, Bian, had not found a husband, he said, because of the war. Dudival began to fantasize that when the war was over and the United States had liberated these people, he would return to court Bian in the Vietnamese fashion, which would require flowers and candy for the parents and chaste walks along the river.

This romantic notion was short lived when the GIs discovered an elaborate network of tunnels right beneath the base that had their own sleeping, eating areas, munitions caches, even hospitals. Unfortunately, they also discovered Bian's father down there with explosives. Dudival's visits to the Trang farm prompted an investigation. Only when Intelligence was certain of Dudival's loyalty did they inform him of Mr. Trang's true identity—that being a decorated colonel in the NVA. Bian was suspected of using her base pass to smuggle medical supplies through the tunnels at night. Intelligence asked Dudival if he was planning on seeing Bian anytime soon. He sheepishly admitted that he had promised to bring the Trangs a set of chaise lounge chairs from the PX. They told him to go ahead and play dumb—which so far, he had been doing admirably. And so they next day, he rode his Honda 50 over to the Trang's farm. He brought the chairs. Bian made tea. Dudival looked around and disingenuously asked after her father—having brought him a gift of Dr. Scholl's foot powder and a carton of Kools. Bian broke down and admitted that he'd been missing for two days. Dudival, reciting the dialogue given him by his handlers, suggested that she tell him the names of some her father's friends—so that he might make inquiries on her father's behalf. Bian abruptly stopped crying and looked up at him with a soldier's face.

"This is our country. You should leave."

Dudival left the chairs and rode his Honda 50 back to the base. There, he conveyed Bian's recalcitrance to the Intelligence Officer. He sheepishly came clean about his feelings for the girl and how he had been duped. Surprisingly, the Intelligence Officer responded with understanding. He told Dudival that if he still cared about what happened to Bian, there was a chance she could redeem herself in the eyes of the US Armed Forces. It was suggested that Dudival escort Colonel Trang and his daughter to Da Nang for questioning. There, with some distance from her comrades, she might, with Dudival's urging, feel more inclined to cooperate. So the next day, Dudival received permission from his Commanding Officer to accompany the group. When the helicopter had achieved altitude over the South China Sea, the Intelligence Officer tapped Dudival on the shoulder and yelled something in his ear that he didn't quite understand over the din of the prop. The Intelligence Officer helped him by gesturing to the Trangs and pantomimed a pushing motion.

"Push 'em out, you fucking lummox!"

Dudival could not recall very much of what happened after that. For years, his mind had tricked him into believing that he had thrown a bale of hay out the door. And that Bian had hugged him goodbye then stepped aboard a Greyhound bus for Denver. But of course, neither was the case.

When his tour of duty was up, Dudival returned to Colorado. He didn't talk about the war or the Trangs to his family—and no one pressed him. They already knew some of it from the doctors at the VA hospital where the corporal spent three months. They didn't know that

Bian was still tunneling—only now into their son's brain—and would emerge every night to commit acts of sabotage—like breaking all the furniture in his bedroom, firing his deer rifle out the window, and urging him to self-immolate like the Buddhist monks she so admired.

ↄ

"YOU ALL RIGHT, SHERIFF?" asked Buster, noticing that the sheriff was tearing up.

"I think a damn bug went up my nose," the sheriff said.

Ashamed of himself, and overcompensating, he stood on the gas pedal. Buster looked on with some unease as the speedometer tickled one hundred and thirty miles an hour.

"Gotta test these mounts for vibration," the sheriff explained in his choked-up voice.

Later that evening, Buster and Sheriff Dudival drove up the Dave Wood Road that traversed the Uncompahgre Mesa where they found a doe that had been hit by a car. They threw it into the back of the truck and when they came upon a natural backstop, tested Sheriff Dudival's new .357 Sig to see how it stacked up against the Colt .45 ACP for bullet penetration and expansion. The sheriff watched Buster empty a magazine into the carcass with adolescent enthusiasm. When the pistol's breech locked back empty, they walked downrange to assess the damage.

"You ever kilt an'body?" asked Buster.

Sheriff Dudival, his head bowed over the dead deer, did not answer. Buster, feeling that he had somehow overstepped the boundaries of their relationship, shut up and bowed his head with him. The two men stood in solemn silence for fifteen, maybe twenty minutes. Finally, the sheriff took a deep breath and looked up.

"You hungry?"

They cruised to the DQ where they ordered hamburgers and a couple of strawberry milkshakes at the drive-up window. The server, seeing it was Sheriff Dudival, practically shoved the bag at him—evidently still smarting from her recent DUI. The rest of the way home was passed in thoughtful silence and the appreciation of scenery too easily taken for granted. Finally, they drove under the Stumplehorst gates, and Dudival stopped in front of Doc and Gigglehorn's cabin.

"Sheriff, ah reckon this was jes about the bes' day of my lahf."

"I enjoyed it quite a bit myself." The sheriff lit a cigarette. "You know, Buster, Mr. Stumplehorst tells me that, despite your earlier problems, you've developed into one real fine cowboy."

"Thank you, sir."

Dudival could see Ned pull the drapes slightly and look suspiciously out the window of the cabin.

"That Gigglehorn's a communist. I hope you don't put any stock in that claptrap of his."

"Tell you the truth, ah really don't know what he's sayin' most of the time, but he seems to really believe it."

"Listen to me, Buster. Private property. You've got to have private property in a democracy."

"Yessir."

"Without private property, there'd be no incentive for people to get off their asses in the morning. You understand what I'm saying?"

"Yessir."

There was another long uncomfortable silence.

"You still pickin' at your nose?"

"No, sir."

"Usin' that hankie I got ya?"

"Yessir."

"Good man. No person with character likes to rub shoulders with a nose picker…or a spitter, for that matter."

"Ah got my eye on it, sir."

"And don't ever fall into that habit of putting a matchstick in your mouth. An intelligent person doesn't walk around like that." Buster nodded, appreciatively.

"All right. I guess that kind of covers things for now."

"Thanks again, Sheriff. Ah know yor a busy man. 'Ppreciate you taken the tahm for me." They shook hands. Sheriff Dudival still looked troubled. All the talk about communists and nose picking had not provided a smooth segue for what he still wanted to get off his chest.

"Buster, don't you know day it is?"

"It's Sunday."

"Yes, it's Sunday, but other than that." Buster just looked at him blankly.

"Buster, today's your birthday."

"Well, ah'll be…ah believe it is!"

"You're eighteen. You're no longer a minor. With that, come some serious responsibilities. Do you understand what I'm talking about?"

"Yes, sir. Ah can get married."

"Yes, you can. And that's sort of what I wanted to talk to you about." What had weighed so heavily on Sheriff Dudival's mind was that today was the day that Buster would officially be let loose on the world. Dudival would no longer be able to protect him as a minor or as his personal ward of the court. "There's some other things to consider as well."

"Ah can buy a gun, raht?"

"Yes, that's right. And you're now eligible to vote, sign up for the armed forces…but also, as an adult, you're eligible for the electric chair—let's say if you ever…*killed someone.*"

"But ah ain't ever kilt no one."

"I'm saying *if.*"

"All right. Thanks for the heads up," Buster said good-naturedly.

"I didn't mean to depress you with this talk. I just felt it was my duty to... Listen, I've got a lot of faith in you. And there's no reason you shouldn't have faith in yourself, too. There's plenty of kids in this town who've had it better than you. No question about it, but you've got a big advantage over all of them. You already know the world can kick a guy pretty good in the ass. You're not gonna fold up like a little baby bird at the first sign of adversity, are you?"

"Fill me in on *adversity* ag'in?"

"When things aren't going your way."

"No, sir, ah ain't lahk that."

"That's right. You *are not* like that," Dudival said, mildly correcting his grammar. "Okay. The next thing I have to tell you is that from this day forward, your relationship with Mr. and Mrs. Stumplehorst is just as employer-employee. They're no longer obligated to keep you as foster parents. They're gonna judge you just like they would any of the other degenerates that work for them. You clear about that?"

"Yessir."

"Good man. Now if it's not too much trouble, I'd be obliged if you'd give me a ride home."

"But, sir, ya got yor own truck."

"Buster, I'm giving this truck to you." Dudival took the keys out of the ignition and handed them to Buster. "The insurance and registration is in the glove box."

Buster just stared at him. The sheriff thought that perhaps he'd given Buster too much to digest at one sitting.

"Happy birthday, son."

Dudival abruptly got out of the driver's seat and went around to the other side of the truck. When he opened the passenger door, Buster had his head in his hands sobbing.

"Now, c'mon now," the sheriff said, his lower lip trembling out of control himself. "Don't be like that. You'll embarrass us both."

"Why're ya doin' this for me, anyways?"

"It's time somebody did something for you."

"But…hadint they already?"

Sheriff Dudival just looked at him.

"Just drive me home," he said.

CHAPTER SEVEN

Eighteen Licks and One for Good Luck

"WHOSE TRUCK IS THAT parked outside?" Gigglehorn said, seated behind his easel, pretending that he hadn't been peeking out the window.

"Ah guess that'r be mine."

"You bought a truck on credit? You idiot! Don't you understand anything? That's how they suck you into the whole rotten system!"

"Uh, what?"

"People pay double for something on credit because they're too stupid to deny themselves something they can't really afford in the first place!"

"Ah dint *buy* it. Som'body done giver to me."

Now he had Doc Solitcz's attention.

"Somebody gave you a truck? Who'd do something like that?"

"Sheriff Dudival. He done it."

"That's a…pretty grand gesture, bonehead. Why?"

"Mr. Gigglehorn, fer the life a me, ah don't know."

Gigglehorn's brain was on the boil now, his eyes blinking uncontrollably.

"Did he say something like, 'Here's this truck. From time to time, I'm going to need information from you pertaining to Ned Gigglehorn?'"

"Nuthin' lahk that…"

"…Nothing about keeping tabs on Ned Gigglehorn's activities on behalf of the International Workers of the World?"

"The who…?" Buster asked.

"He didn't want you to go through my things to find the names of people I…"

"For Chrissake, Ned!" Dr. Solitcz finally cut in. "Nobody cares about your *activities,* aside from the AARP and the Gold Bond chafing powder people."

"That doesn't explain…"

"Why would he spy on you? The man saved your goddamn life!"

"How'd he save yor life?" Buster asked.

Gigglehorn was quiet and tried to keep his hands from touching his 'coon face. "Let's just drop it."

"That's probably a good idea. After all, it *is* the kid's birthday." Doc Solitcz turned to Buster. "And now that you're eighteen, we were thinking you just might be old enough to appreciate a good eighteen-year-old whiskey." Doc Solitcz produced three glasses from the shelf and blew the dust and dead fruit flies out of them. He poured one for Buster, one for himself and an extra large one for Gigglehorn—whose darkened visage indicated the need for an increased dosage.

"Happy birthday, Buster. Cheers."

They raised their glasses and clinked.

"Here's a little something to wear when you're strolling down Main Street."

Doc Solitcz handed him a wrapped box. Inside was a brand new Resistol hat.

"Goll-lee…thanks, Doc!"

Gigglehorn reached under his bed and dragged out a rectangular package carefully wrapped in grocery bag paper. Buster opened it. It was an old rifle.

"The thirty-forty Krag bolt action carbine…" Gigglehorn pronounced, "…was the rifle used by Teddy Roosevelt and the Rough Riders…"

"Jiminy, Ned…thanks."

"The Spanish American War being the first time a politician staged a publicity stunt to kick off a presidential campaign. Nowadays, of course, these cowards just write books."

"How you load this booger?" was all Buster wanted to know.

"The magazine's on the side," Gigglehorn replied, disgruntled, feeling his political assessment had gone unappreciated.

Doc Solitcz got out an old Kodak Retina and composed a picture with Buster in his new hat holding the rifle.

"Wait a minute!" Gigglehorn handed Buster a pamphlet on the *Songbirds of Colorado.* "Hold the rifle in your left hand and this in your right hand." Doc Solitcz looked at him quizzically as Gigglehorn arranged Buster this way and that.

"Our very own Lee Harvey Oswald," Gigglehorn explained, as they recreated a facsimile of the famous photo of the assassin in his backyard.

Gigglehorn and Doc Solitcz had a laugh, but then stopped when they saw an envelope slide under the door. They all just stood and looked at it.

"Very mysterious."

"It says 'Buster' on it," Buster said.

"Then it's probably for you, wouldn't you say?"

Buster opened it. It was a birthday card. At the bottom, all it read was, *Cows need milking.* His roommates were waiting for him to say something, but Buster just put the card in his back pocket. He stretched his arms and performed a big stage yawn.

"Welp, thanks ag'in for ever'thang. Ah'm kinda tucker'd out, so ah'll jes hit the sack if'n ya don't mind."

"Sure. We don't mind."

They watched bemused as he climbed the stairs to the loft, then shook their heads as they poured another drink. Buster quietly opened the window in the loft and climbed out.

The first to hear the noises of Buster and Destiny's lovemaking were the quarter horses in the corral. They had been on edge that night—the slight whiff of mountain lion on the southerly wind. Ears pricked, hooves were stamped restlessly in the mud; a human was moaning in the barn—no, make that two humans moaning in the barn. The horses started to move, slowly at first, then desperately around and around in the corral, whinnying, bucking. A rooster, picking up on the disturbance, came running out from the coop, crowing an hour earlier than usual—and didn't stop. The cows began mooing loudly. The swine squealed and grunted, putting their sensitive noses to the bars, sniffing the human truffles of sex—a smell that had once drifted noiselessly from the second floor of the house many years ago. The horses became more and more agitated. Old Stinker started to kick the fence—others followed suit. Some kicked in the red boards of the barn. As Buster and Destiny reached their climax high above the milking room, every animal on the ranch was bellowing forth a cacophony of protest—that human sex like this should not be taking place in their barn.

In the barn, Buster and Destiny had hoisted themselves up on a hay bay twenty feet in the air. Now shed of their virginity, they lay dizzily on the bale gazing up at the ceiling, pocked with muddy swallows' nests. If it seemed as if they were spinning, they were. And if it seemed that the ceiling was now retreating as if they were looking through the wrong end of a telescope, that's because they were. Mr. Stumplehorst, hearing the racket from the house, had grabbed a shotgun and run to the barn thinking a coyote was in there. Now he was lowering the hay bale and when it reached eye level saw Buster and his daughter in flagrante delicto. Flustered, he let go of the rope—sending Buster and Destiny crashing to earth and he stomping back to the house.

In the morning, Buster was not allowed to say goodbye to Destiny. He wasn't even allowed breakfast. Destiny and her sisters were kept inside while Mr. Stumplehorst had been given the unpleasant task of giving Buster his marching orders. Buster, under the smirking gaze of his fellow cowboys, was loading his few things into the bed of the Apache when Mr. Stumplehorst walked up to him with Stinker.

"What did I say the first day you come here?"

"Stay clear a my daughters," Buster answered glumly.

"That's right. And what did you go up and do? Any fair man would say you brung this on yorself."

Buster looked up at the house. Destiny was standing mutely in her window, crying. He turned back to Mr. Stumplehorst.

"Sir, ah wanna marry her."

"That ain't in the cards."

"But ah love 'er." In the pasture behind them, Mr. Stumplehorst's prize bull, Pepita, was smelling the rear-end of a three-year-old cow that had somehow forced her way through the fence.

"Maybe you do, but that doesn't matter right now. Yor never gonna see her ag'in. Those are my orders from On High."

"Sir, ah b'lieve ah'd maker a good husband."

Stumplehorst put a comforting hand on Buster's shoulder, but when he saw his wife watching from their bedroom window, quickly let it drop.

"I got nothin' against you, personally. Fact is, you and me ain't much diff'rint. Maybe that's why the old lady cast such a powr'ful hate on ya. I tole her that yor one a the best damn cowboys we ever had around here but, sorry to say, that fall upon deaf ears…" The romantic tableau behind them continued to unfold with Pepita mounting the cow and copulating. "The breed that you and me come from…there ain't a lotta demand for it, anymore. So, it's prolly best for everybody's sake to jes…jes let it die off."

Buster hung his head. Mr. Stumplehorst hung his head as well. A few moments passed while both he and Mr. Stumplehorst scratched the dirt with the toes of their boots as if the answer to all their problems could be uncovered there.

"I suppose you think I'm a coldhearted sonofabitch."

"No, sir, ah do not."

"Prolly like to kill me right now, in fact."

"No, sir, thought ain't even crost my mind." Stumplehorst searched his face for veracity, then turned and untied his horse's reins from the fence.

"Well, if it ever does, r'member this was my wife's doin'. You can knock her off anytime without a peep from me. In the meantime, jes so there's no hard feelins, I'm givin' ya Stinker."

Buster waved the offer off.

"No sir, ah couldn't take him."

"You can have that old beige horse trailer to boot."

"Sir, ah jes want Destiny."

"Jes take Stinker and be done with it." Stumplehorst pressed the reins into Buster's hand. "Good bye, son…and good luck."

CHAPTER EIGHT

Exile

FROM THE DAY BUSTER left the Stumplehorst ranch, Mr. Stumplehorst would not sleep until he had strewn crumpled newspapers between the doorway to his bedroom and his bed. He did this as an early warning system in case someone came sneaking up on him in the night, that someone being Buster McCaffrey. There were rumors that Buster was working for a cattle outfit in Disappointment Valley, but that turned out to be false. Then one of the Stumplehorst hands told Mr. Stumplehorst that Buster had been seen riding fence in Egnar (that's Range spelled backwards), but that was also not confirmed—the result of all of these ghost sightings so rattled Mr. Stumplehorst that he began taking horse tranquilizers.

How unnerving it would have been for Skylar Stumplehorst if he had known that Buster's head rested a mere a half-mile away as the crow flew. So ashamed after being cashiered from the Stumplehorst's, Buster's first thought was to leave town. He actually got as far as Gateway then, realizing he couldn't abandon his one true love, turned around. Finding a little-used US Forest Service road behind Jimmy Bayles Morgan's property, he head into the tree line and made camp. From his campfire—where he sat and ate canned beans—Buster could see the twinkling lights of the ranches below and imagined one of those twinkling lights to be Destiny's bedroom.

Stinker whinnied and stamped his feet, rousting Buster from his sorrowful reverie. In all of this feeling sorry for himself business, he had forgotten to take Stinker out of the horse trailer. He apologized as he backed him out and put some oats in a feedbag, but Stinker wasn't interested. He had heard, before he did, the otherworldly, high-pitched whistles of the elk cows and their calves talking to one another as they moved to their evening feeding grounds. Soon they were all around them, making only the slightest sounds of hoof falls through the aspens. Buster stood motionless. The wind was in his face so they couldn't scent him. For some reason he felt the need to follow. He threw on a halter and eased onto Stinker, bareback. Together, they joined the herd that kept multiplying from three different drainages. He had often wondered where the elk fed at night and now they were taking him there. Soon, they emerged from the trees and entered a flat bench invisible to hunters' binoculars from below. That's when Buster saw it—in the middle of this small grassy meadow surrounded by a hundred and fifty elk, an old sheepherder's wagon—illuminated by the moonlight like an enchanted hologram.

Buster guided Stinker through the herd for a closer look. He slowly dismounted so as not to disturb his new family. The wagon's tires were flat. The screen door came off in his hand. Inside, there was a rusted box spring on the floor and a small wood-burning stove that was detached from its chimney. A well-intentioned burlap bag of flour, nibbled to nothing by mice, crumbly safety matches, and a jerry can filled with evaporated water had all been left with worthless good intentions for the next needy traveller. But it was the water-stained calendar on the wall that drew Buster's attention. It was from the Carnation Powdered Milk Company and featured a pretty woman in her twenties giving her tow-headed son a glass of nutritious powdered milk. The year on the calendar was 1988, the year Buster was born. When he was little, he once asked Mrs. Dominguez where he was born and she told him it was up on the mesa in a sheepherder's wagon. Could it have possibly been here that his mother had given her life for him? The next morning, he returned with his things. He dragged out the box spring and swept the place with an upturned mesquite. He reattached the chimney to the stove and cut pine boughs as the cushion for his bedroll. This was where he slept that night, comforted by a feeling that he was somehow near his mother.

Down below in Vanadium, it was 12:30 when Skylar Stumplehorst stumbled out of the High Grade bar. He didn't want to leave. He was having a good time talking marbled meat with his fellow ranchers, but his weekly allowance ran out before closing time. After an adios to every sun-dried miner's widow at the bar nursing their vodka and cranberry juices and a gallant wave of his Stetson, Stumplehorst found himself outside in the darkened parking lot with his bravado ebbing. He squinted into the shadows and must have looked over his shoulder a dozen times expecting Buster with an axe in his hands. When he got to his truck, he quickly jumped in and locked the doors. So as not to supply a DUI-hunting state patrolman with probable cause, he drove the three quarters of a mile home at fifteen miles per hour. Entering his own gates unscathed, he sighed a great sigh of relief. But just then, a Great Horned owl, chasing a small bird, swooped up from the ditch and smashed into his windshield. He screamed like a babysitter in a horror movie and put his foot on the accelerator thinking it was the brake—sending his three-quarter ton truck crashing through the front room of the house—pinning Mrs. Stumplehorst to the living room wall as she watched the *Hour of Power* broadcast from the Crystal Cathedral in Garden Grove, California.

ꙮ

NED GIGGLEHORN AND DOC Solitcz were sound asleep when Buster tiptoed into the cabin holding his boots in his hand. He stood over Gigglehorn, whose tortured expression indicated that he reliving one of his many beatings at the hands of strikebreakers. Buster gently shook him.

"Mr. Gigglehorn…"

Gigglehorn jackknifed upright.

"I'll kill ya! I swear I'll kill ya!!!"

"It's only me," Buster whispered.

Doc Solitcz turned on his light.

"Buster, you're not supposed to be here."

"Ah know that. But ah need to let Destiny know ah'm still here for er."

Buster took a torn piece of grocery bag out of his pocket and held it out to Ned Gigglehorn.

"Raht here. My secret place," he said, pointing to an X on a map that a kindergartner could have drawn. "Will you giver to 'er for me, Mr. Gigglehorn?"

"No. You're being a sap."

Buster offered the map to Doc Solitcz.

"Will you giver to 'er, Doc?"

Doc Solitcz had to chuckle at his persistence.

"Buster, I've been around this family awhile now, so listen to me carefully. Destiny's parents have a great deal of influence over her. And they don't want her to be with you. So you understand where this is going?"

"Sure," he chirped, and held out the map again.

"Okay, I'll give her the map."

The grin returned to Buster's face. Mission accomplished, he headed for the door then stopped, remembering something.

"Think someone should tell Mr. Stumplehorst his truck's in the livin' room."

"Thanks. I think they already know that."

&

THE NEXT DAY, BUSTER prepared for Destiny's arrival. He picked wildflowers, used a couple of rusted coffee cans for vases, and placed them on either side of the wagon's door. He lured a brace of blue grouse into camp with a trail of Stinker's oats then brained them with a rock. Not having pepper or salt, he stuffed their body cavities with wild onions and garlic that Doc Solitcz had showed him how to find. He dug a fire pit and put the birds on a spit; dragged two logs to the fire for a place to sit. He stood back to examine his work. Not bad.

By seven o'clock she hadn't come. Buster turned the birds over the fire for what seemed like the hundredth time. They were more than done. It started to drizzle and he was starting to feel stupid. Gingerly, he pulled one of the grouse from the skewer, held it like it was an ear of corn and took a healthy bite.

"Don't wait for me or nothin'."

Buster almost jumped out of his skin. It was Destiny. She was on foot.

"Ah almost give up on ya."

"Not almost. You *did* give up on me," she said with a laugh. "I left Maple down below. Doc Solitcz said you didn't want anyone to know where you were."

She nodded approvingly as she took in the sheepherder's wagon, the flowers, the campfire, the dinner.

"Looks like you were expectin' a girl or somethin'."

"Matter a fact, yor the third one t'night."

"Buster, I'm really sorry about you losin' your job."

"Feller's gotta make his way into the world sometime. Now's good 'nuff time as any."

Destiny sat down next to him and kissed him on the cheek. He gave her a grouse. She pulled off a piece and chewed it thoughtfully.

"Guess who's pregnant?"

In arrhythmatic space between heartbeats, Buster saw his future play out in front of him. He could see the tense confrontation with her parents, their grudging capitulation to their marriage. They would resent him for years, but would eventually be worn down by his dedication, his resourcefulness, the bevy of children—all sturdy, handsome, polite, churchgoing rodeo champions.

"Maple."

"Beg pardon?"

"Stinker jumped Maple in the corral and got her pregnant. I don't know what got into him. Momma and Daddy are real mad because Maple's a registered quarter horse and Stinker is a God-knows-what."

Stunned by the news that he wasn't going to be a father Buster barely registered Destiny's chatter.

"Hello…? Have you heard anything I just said?"

"Sure, ah heard ya." She didn't believe him.

"I gotta get back."

"When am ah gonna see you ag'in?" Destiny sighed then cocked her head sadly.

"That's what I came up here to tell you. My parents are sending me away."

"Jiminy….to where 'bouts?"

"To school in Junction."

"Oh. Well, ah jes might have a mind to come up and visit with you."

"My parents said if you did that, they'd send me to live with my uncle in the Salvation Army and I really wouldn't like that."

"If'n ya don't want me to come, ah won't."

Sensing his hurt, she put her arms around him.

"Buster, of course I'd *want* you…" They held each other for a little while.

"Ah jes hope you don't come back too smart to be with ol' Buster." Buster said that as a joke, but he kind of meant it.

Destiny made a sad face then kissed him goodbye. When he was sure she was gone, Buster allowed himself to cry. After all, Sheriff Dudival, Buster's personal ideal of masculinity, cried plenty. And what would the sheriff think when he heard of all this? Buster figured that he'd probably wonder why he ever wasted a moment of his time on him.

ℵ

He was at his desk, Sheriff Dudival, the next morning trying to placate an old lady that was accusing her neighbor of stealing water from the irrigation ditch. This was the fourth time she had made the same complaint. Dudival jabbed at his coffee with a letter opener, trying to get a lump of powdered creamer to dissolve while talking to her on his speakerphone.

"Have you talked to your neighbor personally about this?"

"No. I want *you* to. Ain't that what we pay you for?"

Dudival clenched his jaw. This was what he hated most about his job—the perception in the community that he was a paid enforcer. He was just about to tell her as much when he developed a stabbing pain in the solar plexus. He had been having these attacks frequently in the last month or so, but wrote it off as indigestion. He fumbled around in his top drawer for the antacid tablets, but chewing two of them did no good. Suddenly, his face erupted in beads of perspiration.

"Are you there? You better not hang up on me!" the biddy said.

Dudival went to the window and opened it, took several deep breaths of the cool, dry air.

"I need proof before I can accuse someone of stealing water."

Dudival slumped back down in his chair and undid the top button of his uniform.

"Maybe I just won't vote for you next time around."

"Then don't," he said and hung up.

He retrieved his clean hankie and mopped the sweat from his face. The wrenching pain was passing, so he lit a generic cigarette.

"Sheriff, Buster McCaffrey is here to see you," Mrs. Poult said over the intercom. Dudival composed himself as Buster skulked in with his head down.

"Have a seat, Buster. What can I do for you?"

"Ah had sex-shool ree-lay-shuns with Destiny Stumplehorst," Buster mumbled.

"Yes, I'm aware of that."

"They were mighty unhappy with me. Give me my pink slip and an adios y no vuelvas a molestarnos nuevo."

Buster waited for his reaction.

"That's not good, is it?"

"No, it ain't."

"Isn't," he said, correcting.

"Isn't."

"And ah 'spect yor pretty dang disserpointed with me."

"That's an accurate assessment. Yes."

"Well, ah got one thang to say in my de-fense."

"I'm listening."

"Ah love that gal and ah wanna marry her. Those were my 'tentions from the startin' gate." Buster's eyes filling.

"Okay, son. Okay." Now, the sheriff was getting emotional. He took out his hankie again and blew his nose. "Nobody gets through this life without making a mistake or two. I'm glad you thought enough of me to come in here and face the music. It tells me you still care about your character. So, let's try to move forward, shall we?"

"Ah'd shor like to, Sheriff, but it ain't changed my mind 'bout marryin' her."

The sheriff sighed and held his now shaking hand under the desk.

"That's going to prove more difficult than you think."

"Sir?"

"The Stumplehorsts filed a restraining order against you. Know what a restraining order means?"

"Catch me up on that, will ya?"

"A restraining order means you are legally forbidden from being within one hundred yards of them or any of their children. If you see them in town, you've got to cross the street."

"They don't have to worry 'bout me cause ah'm leavin'."

This piece of news did not go down well with the sheriff.

"You don't have to leave. You just have to stay away from them. Understand?"

"Oh, ah unnerstan, all raht. Ah jes need to get me to Utah."

"Why on earth do you want to go there?"

"To find me my real kin."

"Why?"

"It's like this, Sheriff. Right now, them Stumplehorsts're thinkin' ah'm a mutt. Ah don't blame 'em. But ah got a notion my real family in Utah're some top shelf folks. Folks ah could get ta braggin' on."

"Why in the world would you think that?"

"Cause they never wanted anythin' to do with me. If they was low-lifes, they prolly woont give a hang. See what ah mean?"

"I don't know what to say about that. I really don't."

"So, uh, that's why ah'ma hopin' you can send me off with an address or somethin'."

"I wrote your mother's kin when you were born. They didn't…"

"Ah'm jes gonna need that address."

Dudival, visibly flustered by his insistence, pressed the intercom button.

"Mrs. Poult, bring me the address for Buster's grandparents."

The sheriff fidgeted for a generic cigarette and lit one, then realized he already had one going in the ashtray.

"You all right, Sheriff?"

"I'm fine." They just sat and stared at each other until there was a knock on the door. Mrs. Poult stuck her head in.

"I'm sorry, Sheriff, but we don't have an address on those people. Maybe I threw it out?"

"Jiminy."

"Sorry, Buster," she said and made the same kind of sad face that Destiny made the night before.

"You r'member what my pappy's name was?"

Sheriff Dudival put his hands up in exasperation.

"Tom? But I really think this is a fool's errand."

Buster stood and energetically shook the sheriff's hand.

"Sir, ah 'ppreciate all's yous ever done fer me. Ah'll make ya proud."

And with a tip of the hat to Mrs. Poult on the way out, Buster McCaffrey left Vanadium.

CHAPTER NINE

Higher Education

DESTINY'S PARENTS HAD GIVEN her a 1980 orange International Scout Harvester to take to school. She wondered as she drove to Grand Junction—with the windows rolled down all the way—whether the truck's pungence of cow manure was her parent's last subtle way of reminding her where she came from. She also wondered what clothes the other girls would be wearing and if she would stand out as a hick. And she wondered if her mother's Thessalonian home schooling would hold her in good stead for the grueling nights of cramming and writing papers about the esoteric French poets of the eighteenth century and other topics she could only guess; and she wondered what her roommate in the dorm would be like—the usual college stuff. Unlike most kids her age, she did not go on a national college tour with her parents. Her mother had made all the arrangements herself—Destiny's bout of premarital sex had nullified any right to input.

The Rocky Mountain School of the Professional Arts was located in a two story building in the Bookcliff Mall next to Big O Tires. She was enrolled, not in any liberal arts program like she thought, but in a three-week real estate licensing school. And she would not be housed in a dormitory filled with giggling young girls her age, but in the home of a fellow Thessalonian her mother had stayed in touch with—who also appreciated a good fight with the Devil.

"Mother, why did you do this to me?!"

Destiny was calling from the pay phone outside of the GNC Live Well vitamin store.

"Stop this preoccupation with yourself, young lady. I'm giving you a chance to redeem yourself in the eyes of God and your family."

"Why does God care if I get a real estate license?"

"The recent sale of the Puster ranch has made your father and I consider divesting of some of our Vanadian property. Paying a broker 12% is not in the family's best interest. Therefore, once you attain the license, you will do the transactions and that money will stay with the Believers." Destiny just let the phone dangle and walked across the street where she drank seven shots and seven beers—each time toasting. After the third or fourth round, she had all the other people in the bar saying her toast as well.

"To your fucking mother!"

Most daughters get over their hatred of their mothers by the time they are nineteen. By that time, even *they* get bored of the sulking, door slamming, screaming, and crying. Unfortunately, Destiny never had the typical opportunities to vent these emotions—aberrant behavior at home was regarded as Devil's work and treated with powerful tonic enemas if she so much as looked cross-eyed at her mother. Destiny realized that going home without a diploma would be physically taxing in the laxative sense of the word. So, she stayed in Grand Junction and created her own abbreviated college experience by getting high with the college kids at Mesa State and in three weeks, returned home to Vanadium, Colorado—Real Estate License in hand. However, she had no intention of ever living at home again.

"Can I help you?" said Cord Travesty, of Lame Horse Realty. He had heard the doorbell tinkle when he was in the bathroom, but neglected to give himself one last looking over in the mirror before coming out. Two telltale dabs of cocaine remained on either side of his nostrils. Cord Travesty was one of the many real estate agents who were now circling Vanadium. Five years earlier he'd worked for the Telluride Ski and Golf Company. That's where he got his nickname, Cord—for the corduroy he groomed onto the slopes every night in a giant SnowCat. One night, during a storm, as he stared cross-eyed at the snow clinging to his windshield wipers on lower Bushwacker, he received a vision as to how he was going to break out of his working class rut. The answer was right in front of him. Cocaine. In the next six months, he acquired a pilot's license and flew a twenty-year-old Aero Commander under the radar and down the Pacific Coast to Mexico. There, he loaded up at unmarked airstrips and then flew back to Telluride with his precious cargo. His main clients were the hippies in Telluride who pushed the miners out of town, then the TV and movie people who started buying property there, and then the Trustafarians—the kids of wealthy parents who hung out and struck a Rasta pose. The town was crawling with DEA men back in those days, but Cord had slipped through several big busts. However, after fifty trips to Mexico, he started feeling superstitious and sold his plane. With the cash that he kept hidden in the kitchen of his house behind a wall of wine corks, he bought two hundred acres of sheep grazing land that would eventually adjoin the airport. From that deal, he made enough to be a partner in the Staircase to Heaven development—twenty-five ranchettes that sold for a minimum of seven hundred thousand—and the Fool on the Hill Ranch. He now had his grubstake to play with the big boys. If he were smart, he'd parlay it into dirt where he'd have fuck-you money for life. Vanadium, the last big expanse of undeveloped ranch land, in Lame Horse County, was just that place.

"Is the manager here?"

"Yeah. I'm the owner."

Cord didn't look like a manager or an owner. He was dressed in a vintage cowboy shirt, jeans, and old boots that he had bought at a chic resale shop in Telluride. This was his new "look" to make greenhorns passing through think that he was a good old boy from Vanadium who knew what he was talking about.

Cord looked Destiny over as he sat down on one of three moth-eaten couches that surrounded a beat-up table. Not having desks in the office was another one of his ideas. Cord took a sip of his coffee from an Amerfarm Pesticide cup—another phony touch. To Cord, Destiny looked like she could be sixteen, seventeen—eighteen at the most. She was trying to act sophisticated, but he could tell she was wearing her black pants and white blouse from church choir. She, like most of the town kids that came in, was probably here to hit him up for money for the Vanadium school trip or money for the 4H.

"Um, I'm interested in working in your firm...?" Destiny was probably the last girl in the country to have picked up the annoying affectation of ending a sentence on the tonal upswing as if she were asking a question. "Is there any possibility of a position opening up here soon?"

"My firm." *That's a good one*, Cord thought. "Where did you work before?"

"Nowhere."

"Do you have a real estate license?"

"Yes."

Cord smiled.

"So far so good. Where did you go to school?"

"I recently completed the Thessalonians Home Study Course of Oxford, Mississippi."

Cord tried not to laugh as he got up painfully from the couch. He was still having trouble with his ACL. He took Destiny by the arm and started to show her out.

"You're the first person I'm going to call if anything opens up, Miss…?"

"Stumplehorst. Destiny Stumplehorst."

"The Stumplehorsts who live up on the Mesa?"

"The cattle ranch, yes."

Cord gestured for her to wait right there while he ran back in the office for a card. It would be real estate suicide to turn away the daughter of the largest landholder on Lame Horse Mesa.

"Here's my card. Cord Travesty. Do you have a minute for a cup of coffee?"

"Uh, actually, no I don't. I'm late for my meeting with ReMax," she said disingenuously.

"Don't bother with them. They're assholes." He closed the door. "Look. You *do* understand that we don't just send agents out into the field. They have to work in the office for awhile to learn the business."

"Well, sure. I'd be willing to do that," Destiny said, not appreciating the full implication of that.

"Okay, then. It's settled. You can start on Monday."

She took a Spartan room at the Vanadium hotel, which had not been changed since 1946, but her newfound independence made it seem luxurious. She personalized it by putting a picture of her horse on the dresser next to the diaphragm that she had fitted by a gynecologist in Grand Junction when she wanted to strangle her mother.

She sat on the single bed looking down on Main Street and thought about Cord Travesty. He was handsome, and sure knew about 1031 Exchanges and Conservation Easements. Where was Buster, anyway? It wasn't like he was there beating down the door to lay claim to her.

PART TWO

CHAPTER TEN

Hands Up!

It was snowing the night a tall, bearded man wearing a stiff poncho—cut from the hide of an elk—came into Naturita's Suit Yourself Bar. It was only the rougher sorts that drank there. He had ridden in on a horse, the storm having made driving impossible. The stranger sat down in the corner and ordered two shots of tequila. That was just the beginning. For the moment, it was just he and the bartender. The bartender poured. He drank. He drank until his eyeballs rotated independently of each other like those of a horned toad. When he decided that it was time to throw up, he calculated the distance to the front door and then the distance to the men's room. The men's room was closer, and there were chairs and tables to careen off of in support on the way there. In the filthy bathroom, he did what he had to do then rinsed his mouth and nostrils in the sink. Straightening himself, he finally took note of his surroundings and traced his fingers shakily over the black tiles that he may have had a hand in making when he was a boy.

When he came back out to the bar, there were four new customers. They had driven into town in a monster truck with huge utility tires. They were all wearing the same motorcycle jackets that featured a gold beehive with the insignia "The Busy Bees." The leader of the group gestured that they sit at the bar.

It was Cookie Dominguez, now a hulking two hundred and seventy-five pounds.

"Hornitos shots, cherry cokes, and four Ding Dongs!" Cookie demanded as he sat down. His rear end was so big and encompassing that the round seat of the stool completely disappeared beneath him—making him look like a Mexican-on-amphetamines-fudgsicle. The Bees began discussing business when Cookie stopped them, noticing the stranger in the bar's mirror.

"Hey, man," Cookie said, turning around.

"Hey," the stranger said.

"Some fuckin' night, huh?"

The stranger deigned not to reply, possibly thinking that Cookie's question was rhetorical.

"Did you hear what I said, bro? I said 'some fuckin' night.'"

"Yep…it's a booger."

"You from around here?" asked Cookie.

The stranger didn't answer.

"What are you deaf, or something, motherfucker? I *said*, 'are you from around here?'"

"How's Mommy?" the stranger said. The other Bees started laughing.

"Who the fuck are you, man?"

Cookie slid off his stool and knocked the chairs over on his way to the stranger's table. The stranger made no effort to protect himself.

"Yor brother."

Cookie squinted suspiciously. The man before him looked like he had lived under a rock for five years. The other gang members were getting a big kick out of this reunion. Cookie whirled on them, wild-eyed.

"He ain't my fuckin' brother! That fucker killed my fuckin' padre, man! So, shut the fuck up!" They shut up. He walked around Buster, examining him like an exhibit of a caveman at the Museum of Natural History. Still, he couldn't believe it. "The fucker I knew was run off by the Stumplehorsts years ago…"

"Sorry ta diserppoint ya, but ah'm back."

"Then that's gonna be your last fuckin' mistake."

The bartender was nervous. In this snowstorm it would take the sheriff a minimum of thirty minutes to get here—that is, if he had the guts to reach for the phone to call him.

Cookie leaned down to look at Buster, his head slightly bobbing. With a mighty backhand, he slapped the hat off Buster's head, sniffed, and made a horrible face.

"*Tú apestas*, motherfucker!"

Buster didn't respond.

"I said, 'you stink, motherfucker.'"

"Ah bet ah do."

"Here," said Cookie helpfully, "Try some aftershave." And with that, he broke a bottle of tequila over Buster's head—opening a cut five inches long.

Buster fell to the floor, momentarily unconscious. Cookie, now hyperventilating, put a quarter in the jukebox and cranked up Black Sabbath's "Iron Man," his favorite song to fight to. Then, bathed in the neon lighting of the point-of-purchase beer displays, Cookie and the Bees beat the hell out of him—maniacally stomping Buster's head and kicking in his ribs. The bartender, who received a twenty-buck rake off and a small rock of crank when the Busy Bees used his place for business, was sure they were going to kill Buster and possibly kill him for witnessing it. He edged for the phone, but one of the Bees beat him to it and pulled it off the wall. Now he *knew* he was going to die. Cookie grabbed a silver napkin dispenser and squatted down next to Buster and began smashing his skull in beat to the ear-splitting music. He hit him a dozen good times, but on the backswing of number thirteen, the napkin dispenser flew across the room. Cookie felt something funny and looked at his hand. His index finger was gone—as was half of the other finger that he was partial to flipping as an obscenity. The stumps from both were squirting dark blood on his cruel heart's accelerated downbeat. So jacked-up on alcohol and drugs—it took the pain a good fifteen seconds to get to his brain. Confused, he turned to his fellow gang members. They were holding their hands over their heads—looking at the new arrival.

Jimmy Bayles Morgan stood backlit in the doorway wearing his granddaddy's pea-green campaign hat and his heavy wool Doughboy WWI coat. He, too, had come to the bar on horseback for a quick snort and got more than he bargained for. Leveled in his hands were his grandfather's cannons—the two Colt New Service revolvers with staghorn grips and lanyard cords attached to a Sam Brown belt. Smoke was still curling from the barrel of the pistol in his right.

"You shot me!" Cookie cried.

Keeping one pistol pointed at Cookie, he blasted another slug into the jukebox to create some quiet for what he had to say.

"Hittin' a man when he's down…" he said in a hoarse whisper. "Ah cain't much abide that." Jimmy stepped forward into the bar, his hooded grey eyes barely visible. "Listen to me careful. Put yer hands b'hind yor neck and inner-lock yor fingers." They started to do as he ordered, but Cookie stopped them.

"Kill that sonofabitch, you fuckin' cowards!"

One of the Busy Bees reached for his pistol. Jimmy coolly shot him in the face with snakeshot. He screamed and fell to the floor clutching his eyes.

He bent down to address the Busy Bee moaning on the ground.

"How you enjoyin' that 'coon face, sonny? An'body else want one?" There were no takers. "Now turn 'round and do as ah say! Walk to that wall yonder." This time they were obedient. "Closer," he said. "Until your dicks'er touchin' the wall!"

With the compliance of the Busy Bees, Jimmy holstered one of the pistols and threw the bartender a rope.

"Tho' this 'round the poor boy's feet, if you be so kind."

The bartender, with great relief, came around from the other side of the bar and did what was asked. Jimmy took some cash from his vest pocket and threw it on the floor.

"Here's for the damages. We ain't pikers."

Jimmy mused at the unrecognizable bloody mess on the floor and shook his head.

"My, my…lookit what you done did ta this poor bastard."

"I'm sorry I dint kill'm," Cookie Dominguez said half laughing, half crying.

Jimmy lifted his eyes and smiled at him.

"Are ya?"

When the Bartender was finished tying Buster's legs, Jimmy wrapped the other end of the rope around his arm.

"Don't anybody foller me outside unless you wanna spend the night on a slab at Crippner's."

The bartender watched as he carefully backed out of the bar, clicked for his horse to get down on his front legs and then mounted, cinching the rope around the saddle horn—never taking his eyes or guns off Buster's assailants. He gathered his horse's reins then clicked his tongue a couple of times and the horse started to back up. Buster's unconscious body slid feet first across the floor, knocking over the tables and chairs like bowling pins as he exited the bar.

Buster was conveyed, in this fashion, the whole five miles back to Lame Horse Mesa. He was too big for Jimmy to lift up and lay across Stinker's saddle, so he thought, *What the hell?* Buster wasn't going to get any more banged up sliding along the snow than he'd already been in the bar. Besides, Jimmy thought it prudent to ice down some of those contusions.

In the morning, when Buster finally opened his swollen eyes, he didn't know where he was. He hadn't remembered Jimmy coming into the bar, either. Slowly, he focused on his surroundings: there was a smoldering cigarette and a half-drunk cup of coffee sitting on the workbench ten feet away.

"You up?" came a recognizable croak from the other room. Buster swung his legs around to the edge of the bed, but when he tried to sit up, he almost passed out again.

"Whoaa, Nelly," Buster said.

"That noggin' prolly hurts like a sonofabitch, huh?" Slowly, Buster eased himself off the edge of the bed and discovered that he had no clothes.

"C'mon out here."

"Where's my clothes?"

"Ah burned 'em."

In a few minutes, Buster shuffled into his parlor room naked. There wasn't an inch of him that wasn't blue or purple. Jimmy was pouring hot water from a camp kettle into a freestanding cast iron bathtub in the middle of the room. He topped it off with a scoop of Calgon Bouquet and tossed in a bar of Sweetheart soap for good measure.

"Get in."

"Ah ain't gettin' in there. That water's hot 'nough to make soup!"

"Gotta be to kill off them cooties! C'mon Nancy, clamber in there!" Disgruntled, Buster slowly and painfully eased himself into the scalding water. He looked up to see Jimmy stropping a straight razor on a bridle strap.

"This here was Grampie's razor," Jimmy said solemnly as if he were offering Buster the Holy Eucharist.

"Where's Grampie?" Buster asked.

"Six feet south."

"Sorry to hear that."

"They don't make men like him no more. Ah can tell ya that."

Jimmy swirled an old brush around in a shaving mug and applied the lather to Buster's face.

"So, Sheriff Dudival tole me you went off ta Utah."

"Them Mormons was heppin' me find my kin."

"They try ta feed ya that Jesus and the Injuns stuff?"

"No, sir."

"Yor lucky ya got out with your skin. Thar some pee-culiar people."

"They got themselves a big ly-briry with the fam-lee tree of all the people who ever was."

"That's how you found your kinfolk, was it?"

"A feller hepped me. Looked up two hunnert and fifty-nine Tom McCaffreys."

"And which one of 'em was your pappy?"

"None of 'em."

"Ah'm raht sorry to hear that."

"How much did that Mormon feller charge ya…ta hep ya, that is?"

"Oh, he dint charge me nuthin'. He jes axed me fer a d'nation."

"How much was that?"

"Three hundred dollars."

Jimmy whistled between his brown teeth.

"Three hunnert dollars and ya dint find your pappy's kin…"

Jimmy tilted Buster's chin up so he could shave his neck.

"Ah'll bet you cain't even r'member that feller's name in the lybriry, can ya?"

"Heck, ah cain't. His nametag said *Flowers*—and ah thought that there's a funny name for a feller. *Beverly Flowers*."

"Lookit how dirty you was," Jimmy said, changing the subject and pointing to the grey scum floating to the surface of the tub water. "You can git out now."

As Buster stepped out, Jimmy presented him with an old pair of pants and a shirt then left the room. The tan shirt, sans badge, was from the Lame Horse County Sheriff's Department. Buster put it on and wandered over to Jimmy's workbench. There was a brace of large frame Colt revolvers, a little automatic, leather repair tools, gunpowder, bullet-making equipment, and several boxes of Vulcan dynamite blasting caps. There was a cardboard box with a dusty old Contax camera and telephoto lens, a Silvertone wire recorder with earphones, and mounted on the Masonite backboard was a shrine of antique barbed wire surrounding a newspaper obituary for Sheriff James Morgan—a stern looking man with a haircut similar to Jimmy's and a mustache.

"Is this here a picture of yor Grampie?" Buster called into the next room.

Jimmy walked back in and squinted his eyes to see what he was looking at.

"That'd be him."

"Ah see the ra-zem-balance," Buster said, scrutinizing the hawkeyed image in the faded rotogravure. He tried to read the obit. "Says here he was a-sass-i-naded by left wing el-ee-ments."

"That's right. The damn union people."

"How'd that happen?"

"Why don't you ask your friend, Sheriff Dudival, 'bout it?"

"Ah thought he was yor friend, too."

"Yeah, he is." Then he barely heard him mutter, "…Jes caint dupen on him, is all."

"Well, he's been plenny good to me and I don't like you talkin' 'bout him like that!" Buster barked back to him, surprising even himself. Jimmy clenched his jaws combatively then relaxed them into a smile.

"Ah like that…that you stuck up fer a friend. Would you do that fer me, let's say?"

"Ah don't think you should have these blastin' caps jes layin' 'round like this," Buster said, sidestepping the question.

"They ain't hurtin' nobody."

"That ain't the way Mr. Svendergard taught me ta handle dynamite."

"Well, he don't have a lot to say 'bout it no more, now does he?" There was a little coughing laugh from the other room. "Get in here. Ah got somethin' for ya."

"Ah hope it's breakfast."

"Plenty a time for that later. C'mon now…"

When Buster came back into the other room, he was surprised to see Jimmy grab for a nasal cannula attached to an oxygen tank.

"What's wrong with you?" Buster asked.

"What does it look like? Ah cain't breathe." He took a couple of deep sniffs then twisted the outflow valve shut so he could light a cigarette. Buster's eyes tracked to an army surplus medical kit that Jimmy had laid out on a towel with sutures and several feet of catgut.

"What's that all for?"

"Need to do some work on yor face."

"Cain't ah go to the doctor?"

"We ain't payin' those bastards a hundred bucks for an office visit! Now, set down here and stop bein' sech a weak tittie."

Buster sat down on the chair and looked warily as he strung the catgut through the first hooked suture.

"Where'd ya learnt to do this?" Buster asked, not unreasonably, as Jimmy daubed his face with rubbing alcohol.

"Haven't ya ev'r darned a sock?" The bedside manner part of the procedure over, Jimmy jabbed the first suture into the ugly cut above Buster's eyebrow.

"Jiminy Christmas!" Buster yowled.

"This might sting a little."

"Good gravy! Ain't you gonna give me somethin' for the pain?"

"You had enough of that last night."

And with that, he plunged the suture into his face again. Buster yowled and Jimmy just left it there while he retrieved his Chesterfield Commander that had been left smoldering in the ashtray and took a drag. Tears were running down Buster's face, and his nose was dripping like an icicle on a south facing roof.

"So, you wanna be known as the town fool."

"No, sir."

"Well, yor winnin' the e-lection, unopposed."

"What's it to you, anyways?"

"Makes me sick to see a man makin' a fool of hisself over a dumb girl."

"What ah do, or don't do, don't concern you."

Jimmy was going to say something, but didn't.

"And Destiny ain't dumb. She plumb gone to college!" Buster said, defensively.

"What're you talkin' 'bout? College! She jes went and got herself a fuckin' reelstate license! And if you think sellin' our land's any proper way to make a livin', yor a bigger ass than I give you credit fer!" Jimmy plunged the suture into his eyebrow once again. With all the jagged black catgut sutures bristling from his face, he was starting to look like a rag doll at an amateur craft fair.

"Ow, ow, ow!"

"Lemme ask you somethin'. You gotta a job?"

"Ah'm fixin' to git me one."

"Yor fixin' to git one."

"Why?" Buster asked suspiciously.

"You ain't gonna git one 'round here."

"And just how are you so sure a that?"

"The Stumplehorsts put the word out. They don't want you bird doggin' their daughter. An'body give you a job gonna be on their shit list."

"But…but ol' Pop likes me."

"Ah see ah'm gonna have to curry the kinks outta you," he said, turning on his oxygen for a quick pick-me-up. "Stumplehorst likes you to *yor face*, unnerstan? To yor back, that's 'nother thing 'ntirely. A two-faced man…well, that's one thing ah truly cain't abide," he said, his irises slowly narrowing darkly.

In fact, as we now know, there was not just one, but many things Jimmy Bayles Morgan could not abide. And these defects that he found in Man's very nature kept him in a constant state of deadly vexation. Over twenty years had passed since the town biddies had refused his custody of the McCaffrey baby—the baby *he* had found. But that didn't stop him from monitoring and surveilling him—the way he had learned at Sheriff Morgan's knee. So, it should come as no surprise that he could not abide the child molester, Carlito Dominguez—who he blew up with dynamite before he could get his hands on Buster. Nor should it be surprising that, nudity aside, he could not abide Gil Svendergard denying Buster an education—and gave him that little push off his perch and into his cement contraption. And despite his tough veneer, Jimmy Bayles Morgan could not abide Buster living under the roof of a wife-beater. And so, he did a little work on Bob Boyle's brakes. But as far as Stumplehorst was concerned, he had let him live. After all, he finally had the boy back under his control, so why not be magnanimous?

"Have you seen her?" Buster asked.

"Seen who?"

"Destiny."

"Oh yeah, ah seen her."

"How is she?"

"All right, ah guess."

"Does she ever ask 'bout me?"

"Fuck no." The catgut was holding Buster's brow from drooping. "But, she's prolly pretty busy…whorin' for cocaine from that real estate guy."

Buster looked at him wide-eyed for a moment, and then started to blubber.

"C'mon, now. This is disgraceful! Cryin' over Destiny Stumplehorst, my goodness!"

Buster was inconsolable. Jimmy sat back and watched him cry and cry while he reheated his coffee and chain-lit another cigarette. "What about that VonMorsch girl? Seen her lately? Ah'll tell ya, she's a pretty good looker. Got a nice little ass on 'er, too—*and* she was the 4H swine champion—six years runnin'! Lemme tell you somethin,' friend, that's three good qualities in a ranchin' wife right there!"

"Ah don't wanna be with any other girls," Buster said quietly. Jimmy shook his head at the hopeless lump in front of him.

"Here. Have something to eat. You might even grow a ball or two." He grabbed a bowl and poured some Lucky Charms into it, then noticed some mouse turds speckling the presentation and gave them the boot with a flick of his finger before pouring on the powdered milk and water.

"Much obliged," Buster said, sniffling. Jimmy was studying him now.

"Here's a thought. Why don't you throw in with me?"

"Takin' folks on pony rides?" Buster guffawed, milk dribbling out of his mouth. "Thas no job for a real cowboy. No 'ffense."

Jimmy had to bite his lip. "None taken. 'Course, it'd only be temp'rary 'til you got back on yor feet…"

"Yeah, ah don't know 'bout that…"

"There's probably some advantage to bein' in proximity to your *amor verdadera*, but who am ah to say?" Buster considered that new wrinkle for a moment, while Jimmy considered pulling the stitches out of his face.

"All raht," he finally conceded. "But jes 'til ah get back on my feet."

CHAPTER ELEVEN

Cabin Fever

JIMMY CLEARED A TACK room for Buster to bunk. His shack—it wasn't quite accurate to call it a house—was erected in 1883, as the date on the newspapers used as insulation inside the walls could attest. There was no foundation, just four piles of rubble under each corner. The front of the place was constructed with split logs, but the sides and back were a hodgepodge of materials that looked like the original builder had panicked—with winter quickly approaching—and nailed up anything he could find to have a roof over his head by first snow. The ruin owed its structural integrity to a century-old Peking Cotoneaster shrub that had grown into a thicket surrounding the tumbledown's perimeter—holding its warped and rotting bits in place like a soiled dove's corset.

There was telephone and electricity at the shack, but Jimmy had only paid for their initial installation and never a penny more. In his mind, the power and telephone companies had traversed his land, so in exchange for that, his fee would be free service and telephone for the rest of his life. What utility company would agree to a deal like that, you wonder? A utility company that wasn't just a recorded voice on the phone, but an actual person sitting in an office in town—who knew very well what a Morgan was capable of doing when crossed.

Jimmy was like no other person Buster had ever known. He never saw Jimmy put anything in his mouth besides coffee and cigarettes. The only food in the cabin all winter was a fifty-pound bag of flour and a fifty-pound bag of Anasazi beans. Jimmy supplemented their diet with deer that he shot in any season—not feeling he had to hew to game laws dictated by the state. When Buster complained about eating the same thing every night, Jimmy went out and rammed one of Stumplehorst's Angus with his truck. Buster was mortified and called Jimmy out to explain himself.

"Ol' Stumplehorst had it comin'...firin' you jes b'cause you poked his daughter."

"What if they find out? They might think ah did it!"

"Nobody's gonna find out. Ah removed the ah-lids and the gani-tayla to make it look like an alien moot-il-ayshun."

For several weeks after the beating Buster received, at the now eight-fingered hands of Cookie Dominguez, Buster walked hunched over like an old man. His pummeled kidneys produced an alarming cabernet-colored pee. He couldn't ride his horse for fear of puncturing a lung with his broken ribs. His teeth were tender and loose. Repeated blows to his skull gave him unexpected dizzy spells—forcing him to suddenly grab the nearest object to stay upright. Jimmy didn't like it when that object was him.

"Brisk up!" he'd say, and push Buster off.

Jimmy couldn't abide a freeloader, so Buster helped out when he could with simple domestic chores. Jimmy had lived alone in the shack all these years and had probably never swept, washed, or fixed anything. A wet, soapy rag, when wiped across any surface, yielded the tacky burnt sienna of thousands—if not hundreds of thousands—of cigarettes. Buster, well trained by Edita Dominguez, scrubbed and swept every inch of the place. A normal person would have welcomed the new hygiene of his surroundings, but not Jimmy. It rankled him when he saw Buster cleaning.

"What the goddamn hell're you doin'? That's what we got Messicans for!"

Of course, Jimmy would never think of actually hiring anyone to do the cleaning, he just didn't want to miss the opportunity to take a racist shot. And when he caught Buster doing his washing, he really hit the roof. Buster had taken it upon himself to drag out an old washtub and washboard. Jimmy only had two changes—work jeans, work shirt, newer jeans, and an Indian-patterned western shirt for Saturday night at the High Grade. There were some other items whose purpose to Buster seemed mysterious—a couple yards of cotton swaddling and some Ace bandages. Jimmy happened to come outside while he was examining them and angrily threw his cigarette in the wash water.

"What in Christ's name!"

"Thought ah'd do some warshin'."

"Don't you unnerstan? Men don't do laundry. That's what we got chinks for!"

Jimmy hurried the soapy pile back into the privacy of his room. *What was all that about?*

The answer came two weeks before the ranch's Memorial Day opener. While prying up a crumbling piece of planking on the front porch, a sizeable sliver found its way into Buster's finger and broke off when he tried to remove it. Minor surgery was called for. He looked around for some disinfectant to sterilize his penknife. There was a closet outside Jimmy's door that he postulated might hold such a thing. As he was perusing the shelves—cluttered with prescription medicine bottles and oxygen equipment—he was surprised to discover the same kind of device that Jimmy had once identified for him at the Puster auction. A douche bag. What was Jimmy doing with that, he wondered? And then he came across box of Tampax sanitary napkins. Had Jimmy once shared this cabin with a lady friend? In all the time he'd known him—unlike other cowboys—Buster had never heard Jimmy brag about his female conquests, but here was now evidence of a past relationship. Buster smiled at Jimmy's caginess and thought he'd call him on it. Jimmy was in his room when Buster burst in excitedly with the incriminating Tampax box.

"Hey, you ol' cayuse. You never tole me..."

But he never got to the end of the sentence. There, standing in the middle of the room was Jimmy—wrapping the Ace bandage around his chest, binding and flattening her unmistakabe women's breasts. Jimmy quickly covered up.

"Get out!"

Buster shut the door in a panic and tried to close his gaping mouth. How could it be? The swearing, spitting, threatening Jimmy? The Jimmy at the auction, sitting on the fence like a man, cowboy boot hooked on the bottom rail firing up a smoke? The crotch-grabbing, gun-toting Jimmy—riding full blast down a sixty degree canyon wall? That was no woman. That had to be a man. But Jimmy Bayles Morgan was not, in fact, a man—although everyone on the mesa treated her as one.

In Buster's defense, Jimmy didn't make it easy for people to identify her gender. A dress had never graced her boyish figure, not even when she was a little girl. She had always preferred rodeo-cut jeans and cowboy shirts neatly rolled to firm biceps. Her once blonde hair was worn in a fifties flat top—cut by a barber in Naturita. He had a faded style chart on the wall of his shop from which his customers—most of whom couldn't speak English—picked what they wanted.

Jimmy always chose the "Lee Marvin." She slicked it with butch wax and toughened up the look with dark Ray Ban Aviators. Tomboys of Jimmy's stripe were not uncommon in these parts. Girls with given names like Maureen often shortened them to "Mo," Josephine to "Jo", Wilhelmina to "Billy"—especially if they came from families where boys predominated. In Jimmy's case, she was an only child. When she was four, her parents, raging alcoholics, left her to be raised by her grandfather, the Sheriff James Morgan. Before the advent of day care, Jimmy was forced to spend the entire day in her grandfather's patrol cruiser—a front seat witness to untold acts of sadism and brutality. Jimmy emerged from adolescence as a swaggering, violent, bowed-legged, profaning, cigarette smoking copy of her grandfather and near proof of the Konrad Lorenz theory of social imprinting. But that still didn't change the fact that she was a woman.

What was he to do? Jimmy would be coming out of her room soon. Red-faced with embarrassment, the little boy in Buster was urging him to run away, saddle a horse, gallop a few miles, and scream. But after pacing in the kitchen a bit, he decided against that. He decided to sit down, drum his thumbs on the table and act like nothing out of the ordinary had happened.

The door to Jimmy's room opened. Jimmy cast a quick look at Buster then went around behind him to the cupboard. She uncorked a pint of Crazy Crow then splashed three fingers into a dirty enameled coffee cup. She stood there looking at the back of Buster's head—he remaining motionless, looking straight ahead.

"Ah don't know how it was with them fuckin' Dominguezes, the Svendergards, or them fuckin' Boyles, but 'round here…we don't go bargin' inta other folks's rooms without knockin'. Got that, pard?"

"Yes, sss…uh…ma'am."

"Jimmy," she said quietly.

"Jimmy."

Jimmy poured him a slug of whiskey and handed it to him. He quickly gulped it.

"Ah'm awful sorry."

Jimmy refilled his cup and slipped into the chair facing him.

"We don't ev'r haveta menchun this ag'in," she said, lighting a cigarette.

"That'd be jes fahn by me," Buster said. And they sat at the table in silence, not leaving until the whiskey was finished.

ꝏ

IN THE WEEKS AND months that were to follow, Buster's familiarity with this strange character began to breed a litter of contempt between both of them. Buster never considered Jimmy's gangrene material about Mexicans, Afro-Americans, the Jews, and the government funny, but at first, he let it slide. Maybe something had happened to her to make her like this. Whatever it was, he figured her enmity was the fire in her belly that kept her alive. If that had been true, it was failing her now. Jimmy's skin stubbornly remained gray—no matter how much time she spent with the horses under the blazing sun. Buster didn't have to be a doctor to know she was sick, something serious. But whenever he asked her about it, she wouldn't give him a straight answer. All he knew was she took a lot of medicine and drove to the hospital two times a month for treatments. Exposure to her toxic pronouncements about people—people with whom she had no first hand knowledge—began to weaken Buster—as if *he* was the one having the hospital treatments, not her. No dummy, she could tell from the sour expression on Buster's face that he didn't approve of her, but she persisted anyway. Buster began to suspect that her slurs were really meant for him—finger pokes at a softness in him she could not abide.

By the end of May, he dreaded every evening with her. There were only two ways to escape her company—a well-worn muddy path to the corral to feed the horses and the well-worn muddy path to the putrid outhouse. His room was not an option for sanctuary—it being only six by nine. That left the workshop—where they both converged every night.

Jimmy wasn't lazy; he could say that for her. She always had a project. Those projects unfortunately involved the killing or maiming of poor animals that had managed to get on her bad side. She referred to these hapless "critters"—skunks, weasels, opossums, raccoons, beavers—as "needin' fixin'"—as if she was graciously filling a request, by the animals themselves, for their own mutilation or demise. She would patiently explain to Buster that these animals couldn't help being the way they were. They couldn't be talked out of stinking under the shack. They couldn't be convinced to stop chewing down her trees. They couldn't be cajoled out of slaughtering her chickens. And so, she was left with no other choice than to "fix" these immutable defects in the animal's very nature. Confusing Buster's silence with acceptance, she cannily presented him with the logical follow up.

"People ain't much diff'rint, ya know."

"How ya mean?" asked Buster.

"Off'n times there's a prollem with a feller's very nature."

"Not much you can do 'bout that," Buster said.

"Maybe. Maybe not," was all Jimmy said, as she completed a wire noose made from fishhooks for the weasel living under the loafing shed. She dangled it proudly for Buster to see, but was chagrined to find him, once again, scribbling away in a child's spiral notebook—his tongue stuck out in concentration. She took a deep drag on her cigarette, the smoke forcing its way through gummy alveoli.

"Thought 'bout whatcher gonna do 'bout Cookie Dominguez?"

"Ah ain't gonna do nothin'."

"Why not?"

"Cause ah ain't."

"Ah b'lieve that sonofabitch is gettin' up a head a steam to kill you."

"Ol' Cookie's allus been like that. He's jes unhappy with the way he looks. That's what Momma Dominguez used to say."

"That's right. An he won't be happy 'til he sees you dead."

Buster laughed.

"Next yor gonna tell me he needs fixin', too."

Jimmy swelled with expectation. The fabled horse had been led to water. Buster looked up from his notebook.

"Hey…that's what you *are* sayin.'"

"Nev'r say nothin' that can be used agin' ya in a courta law," she cackled proudly while liberating some bloody lung matter that she spat into a shop rag. "Ah jes hope yer not makin' notes of this conversation!" she said, when she caught her breath.

"I'm writin' Destiny a letter."

"Not 'nother goddamn letter!" Jimmy just threw her head back and laughed. "You weak godamn tittie!"

This would be Buster's thirty-fifth letter. The previous thirty-four were written with the conceit that he was still in Utah pursuing his bona fide ancestry—even though a Vanadium postal stamp would have indicated otherwise. Those early letters, while he recuperated, were written in the style of a foreign correspondent's reportage: what it was like inside the Mormon Tabernacle, how the Chinese buffet restaurants charge by the age of Mormon kids in a "combined" family, how a teenage Mormon girl snuck up to him at a gas station in Colorado City and asked that he help her escape from her polygamous marriage and how those folks stopped his truck and had Buster arrested for interfering with a minor—and all the interesting people he met in jail! How he had run out of money and what lizards and roadrunners taste like. Things like that. Some of the letters asked for news of home.

How was Maple's foal and if she would like him to train it when he got back? How he missed her pancakes. How were her parents? How were Doc and Ned Gigglehorn? Things like that. But letter number thirty-five was a full-blown love letter.

In this letter, he came clean and admitted that he'd been in Vanadium all this time and that he'd been in a fight and didn't want her to see what he looked like until his face healed. He told her that, wherever he had been, he thought of her every day and every night before he went to sleep and how he wished he could hold her in his arms. He told her how he remembered every detail of their lovemaking. He told her he imagined touching her and kissing her all over her body and shyly asked if she thought of him that way. He congratulated her on her new profession and told her to keep an eye out for a piece of land that he could buy for raising their family one day. He ended the letter by pledging his undying love for her and including a piece of the catgut from his face—a poetic gesture, he thought, to say that their two hearts would be stitched together as one. Maybe including a bloody piece of string wasn't such a good idea, but he'd already licked the envelope closed.

"Woodja mail'er fer me?"

Buster held out the envelope.

"Why don't you jes give it to her yorsef, ya damn pussy?"

"Ah don't wanner to see me lookin' like this."

"If you en-sest on it," she said, sourly taking possession of it.

"Don't read it, though," Buster said.

"Why the hell would ah?"

That night, after reading it, Jimmy burned number thirty-five in the same oil drum she had burned all previous thirty-four.

CHAPTER TWELVE

Mr. M

THE MUD SEASON THAT kept Buster and Jimmy from getting any outside work done was now over. The rush was on to get the place ready—to transform it from its muddy derelict state to something resembling a set in a John Ford movie—which was what the tourists liked. Horses were curried, washed, and re-shod. The gravel parking lot was dragged level, potholes filled. Dust and mites were beaten out of old Navajo blankets and were laid across the chairs on the porch in case a customer wanted to put his feet up while toking on a Cubano Esplendido. Buster could stick his nose up all he wanted at the pony ride industry, but Jimmy had a sweet little deal on Lame Horse Mesa. Telluride's second homeowners, many escaping the summer heat of Chicago, New York, Dallas, and Houston provided her with steady business from June to October. These people, many of whom suffered awkward and fearful childhoods, found themselves emboldened by their success in later life, eager to remediate their past teenage intimidations. Jimmy's hokey ad in the area's yellow pages "for an Authentic Western Experience" dog whistled to that. The Trail Ride package came with a grilled chicken dinner and cowboy singing for one hundred twenty-five bucks a head. For the fly fishermen, she led pack trips to not-so-remote mountain lakes that she personally stocked with her favorite named fish—cutthroat. An overnight belly-boat trip cost five hundred per and she never had an empty slot on the calendar—not just because the fishing was great, but Jimmy's odd character and foul mouth were the stuff of legend at Telluride Mountain Village dinner parties. She didn't accept credit cards. It was an all-cash deal, and Jimmy took great pride in the fact that she had never paid federal income tax and only took 40 percent from Buster's tips jar for herself.

Buster's knowledge of every plant, flower, bird, and animal—stemming from his time with Ned Gigglehorn and Doc Solitcz—held him in good stead with Jimmy's clients. Despite the fact that Jimmy had guided these horse rides all her adult life and fielded thousands of questions from snotty-nosed rich kids, she took great pride in never having bothered to know the real name of any bird or plant in Colorado. She preferred to make them up on the fly.

"That there is a Speckle-assed Pudsucker," she would tell a precocious seven year-old boy from San Antonio. "That there is a Periwinkled Pipewiper. We cowboys use it for toilet paper in a pinch," she would tell a five year-old girl from Darien, Connecticut. "That there is a Feral Nutlicker," she once informed the wife of the retired CEO of Exxon when asked to identify a coyote.

A black Land Rover pulled into the parking lot. Jimmy slung her portable oxygen tank over her shoulder and got up from her desk to meet her nine o'clock—the Mallomars of New York. It was serendipity that Marvin and Dana Mallomar had found their way here. The couple had considered Aspen, Steamboat, and Santa Fe. She liked Aspen, but he didn't like competing socially with the film people. He liked

Steamboat, but she didn't like the fact that there were only two Chinese restaurants in town and both of them were Mandarin. She liked Santa Fe, but he got "a vibe" that the local Hispanic population had, what he called, a "hard-on" for Anglos. That led them to undiscovered Vanadium. Perusing a real estate brochure that only seemed to highlight the limited activities in the area, Mallomar spotted Jimmy's already-mentioned ad for an "Authentic Western Experience." Once assured that horses didn't carry Lyme disease and that his wife could have their picnic food prepared by a caterer, Mallomar signed on for opening day.

Jimmy's fast draw was only second to her "fast take" on people, and there was no one faster from the hip or more deadly than Jimmy. Under the wide brim of her sombrero, she snuck sly peeks at the Mallomars and, in an instant, had all the information she needed to trap her unwitting subjects in the amber of her misanthropy.

To Jimmy's lights, the mister was overweight. That meant he indulged himself and was slothful—two more things Jimmy could not abide. He also wore Levis. People around here wore Wranglers. And cinching his flabby waist was an expensive hand-tooled silver belt, "the kind they sold in Aspen and Santa Fe to faggots," she explained later to Buster. Jimmy didn't abide with ostentation, either. When he took off his hat to wipe away the perspiration, she noticed a D-Day formation of tiny circles where he'd had hair seedlings punched into his head. Men around here were compliant with their baldness. Vanity was another thing Jimmy could not abide. Then there was the matter of his face. It reminded her of a horse she once knew with a "Roman nose." A nag with a Roman nose meant it had a stubborn or obstinate personality—two more things that Jimmy could not abide.

As for the wife, she was attractive and a lot younger than Mallomar. That probably meant she married him for his money. Jimmy did not abide women who married men for their money. Women who married men for their money lowered men's opinions of all regular workingwomen. And Mrs. Mallomar didn't wear underwear under her tight-fitting Hermes riding breeches—the outline of her genitalia showed through, like the track of a young antelope in a dry streambed. Jimmy did not abide with immodesty in dress and deportment. And she did not abide with Mrs. Mallomar trying to catch her husband's eye so they could have a private little laugh at her manly expense. But as far as these Mallomars were concerned, she would bear their effrontery with absolutely no visible sign of indignation, for they were just visiting. Tourism, she intuited, had the potential for being Vanadium's second act after mining.

Jimmy unplugged her oxygen, wrinkled up her brown parchment face into a smile and extended her hand to shake.

"Good mornin to ya'll! Ah'm Jimmy."

At the sound of Jimmy's mannish voice, Mrs. Mallomar let loose a little snort through her nose like a stupid third grade girl. Mallomar looked at his wife sternly and turned to Jimmy.

"She's a little nervous. Never been on a horse before," Mallomar said, covering.

"Don't you worry, honey. We got a horse for ya'll that's like sittin' on a rockin' chair," she rasped. "Or like sittin on a vibrator if that's more to yor likin," she camouflaged with an emphysemic hack and a phlegmy spit as she walked away from them to the corral. "Hey, Buster!" Jimmy bellowed. "Come over here and meet your clients!"

Buster was in the corral lifting a pannier onto a mule that held their '88 Grgich Chardonnay, fresh baked baguettes, a marinated eggplant with tarragon chicken, arugula with shaved parmesan, and some brownies—all demanded by the Mallomars and created by Mary Boyle—who, after finally losing the Buttered Roll, was now the head cook at the High Grade. Buster swung himself up on Stinker and rode over to meet the man who was going to change his life.

"Buster, this here's Mr. Mallomar and his missus, Mrs. Mallomar."

"Mornin' ma'am," Buster said tipping his hat to Mrs. Mallomar, who ever so slightly arched her back. Mrs. Mallomar deigned not to reply, letting her body do all the talking. Buster struggled, but maintained steady eye contact—unaware that Mallomar was watching to see where his eyes went. "Mornin', sir."

"Mornin'," Mallomar grunted, dropping the *g* because he was in the West.

Mallomar had begged his wife to be more conservative in her choice of clothes, especially her blouses and sweaters. But she had a beautiful body and didn't care if everybody knew it. It was all hers—if one didn't count the little lift she had for her thirty-fifth birthday. Dana's appearance, which had once been a source of pride for Mallomar, was now his bane. When they were together, people seemed to forget that *he* was the one who gave twenty million dollars to Cedars Sinai for the Children's Burn Unit, or that *he* was the one who scooped Modigliani's "Nude on a Divan" out from under the noses of the Bass Brothers at Sotheby's for the Met, or that *he* was the one who brought a secret message to the Pope from Catholic venture capitalists meeting in Montenegro during the UN occupation—*get rid of Milosevic and we're in*. No one ever remembered his being there if she was there. Wherever they went together, all eyes followed her beautiful breasts like they had an important message for the world.

"All right then, trail ho!" Jimmy said, in her most fake upbeat. Jimmy grabbed Buster as they mounted up and hissed. "The missus is allergic to wheat. Don't let her eat any, or she'll swell up like a Spanish wine bag."

And with that, stirrups were adjusted, liability releases were signed, and the three headed out on the ten-mile trail to Hope Lake, which was a real place and not a metaphor for anything. Mr. and Mrs. Mallomar bickered most of the way up.

"I don't know how comfortable this saddle is," Mrs. Mallomar whinged.

"It's a saddle. It's not a lounge chair," Mr. Mallomar snidely shot back.

Then there was the difference of opinion as to how the mountains were formed. Mrs. Mallomar felt that they had been pushed up from plates under the surface. Mallomar didn't agree.

"These peaks are old volcanoes, for Chrissake. And these valleys you see here were scoured by receding glaciers."

"What fucking Discovery Show did you watch? The volcanoes are in Maui."

"Okay, let's ask somebody who lives here," Mallomar said. "What do you say, Clem?"

Buster turned around in his saddle to answer. The volcano answer sounded good. He sort of remembered somebody saying something about that. But it would be a long day if he aggravated the missus so early in the ride, so he replied in the way Mrs. Stumplehorst might have if she were sitting in his saddle at this moment.

"Ah b'lieve the good Lord cr'ated 'em." Buster smiled sweetly and turned back around in his saddle. Mrs. Mallomar didn't use any more four-letter words after that. As a matter of fact, the ride went smoothly for the rest of the way. Buster was able to lean back in his saddle and enjoy himself. He puckered up and whistled to a lark bunting perched in a juniper, he warbled to a mountain chickadee and screeched teasingly to a pine Grosbeak. Mrs. Mallomar was at it again—rolling her eyes to her husband—as if to say, "Get a load a *him*." Mallomar refused to be a co-conspirator in his wife's snobbery and wouldn't give her the satisfaction of a response.

Mallomar had taken five hundred milligrams of Elavil and a Percocet with his egg white omelet that morning and really didn't feel like tilting the little bubble in his psychoneural carpenter's level. The

Mallomars had been having marital problems as of late and dabbled in many kinds of therapy. Like much of life, things boiled down to "the chicken or the egg" concept of cause and effect. Was Mrs. Mallomar a substance abuser because their marriage was in trouble, or was their marriage in trouble because Dana was a substance abuser? Was Mallomar's uncontrollable anger a result of a troubled marriage or was the troubled marriage the reason for his uncontrollable anger? After a combined four hundred man-hours of therapy discussing these things and much more, they were still at an impasse. To be fair to their psychiatrist, despite a great deal of shouting, accusing, and soul baring, Mallomar never told the complete truth about himself. Even though his tax return had him listed in prosaic terms as a venture capitalist, he was really an accomplished actor. This was the secret to his success—the roles he had performed to the world: The Great Charging Bull, The Humble Before the Great, The Hale Fellow Well Met, and the award-winning Sentimentalist. How convincing he could be as that character when speaking of the Truly Important Things in Life: Family, Health, and the Belief in a Greater Power. Mallomar didn't personally believe in any of it himself, but the performance he offered to the world, standing upstage and bellowing to the cheap seats until his lungs burned, had so much conviction that no one ever had the impertinence or cynicism to call him on it. That is, except Mrs. Mallomar. She knew him for the emotional fraud that he was—no matter how he tried to convince her otherwise. The fact that she didn't believe in him anymore was particularly galling. Angered by this inner dialogue, Mallomar wrapped the reins tightly around his fist and gave his horse a commanding giddy-yap and went ahead of his wife, making her gag in a cloud of his dust.

That was typical, Mrs. Mallomar thought. From her dusty vantage point she fumed in silence as she watched him steer his horse around every rock and bush—as if the horse didn't know where the hell it was going. Yes, and as if *she* didn't know where she was going. She got along fine before she met him. She even made some decisions on her own. Controlling bastard. She chortled at how the fat of his hairy neck folded back on itself like a shar-pei. If she divorced him, she'd get half of everything since 1994. He'd fight it. Marvin knew how to fight dirty. He'd probably bring up how they met.

At lunch by the lake, Buster watched nervously as Mr. Mallomar sullenly picked the grapes out of his salad. Mrs. Mallomar, in the meantime, was segregating the wheat croutons from hers.

"Didn't anyone tell you I was allergic to wheat?"

"It's just four fuckin' croutons. Don't make a Federal case out of it," Mallomar said, slapping at caddisflies as if they were yellow jackets.

"Uh, would you like me to take a picture of you two as a mo-min-toe?" Buster said, noticing Mr. Mallomar's camera.

Mrs. Mallomar shrugged listlessly.

"Why not?" Mallomar put his food down and moved closer to his wife who stiffened. After several attempts to satisfy Mallomar's specific sense of composition, Buster was finally told to snap the picture. Unfortunately, after he did, he fumbled the camera and it fell to the ground. It would have survived if Stinker hadn't stepped on it.

"Jiminy. Sorry," said Buster.

"What'd he do?"

"His horse stepped on the camera."

"Just as well," said Mrs. Mallomar.

"What's that supposed to mean?" asked Mallomar.

"It means…maybe I don't feel so compelled to capture every sad, banal moment of my fucking life. Copy that, Bunky?" Mallomar just stared at her. Buster shifted uncomfortably.

"She's kidding," Mallomar said. "Where can I take a leak?"

"Men's, to the left. Ladies', to the right."

Mallomar blinked, not getting the tried and true guide's joke.

"Anywhere you please," Buster said, by way of clarification. Mallomar couldn't believe that something like that wasn't, in some way, regulated. So to get things rolling, Buster walked off a discrete distance from Mrs. Mallomar behind a juniper where Mr. Mallomar joined him. Both men unzipped and when it became clear that they were passing water through disparate-sized equipment, Mallomar—the possessor of the smaller—felt the urge to compensate.

"I financed a search engine, drlivingstonipresume.com. Ever hear of it? The IPO opened at four and an eighth and shot to sixty-five by twelve-thirty the same day. Six hundred and fifty million."

Buster didn't seem to fully grasp the extent of Mallomar's Wall Street derring-do. He just smiled pleasantly, shook, and zipped up.

"Six hundred and fifty million. Ain't that the number a Chinamen they got over there?"

Mallomar just looked at him dumbfounded. Was he kidding? On the ride back down, Mrs. Mallomar complained about Buster's horse's gas. Then she complained that Mallomar had been given the good saddle. Not wanting to hear her whine about this for the next five miles, Mallomar asked Buster if he'd mind stopping to switch them. Buster politely obliged. They remounted and continued down the trail. Mrs. Mallomar had a light-hearted moment commenting on Mallomar's jiggling love handles and belly. Mallomar smiled good-naturedly, but Buster could see his jaw muscles tighten as if he they were receiving electric shocks.

"They have the death penalty here in Colorado?" Mallomar said, looking at his wife.

But Buster wasn't paying attention. He was leaning over in his saddle, scrutinizing tracks in the trail.

"What're you looking at?"

"A doe and her fawn were coming down here this morning prolly headed for the lake. Now look at this here. A big cat cut their track."

Mallomar was agog.

"A cat?"

"Mountain lion."

"What do you think's going to happen?"

"Somebody's gonna get et," Buster said casually.

"What did he say?" Mrs. Mallomar said, not wanting to miss out on anything.

"We just found some mountain lion tracks," Mallomar said, appropriating. "A lion. He cut the track of a couple of deer. Probably gonna eat them."

"Oh my god...does he know *we're* here?" Mallomar looked to Buster. Buster nodded.

"Oh, yeah," Mallomar said. He enjoyed stoking her fear. It got her mind off of him for a while. "Have you ever shot anything with that thing?" Mallomar asked, gesturing to the Krag .30-40 in Buster's scabbard.

"Yessir."

"Mountain lion?"

"No, sir."

"What exactly?"

"Ev'r year ah get tags to shoot a couple elk and a mule deer. Keep some of the meat for m'sef and swap out the res' for other things ah need—flour, saddle equipment...what not. Don't need much."

Buster was telling the truth. It was Jimmy who wouldn't stoop to eat game and preferred hunting with her truck.

"You don't use cash?"

"Well, of course. Ever'body got to have cash!" Buster guffawed. Mallomar guffawed, too—looking at his wife to make sure she got the joke.

"How much, if you don't mind me asking?"

"Beggin' your pardon?"

"What's your nut? How much do you need to get by on?"

Buster recalled from Mrs. Humphrey's *Manners for Men* something about never talking about another fellow's money. But he also didn't want to make Jimmy's client think he was uppity.

"Well, my goal's twelve hunnert."

"A week?"

Buster leaned back in his saddle and hee-hawed.

"No, sir, a year!"

Mallomar just looked at him in disbelief.

"Very interesting," was all he could muster saying, "Very interesting." It was as if Mallomar had been struck by lightning. How simple life could be, if one's wants were simple. "What else can you point out to me?"

Buster continued to point out the tracks of at least a half-dozen other animals—from chipmunks to black bears. He taught Mallomar how to tell the difference between a crow and a raven. He told him why ranchers didn't mind having coyotes around, but happily shoot porcupines. Now showing off, Buster identified skunkgrass, pigweed, beargrass, and kinnikinnick. He lowered his voice with reverence when they rode through remnants of an old growth forest. And always the gentleman, he stopped to pick a posy of columbines, bluebells, and paintbrush for the missus.

Mallomar found it peculiar that he did not take exception to Buster's attention to his wife the way he did with other men. He found it even more unusual that he found himself—though older, smarter, and richer—actually looking up to Buster for some reason—even *admiring* him. As the corral came into sight, his heart sank. The ride was over. He didn't want it to be. He looked over at Buster. He had his hat tilted back on his head, right leg hooked over his pommel rolling a cigarette. Mallomar chuckled to himself and shook his head. Only hours earlier, he had considered Buster an unalloyed idiot. Now, he was surprised to find himself wondering what Buster thought of *him*.

When they arrived at the stable, Mallomar gave Buster a $200 tip that he'd folded into a packet the size of a stick of Wrigley gum. He'd seen a wiseguy tip the maitre d' at Sparks Steakhouse that way and decided to make it his own. To Mallomar's chagrin, Buster put it in his pocket without checking to see how much it was."Much obliged," he said casually.

"That was a great ride," Mallomar said.

"Glad ya lahked it," Buster said as he slid off Stinker's saddle.

"You, uh, never stared at my wife's ass when it was slapping up and down in the saddle. I appreciated that."

"No problemo."

True, Buster had not stared. The thought did occur to him, however, as to what it might be like to have sex with Mrs. Mallomar. But his mind entertained the sinful notion no longer than it took a grouse to flush and vanish into the darkened ponderosa. He wanted Destiny and a ranch. It was best to keep his aim steady on that.

"Look at her over there," Mallomar said discouragingly and pointed in the direction of Mrs. Mallomar. She dumped her bouquet in the horse trough then moved to the side mirror of the Land Rover to freshen her makeup.

"She doesn't *get* any of this."

Buster didn't feel he should comment.

"Tell me, what would you do with a woman like that?"

Buster looked away. "Ah really coont say, sir. Alls ah know about's horses."

"Okay then, what would you do with a pain-in-the-ass horse like that?"

Buster pushed his hat up exposing a fine line of dirt across his forehead. It looked like the line drawn by a coroner with a black magic marker just before sawing the skull in half for an autopsy. And that was what Buster wished would have happened before he opened his big mouth.

"Well sir… Ah'd bite down hard on her ear. They don't like that."

Buster realized his faux pas as soon as the words launched off his dust-covered tongue. Normally, he spoke no more than a dozen words a week, but somehow being around Mallomar, discussing the Internet and showing off about his tracking skills, made Buster feel smarter than he was—like he had been given membership in a whole new level of society. In anticipation of Mallomar's reaction, Buster reached into his pocket to give his tip back. But Mallomar just looked at him with no more expression on his face than a man wearing a brown paper bag with the eyes cut out.

"You'd think a man with as much going for him as me…could find someone who loved him."

And with that, he turned and walked back to his car.

CHAPTER THIRTEEN

Restrained

The Mallomars' exhaust had hardly cleared from the air before Jimmy descended on Buster as he saw to the horses in the loafing shed.

"How'd it go with them folks?"

"Perty good."

"Oh yeah? What'd you make of the mister… dago or Hebe?"

"Ah don't know."

"Ah figgered him fer a Hebe at first, but ah changed my mind to dago. Both a those races'r bluebearded."

"Don't talk lahk that, okay?"

"Whatsamatter? He stiff you?"

"He do what?"

"Dint he tip ya, for Christ fuckin' sake?"

Buster tossed Mallomar's saddle onto the rail and started to brush his horse.

"Yeah, he tipped me," he said laconically, patting his shirt pocket.

“Well, cough it up. All fer one, all fer all, amigo.”

Buster sighed and reached into his pocket extracting the two Benjamins. Jimmy snatched them, her yellow eyes popping.

“Well yor a cool customer! Sonofabitch give us two hundred dollars!”

“That a lot for somethin’ like this here?”

“Ah’ll say! Ah reckon the sonofabitch’s queer for ya!” Jimmy laughed and laughed until she ran out of oxygen and had to quickly stick the cannula back in her nose. “Tell you what ah’m gonna do. Ah’m jes gonna take jes oner these hunnerts and you can keep th’ other if you take me out to supper with yor share.”

“Ah already tole ya. Ah ain’t goin ta town.”

“Did any of them say anythin’ ’bout yor face?”

“No.”

“Course not. That’s what ah’ve been tryin’ to tell ya. It’s all in yor head. Yor mug’s fine. So let’s go and have ourselves an openin’ day celer-bray-shun!”

“Ah don’t feel like it.”

“Okay, don’t wanna drag ya,” she said. “Ah’ll jes take the Ford and go get us a couple of steaks…”

“Never mind,” he said quickly, knowing what that meant. “Ah’ll go.”

Jimmy arranged dinner with Sheriff Dudival at the High Grade. In the hopes that he would run into Destiny, Buster spent hours bathing, shaving, combing his hair, and finding cowboy clothes appropriate for a night out.

“Let’s head out!” She barked. “You’d think you were a damn girl the way you fuss ov’r yor ’ppearance so!”

The High Grade Bar was the only place in Vanadium that had both a liquor license and a kitchen that cooked non-microwaved food. To this point the locals, out of respect, took great care to not tear up the place if they could possibly avoid it. If they had to fight, they did it in the gravel parking lot. Other than the obligatory initials, hearts swearing devotion, or the occasional swastika carved into the Formica tabletops here and there, the place was exactly the way it had been fifty years ago—unlike its two original waitresses who had not held up as well.

Jimmy walked to the rear of the restaurant and slid into the back booth. It was her grandfather that insisted on sitting with his back to the wall for good reason. And Jimmy was never one to break with tradition. She signaled for the waitress to come and wipe off the table.

"Be a good girl now and bring us a coupla longnecks."

She waited for Sheriff Dudival before ordering, Buster keeping his eyes glued to the front door for a flash of braided blonde hair. Quietly, the back door opened and Sheriff Dudival appeared, stood perfectly still, scoped every last person in the place then slid alongside her in the booth.

"He allus does that. Learnt that from Grampie," Jimmy said, with a wink to Buster.

Dudival extended his hand to Buster.

"Welcome back. I see Jimmy's been taking good care of you."

"Yes, sir," Buster said, not knowing what else to say. Dudival put on his reading glasses and perused the menu he already knew by heart.

"Everybody know what they want? Tonight is my treat."

"You don't have to do that, Shep. Buster's payin'."

"I won't hear of it," he said calmly.

"He got hisseff a big tip t'day. Let'm git it."

"I said…I'd…get…it." He didn't quite shout, but he pronounced his intention adamantly enough to set Jimmy back on her opposing scrawny ass cheek and look at him oddly. Buster had never been around the sheriff when he was in her company. Strangely, for all the talk about them being such good friends, he wasn't really relaxed around her—or she with him. However, that was not always so.

When Dudival was a green deputy and Jimmy a teenager, they couldn't get enough of each other. Often, she would sit with him on stakeouts or join him with sandwiches at the speedtrap behind the John Birch Society billboard exhorting the US to get out of the United Nations. They giddily found themselves agreeing with each other on just about everything. Mayonnaise, good. Miracle Whip, bad. Segregation, good. Civil rights, bad. They both agreed that it was preferable to be shot, rather than stabbed. Property rights, good. Immigration, bad. The .45 auto, good. The 9 mm, bad. The death penalty, good. Gun control, bad. Personal responsibility, good. Welfare, bad. They talked about their dreams: his, wanting to get married and start a family. Hers, wanting to start a bounty hunter business. Never once did her dreams mention a man to share her life or the desire to have children—not counting her opinion of corporal punishment in public grade schools. Good.

One night after the completion of their Sunday dinner, Sheriff Morgan took Deputy Dudival up to the roof for a brandy and cigarette.

"You shared any form of sexual intimacy with my granddaughter?"

"Beg your pardon, sir?"

"For godsake, man, have you two done the business?"

"Uh…no."

Sheriff Morgan took a thoughtful drag on his cigarette. "There haven't been very many women in the life we've led. As a result, she's somewhat *tabula rasa* in regards to sexual role-playing."

"What are you saying, sir?"

"You may have to force yourself on her until she warms to the idea. You have my permission to do so. That's what I'm saying."

This kind of behavior, of course, ran counter to everything set forth in *Manners for Men,* but Dudival trusted the sheriff's opinion and decided to take a stronger leadership role in making intimacy happen between him and Jimmy.

The opportunity provided itself at the town's Fourth of July picnic. Jimmy was particularly buoyant that day having won the Olathe corn-eating contest. Deputy Dudival put his arm around her shoulder like a congratulatory pal and led her away from the crowds down a path toward a stretch of willow-lined river. Jimmy, for reasons even unknown to herself, was getting nervous. Maybe it was the sudden lack of confidence in Dudival's face. He was up to something, and she couldn't figure out what. She took a step ahead of him—sliding out from under his heavy arm. He went to grab her around the hips, but she giggled and pulled away. The game was now on. Dudival dove for her legs, but she slipped out of his grasp and ran into the river. He followed after her, sliding on the slick stream rocks and catching a mouthful of water that gave him fits of diarrhea for the next three weeks. Now, on his hands and knees, he pulled himself onto the bank. Jimmy was on the other side of the river, her hands on her hips, smiling.

"Shep Dudival! Are you crazy?" Dudival didn't answer. He stumbled to his feet and threw himself across the river once again in hot pursuit. Using his head now, he herded her toward a patch of wild rose bushes. She tried to run through them, but found herself painfully caught. Dudival grabbed her, threw her down on the grass and put his full weight on top of her. She was still trying to catch her breath when he kissed her on the mouth like he'd seen Rosanno Brazzi do with Mary Martin in *South Pacific*. The kiss, despite all the sidespin and English he put on it, came in DOA. When he ceased and desisted, Dudival opened his eyes to find that Jimmy had had hers open the whole time. Her expression was of confused amusement, as if she had just seen a drunk, bare-assed Indian run down Main Street wearing his red long johns on his head as a headdress. This was exactly the problem her grandfather had warned Dudival about. It was time to be forceful. With shaking hands, he reached down to unbuckle her pants, but she started squirming around and giggling like he was trying to tickle her. He tried kissing her again, but finding her mouth now was like hitting the ducky at the carnival sharp shooting booth. Finally, he just stopped. He didn't mind roughing up the occasional leftist at the uranium mine, but he couldn't do this to a woman. Attempting to reintroduce decorum to the proceedings, Dudival performed a rigid military-style pushup, lifting his body off of hers then rolling off as if leaping from a moving car. They were both lying on their backs now looking up into the swishing willows. "Shep, what the hell's gotten into you?"

"I don't know." Dudival was disgusted with himself and angry that he had blindly followed Sheriff Morgan's advice. Jimmy leaned on one elbow, studying the tortured look on his face. She thought about kissing him on the cheek, but then dismissed the idea as being silly. Besides, she really didn't *feel* like kissing him. She didn't know why, but she didn't. She only knew that, besides her grandfather, Dudival was her best friend in the world and she hated seeing him miserable.

"Shep…?"

"What?" he said after a long interval.

"If you had your druthers, you rather be shot or stabbed?"

"Haven't we already gone over that one?"

"I didn't know it was a matter of public record," she said feigning huffiness. Finally, he turned to face her. She had an impish toothy grin—that still showcased the yellow remnants of her corn-eating victory. Pathetically, he couldn't help himself from loving her.

"Shot," he said. "I'd rather be shot."

Now one of the waitresses brought their food and whispered something in Sheriff Dudival's ear. He nodded. Buster was taking his first bite out of a double cheeseburger with grilled onions.

"Buster, the Stumplehorsts are here at the restaurant," the sheriff said, not wanting him to have food in his mouth in case he choked.

"Is Destiny with 'em?"

"Yes, she is." Buster blushed, composed himself and then started to get up. The sheriff held onto his arm.

"Here's the complication, Buster. There's still a restraining order against you. So, you have a choice and I want you to consider this carefully. I could go out there and say that you were here first, so they would have to leave or…you could leave."

"But ah wanna see Destiny. See how she is and all." Buster craned his neck around to the front door to see if he could catch a glimpse of her.

"They're waiting outside for an answer. How do you want me to handle this?"

Buster didn't really have to think about it.

"Ah'll go."

"I believe that's the gentlemanly thing to do."

"See how much damn trouble that gal is?" Jimmy offered, to make it worse.

"I'll have them wrap up your dinner and bring it out to you."

Buster started for the front door. The sheriff stopped him.

"Best to go out the back."

Buster hesitated, then capitulated and skulked out the back door. "Jes cain't figger it," Jimmy said.

"He's in love," Dudival said, turning to make eye contact with her. "You're capable of doing a lot of ill-considered things when you're in love," Dudival said pointedly. Jimmy shuddered, like ants had just crawled up the back of her shirt.

"Well, thank you, Ann Fuckin' Landers!"

Dudival just stared at her. Defiantly, she put a big piece of chicken-fried steak in her mouth and chewed it open-mouthed, being intentionally obnoxious in a childish attempt to get him to pry his eyes off her. Finally, he shook his head and returned to his own supper.

"Ah need ya to run a name for me, compadre."

"I'll have to think about that."

"He's jes an old friend ah loss tech with."

"I'm not doing that for you anymore."

"C'mon now. But lookee here, a feller in my perzishun has to make shor he's prop'rly said all his g'byes."

"You're not going anywhere, Jimmy. So don't give me that bunk," Dudival said, his eyes getting moist.

"So yool do this fer ol' Jimmy?"

"This is the last goddamn time." Jimmy gleefully reached into her shirt pocket and gave him a slip of paper. Dudival readjusted his glasses, having trouble reading her chicken scratch.

"What's this say?"

"Flowers," she said. "Beverly Flowers."

ꙮ

BUSTER SAT GLUMLY IN Jimmy's truck. She had parked it in the back by the dumpsters so no one with bad intentions could identify her truck from the highway. She was always thinking of things like that. Mary Boyle, Buster's third mother, came out the back with a tray of food.

"Hey, Buster. I heard what just happened so I made up a fresh burger and fries for you."

"Much obliged, Mom, but ah kinder loss my apper-tite."

"Just for the record, I don't think it's right what they're doing. They should kiss your feet to have a nice boy like you be interested in their daughter."

"'Course yood say that. Yor my mom."

Their conversation was interrupted as the window to the ladies' room suddenly screeched open. Buster and Mary watched as a woman's leg dangled out of the opening followed by another leg. Someone in a dress was awkwardly attempting to exit through the window backward. Her dress got hung up over her head exposing sensible white underpants. The figure hung there like that for a moment.

"Who's that?"

"Destiny."

"I'll leave you two to talk." Mary gave Buster a couple of extra napkins from her waitress apron then went back inside the regular way.

Buster quickly got out of the truck to help Destiny down from the window.

"I told my mother I had to go to the bathroom."

"That s'plains it," Buster said.

They stood looking at each other—the parking lot's yellow sodium light making the mayflies and miller moths swirling around her head look like a halo. They kissed.

"I shouldn't do that," she said, pulling away.

"Why not?"

"I'm seeing somebody."

"Well, jes stop seein' him then."

"It's more complicated than that."

Destiny saw something over Buster's shoulder that made her duck down behind the truck. She motioned to the ladies' room window. Buster turned to see an irritated Calvina Stumplehorst craning her neck outside the window looking for her errant daughter. Buster and Mrs. Stumplehorst's eyes met. He smiled at her. She gave him nothing back—then slowly closed the window. Buster helped Destiny to her feet.

"You just can't come home and expect me waiting for you. I didn't hear from you for almost two years."

"But ah wrote you. Ah wrote you thirty-five goldarn letters."

"Well, if you did. I never did get one of 'em."

Buster considered that. He looked back to the restaurant. "Jimmy."

Buster took Destiny by the hand and dragged her through the back door of the restaurant.

"What're ya doin'?"

Sheriff Dudival and Jimmy had just been served their coffee and pie a la mode when Buster appeared before them with Destiny.

"Buster, you're willfully violating the restraining order," Sheriff Dudival said, getting to his feet to do his duty. Buster ignored him.

"Tell'er, Jimmy," Buster demanded.

"Tell'er what, pard?" she said, as sweetly as the untouched pie in front of her.

"Tell'er 'bout the dang letters ah wrote."

Jimmy leaned back casually addressing Destiny.

"The boy here wrote a shitload a letters." She turned to Buster. "Satersfied?"

"What'd ya do with 'em?"

"Truth be tole, ah burned ev'r lass one them weepy cocksuckers."

Destiny looked at Buster, burst into tears, and ran out.

Sheriff Dudival threw down his napkin in disgust.

"Jimmy, how could you do something that?"

"Ev'rbody's mad at Jimmy." Jimmy took a few sniffs of oxygen. "This gal's no good. Ah coont wait fer a fuckin' Act a Congress b'fore the doofus figgered it out for hissef."

"You dint have no right!"

"You owe this boy an apology."

"Doin' the tough thang aint allus pop'lar. They'll be no 'pologies forthcomin'."

"Thas it fer us, Jimmy. Ah'll pack my thangs and move off t'night!"

"Don't be sech a ninny. Sit down and less disgust this."

"Ah'm thoo with ya," Buster said as he headed out the door.

"Ah was jes lookin' out fer ya, ASSHOLE!" she yelled after him.

CHAPTER FOURTEEN

Stalking Destiny

BUSTER HITCHED A RIDE on a lumber truck that was taking the shortcut across the Lame Horse Mesa to Cortez. He walked the rest of the way to Jimmy's then packed his few possessions, loaded up Stinker in the trailer and returned to his sheepherder's campsite. It was a little worse for wear after the winter, but he didn't care about his own comfort. All Buster could think about was Destiny. For the first time in his life he was angry and heartsick at the same time—angry at Jimmy, heartsick at losing Destiny to a real estate salesman. The whole idea of finding his real family to impress the Stumplehorsts had backfired badly. Now he was faced with a choice. Should he fight back and try to reclaim Destiny or should he take the beating—like he had with Cookie—and chalk it up to one of those lessons in life? He decided that this time he would fight back. Destiny was meant to be with him. He had to save her. To anybody else, it would seem clear that she didn't want to be saved. But in Buster's particular upside-down way of thinking, Destiny had supplied a small clue as to why he should continue his pursuit. It was the fact that she had climbed backwards out of the lavatory window in a dress. To Buster, that told him that, despite her new position as a real estate executive, she was still at heart, the girl in the barn. So pride and commonsense would have to hold his coat while he fought for her.

He was going to need a job. Pragmatically, he drew a twenty-five mile circle on a map around Vanadium and drove to every cattle operation within that. Only one of the cattle bosses didn't give him a flat out "no." That guy backed out at the last moment.

"How come you changed yor mind?" Buster asked.

"Look, kid, I hear you're a top hand, but I buy my hay from Stumplehorst. Do I need to draw you a picture?"

Buster increased the circumference on his map to fifty miles with no greater success. Jimmy was right about how no one wanted to go up against the Stumplehorsts. But then again, Jimmy could go to hell.

Buster stopped off in town to pick up supplies and check his post office box. There was some mail that had been forwarded from Jimmy Bayles Morgan's box number. He was about to read it when he caught sight of Destiny's photo on the front page of a free real estate flyer. It was an ad for an open house that Destiny's real estate company had scheduled for that very same day—a little farmhouse just outside of town with five acres for $149,000. Was it unreasonable to think that such a place was within reach of a young cowboy without a job? What was the harm in dropping by in taking a look? And if he happened to bump into Destiny—well, wouldn't that be a funny coincidence?

Buster drove over up to the house in his Apache and parked on the gravel county road. There were a few cars in the driveway. Buster decided, for the maximum dramatic effect of his reappearance, to wait until they had left. He passed the time braiding strands of horsehair for a fob for his truck keys. When every car had driven off, leaving a lone copper colored BMW X-5, he got out of his truck and walked up to the front door.

Downstairs was a little walnut table in the entranceway. There was a silver tray with Cord Travesty's business cards fanned across. There were some plastic glasses with dribs of white wine left in them by the potential clients who decided they'd had enough of looking at this sad and dingy house. Buster looked in the kitchen. The faucet was leaking. He tried to turn it off. It still dripped. Probably needed a new gasket. No one was in the pantry. No one was in the spare downstairs bedroom, either. That meant that there was only one place left for Destiny to be, the upstairs bedroom. Buster ascended the stairs quietly—hoping to surprise her. The door was closed. Buster eased the door open slowly—just in case she was on the other side of it with a tape measure or something. Instead, he found her on the bed with Cord Travesty. He was copulating with her very quickly from behind as if he was competing in some crazy athletic event. Buster stood there until his eyeballs filled with tears and quietly closed the door.

At his camp that night, he sat for hours looking into the fire. Not giving up was proving to be a more painful proposition than he originally imagined. Then he remembered his groceries were still in the truck. He retrieved a package of hot dogs, some potato salad, which he sniffed, and a pint of vanilla ice cream—which was now completely melted. Down at the bottom of the soggy bag was his mail. There was a notice for jury duty, an offer for a credit card with 0% interest for three months, and a letter. He tossed the jury duty notice and the credit card offer in the fire, put three hot dogs on a cottonwood skewer, and opened the letter. It read:

Dear Buster,

I remember you telling me that you didn't use the Internet, so I am writing this the old-fashioned way with paper and a fountain pen. This particular pen that I acquired at auction was said to have belonged to Secretary of State, George Marshall. Anyway, I enjoyed myself very much on our little ride up the mountain. It kind of got me thinking. This is going to sound crazy, but what if you and I went elk hunting together? If I was so lucky as to catch one, I would like the proceeds to be "swapped out" for some canned goods and other essentials the same way you do. We could go 50-50 on it. Please arrange this for me.

P.S. Don't worry. I'm not bringing my wife this time.

Sincerely,

Marvin Mallomar, New York City

Buster folded the letter and tucked it in his jacket. Mr. Mallomar on an elk hunt? The notion seemed preposterous. Arranging it wasn't the problem. He was surrounded by one of the largest elk herds on the western slope. The problem was whether Mr. Mallomar would survive the heart attack he would most likely have while traipsing the eleven-thousand-plus-foot mountain ridges in the coming snow.

Buster wrote Mr. Mallomar back on a postcard depicting an old photograph of a stuffed black bear sitting in an outhouse.

Dear Mr. Mallomar,

Ah'd be tikkled to set you on an elk this fall. Jes hope you know what yor in for. Yor gonna be trakin these animels in freezin cold wether pretty high up. Ah'd feel a hole lot better if you got yoserf in shape a bit.

Ceerly,

Buster McCaffrey, Vanadium

Even though Buster meant well, Mallomar was rankled by the insinuation that he was out of shape. He was a pretty strong guy for his size. He didn't drink all that much. Well, maybe he drank, but he never smoked besides the odd Cuban. In business, he had the reputation of being a tough guy. When he gave his *look,* people would want to shit their pants. But even Mallomar had to admit that intimidating people and coping with the elements—high altitude and steep terrain—were not the same. Grudgingly, he admitted to himself that Buster might be right—although, this assessment only came after he'd taken his Lexapro for depression (he discovered he liked it better than his old Elavil) and paced for two hours. And pacing wasn't going to get him in shape either, so for the next four weeks he walked the six blocks to his office building. When he got there, he took the stairs to the fifteenth floor—muttering every step of the way about Buster underestimating the determination of Marvin P. Mallomar.

ꕥ

IN VANADIUM, THE FIRST rifle season had begun. Lame Horse Mesa's surrounding mountains provided the best elk hunting on public land that any workingman could ask for in North America. From October 12 to the end of December, a continuous elephant walk of Texas and Oklahoma trucks circled Vanadium's downtown looking for a parking place. The two restaurants and hardware store were filled from ten o'clock until three—because if a hunter hadn't filled his tag by morning, he usually came into town to warm up or nurse a few beers and watch the Fox Channel before heading back to his freezing tent. But it wasn't only the hardware store and restaurants that benefited from the orange "Welcome Hunters" banner that hung across Main Street.

Cookie Dominguez and the Busy Bees operated two jerky stands at either end of town. Originally, the Bees sold topographical maps of the area—Cookie's version of *Hollywood Maps to the Stars.* Hunters would stop to get a map of the BLM and National Forest lands that were available to the public. They would then show Cookie, on those maps, where they were camping and place their orders for liquor and prostitutes. Cookie would ride the women up the mountain on ATV's and pick them up in the morning. With the Christmas only two months away, there was no shortage of women needing cash. The hunters, most of them sorely lacking in outdoor skills, stood no better than a 10 percent chance of getting an elk. Those lucky enough to get one either shot theirs illegally in the middle of a county road or in someone's yard. The brilliance of Cookie's service was that even those who were unlucky could still go home with a wonderful memory of Vanadium. Unfortunately, over time, the hunters began to prefer Internet pornography to his flabby-fleshed lineup. Cookie, too smart a businessman to buck a trend, replaced prostitution with selling jerky. The Busy Bee vacuum-packed jerky was, of course, a loss leader. The real sales were in meth rocks and loose joints.

Each of Cookie's jerky stands was positioned over a storm drain. The counter man had a piece of kite string tied to his finger. At the end of that string was a daisy chain of Ziploc bags containing several thousand dollars worth of black market goods hanging inside the storm drain. When a customer requested some weed or methamphetamines, the counter man would simply reel up the bags and package it with a small bag of jerky. In the event of a bust, the Busy Bee would simply release the string, make note of the amount and report it to accounting as a write-down. This system worked so well that Cookie decided to expand his drug franchise over the Fourth of July weekend by selling meth along with fireworks.

Buster had spent the last couple of weeks frantically preparing his spike camp for Mallomar's arrival. He was making his last trip to the grocery store when he happened to see Cookie serving up his special jerky to a young hunter with "Sooner" plates. Their eyes met momentarily as he drove past and Cookie glowered at him. Buster thought about what Jimmy had said regarding Cookie's intentions to kill him and quickly decided to go have a word with him. Buster hit the brakes and made a U-turn. The screech of the brakes startled Cookie and he reached reflexively for his baby Glock embedded above his fat right butt cheek. It wasn't there. He panicked. He'd forgotten that he'd moved it to his left butt cheek since the loss of his two right fingers. Cookie's customer seemed uncomfortable with a stranger walking up and he made a quick exit to his fifth wheel.

"What the fuck do you want, fuck face?" Cookie said, as Buster sauntered over, unaware of Cookie's real enterprise.

"Ah was jes thinkin' that this here's gone far 'nuff—with you and me clashin' like."

"Why don't you learn to speak English, *joto*? This only gets settled one way. Now fuck off."

"C'mon now, Cook. Why you talkin' like that?"

"You want me to put you down right here? Is that what you want, *culero*?"

Cookie yanked his pistol out if the holster and let Buster have a peek at it under a laminated jerky menu.

Buster put his hands up. "Easy there, bollito."

"Now you've done it!" *Bollito*, Spanish for cookie or biscuit, was what he only allowed his mother to call him. "Now you're dead." Buster closed his eyes and waited for the shot to ring out, but it didn't. "Oh shit," he heard Cookie say.

Buster opened his eyes to see that Sheriff Dudival had pulled over. He had not yet seen the gun. He had been distracted by a dead yellow bug on Buster's right fender and stopped to scratch it off with his thumbnail. Cookie had the gun in his left hand and held the string to his drugs in his right.

"Uh, ah'd like to buy some jerky," Buster said, trying to help everyone concerned. Cookie slid the gun back off the counter and held it at his side.

"Just take it and get the fuck out of here."

"Ah 'spect to pay fer it." Buster took a ten-dollar bill out of his wallet. There was no way Cookie could make change with his hands filled as they were.

"Did you hear what I said, you fuckin' idiot?"

A customer slowed down to pick up some of Cookie's fast-paced jerky, but when he saw the sheriff waiting at Buster's truck, he sped up and drove away.

"Ah'm payin for it. No ifs, ands, er buts."

"Just go, faggot. I don't have change."

"I have some change," Sheriff Dudival said, overhearing.

Dudival reached for his wallet as he approached the stand. Cookie realized that his best option was to drop the gun in the grass behind him, but used to holding it in his right hand, he released the string by mistake. He shuddered as thirty thousand dollar's worth of crank disappeared down the storm drain and splashed below. He wanted to kill both of them or kill himself—he was so angry but, after considering all outcomes, dropped the gun into the goldenrod behind him. "I've got ten singles. That any help?"

"Yeah," Cookie said hoarsely.

Buster handed Cookie the ten and opened his package of jerky, tore off a piece with his big teeth and chomped it.

"Say…this here's top shelf!"

Cookie smiled weakly as the sheriff provided the change.

"Buster, do you mind if I have a word with you…in private?"

"Nice visitin', *hermano*," Buster said.

"Yeah," Cookie said, his mouth spitless.

Buster and the sheriff walked back to his truck.

"You're working as a game guide now. Is that right?"

"Yessir. Elk and the like."

"I presume you have a guide's license?"

Did he have to ask that? Of course Buster didn't have a guide's license.

"Ah kinda don't, seein' as how ah'm doin' this for a friend like."

"Oh," the sheriff said, wincing at his speech as much as his disregard for the law. "But…*if* you decide to make this a permanent commercial venture, you *will* need to file the proper paperwork. The Department of Wildlife is very specific about that."

"'A course."

"Do you have a tent cabin for your client?"

"Not yet, ah don't."

"I have one if you want to make use of it."

"Golly, how'd you come acrost one a them?"

"Two hunters from Oklahoma went missing. They were found on Lone Cone this morning—all cozied up in their sleeping bags—dead. From what I could gather, asphyxiation. They must have closed the tent flaps and had the propane heater on all night. I contacted the family. They're obese and can't make it up the mountain to retrieve the tent. So, it's yours for the asking."

"Gosh…ah'm much obliged…"

"Come by the office and I'll give you the map coordinates so you can haul it out."

"But uh…what do ah owe ya, fer it?"

"Nothing."

"Jiminy. Really? That booger gotta be worth a grand er more."

"There's just a small thing I'd like you to do for me."

"Shoot."

"This unpleasantness between you and Jimmy. I'd like to see it end. She feels sorry about what she did."

"She can jes tell me that himself then."

"You know her better than that."

"Well, if she ain't man 'nuff to 'pologize…" Buster got into his truck and rolled down the window. "Ah'd like to give you a side of elk in 'xchange for the tent, if you don't mind…jes to keep thangs straight."

"The rightful recipient of that would be Jimmy," the sheriff said as Buster kicked over the engine. "She's the one who found them."

"Found who?"

"The dead hunters."

CHAPTER FIFTEEN

Dang Fool

THE DAY BEFORE THE season opened, a Gulfstream IV flew into Montrose airport. The employees at the APO were waiting on the tarmac with disposable cameras. There were rumors that the plane belonged to Telluride property owner Oprah Winfrey. Some of the women employees brought out her latest book for her to sign personally. Then the plane landed, and Mallomar appeared at the top of the gangway waving to them like he was the president of the United States. They dispersed with disappointment and some with disgruntlement. But Buster got a small thrill driving his pickup truck—on the normally verboten tarmac—right up to the plane. The excitement turned to befuddlement, however, when he saw Mallomar's crew unloading boxes and boxes of brand new equipment from every outdoor company known to man.

"Howdy, Buster!"

Buster winced as Mallomar approached the truck wearing a brand new plaid guide coat and a red Filson wool hat replete with earflaps.

"Uh, howdy there, Mr. Mallomar..."

"Why the look of consternation?" Mallomar said as he placed the same gum-shaped packet of hundred-dollar bills in his pilot's hand.

"What's all this stuff for?"

"It's for our trip...why?"

"We'd need a mule train to carry all that stuff... Besides, you don't need nuthin' much more'n a pair of boots."

Mallomar's face clouded. He looked lovingly at the boxes containing the sub-forty-degree sleeping bag, the collapsible cooking stove, the portable shower—all the stuff he had had so much fun buying.

"What do I do for clothes, then?"

"Ah got some clothes for ya that ah've had settin outside unnerneath a pile of pine boughs to get the scent off 'em."

Mallomar thought about that for a moment. A big smile grew across his face. He ordered the pilot to put all the boxes back on the plane.

"I'm leaving my scent behind," he explained to the sangfroid crew.

Everything went back in the plane except a pair of boots and two bottles of Macallan whiskey. Buster got back in the truck and was ready to roll, but Mallomar just stood outside the driver's door.

"*Problemo*, Mr. Mallomar?"

"Uh...can I drive your truck?"

Mallomar owned two Mercedes, the twin to Prince Charles's 1969 Aston Martin DB6, a Ferrari 380 GTS, and a 1934 Bugati. Why he wanted to get behind the wheel of Buster's Chevy Apache was anybody's guess.

"I never drove a pickup before," he said shyly.

"Okay," said Buster. "But go easy on 'er."

Buster slid over on the bench seat and started to roll a quirley. Mallomar ground the Chevy noisily into reverse, then first. He looked around for his seat belt. There was none—the truck being manufactured before the mandate for safety regulations. Mallomar practically squealed with delight at this. And he had Buster roll him a cigarette even though he hadn't had one in twenty-five years. Then he cranked open his window and stuck his arm out into the freezing night. Down the main drag they went—the radio tuned to "Maverick Country"—past McDonald's, Taco Bell, Super Wal-Mart, past the Cattleman, the Dairy Queen, and the Red Barn. Mallomar was smiling so hard he looked like Arthur Bremer on his way to shoot Governor Wallace.

"I want to buy this truck."

"Sorry, it ain't for sale."

"Give you thirty grand for it."

"No thanks."

"Fifty."

"Sorry. It was a present from someone."

"That's twenty grand more than it's worth!"

"Caint."

When they pulled up to the first red light, Mallomar's smile faded slightly as he looked over to see the demonic face of Cookie Dominguez framed in the window of his monster truck next to him. Cookie rolled down his passenger side window and leaned over.

"Hey!" he said making sure he had their attention. Then he motioned for Mallomar to lean over.

"What can I do for ya?" Mallomar said, colloquially.

"Do you know what this means?" Cookie made a "V" with his two blown off fingers.

"Don't imitate Winston Churchill while operating a punch press?" Mallomar said, thinking he was being funny.

"It means you're a fuckin' dead skunk!" Cookie yelled and threw something furry through Mallomar's driver's window and then squealed off in a cloud of diesel and burnt rubber.

Mallomar practically had a heart attack. Buster calmly opened his door and toed the creature out his side. To carry a dead skunk around in a new truck with the slim chance of using it as an act of terrorism was testament to Cookie's psychosis.

"What the hell's his problem?"

"He wants to kill me."

"So you know the guy?"

"Yessir. He's my 'dopted brother."

As far as Mallomar was concerned, the trip was already worth the twenty-seven thousand dollars he paid for jet fuel. He had only been off the tarmac for five minutes, and his intuition to come and experience life in its rawest form was paying off in spades.

Leaving the big city lights of Montrose behind, Buster and Mallomar arrived at their trailhead and began their horseback ride to the spike camp in Disappointment Valley. Buster had to remind Mallomar half a dozen times not to talk lest he would spook the game. Mallomar couldn't help himself. He was too jacked up to keep his mouth shut.

As soon as they arrived at camp, Buster got the wood stove going for hot water.

"Saw some big bulls comin' down this trail jes' the other day," Buster observed as he offered Mallomar hot decaf and a plate of Lorna Doones arranged in a daisy pattern.

"Do they still make Lorna Doones?" Mallomar said. "Fan-tas-tic!"

By ten o'clock the next morning, Mallomar had fired his custom-made Cooper .300 magnum rifle a total of eleven times, which was ten times more than necessary. No one could have predicted the Hulk-like effect Mallomar's prescription medications would have on his body in combination with the altitude and his own adrenaline. In the dim light of the tent cabin, Mallomar opened his compartmentalized plastic pill container and mistakenly took seventy-five ml. of Marplan—his old monoamine oxidase inhibitor medication for depression—along with 125 ml. of Lexapro—his new medication, along with a Tagamet to ward off the heartburn he would certainly encounter during the day. Little did he know that within two and a half hours he would be sending his body into extreme hypertensive crisis. The result—Mallomar's sudden murderous zeal coupled with his labored breathing and blurred vision—so unnerved Buster that he decided to keep his rifle chambered just in case Mallomar decided to start shooting at *him*. Fortunately for the elk and Buster, Mallomar's shooting was about to cease.

It had just started to snow. Buster peered through the white veil with his binoculars. He was glassing the edge of the timberline where he'd just heard some bugling. A large seven-by-seven with tines and beams that would've scored at least a 280 on the Boone and Crockett was staring back at him. The bull's nose was in the air trying to scent, but the wind was at his back. At 175 yards, it was an easy shot—even for Mallomar.

"There's yor elk, Mr. Mallomar."

Buster slowly took off his pack and nestled it into the snow for Mallomar to use as a rifle rest.

"Now this tahm, don't shoot so dang fast. Take a breath, relax, and squeeeeeze..." Buster stuck his pinkies in his ears and waited and waited for the gun to go off. After thirty seconds Buster turned around to see Mallomar—red as a crayfish, his eyes rolled back in his head, unconscious.

When Mallomar opened his eyes two nights later, he was on an army cot swaddled like a baby in horse blankets. Not being able to take any more medication, his convulsions finally ceased. Buster, trying to calm himself, was sitting at his side tapping out a portrait of Destiny and Maple on a pie plate with a hammer and awl. Mallomar opened his crusted eyes.

"How ya feelin' thar, Mr. Mallomar?"

"I feel like taking a crap." Buster grabbed him by an elbow and led him around the tent to a place in the trees. "What the hell is that thing?" Mallomar felt like he was hallucinating. Buster's usual privy was a guide's "groover"—a .50 ammo can so named for parallel grooves it left on the user's buttocks. But anticipating Mallomar's discomfort, Buster topped his groover with a scrounged toilet seat and jury-rigged a pink plastic shower curtain around the whole affair to provide privacy. Charmin Extra Soft toilet paper and a magazine rack with a few American Rifleman magazines were added as a finishing flourish.

Once satisfied that Mallomar was properly enthroned, Buster moved off to the cook tent to prepare the hors d'oeuvres. Mallomar had missed the first night's round—which was cheddar cheese on Triscuits with a crisscross of roasted red peppers and a dot of caper. Tonight's menu would begin with sautéed mushroom caps stuffed with artificial crab salad and celery stalks filled with smoked oysters and cream cheese. He hoped that Mallomar's hunting experience hadn't been ruined by the fact that he had almost died.

Mallomar made it back to the tent by himself and collapsed back on the cot. There was a glass of single malt whiskey with one cube—the way he liked it—sitting on top of a chunk of pine. He swallowed his drink and within two minutes was noisily asleep—missing dinner again. Buster didn't wake him, for he was pretty wrung out himself. So, after he had fastidiously cleaned all the dishes and utensils and re-hung their food in a tree, Buster climbed into his bedroll and finally got to sleep himself.

In the middle of the night, Mallomar awoke. He was feeling better, and his appetite had returned with a fury. He was going to wake Buster, but when he saw how soundly he was sleeping, he decided to forage in the cook tent for himself. Not fully appreciating why Buster had hung all of their food in a tree, he was about to give up when he found an unopened bag of snack crackers. He crammed the whole package into his mouth like a madman, crawled back in his sleeping bag and returned to sleep.

Around two in the morning, Mallomar found himself in a disturbing dream. He was looking at the elk through his rifle's crosshairs. There was a report, and the elk teetered and fell. A knife came into view and cut from its sternum down to its pelvis. The intestines, stomach, and liver were removed. Finally, the heart was wrenched free and held up in bloody hands. The elk, despite its vivisection, lifted its mighty head. But it was not the elk's face he saw, but his own. *If this elk is me*, he wondered, *who's doing the cutting?* Then he recognized the wedding ring that he had purchased in Johannesburg on the hand that was holding his heart.

"Why are you doing this to me, Dana?"

"This is what you get for enforcing the pre-nup."

"But I haven't divorced you!"

"No, but you're thinking about it."

"That's not true. I love you."

"We can't have children."

"I never held that against you."

"Marvin, did you ever think it could be *you* that couldn't have children?"

"It couldn't be *me*. I knocked up my girlfriend in college, for chrissake!"

"Really? Let's just take a look at your penis, then." And with that, Dana took her drop point knife and started separating Mallomar's genitalia from its abdominal fascia.

A sharp pain radiated from Mallomar's groin all the way to his feet. He moaned in agony. This monstrous hate! What had he done to deserve it? Then, as his mind swam to the surface of consciousness, he realized that the pain he was feeling was real. He reached down with his hand and felt fur. An animal was inside his sleeping bag biting his testicles—testicles that had been inadvertently flavored with the artificial cheese seasoning from Pepperidge Farm goldfish. Mallomar let out a scream so high-pitched that Buster, sleeping next to him, almost wet himself.

"Oh my God, she's killing me!"

Buster jumped out of his bedroll and clicked on his flashlight. All hell was breaking loose at the foot of Mallomar's sleeping bag. Buster grabbed it with his big hands and pinched it off. Mallomar, quaking and blubbering, slipped out of the bag and quickly put on his boxers and boots. Buster looked at the screeching lump that he held at arm's length. He considered smacking it on a rock, but thought better of it. It was Buster's rule to never kill anything he wasn't prepared to eat. So he walked the sleeping bag away from camp and released the bottleneck. An aggravated pine martin—a cat-sized cousin of the weasel emerged, hissed at him then scurried up a blue spruce releasing a shelf of snow from a bough that fell on Buster's head as a final insult.

Buster sprinkled white gas on some damp wood and got a fire going, while Mallomar, hands trembling, uncorked his whiskey and took a long pull.

"Jesus Christ," Mallomar said after he had calmed down and dried his eyes.

"Mr. Mallomar, dint ah tell ya not to bring any food in the tent?"

"You did. But I was hungry."

"Ah guess so was that pine martin."

"That's what that little fucker was? I'm lucky I still have my balls."

"Yeah, and one of 'ems not in such great shape," Buster said, gesturing to one of Mallomar's abraded testicles that was hanging errantly from his shorts.

Mallomar finally saw the humor in all this and gave a wheezy chuckle.

"I'm going to dine out on this story for the rest of my life!"

"If it were possible to 'dine out' on all the dumb things *ah* done in my life, ah could jes quit workin' entahrly."

He passed Buster a tin cup that was filled to the top with whiskey, but Buster thought one of them should be sober and demurred.

"A pine martin."

"Yep."

Mallomar shook his head and then got very serious. "My wife and I are having some problems. I'm probably the one to blame. She's very sensitive to the world. Me, I'm like a horse."

Jiminy, that's not true, Buster only thought, but didn't say. Mallomar was as complicated and delicate as a Swiss chronograph that had mechanisms for the day, the date, the tides, the phase of the moon, and five different time zones.

"Goddamn! Life's problematical, don't you think?"

"It's a booger, Mr. Mallomar."

"I had this crazy notion that if I came out here and got rid of all the crap…separated the wheat from the chaff so to speak, I'd…" Then he trailed off without finishing his thought. "Anyway, I'd appreciate it if you never mentioned me crying to anyone."

"As far as ah'm concerned, you were cryin' outta happiness," Buster assured.

"Goddamn pine martin," Mallomar said once again.

They sat quietly for a while. Buster caught a glimpse of Mallomar staring at him from across the fire.

"You know, for some crazy reason, I honestly believe that you and I were meant to meet."

Buster kept a straight face and looked at the big cup of whiskey now in Mallomar's hand. He wondered whether his client was capable of pulling off some kind of funny business. He decided to eliminate the alcohol part of the program.

"Ah'll jes stow this here bottle of whiskey away, Mr. Mallomar. Shame if a body stumbelt ov'r it in the night and cut a toe or somethin'." Mallomar was watching him intently.

"Ever hear of a place on Lame Horse Mesa called the Puster Ranch?"

"Yessir." The lack of enthusiasm on Buster's part was telling.

"Not a very good place?"

"Well, ah really don't want to speak ill of the place, considerin' how poor ol' Mr. Puster had to give 'er up."

"But you don't think too highly of the place..."

"It's easy to lean back in the saddle and critic-size another feller's effirts...when you don't know how you woulda done."

"I get it. You don't want to shitcan another man's deal. Hey, if it will ease your mind, Mr. and Mrs. Puster are living in a million-dollar house in Naples, Florida—so I wouldn't get too choked up about poor ol' Mr. and Mrs. Puster."

"They live down in Florida?"

"On the beach, baby."

Buster reconsidered the situation, not stopping to ask how Mr. Mallomar knew that.

"Well, he was a nice man and all, but ah caint say Mr. Puster was much of a rancher. Fact is, the place when I saw it, was a damn fallin' down wreck. Anythin' that ever give out was dropped from the hand right where it broke!"

"Uh huh."

"And 'nother thing...people get all gooey-eyed when they see all that sagebrush. Fact is, when you have that much of the dang stuff, it means the place's been over-grazed. It ain't fit to feed anythin' on 'cept mule deer."

"It's not, is it?"

"No, it ain't. And that ain't the worst thing about that place."

"I'll bet it's not." Mallomar was looking like he couldn't find a comfortable position to sit in.

"There aint no water 'cept a little creek that runs dry by June. The last well they dug out there—they had to go down twenty-five hundred feet—cost 'em thirty *thousand* dollars. Water didn't last a year!"

"You make it seem like the place's a complete loss..."

"Well, ah wouldn't go as far as that," Buster said, now thinking he was some kind of genius. "See, they never changed anythin' up there for over a hunnert years. A lot of these ranchers 'round here...they get onto one thing and they just stick with it and ride it into the ground. The sorry fact is thar too ig-or-ant 'n' stubborn ta try anythin' new."

"So, what would you do?"Buster stroked his chin pretending like he was thinking about it for the first time.

"Well, first off, ah'd hire a bunch of kids to come up thar and pick up ev'r piece of scrap, ev'r piece of junk that's layin' around thar...haul it off in thar own trucks—wouldn't even have to pay for a dumpster. Then ah'd bush hog the sage and get one of them Forest Service fellas to put me in their Native Grass Seed Program—the government's kind enuff ta give ya money for sech things. And once that grass come in, well sir, that's when ah'd start me a cattle ranch."

"Well, Buster, I believe you've got yourself a good plan. I think you should implement it."

"Sir, that ain't gonna be posserbull, some dang fool bought the place for five million dollars!"

"Yeah…that was me," said Mallomar, staring into the fire. Buster's eyes widened.

"Oh, Mr. Mallomar, please fergive me, sir. Me and my big dang mouth…"

"No, you had it right. I am a damn fool for buying that place. I had some stupid idea about simplifying my life…"

"Nothin' wrong with that, ah guess…"

"But what the hell do I know about ranching?" They both sat and looked into the fire. "That's why I need someone who knows as much as you do."

Buster had no clue that Mallomar was guiding him ever so slowly into his dilapidated barn.

"That's prolly a good place to start. Git yourself a good foreman."

"Maybe it won't be so much of a goddamn disaster if I get myself a good foreman. You're right."

They sat and stared into the fire a few minutes more.

"Say, why don't you be my foreman?"

"Aw, shucks, Mr. Mallomar, ah don't reckon ah could do that."

"Why not?"

"Ah never done nuthin' like that before. Allus worked *for* a foreman."

"You've got great ideas…so it can't be you don't think you're smart enough."

"Well, thank you, sir, but a lot of people 'round here might disergree with you on that one."

"I don't give a rat's ass what people around here think. And here's a tip. If you want to get anywhere in life, neither should you."

"Ah'm pretty comferbull in the sich-eee-a-shun ah got right now," Buster said unconvincingly.

"Which is what?"

"Well, nothin' raht now, but…"

"If you helped me turn that ranch into something, I'd be willing to pay you seventy-five thousand dollars."

Buster sat up. Seventy-five thousand! That was unheard of. There was no doubt in his mind that he'd be taking advantage of Mallomar at that kind of wage. On the other hand, the way Mallomar had been so sanguine about being taken for a ride on the Puster deal, Buster had the impression that no matter how hard Mallomar tried to get rid of his money, it would just keep sprouting back up like the hair on a woman's legs.

"Ah gotta be honest, Mr. Mallomar. You could find a lot of fellers 'round here that would do that job for a lot less."

"That's true. But they're not you. Five minutes ago you just gave me the whole operational plan—for free. Why should I trust anybody else?"

"That beats me…"

"Let me put it another way. I'm going to give that ranch two years to pay its own way. If it's not self-sustaining by then, I'm dumping. And who's going to buy it? Someone who can get their money back by carving it into thirty-five acre ranchettes. Is that what you want to see happen out there? Or would you like to see the ranch kept intact?"

"Intack, ah guess, but…"

"But what?"

"Ah jes never thought a mysef as a foreman of a ranch and sech."

"I guess you're holding out for an offer to run General Electric or something."

"No, sir. Ah dint mean it like that…"

"Or maybe you don't like me. You wouldn't be the first person I rubbed the wrong way…"

"Naw, ah like you fahn."

"Then what's stopping you from taking advantage of a gigantic opportunity for yourself?"

"Ah'll be honest with you, Mr. Mallomar. Ah was kinda hopin' to have a ranch of my own some day."

"How did you plan on paying for your ranch? Don't you need money? How can you make money if you don't want to work for someone?"

Buster's hands were shaking. He was not in Mallomar's negotiating league. He haggled for a saddle once and wound up paying more for it than the original asking price.

"How's this? We build in a performance bonus of a hundred grand if you can get this place into the black in two years." That sounded pretty good, even though Buster did not know what "in the black" meant.

"Mr. Mallomar, ah ain't a smart man. But, ah'm smart enough to know that ain't a good deal for you."

"We're in uncharted altruistic waters here, I admit. So do we have a deal?

Mallomar reached across the fire to shake Buster's hand. Was that the one that he used to touch his testicles?

The image of Destiny having sex with Cord Travesty popped out of the fire and then crackled into the night air. Buster knew he could never win her back unless he proved himself in some way that captured the Stumplehorst's imaginations. Or, he could remain just another cowboy sitting at the High Grade bar complaining about his boss and the way the world had gone to shit.

"Well, okay… You got yorself a dang foreman."

CHAPTER SIXTEEN

The Big Dog

BEFORE THE GROUND COULD harden, construction of what was to be the Mallomar Residence began. Mallomar was serious about leading the minimalist lifestyle that he so admired about his new foreman, Buster. So in earnest was he, that he divested himself of all his worldly possessions. Various Catholic and Jewish resale agencies came to his Fifth Avenue apartment and collected all of his and his wife's expensive clothing. Sotheby's was called as well. They catalogued and crated all of the Mallomar's paintings (twentieth century landscape through WPA), their silver service collections (English and French), their antique glass collections (Tiffany and Lalique), rare watches, Biedermeier furniture, Pahlavi rugs, and all of Mrs. Mallomar's fine jewelry that she had received as birthday and anniversary presents over the years. Unfortunately Mrs. Mallomar was not present to share the joy of unburdening. She had had a setback with her drinking. Her five bouts of rehab clinic having failed, this time she was sent to an ashram in Fish Kill.

The original concept of the new dwelling was to gut the old Puster ranch house, lift it up off the ground and set it back on a concrete foundation. The new basement, dug out of rock, would radiate a steady temperature of fifty-seven degrees—substantially reducing energy consumption. Native stone and salvaged barn wood was to be used in the interiors. The plans called for a modest kitchen with old-fashioned linoleum floors and two nice bathrooms with matching soaking tubs. Mallomar insisted that no modern telecommunication devices be present on the premises and had the interior designer comb the area's antique stores to find old black rotary telephones. This was the house where Mallomar and Mrs. Mallomar would finally be able to get in touch with their real selves.

For a while, Mallomar even toyed with the idea of going without electricity. But his resolve to live his life with simplicity was worn down by his Aspen architect's resolve to have something to show in the upcoming "Ranch Edition" of *Architectural Digest*. He harangued Mallomar from morning till night with blueprints. Time and time again, he complained that Mallomar "wasn't doing right by the site," that putting a plebian house on a magnificent property was "cutting the legs off its resale value," that for a renowned collector of art he was "missing the opportunity to create art himself." The architect was relentless as the groundbreaking day approached. "Where were they going to put his office? Where was Dana's yoga and workout room? Where was the home entertainment area going to go—with its twenty-five motorized leather seats, THX Surround, and its thirty-foot screen? Have you ever actually *lived* in a twenty-five-hundred-square-foot house?" His architect threatened to resign. "What you want is a kit house!" Mallomar blinked. By June, the simple plan had metastasized into forty thousand square feet with ten bedrooms, twelve bathrooms, a fully equipped gym, a gunroom, a fly-tying room, a state-of-the-art observatory with a computer-controlled telescope, and a four-thousand-square-foot Great Room modeled on the main dining area of the Ahwanee Hotel in Yosemite National Park.

With quiet disapproval, Buster bulldozed the Puster ranch house and razed it on the following burn day. Realizing how much Mallomar was under the spell of his architect, Buster decided to plead his case to him. He mildly suggested to the architect that the barn and various faded, red outbuildings be saved for their "at-mo-spear." Grudgingly, the architect agreed and told Mallomar he had an idea as to how to retain the historic ranch's authenticity. Despite this small victory, the house became the talk of Vanadium's Main Street, every day bringing a new rumor about a more outrageous Mallomar extravagance. Buster's unease was compounded by the guff he was getting from cowboys in town who'd begun referring to him as Mr. Mallomar's "caretaker"—a job title generally attributed to women. Mallomar could tell something was eating Buster and finally confronted him.

"You don't approve of this house. I get it."

"Mr. Mallomar, what you do ain't none of my bidnis one way or 'nother."

"How much of your pay have you spent so far?"

"Dang near none of it."

"How's that possible?"

Buster shrugged.

"Ah got a place to sleep. You feed me…"

"Isn't there anything you want?"

"A ranch. That's what ah'm savin' up for."

"But nothing other than that."

"Nope."

Mallomar started taking Buster's frugality as a slight.

"I'm picking up a moral superiority thing from you that I don't like."

"Mr. Mallomar, that ain't even posserbull."

"It ain't? Well, then what's eating at you?"

"Ah'm sorry, sir."

"You're like a goddamn priest, with this vow of poverty bullshit."

"Ah don't mean to be. Ah jes need to save my money."

Mallomar eyed him coolly.

"What are you hiding? What's the real reason for this crazy acorn burying? What is it? A gambling debt? Blackmail? A woman? What?" Buster shifted his gaze to the ground and remained silent,

"Okay, I'm going to let you in on something very important. It's as important as the very air we breathe." Mallomar took a deep breath as if he was going to blow out all the candles on a birthday cake. "To have our *needs met*…we have to make our *needs known*." He waited for that to sink in. "It's a simple, elegant idea, isn't it? It's Ebay, baby."

"Ah need her folks to think ah'm somebody."

Mallomar clapped his hands together with joy. Nobody loved it more than Mallomar when he was right about something. He grabbed Buster by the arms and shook him, hugged him.

"Let me tell you something, sport," he said with great sincerity. "More fortunes have been built upon what you just admitted than any other motivation in the world! I'm proud of you. I didn't think you had the shit in you, but you do. Buster, my friend, don't ever let anyone deny that you have a dick and a brain. We're going to take care of this woman issue. Marvin Mallomar is here to the rescue!"

The next day Mallomar handed Buster a business-sized leather checkbook with the words "Big Dog Ranch" hand-tooled on the cover.

"I put your name on the account. There's five hundred grand in there. Next week there'll be another five hundred. From now on, you're writing all the checks around here."

"Why?"

"You'll see why."

ꙮ

Later that day, Mallomar's architect came to the barn where Buster was working.

"Mr. Mallomar said I was to come to you." The architect was smirking. Buster didn't care for him much to begin with. He was sixty years old and wore gaudy basketball shoes and dressed like a teenager at the Mesa Mall. "I need you to write a check for two hundred forty-three thousand dollars and twenty-seven cents."

"What for?" Buster had the temerity to ask.

The architect tossed a thick printout on the ground where Buster was shoeing a horse.

"That's the production schedule for the house. Why don't you figure it out?" And with that, he whirled around and headed for his prefab office.

Buster picked up the itemized schedule as if it were a snake and tried to decipher it. Most of it was Greek to him, that's for sure. But he did see that Mallomar was paying over triple for what he should have for concrete. And he understood that he could supply the "weathered barn wood" at a fraction of the price that the architect had budgeted for—shipping it in from Canada of all places. And having spent some amount of time in a tile-making family, he knew he could do a lot better than what was itemized there.

The first thing Buster did was drive into Vanadium and round up every unemployed teenager loitering around town with their jeans hanging down below their asses. He gave them the names and addresses of every ranch and farm that that had a sagging, dilapidated barn or shed they wanted to get rid of. As he'd previously arranged, the teenagers dismantled the boards and brought them back to the ranch where Buster paid a dollar a pop at a savings of close to a hundred thousand dollars. The same was true for the concrete. Gravel and stone were quarried and mixed at the old Svendergard place. What Buster had learned from Mr. Svendergard he was now able to pass on to some of these kids who had a chance to earn some real money before school started. Vanadium's blacksmith, whose business had shrunk to bending an occasional horseshoe, were called in to create one-of-a-kind hinges, drawer pulls, and stairway rungs. The tiles were custom-made by the Dominguez family. The copper drains and downspouts alone—jobbed out to Vanadium Heating and Downspouts—saved Mallomar another fifty grand. All the barbed wire replaced with old-fashioned worm fence. Unfortunately, Mallomar didn't like the fact that the fence looked new and had the men stain it by hand to make the wood look old. No one in town joked about Mallomar's house when they were making a fortune building it.

Now, in the evenings, when Buster strolled down Main Street, the leather-bound checkbook under his arm, the local populace welcomed him as if he were a one-man government program without the bureaucratic paperwork. New cars and trucks, which had not been seen cruising Vanadium since the late sixties, were now ubiquitous. People had money to do work on their own houses and as a result, the whole town started to look a lot less tired. There was a spring in the step of Vanadium again. Everyone seemed pleased with their new free spending resident, everyone except Jimmy Bayles Morgan.

"It aint nothin' but a house a cards," she dissented to Sheriff Dudival.

"C'mon, Jimmy, loosen your girdle. You've got to admit he's done all right by this town."

"He ain't the one who decides what's right for this town."

Jimmy threw down a buck for her coffee—even though coffee was now $2.50—and squeakily wheeled her oxygen tank out the door.

In Telluride, the story of Mr. Mallomar had hit the trip wire. Many a dinner conversation was spent debating whether the famous

Vanadian was a Republican or a Democrat. The Republicans claimed him because he had used capital to create a market economy in Vanadium where there was none. The Democrats claimed him because he was a social engineer. Both groups vied to put the Mallomar feather in their caps. The Democrats' first gambit was to ask Mr. Mallomar to lend his name to a petition that called for the immediate cessation of coyote poisoning. After he wasn't heard from, they tried to recoup by asking him to a thousand-dollar-a-plate gourmet charity dinner—"The San Juan Soiree"—to help finance the purchase of a high-tech MRI for their two-thousand-square-foot clinic. The ranking Republicans—a retired Four-Star General, a retired CEO of a blue chip communications company, the owner of a large Napa winery, and two owners of the biggest real estate companies—invited him to their weekly high-stakes poker game. Mr. Mallomar was neither a gambler with money nor his health. And given the fact that his wife was still "under the weather," he declined all offers to mix and mingle with the people on his supposed level.

As for the coyote petition, Mr. Mallomar demurred from adding his name to any list outlawing poison or traps. He tried to explain to an uncomprehending Buster that it wasn't that he disliked coyotes, but merely that he admired them so much that he wanted the poisoning to continue. Coyotes, he said, were inspired by the impediments put in their way to identify opportunities. Ensuring their safety would only have the deleterious effect of tilting the dynamic and hindering the coyotes' ability to act as "fringe players" in the mesa's food system. Mr. Mallomar did not have to know anything about nature to offer up this notion. He knew what he knew, and what he knew he always applied to what he didn't. So what if the ranch missed a cat or two to fringe playing market opportunists? His notion of using Vanadium as a palette for his frustrated creativity was working. The ranch reinvigorated his waning middle-aged self-confidence, and for the first time in his life, he had one other person in his life, besides his lawyer, with whom he could trust.

The next week, Buster stopped at the old Vanadium Potato Company—a large, sturdy limestone warehouse that had been built in the 1880s and had been used over the years as the This 'n' That Resale Shop. For years, they'd been lucky to see three customers a week. Mr. and Mrs. Moulder, the owners of the building and the shop's proprietors, had sat in the same position for so long, they both had permanent vertical welts on their behinds from the slats of their wooden deck chairs that had found their way to the store from the HMS Liverpool.

"Good day to ya'll," Buster said, hoping their response would identify them from the dusty mannequins.

"Good day, Buster," one of the human beings said.

"With all due respect, ah'd like to inquire 'bout purchasin' this here buildin' for Mr. Mallomar." Mr. and Mrs. Molder laughed, albeit weakly.

"Now what the heck would anybody want this ol' buildin' for?" Mrs. Molder said.

"Are you innerested in sellin' er not?" Buster reiterated.

"Well, sure. How much you willin' to pay?"

Buster laid out his checkbook on the counter.

"Two hunnert thousand dollars."

"Two hunnert thousand dollars! Good gracious!"

"You ain't foolin with us now, are ya, Buster?"

"No ma'am, ah ain't."

Mrs. Molder started to cry.

"We'll take it."

"All righty, then." Buster wrote out a check for two hundred thousand dollars, had them sign some papers and that was that. Buster tipped his hat politely to them.

"Thank you kindly."

Buster turned to leave.

"Buster, you never said what he wanted with it."

"This here's gonna be a foreign movie thee-yator."

The transaction completed, Buster smiled and walked out the door. He was to meet Mallomar at the High Grade for dinner—where it was his custom to dine almost every night. As Buster entered, a long procession of folks stopped what they were doing to come greet him and shake his hand. This was Mallomar's plan to re-groove Buster in the eyes of the town as a key player in Vanadium's renaissance. He could have easily hogged the kudos for himself, for Mallomar was no shrinking violet when it came to taking credit due or otherwise, but in Buster's case, he had a higher purpose. Only three short months ago, most Vanadians considered Buster to be a moron if not homicidal, but now some of the most highly regarded ranchers sought his advice about cattle and feed prices. Single women who had previously dismissed Buster as a backward oaf were now vying for his attentions. But there was only one girl, of course, whose attention he ever wanted.

ꟾ

Destiny Stumplehorst was sitting in booth number one with her parents, Skylar and Calvina, when Buster walked in. Since Mary Boyle had taken over the High Grade's kitchen, it had become the custom on Friday nights, for anyone who was anyone in Vanadium, to be seen over a plate of her chicken-fried steak, cream gravy, and garlic mashed potatoes. The Stumplehorsts, in the old days—mostly due to Calvina's parsimony—eschewed dining out, but now in the era of Vanadium's sudden wealth, felt the need to establish themselves as "old money." Buster tipped his hat to the mister and missus. Destiny kept her eyes fixed on the menu.

"Evenin', folks."

"Evenin', Buster."

"I heard a rumor they have you running for Vanadium School Board," said Mrs. Stumplehorst approvingly.

"Shucks, ma'am, guess we got the Thessalonians Home Study Course to thank for that."

That was rank flattery, for Buster's popularity with the high school—which was slated for an expensive expansion—was largely based on the infusion of fresh property tax revenue from Mallomar's Big Dog Ranch. Nevertheless, there was a slight thaw in the way Mr. and Mrs. Stumplehorst regarded him. They were starting to view Buster nostalgically in contrast to the real estate agent and former drug dealer, Cord Travesty.

"May ah borrow this young lady for a moment?" Buster inquired, like a gentleman straight out of Mrs. Humphrey's *Manners For Men.*

"Go right ahead," Mr. Stumplehorst and Mrs. Stumplehorst, answered eagerly. Destiny shot them a betrayed look. In the last two years, Destiny had dropped nearly twenty pounds, hardly resembling the apple-cheeked farm girl Buster had fallen in love with a girl who could down a stack of Jesus cakes smothered in maple syrup and polish it off with a glass of fresh milk.

Gallantly, Buster offered Destiny his arm and she slid out of the booth.

"Ah won't keep you," Buster said in the way he'd heard Mr. Mallomar say while on the phone. He took Destiny around to the saloon side of the restaurant, which was raucous enough to provide privacy.

"How are you, Destiny?"

"I'm still with Cord, Buster."

"Ah know yor with him."

"You should stop thinking about me. And stop following Cord."

"Ah ain't follerin' him. Ah can tell you that."

"He says someone is following him and he thinks it's you."

"Well, it ain't. Look here, Destiny, yor a bidniswoman. Ah'm a bidnisman. The only reason ah brung you over here is to let you in on a sweet little deal. An op-er-toon-itty."

"Oh yeah?" she brightened. "Your Mr. Mallomar wants to buy some more land?"

"That aint 'xactly it." Buster pushed his hat back on his head. "We're lookin' to hire a new 'ssistant to hep manage thangs up there. The whole shebang has gotten too much for yors truly to handle by hisself. The job pays thirty-five grand." Buster considered splitting his salary with Destiny a small price to pay for getting her away from Cord Travesty. "Course, yood have ta move in up thar on the premeeses."

"Thirty-five thousand?"

"We could go forty," Buster quickly countered—employing the same bargaining technique he'd used when haggling for his saddle.

Destiny's eyes softened, and Buster's heart bounded at the possibility that there was still a wisp of something there for him.

"That thirty-five thousand…is that comin' outta your own pocket?"

"Why heck no! Ah ain't that dumb!"

She smiled, her eyes quickly filling with tears.

"Buster," she said in a choked-up whisper. "I ain't worth the trouble." She touched his arm gently and then walked back to her parent's table. It must have taken him a good five minutes before he could tear his eyes away from the empty space where she had just stood.

Mallomar was at the counter having the fried abalone that he had specially flown in from San Luis Obispo. He had also installed, at his own expense, a nitrogen wine storage system where he kept his own vintages—some of them costing more than an average Vanadian could make in six months. As Buster sat down to join him, Mallomar swirled an $800 bottle of Chateau Cheval Blanc around in his glass.

"How'd it go?"

"Not good."

"They wouldn't sell?"

When Buster realized he was talking about something else, he slid the signed purchase papers for the potato warehouse over to him.

"Good man. Care for a glass of wine?"

"Ah'll have a beer, jes' the same," Buster said.

Mary Boyle, seeing Buster sit down, took off her apron and came over to say hello.

"Hey, Buster."

"Hey there, Mommy."

"You'll never guess what Mr. Mallomar told me." Buster looked at Mallomar a bit uneasily.

"What's that?"

"Mr. Mallomar says that he'll supply the financing to franchise my chicken-fried steak recipe! Isn't that exciting?" Mallomar seemed slightly embarrassed by her disclosure. It was then Buster wondered whether something else was going on between them that was more than financial.

"That's real good news."

Mallomar had enthralled her, much as he had Buster, with the notion that she could improve herself. Mallomar's ideas about franchising the High Grade as an old-fashioned supper and dance club made Mary dizzy with possibility. How sincere Mallomar was about all this was uncertain. In the short time that Buster had known him, he had seen Mallomar concoct business deals out of thin air just to impress someone. He feared that this was the case with his adopted mother—she was, after all, still an attractive woman. Mary leaned into Buster's ear to whisper something.

"He's even offered to fix my nose that Bob broke."

Now Buster was really worried. Until now, it had just been buildings. Now Mallomar was folding Mary into his Vanadium renaissance project.

"Hey, Mary, I'd like a glass of that good wine you got back there!"

Suddenly the place got quiet as Cookie Dominguez padded in and sat on a barstool next to Mallomar.

"That wine isn't for sale, Cookie," said Mary. "It's Mr. Mallomar's." Mary looked tensely to Mallomar who, ever so slightly, nodded that it was okay.

"I can't turn down a fellow wine connoisseur," said Mallomar with bonhomie. Everyone in town knew from years of experience with Cookie that he only started conversations to pick a fight. Buster stuffed Mr. Mallomar's biscuit into his mouth. This might possibly save a few teeth when all hell broke loose.

The room watched with anticipation as Mary gave Cookie a clean glass. Cookie, eyes already glazed and somewhat crossed, made a big show out of swirling the wine around, smelling its nose and gargling loudly. Folks thought that was pretty funny.

"I hope this vintage meets your approval," Mallomar said, trying to build on the laughter. Mallomar clearly did not understand how much trouble he was in.

Cookie stopped gargling. "Are you fuckin' with me?"

"No, I..."

"Yes, I believe you *are* fuckin' with me. Do you know what happens to people 'round here who stick their noses up at poor folks?" Cookie held up his bratwurst-shaped finger stubs in the familiar victory sign. "They get a Winston Churchill. Remember that, wiseguy?"

"I vaguely recall something about a skun..."

But before Mallomar could finish the sentence, Cookie jammed his stubs—all the way up to the knuckles—into Mallomar's nose.

Mallomar screamed in agony as Cookie began to lift him off the stool by his nostrils.

"All right, Cookie. Fun's over, let'm go," said Buster as he flanked him. Still holding Mallomar, Cookie gave Buster a quick jab to his Adam's apple. Buster choked, but regrouped quickly enough to land a right hook to Cookie's ear. The discomfort and ringing that followed was enough of a distraction for Mallomar to get off the hook. Blood was pouring out of Mallomar's nose as Cookie now turned his full attention to Buster.

"Remember what I tole you?"

Buster figured it was no use trying to make a fair fight of it. He swung his barstool up in the air and conked Cookie squarely, but it only dazed him. Cookie reached down and grabbed Buster by the legs and started swinging him like an axe with which he intended to chop all the tables into kindling.

Across the counter, one of Sheriff Dudival's reserve deputies was having a grilled cheese and bacon sandwich with a chocolate milkshake. People said the deputy had been a Hollywood screenwriter before moving out to Lame Horse Mesa and was looking for "material" for a buddy comedy. He was not happy to see this fight break out—him being there all alone. Discretion, the better part of valor, he crouched under the counter and called dispatch for back up on his radio.

"Aren't you gonna do something about this, Deputy?" Mary said standing over him.

"Yes, ma'am." *When,* was the question. The deputy thought prudently that the Hispanic gentleman might tire himself a bit before he tried to represent authority. He looked down at his duty belt. The 9mm? No. The ASP? It probably wouldn't make a dent on him. The Taser? Yes. Surreptitiously, he slid it out of its bracket holster and pointed it at Cookie's back as he approached.

"All right! That's enough! You're under arrest!" Cookie had caught sight of the nimrod in the bar's mirror and, without turning around, grabbed the Taser out of the deputy's hand and shot him with it. The deputy immediately fell to the floor with electrostatic convulsions. Try as he might, he was not able to conjure up this colorful detail when finally regaining consciousness. Not that he wanted to include it in his police report. He had been struggling to come up with a decent demonstration of evil for his bad guy in the first act of his screenplay called, *Demon Run*.

Cookie pulled the unconscious deputy's gun from its holster and was just about to shoot him in the head, when four farm-sized deputies from the SO showed up. One of the deputies grabbed his hair. The other two grabbed his arms and tried to twist them into bent wristlocks, a pain-compliance technique that quickly put most normal people up on their toes. The third stood in front of him and hosed his face with a can of pepper spray.

"Racist pigs!" Cookie screamed with his eyes closed. "This is how they treat Hispanics!" Finally, to everyone's great relief, Cookie put both of his hands behind his back, palms touching, and submitted to being handcuffed. As one of the deputies led him out, the other two turned their attention to Buster. They found him out cold under a slash pile of broken barstools and tabletops. He wasn't as surprised to be arrested as Mallomar was—for it was the rule in Western bar fights to arrest everyone regardless of who started it.

Down at the sheriff's office, Buster and Mallomar shared a cell. Cookie sat down the row, carving his name and the date into the wall with his own tooth that Buster had been lucky to dislodge. As for Buster, both of his eyes were swollen shut, his temples blue, his lips cracked and bleeding, and his right ear partially serrated—the result of Cookie's King Salmon-like underbite.

Mallomar was dazed, his nose crusted with blood. A few of his hair plugs had been deforested—a routine forensic examination would find them under the dirty fingernails of Cookie's good hand.

"Hey," Mr. Mallomar finally said, "I did pretty good, huh?"

Buster stuck a finger into his mouth, scooping out the remnants of the sourdough biscuit. He was happy to find his own teeth tight in their sockets and in good working order.

"Oh, yor a reg-lur whirlwind, you are, Mr. Mallomar."

"And I'll tell you something else." Mallomar held a finger along his right nostril and sniffed. "I can breathe out of this sinus. I've never been able to do that in twenty-five years—even after turbinate reduction surgery!"

All Buster could muster was a weak smile. But nothing was going to throw a wet blanket over Mallomar's joie d'vivre. To him, everything about being in the eighty-year-old jail was fascinating—from the thirty coats of pea-green puke paint on the walls, the marks on the bars where other criminals before them had gripped and yelled for a lawyer or a cigarette, the toilet without a seat, to the Draconian locks. He stopped to contemplate each item as if he was an art student on a field trip to the Museé D'Orsay.

"Hey," he said turning to Buster, "…thanks for all this."

By the time they had made bail, Mallomar had already figured out that if the inmates were allowed to make their own lunch, the jail could save as much as $120,000 a year. Sheriff Dudival may have been the only person in town who wasn't swept away by Mallomar's whirlwind even when Mallomar presented him with—on the back of his paper lunch plate—preliminary designs for a state-of-the-art new jail and offered to arrange a low-interest bridge loan. As Buster hobbled to his truck, impounded in the jail parking lot overnight, he looked back to see Mallomar—hands framing the future site of the new jail like a film director. He turned to Buster and winked.

"It needs to be built *into* the hill, don't you think?"

CHAPTER SEVENTEEN

Work Begins

WITH THE BIG DOG house well under way, Buster began his work to resuscitate the Big Dog land. As he had promised that night on the elk hunt, the sage was bush-hogged, and native grasses were planted. The place was finally taking shape and he was proud of his work. It was only natural that he'd want to show the place off a bit. So he invited his old bunkmates, Ned Gigglehorn and Doc Solitcz, over for lunch.

"How many people live here?" Gigglehorn asked as he stood before the Mallomar residence regarding it somewhat like an archeologist might regard a Mayan pyramid in Tikal.

"Two," Buster said.

Gigglehorn turned to Doc Solitcz. "Two people live in this house."

"I heard him."

"Almost ev'r'body in town worked on the dang booger," Buster said defensively.

"Trickle down economics" offered Doc Solitcz. "Can't quarrel with that, Ned."

"How much does it cost to heat this behemoth?"

"Ah don't rahtly know."

"You must have some idea, you're the damn foreman."

"Somethin' like…eighty-five hunnert a month," Buster admitted sheepishly.

"That's over a hundred grand a year, for chrissake!"

"All right, Ned. That's enough. He invited us over for lunch not a damn audit."

But Ned had to admit that Buster had done well by the land. If one were to place a thumb, using the old oil painters' trick of judging scale, over the house—a stunning landscape of rock outcroppings, rolling hills and wildflowers were revealed. The place had drastically changed since that day of the Puster auction—they had to give Buster that.

Buster had prepared a picnic of elk sausage, baked potatoes, heirloom tomatoes, and a bottle of Mallomar's wine for his old friends. The three rode to an earthen bench two hundred yards above the house. After they ate, Doc took a nap while Buster tapped out a portrait of them on a pie plate, and Ned unpacked his easel to paint. He put a friendly arm on Buster's shoulder as they walked the bench to find a good spot for composition.

"Kid, you did good with this place, but will you let me give you a little piece of advice?"

"Sure."

"Get the hell outta here. This is no place for regular people like us."

"Mr. Mallomar's done a lot for this town. He's not what you think."

"This is all an *amusement* for him. But this is our life. A guy I grew up with on the commune has a cattle ranch in Paradox. He's looking for another hand. Let me tell him you're interested."

"Ah ain't a hand no more. Ah'm a foreman. And ah ain't goin'."

"You dumb cluck! Listen to me before it's too…too…"

Suddenly Ned's eyes started blinking rapidly, and his legs started to wobble. He keeled over and vomited. Doc woke up and ran over to him, calmly knotted his napkin and stuck it in Ned's mouth so he wouldn't bite off his tongue. Once that was accomplished, he patted Buster on the shoulder.

"Congratulations. Looks like you have water here."

When Buster brought the drilling company back to the spot Ned Gigglehorn had his seizure—which was carefully marked by an empty bottle of Mouton Rothschild 2000 Pauillac—the drillers hit water going only fifty feet down. The well supplied a generous three hundred gallons a minute through a six-inch pipe. And so it was here above the house, that Buster made the fateful decision to build a reservoir. Mallomar leaped at purchasing his own bulldozer. He chose the Caterpillar D-9, the model favored by the Israelis for removing the homes of Palestinians whose relatives had been connected to acts of terrorism.

Second only to the Miramonte Reservoir in neighboring San Miguel County, the Big Dog was to be the largest private reservoir in all of southwest Colorado. Since Mallomar contributed the first real funds to the building of a new jail, Sheriff Dudival reciprocated by allowing a chain gang of able-bodied convicts to lay the reservoir bottom. Rolls and rolls of heavy-duty plastic sheeting were laid down to prevent the water from seeping into the soil. In fact, so much plastic sheeting was ordered that it forced the plastic company's other big customer, the conceptual artist, Cristo, to postpone his wrapping of Fort Knox. In true Mallomar style, lunch for the County jump-suited group—primarily drunks and wife beaters—was catered.

Cookie Dominguez, who'd heard about the deal from one of his Bees incarcerated for pandering with a minor, drove the delivery truck and used the opportunity to transfer a half of a kilogram of meth to the jail population by way of four Trojan chicken burritos. Neither Mallomar nor Buster saw him in his white kitchen outfit. On the drive out, he stopped at the Mallomar house. Knowing that no one would disturb him, he took an unhurried tour of the place that so many people in town had been talking about.

"*Así que esto es como un hombre rico con una gran cantidad real de dinero vive,*" he said approvingly. He appreciated the interior color scheme that utilized colors derived from their outdoor surroundings. And the Western paintings were similar to the ones that he'd seen in a museum when his fifth grade teacher took him to Denver on a school trip. In Mallomar's office, he helped himself to a handful of cigars and noticed some opened mail. Of particular interest was a bill from Mrs. Mallomar's psychiatrist in New York and a corresponding payment from an insurance company. The diagnosis by the psychiatrist was in code, but the letter the insurance company sent stated plainly that they had paid for psychiatric treatments for "substance abuse."

ꟹ

MRS. MALLOMAR, MEANWHILE, RETURNED fresh from the ashram to her Fifth Avenue apartment overlooking Central Park. For five months, she had kept an oath of silence and ate only brown rice and vegetables. Finding the apartment empty except for a bed and a few articles of clothing, she assumed that either they had been robbed or her husband had put everything in storage for redecorating.

"How are you feeling?" Mallomar asked when they later spoke on the phone.

"I feel recharged. Strong."

"That's great, Dana. I am so glad to hear that. How did it go at the ashram?"

"It quieted me. I liked not having the distractions."

"I think I know what you mean."

"By the way, where is everything?" she asked.

"It's all gone."

"I know it's gone. Where did it go?"

"Sotheby's, mostly."

"All my jewelry and clothes?"

"Yes."

"All our paintings?"

"I wanted to simplify our lives."

"Those were my things. How dare you take it upon yourself to…"

"Dana, get a good night's sleep and hop the plane to Montrose. We'll both be a lot happier at the ranch. You'll see. I'm very proud of this place. We've just finished the reservoir. We've got native grasses coming in. A five-acre organic food plot I put in just for you. And in a couple of months, we're going to have our first yearlings for sale. It's all so beautiful. New businesses on Main Street… We even sponsor the rodeo, for chrissakes."

"You sold all of our things," she responded in a depressive monotone voice.

"That's not who we are."

"Marvin, I could fucking kill you!"

"This, from somebody who just came back from an ashram."

"Don't you think you owed it to me to tell me you were going to do something asinine like this?"

"How could I? You took a fucking oath of silence!"

She hung up and looked for a vase to smash—but they were all gone. So, she sat on the floor cross-legged, concentrated on her breath and cleared her mind. Three minutes later, she was swallowing tranquilizers. By morning, the doorman alerted Mallomar to his wife's odd behavior. Apparently, she came down to the lobby in her bathrobe and ordered a taxi in a language that sounded like Swedish, but wasn't.

ꝏ

DESPITE THEIR ACRIMONIOUS RELATIONSHIP, the news of Dana's recidivism caused Mallomar untold anguish. He immediately called the FBO in Montrose to fuel his plane for takeoff. His second call was to Sidney Glasker, to find yet another addiction specialist and to get the ball rolling on the necessary paperwork.

Four hours later, Mallomar stood at the foot of Dana's bed. She had been intubated and heavily sedated to calm her down. Mallomar had seen versions of this before, but this was truly one for the books. She had a couple of shiners, a big, bloody scab on the end of her nose and stitches on her chin—the result of a header into a curb? The skin on her knuckles was raw—from punching something or someone? Mallomar pulled up a chair next to the bed, holding her non-IVed hand.

Dana Karlsson—her stage name metamorphosed from the original Donna—grew up in Shaker Heights where her father, Don, created a middle-class life for his family from a middle-management position analyzing land leases for Standard Oil. Dana's mother, who began as a dedicated homemaker, came to express her wild side by watching *The French Chef* in the morning and hosting martini klatches comprised of fellow Standard Oil wives in the afternoon. Dana's younger sibling, a brother, having escaped the fuzzy attention of his Boodles inductee-mother, became an ardent liar and defacer of public property. But Donna was a star in the community. She had a B-plus average, a diversified portfolio of volunteer work through the church, and a position as the youngest dancer with the Buckeye Ballet. Things took an unexpected turn for the worse, however, when

Dana, by the age of twelve, had become preternaturally beautiful. What would ordinarily seem like a blessing became the beginning of a curse over which she had no control. Up until this time, her father had no problem hugging her, holding her on his lap, and telling her how proud he was of her. But when she became beautiful—a younger and more refined version of his wife—he became uncomfortable expressing physical affection toward her. Instead, he suddenly adopted a stern, arm's-length attitude. She was not allowed to wear any kind of makeup, even lipstick. She was not allowed to go out on dates. He pushed her into sports, for he thought that a young girl, who looked like Dana, should have something to redirect sexual energies—when it was really his sexual energies, or at least his subconscious—that was the problem.

Dana's perceived rejection by her father had the effect of wanting to please him even more. She tried out for the gymnastics team and showed a particular talent for the uneven bars. To say she threw herself into it was no exaggeration. When Dana was competing, she came out of a pike with such velocity—throwing her pelvis into the lower bar with such force—that people in the audience would audibly gasp. Dana's performance won her team the All-State Women's Finals two years in a row.

Her coach, a one-time state champion himself, believed Dana had a shot for the Olympics. This, of course, required even more work and dedication. It also required of Dana more time spent with her coach—who, while trying his best to look upon Dana's form clinically, was also having a problem. He was thirty-five and Dana, by this time, was fifteen. The other girls on the team, who giggled over how handsome he was, also took notice of the singular attention he paid Dana. There was an undercurrent of gossip. Dana's father and mother questioned her and made her feel badly. And while the coach was circumspect, he admitted to himself and his priest that occasionally he did have improper thoughts. The priest suggested that he find employment elsewhere. He did, at a competing school, and left Dana hanging as the person responsible. The kids on the team now hated her. Many unkind things were said to her and her parents. Dana had her first nervous breakdown.

Her parents sent her to a school that specialized in uncontrollable girls. There, she discontinued her interest in gymnastics, but not her desire to escape gravity. In fact, for the rest of her life she was determined to regain that feeling of freedom that she experienced when she left her body. She studied yoga and meditation. When she got lazy, she achieved her out-of-body experience by getting loaded.

The men, that were to follow in her life, offered her positions in the chorus line, trips to Mustique, and apartments in unsold condominiums. All of these affairs ended the same way—with the men discovering that she was just a nice girl from Ohio with a B-plus average. And then she met Marvin Mallomar. He was, by no means, the best looking of the men she had previously known. He was rich, but that wasn't what she was attracted to. What impressed her was his ability to defy his own gravity—that of being a stubby, ill-educated man with tufts of hair on his back—and his facility for self-reinvention. Unfortunately, it was an art he didn't care to share with anyone else, not even his own wife.

ꕤ

THE DOOR TO THE room opened and a doctor accompanied by two orderlies wheeled in an impressive machine—requiring Mallomar to move into the corner to provide them room. He had found, through Sidney Glasker's contacts in the medical world, an experimental detox therapy that involved the use of ultraviolet blood irradiation. It had been a promising direction for addiction under study by the

Germans in the 1940s, but was discredited because of the stigma it carried—it being tested on people in concentration camps. Mallomar stayed in her room while Dana received her first treatment that night then went home.

The next morning, Mallomar called the hospital to check on his wife's condition. The nurse said that she was awake and was in the middle of telling him that she had eaten a nice breakfast when Dana grabbed the phone and demanded that Mallomar have her released immediately. He refused. She called him many names. He responded calmly to her, making her want to slam down the receiver, but it wasn't the kind of phone that could be slammed down. *Why did she have to be like that,* Mallomar wondered. *Why couldn't Dana be the sweet and adorable woman that she was when she was unconscious?* Mallomar showered and dressed himself for the day. In his vast dressing room there hung one lone suit—his sole holdout from Goodwill. He grabbed his wallet, a few thousand for walking-around money, and his phone. He saw that, while he was in the shower, he'd had a message from a friend who worked at the Fed. Was he free for dinner? Right now, he just wanted to walk.

It was the kind of day that Mallomar used to love—when the wind was blowing off the harbor making the Manhattan air smell as if one was walking on the deck of a ship at sea—rather than the usual sensation of walking on the deck of a garbage scow. Even with his medication, recent events with Dana had jangled him and pulled him downward to the bad pole. He sighed so loudly with melancholy that the people walking ahead of him actually turned to see whom it was.

Next, he swung by Georgette Klinger's on Fifth. The receptionist greeted him like the past recipient of his extravagant gratuities that she was.

"Good morning, Mr. Mallomar. Welcome back! Natasha will be right with you." He followed her to a private room where he changed into a robe and slippers. A few minutes later, Natasha, a zaftig bleached blonde woman in her late forties entered. Mallomar had found her years ago working at a high end Russian call out service. He saw something in her and arranged for Natasha's enrollment in a cosmetology school.

"You lose too much weight," she said, in a blunt Balkan accent. "When a man reaches fifty, he must choose between his ass and face. You have chosen the wrong one." Recently a citizen, Natasha had yet to adopt the diplomatic affectations of everyday American life.

"Do what you can with it."

Natasha put on her magnifying goggles and aimed a bright circular lamp on his nose.

"Oh boy," she said. "Blackheads 'R' Us."

What he had thought was going to be a relaxing interlude turned out to be an eye-wateringly painful forty-five minutes. Natasha's habit of knitting her eyebrows and crossing her eyes in deadly concentration, gave Mallomar the impression that she was not just eliminating blackheads, but cleansing the Serbs responsible for the death of her father and brothers.

"Still living in Queens?"

"I move to Fort Greene. Buy condo."

"Huh. Well, good for you."

"Two condos—one to rent, one to live. Fort Greene has many blacks but changing."

"How'd you pull that off? Mortgage-wise."

"Countrywide. No problem."

"A fixed?"

"Adjustable, sub-prime."

"You don't say?"

"Why do you have such dirty skins?"

"I'm a rancher now."

"You don't say," was now her turn to say.

After she steamed and excavated every pore of his face, applied an astringent to reduce the redness and calmed it down with a vitamin-rich moisturizer, she saw he was still tearing, which may or may not have been the result of her work, and gave him a tissue.

"I'm sorry this so painful. Can I do something to make you feel… *happy*?" Mallomar demurred and reached into the pocket of his robe—placing five, neatly folded hundreds into her moisturized hand.

"Thanks. You already have."

Mallomar was a feel player and Natasha had unwittingly given him something substantial to feel. Returning to his apartment, he immediately placed a call to his consigliore, Sidney Glasker. They briefly discussed Dana's health situation—the doctors were pleased with the photo-radiation blood-cleansing progress Dana was making and how they were wondering if Mallomar might be interested in helping them obtain FDA approval for their patent.

"Sidney, c'mon. You and I both know these guys are quacks."

"I told them you could see your way clear to give them something."

"Then I won't embarrass you. Cut them a check for a hundred grand. By the way, Sidney, how much is drlivingstonipresume.com worth right at this moment?"

"I don't know. Somewhere between eight hundred and fifty million and a billion. Why?"

"I want you to sell it. Tomorrow."

"You're kidding."

"I couldn't be more serious. Sidney, listen to me carefully. We are on the precipice of a banking disaster that's going to rival the Great Depression."

There was silence on the other end of the phone.

"Marvin, anti-depressants aren't like baby aspirins. You can't just stop taking them. You can have a psychotic episode."

"Today, my facialist, who makes no more than forty grand a year, told me that Countrywide gave her mortgages for two condominiums at sub prime. How is that possible?"

"The government is encouraging home ownership."

"That's the Kool-Aid. We're going down the tubes. I can feel it."

"Marvin..."

"Leave me a hundred million to live on, and sell everything else."

"What am I supposed to do with all that money?"

"Short Freddie and Fannie. But do it in ten tranches so no one knows what I'm up to."

"Could you please give this the twenty-four hour test?"

"Sell drlivingston, Sidney. Tomorrow."

ꝏ

MALLOMAR FLEW BACK TO Colorado at daybreak. That morning, on the floor of the NYSE, his instructions to sell drlivingstonipresume.com were carried out at the sound of the opening bell. Serendipitously, fifteen minutes later, Google announced news of an improved algorithm that would revolutionize search engines, and the stock price of drlivingstonipresume.com plummeted 35 percent by the close. The Securities and Exchange Commission, as well as the New York District Attorney's Office were quite interested in Mallomar's exquisite timing. They contacted Sidney Glasker and suggested that his client return to New York for a frank discussion.

"What do you want me to tell them?" Glasker asked Mallomar.

"Tell them I'm busy."

"They won't want to hear that."

"Did you place the short?"

"Of course, I did. By the way, today's *FT* says constructions starts are on the rise and real estate is up another nine point five percent across the board."

"There's always a head fake before a crash."

"A billion dollars, Marvin. That's an awful lot of money..."

"Sidney, are you tryin' to make me go wee-wee?"

"I'm just wondering if we committed the wrong Mallomar."

"How much of your dough did you put in?"

"What are you talking about?"

"Didn't you use any of your own money to short Fannie and Freddie?"

"Fuck no, I didn't. It's insane."

"Let me ask you something. How much did you make riding my coattails into drlivingstonipresume.com?"

"I don't know...maybe three and a half million."

"Toss it in the pot, Sidney."

"Three and a half million has a different meaning to me than it does to you."

"Toss it in, you fuckin' chicken." And Mallomar hung up.

His business in New York finished, Mallomar flew his plane back to Colorado that afternoon, but not before stopping at Russ and Daughters to pick up five pounds of Irish organic smoked salmon.

It was unusual for Buster to pick up Mallomar at the Montrose FBO, but he had an ulterior reason. There were still three of the original rust-colored Puster outbuildings on the property and the architect wanted them torn down for aesthetic reasons. Buster wanted them to remain for authenticity reasons. Their only chance of survival rested with the Big Dog himself, so on the way home, Buster pretended that the lugs were loose on his left front tire and pulled off onto the shoulder of the highway. The location was no accident. While Buster play-acted with a lug wrench, he waited for Mallomar to notice what he had led him here to see. Across the highway was the Double RL, belonging to Ralph Lauren. Lauren had kept the outbuildings from the ranch that he'd bought from its original owner.

"He's got all his old buildings," Mallomar said.

Buster stood up and squinted across the highway.

"Ah do b'lieve he has."

There was no need to say anymore. When they got back to the ranch, Mallomar put the kibosh on the demolition of his original buildings—much to his architect's chagrin. However, it was conceded that if the dilapidated buildings were to stay, they would need reinforcing and rehabilitation. The fly in the ointment was that Mallomar had decreed that he was to be a member of the construction crew. Buster was sorry that he agreed when Mallomar showed up for work wearing a tool belt and the chrome-plated tools that he'd been gifted for his five-million-dollar contribution to Habitat For Humanity.

Each of the rickety buildings was painstakingly lifted off the ground and reset on newly poured concrete slabs. The rotted wood was replaced. The barn walls, as well as the roof, were re-plumbed, shimmed and insulated. Mallomar, silver tools in hand, insinuated his position into every one of these tasks. It was clear that he wanted to show the locals working on this project that he was just "one of the guys."

However, his constant self-aggrandizing began to militate against the desired effect.

No matter what the men were bullshitting about as they worked, Mallomar would find a way to free-associate a story involving some great achievement of his, a famous person he knew, a beautiful woman he had had sex with, an expensive item he once owned, an extravagantly crazy thing he once did, or some really wonderful food he once ate. Buster didn't mind this when they were alone, but he became embarrassed for him when he did this around the other men. He tried to gently head off the conversation—the way a cowboy moves a straggler out of the trees and back with the herd. Eventually, Mallomar noticed.

One afternoon while they and the crew were tearing out the asbestos roof tiles on an old chicken coop, Mallomar began to decry the quality of local meat.

"The irony," he said through his safety mask, "…is that here we are in the middle of beef country—and you can't even get a decent hamburger. I had the guy at the meat counter grind up ten pounds of sirloin and it still tasted like I was eating a goddamn Dr. Scholl's insole!"

Buster could see the other fellows' eyes widen and leaped in to say how many wild strawberries he'd run across while up in Beaver Park. Mallomar just stared at him, and then asked him to step outside for a moment.

"What's the problem?" Buster asked as he lifted his mask.

"I'll tell you what the problem is. Every time I start telling a story, you change the subject."

"Well, if'n ah do, ah ain't aware of it."

"*I'm* aware of it. Trust me, you do it all the fucking time."

"Well, Mr. Mallomar, ah'll try to keep an eye on it." Buster turned to go back in the chicken coop, then stopped. "Tell you what…ever' time you start to tell these folks, who mostly live offa food stamps, how you take perfekly good steaks and grind em up into burgers—or how you have some lil' guy in Italy make two-thousand-dollar shoes for you cause you got 'specially skinny feet…ah'll jes kep my mouth shut and let you go on makin'a dang fool of yorself."

"Are you saying I've got a big mouth?"

"You prolly know someone in New York who's got a bigger one, a better one, one that can eat breakfast, lunch, and dinner at the same time whilst recitin' all the companies on the dang New York Stock

Exchange—but, yessir, that's what ah'm sayin'." Buster had never stood up to anyone like this before. Sarcasm, in Buster's upside-down brain, had finally come onstream.

Mallomar sputtered, at a loss for words.

"I was just trying to hold up my end of the conversation," he protested weakly.

"We ain't on a talk show, Mr. Mallomar. These men are only here cause yor payin' em. You don't need to impress 'em any more'n that."

Mallomar swallowed the lump in his throat. The doleful look on his face was a pitiful sight to behold.

"Well, I'm...I'm not going to say another fucking word," Mallomar said petulantly.

Buster raised an eyebrow and pig snorted.

"Now, Mr. Mallomar, we both know *that* ain't true."

"I mean it, goddammit! I've got a big mouth and I'm not going to say another word!"

"Now really, Mr. Mallomar, that ain't dang posserbull."

"I'm not going to say another word for seven days and seven nights."

"You cain't do it."

"Yes, I can."

"Cain't."

"Can."

"Cain't."

"Can."

Then Mallomar broke a hunk of asbestos over Buster's head. Buster, deadpan, broke some asbestos over Mallomar's head. The others came out of the chicken coop and stood in silence watching the two men crack each other over the head at least a dozen times and bray with laughter until the air had been squeezed out of each others' lungs and they fell to the ground. They then proceeded to heap dirt on each other until their ears, nostrils and mouths were filled with the stuff and they spat out dirt-colored drool like two hydrophobic dogs. The help could see that this was not an ordinary relationship between a ranch boss and his foreman. They just didn't know what exactly it was.

"Seven days and seven nights without talking," Mallomar gasped.

"What's the bet?"

"I'll bet you one hundred acres of my land."

"And iffin' ah lose…?" Mallomar knew exactly what he wanted from Buster. And it had been sticking in his craw from the day they went elk hunting.

"I'll take your truck."

All the men looked at Buster. It was too late to back out now.

"All right…it's a bet," Buster said.

Suddenly, the ground started to rumble and the ranch dogs woke from their naps under the deck and started barking. Mallomar's face took on a glum expression that Buster hadn't seen in weeks as a black Suburban worked its way up the road. Buster recognized the logo on the door as belonging to the local limo company.

Six full-sized Halliburton cases were eased down from the luggage rack, but the main cargo still hadn't shown herself. Mallomar shooed the barking dogs away, then tapped on the blacked-out window. He found himself in the very difficult position of wanting to yell at her, but holding to the bet, not being able to speak. Tapping on the window wasn't getting him anywhere with the occupant. He looked at Buster, entreatingly.

"Hmmm mm mmmm." *Have a heart*, he said with his lips closed. Buster stepped forward, not wanting to take unfair advantage of the situation.

"Uh, you can come out now, Mrs. Mallomar."

Buster shaded his eyes and peeked into the blacked-out car. He could make out the form of a woman in the back seat, but she wasn't budging. Mallomar's jaw muscles tightened, and he rapped on the window again. This next time, a bit more impatiently. Buster and Mallomar could hear the electric doors lock again.

"Hmmuhmmm." *Sonofabitch*, it can be assumed he said.

"Hello there, Mrs. Mallomar…'member me? Buster McCaffrey? Welcome to the Big Dog Ranch! If ya'll kindly unlock them doors we can get you sich-eee-yated in the main house," Buster said as sweet as coconut pie. But Mrs. Mallomar didn't budge. Mallomar sighed and shrugged his shoulders. He started to walk away from the car and then stopped. His face turned purple and contorted. He charged the Suburban kicking and clawing at the door like an animal.

"Do you have any idea what you put me through? Well, that's enough goddammit! That's enough! If you don't get out of this car right now—I'm going to break the window and pull you out by your fucking hair!" Mallomar couldn't believe what had just burst from his mouth. Buster raised an eyebrow and smiled to the other men. They nodded as if to say, *Yep, we heard him, all right*. The Big Dog Ranch was now minus one hundred acres.

Now, the damage done, the locks clicked up, and the door opened. A skinny white leg in black shorts swung out and paused as if testing to see if the atmosphere on earth was safe. An empty bottle of Ketel One toppled to the ground. Finally, the sum of Mrs. Mallomar's Giacometti-thin figure emerged and steadied itself against the car. She jauntily adjusted her black Oakleys. She was wearing a black baseball cap that the hospital had given her as a going away present, heralding the generic version of "AMITRIPTYLIN."

Swaying as if in a breeze, Mrs. Mallomar's sunglasses took in her surroundings: an almost finished house in the middle of nowhere, the husband wearing cheap western clothes covered in filth, and some tall cowboy—also dirty and smiling at her through tobacco-stained horse teeth.

"Fuuuuuuuck," she said, and threw up all over Buster's boots before passing out.

Buster and Mallomar caught her before she face-planted. Together, they fireman-carried her into the house.

"Look at what she's done to herself!" Mallomar said, shocked at how much weight she'd lost during her experimental treatment. "She's got a substance abuse problem. Had her in the best…" Mallomar caught himself before bragging. "Had her in a nut hospital. I guess we know how well that fucking worked."

Like biblical handmaidens, they carried her up the stairs to her own room.

"Last year they arrested her for shoplifting. Can you imagine that? One of the wealthiest…" Once again, he stopped himself from bragging. "They caught her stealing shoe samples on display at Barney's. Her closets were filled with three hundred of the damn things—no pairs—just tiny single shoes. After they pinched her, I said, 'Dana, you had no possible use for the fucking things. Why in God's name did you take them?' She just shrugged her shoulders and looked at me like I was the biggest lox in the world and said, 'Why do you think?'"

Once they had her tucked in, her hospital-white skin against the white sheets made her appear chroma-keyed and invisible save for her eyebrows.

Buster thought it best that he step outside to give the Mallomars some privacy. Mallomar looked down on Dana, dead to the world, and noticed that she still had her shoulder bag on her. Gently, he lifted the strap around her neck and pulled it up from below the sheets. He threw the bag on the chair and was about to leave the room, when he had a thought. He went back to the bag and emptied its contents on the dresser. There were the remnants of her hospital hygiene kit, the plastic ID bracelet that she had decided to keep as a souvenir, and a package of beef jerky. Beef jerky? She had never eaten beef jerky in her life. He turned the package over and a white powder cascaded from it. Dana had been under close supervision from the time she left the hospital, to his own driver, to their private airplane. From Montrose, the only person with whom Dana had contact was the limo guy.

"This is Marvin Mallomar," he said, on the phone in his office. "That's right, you just brought my wife up to the ranch in Vanadium. Hey, in all the commotion of the happy homecoming, I forgot to tip your guy. Got his name and address handy?"

Mallomar put the jerky and drug remnants in a FedEx envelope with a note.

He wasn't going to bother with the local constabulary when he already had connections at the DEA. Whoever that driver was, Marvin Mallomar intended to fuck him up good. When he finished, Buster was waiting for him on the front porch with two cold beers.

For the first time since Buster had known him, the arrival of his delirious wife had put Mallomar truly at a loss for words. As the sun set and the San Juan's were slowly turning Venetian red with alpenglow, they drank their beer in silence.

"So, where do you want your hundred acres?" Mallomar asked, finally.

"At the edge of the canyon, by that old sheepherder's wagon."

"Done."

"But Mr. Mallomar…?"

"Yeah?"

"Now ah'm givin' it back to you."

"What're you talking about?"

"Since it's mine, ah'm free to do whatev'r I dang please. So, ah'm makin' a little present of it for ya."

"You're crazy. It's worth seven hundred thousand dollars."

"Beggin' yor pardon, sir. Ah ain't settin' out to get my ranch thataway."

"You really…want to give it back to me?" Mallomar seemed to suffer from the same problem Sheriff Dudival had and turned away from Buster to clear the lump in his throat.

"Yes, sir."

Buster could see Mallomar's hand go up to his face as if he were brushing something away. Finally, he turned around and offered his hand.

"Thank you."

CHAPTER EIGHTEEN

Hell to Pay

Mrs. Mallomar woke up the next day with no clue as to where she was. Her mind shuffled through her Rolodex of hospitals, first, second, and third homes, development sites, and hotels—and drew a blank. Wherever she was, her arms were not restrained, she noticed. That was a good sign. And it was quiet. She smelled fresh paint and the pleasant aroma of newly laid wood flooring. Slowly, she untangled her bony legs from the sweat-knotted sheets, stood up and walked to the door. The hallway led to the overview of the house's Great Room: an architectural assembly of trusses and beams that arched cathedral-like over a two-thousand-square-foot living room complete with a ten-ton fieldstone and blackened-iron fireplace.

"This is the fucking cabin?" she mumbled to herself as she held on tightly to the railing trying not to slip on the just-polished stairs. Mrs. Mallomar, no slouch when it came to interior decorating herself—

having previously decorated four of their part-time houses—took note of the salvaged barn wood he had used extensively on the interior walls. "I know where you got that idea, Marvin," she grumbled. It was at the Democratic Fundraiser at the teen-movie director, Adam Schreifeldt's house on Long Island. He had bought the barns from four different defunct potato farms that could no longer afford the increased Hamptons real estate taxes.

When Mrs. Mallomar finally made it to the bottom of the stairs, she stood mind-boggled, facing what could still be identified as a hundred-thousand-dollar Frank Lloyd Wright dining table—its legs having been cruelly sawn off by her husband to create a coffee table large enough to fit the scale of the oversized room. The monster. Was he in the house? She couldn't wait to scream at him for the nouveau-riche boor he was. Unfortunately, he was nowhere to be seen. She was alone except for the two Ute girls who were washing the windows in the Great Room.

Not many rich people used Utes as domestics, she would learn, generally favoring the less expensive illegal Mexicans, but Mallomar had found, after going through every able-bodied woman from Ridgway to Egnar, that the Ute women were the only ones with the requisite courage and balance to ascend the thirty-foot extension ladders needed to wash his Great Room's twenty-five-foot picture windows. Lolly and Lily Longfeather, chammies clutched in puckered brown fingers, were perched atop twin ladders looking very much like their cliff-dwelling ancestors depicted in the clay model at the Anasazi Visitors Center in Mesa Verde. Unaware of Mrs. Mallomar's pale-faced presence, they paused for a moment to look through the just-cleaned upper portion of the windows and contemplated the clouds drifting by Sunshine Peak, Lizard Head, Mt. Wilson, El Diente, and Lone Cone Peak—the sacred gateways of the Ute and Navajo Indian Nations. Suddenly, a blue jay, fooled by his reflection in the sparkling clean window, smacked into it and fell to the ground, its neck swizzling 180 degrees. Shocked by the impact, the Ute women wobbled on their ladders for a moment, but regained their balance. They looked at the dead jay, and then at each other with horror. This was bad Ute juju. Even Mrs. Mallomar sensed it—in her first sober moment in forty-eight hours.

In the meadow behind the house, Buster and his horse, Stinker, were inspecting the ditch line for blockages. Buster was proud that the work he had done on the irrigation system might last for generations. But something was wrong with Stinker. He wouldn't stop fidgeting and cantering sideways from the house. The more Buster tried to get him to go closer to the house, the more agitated he became.

"Something wrong, old boy?" Buster said, trying to soothe him. His eyes were wide with fear, and his nostrils flared. Buster quickly looked around to see if there were any mountain lions. Stinker started gagging on his bit, backing up. Buster squinted in the direction of what was spooking him. About twenty-five yards away, the ghostlike figure of Mrs. Mallomar could be seen in the window, looking down at the hapless feathered aviator. Stinker, it seemed, had never seen a human being as skinny and pale as her before and bucked with such ferocity that his bridle broke. Off he went, Buster holding on for dear life, as the horse leapt over the river-rocked garden wall, smashing two $3,500 teak chaise lounge chairs that Mallomar had just uncrated from Smith and Hawken.

Mrs. Mallomar screamed so loudly, and so unexpectantly, that the Ute women fumbled their Rubbermaid buckets of vinegar and water. The ladders waved together then parted like knitting strands of DNA—and then women, buckets, and ladders crashed to the floor. The buckets, smashed the Frank Lloyd Wright coffee table in half soaking the forty-by-sixty Persian rug with vinegar. The overstuffed leather sofas fortunately broke Lilly and Lolly Longfeather's fall. They were unhurt, but had trouble catching their breath. The damage would clearly cost twenty years of their combined salaries. Numbly, they looked out at Buster, now on the patio, who had dismounted to look for his hat. Sadly, he found the little bird instead, picking it up in his big hand. He gazed up at the Ute girls through the window and pantomimed to the dead bird. "Did I do this?"

The Utes mutely shook their heads. Relieved, he smiled. That is until he saw Mrs. Mallomar. She stormed out the patio doors, scaring Stinker away.

"Uh, afternoon, Mrs. Mallomar. Sleep well?" Buster said, holding the jay behind his back so as not to further upset her delicate constitution.

"Who the fuck are you?"

"Well, ah'm Buster. We, uh, met…already."

"Is this my house?"

"Uh, yes, ma'am."

"Do you work here?"

"Yes, ma'am."

"Then you're fired."

"Yes, ma'am," Buster said, and stuck his hat back on his head. Then he laid the dead bird on top of the covered Wolf gas grill like a Raja on a funeral bier. Stinker had run all the way back to the barn where Buster retreated as well.

About an hour later, Mallomar, who'd been in town ostensibly discussing chicken-fried steak franchises with Mary Boyle, found Buster's pickup and trailer next to the barn. He was inside packing up his horse tack.

"My wife said she fired you over some crappy furniture you broke. Is that what's going on here?"

"Yessir. Ah'ma leavin'."

"Did you tell her you were the foreman of this place?"

"No, sir."

"Don't you think you should have conveyed to her, in all her fucking dazed glory, that you run this place…that you're my partner?"

"Dint wanna rile her no further."

"You're not afraid of her, are you?"

"No sir, not 'xactly."

"Well, tell me something. Would you turn your back and run away from a mountain lion?"

"No sir, ah sure would not."

"How about a grizzly bear?"

"No, sir."

"Then why, in the fucking world, would you run away from a ninety-five-pound drug-addled woman?"

CHAPTER NINETEEN

Dangerous Quarry

MARVIN MALLOMAR WAS A fixer by nature, so one can only imagine his frustration in not be able to fix his wife. There she was, sleeping in another room down the hall, craving something day and night that would probably kill her and so far he hadn't been able to do anything about it. Why not? Why couldn't he solve this? Then the answer came to him during a restless night's sleep. It was simple. He had outsourced her. No more, he thought. No more doctors with experimental cures, no more half-listening headshrinkers. He would put his own hand to the till and he, Marvin Mallomar, would concentrate his full powers and attention to Dana's cure.

That said, Mallomar's powers and attention were sorely being tested on several other fronts. First, there was the SEC. He'd denied their request for a friendly conversation, but now they were demanding—by way of a subpoena—his appearance before the Commission on allegations of insider trading. On top of that, his impulsive decision to send the jerky/drug sample to his friend in the DEA had boomeranged into a full-blown investigation. His connection phoned to warn him that a team of agents had been dispatched to Lame Horse County—without Sheriff Dudival's knowledge—to investigate Dana's limo driver, who it turned out, had been named Cookie Dominguez's "Salesman of the Month" for expanding the Busy Bees' methamphetamine business into the Four Corners of Colorado, New Mexico, Arizona, and Utah. In fact, an assault on Cookie's crank farm was already in the works and it was suggested that Mallomar leave town for a few days. Mallomar, concerned about the possibility of a murderous backlash, purchased a handgun. He trained himself to use it by dry-firing it at the TV image of Maria Bartiromo when she appeared on CNBC's *Squawk Box.* He found her particularly annoying—crowing daily about the upswing in housing starts. Add to all of this, an excruciating spray of shingles appearing across his stomach and love handles—in the exact same place he wore his money belt when he travelled in developing nations—and you would have the sum total of a man at his limit. But then, Marvin Mallomar was no ordinary man. He knew how to compartmentalize. He knew how to triage. He knew how to talk himself down from his own tree.

The billion-dollar investment? In his mind, there was nothing he could do about it. If he lost it, he lost it. He'd still have a hundred million in the mattress. Hell, his parents had lived through the Great Depression. He'd manage. The SEC? They didn't have the resources in their department to go after him *and* Stevie Cohen at the same time. Cookie Dominguez? Not that he condoned capital punishment for nonviolent crimes, but maybe he'd get lucky and the Feds would blow his head off. The shingles? He'd live. How easy was that? Now, back to Dana.

Mallomar handed down the edict that, until further notice, no one was to disturb Mrs. Mallomar. That included the animals—which were all moved outside of earshot to the furthermost field. Buster was told to continue to pay Lilly and Lolly Longfeather's weekly salary, but under no circumstances were they to enter the house to clean or cook. Mallomar, himself, would do the cooking—but there was a minor glitch. For three days straight, Dana Mallomar refused to eat.

"I had this chicken flown in from D'Artagnan in New York," Mallomar said. His wife remained silent, offering only a sad, blank stare. "It's organic, if that's what you're worried about. Or you can just eat the vegetables."

"I'm not very hungry," she finally said.

"I'm not letting you leave this table until you eat something." That may have sounded like something one says to a child, but since they never had any children, Mallomar felt it was there for him to use.

"Then be prepared to wait a long, long fucking time."

"I've got all the time in the world. I'm a patient man."

"Marvin, you're a fat man—a selfish, narcissistic, badly tempered man. But you are NOT a patient man."

Mallomar smiled slightly, not wanting to give her the satisfaction of seeing just how badly tempered he could be. Dana looked at his right hand and slightly raised her eyebrows. Unbeknownst to him, he had strangled his fork, bending the tines backwards like Uri Geller.

"What are you trying to do here, Marvin?"

"I'm trying to make you well. Be a sport and lift a tiny finger to help me."

"Can I tell you something…as a friend?"

"What?"

"Let go of the rope."

"No."

"I'm never going to fuck you again."

"Who do you think you're talking to…your father?"

"That was not…" She waved the rest of the sentence off with her hands and started crying.

"I didn't mean that. You wound me up."

"I hate you."

"Happy to see you're getting back to your old self. Will you be all right here for a couple of days?"

"Why? Where are you going?"

"I have to go to New York tomorrow to take care of something."

"Working on your divorce strategy with Sidney?"

"Don't flatter yourself. You're not my only ass cancer."

Mallomar got up from the table and smiled.

"Try to eat something."

ஐ

MALLOMAR STOPPED OUTSIDE THE house to take a few deep breaths and shake it off. He walked across the driveway to the barn where he found Buster currycombing his horse.

"How-dee," Mallomar chirped like a Minnie Pearl, as if he didn't have a care in the world. Mallomar sat on a bale of hay. "What's the good word, brother?"

"You have any inneress in perchissin' Belted Galloways?" Belted Galloways were the distinctive breed of black Scottish cattle with white bands around their middle.

"I don't know… Are they any good?"

"They say thar the best eatin'… Mr. Ralph Lauren has a hunnert of 'em."

"He does, does he?" Mallomar thought for a moment. "Let's get some. A hundred and fifty," Mallomar said, not too opaquely.

"Ah'll take a look a that."

"Hey amigo, I just wanted to give you a heads up…I have to go to back east for a spell." Mallomar had not only bought up the real estate in town, but had started to appropriate Buster's lingo.

"How long you gonna be gone for?" Buster said, feeling his pulse quicken.

"I'm not at liberty to say."

Mallomar could see the panic in Buster's eyes at the thought of being left alone with his wife and was frankly comforted by it. "I hid all the booze and meds in the chicken house."

"Mr. Mallomar," Buster said, "ah ain't comferbull bein' alone up here with her and all."

"You'll be okay."

"Ah really think you should getta nurse or some woman to come out here."

"She'll only rebel if I do that."

"Maybe we can bring Mrs. Boyle up here to cook for her and all."

Mallomar's face darkened.

"What's your next fucked up idea?" He handed Buster a cell phone. "Look, if there's any trouble—not that there will be—call me on this phone. And, uh…if anything bad *does* happen…just make sure you document it."

There was a lot going on that Buster didn't understand. Mallomar patted Buster on the shoulder. "C'mon… you'll be okay as long as you remember one thing…"

Mallomar locked eyes with Buster and leaned in menacingly. "Don't…fuck…her." Mallomar held this look for about five seconds then burst out laughing so hard he could hardly contain himself. "Jesus Christ, you should see the look on your face!"

The next morning, Buster rushed out to the front pasture to lower the irrigation headgates. Rain was in the forecast and they wouldn't be needing to use their reservoir water. He stood up to see

Mallomar drive past and beep his horn, then gesture to the house. Buster panicked. Mallomar meant that his wife was now all alone. Buster jumped on Stinker and raced back. When he got there, he was relieved to discover that she hadn't yet left her room. Honoring his promise to keep an eye on her, Buster sat down in the living room and obediently waited, slowly leafing through the many Mallomar coffee table books. A book of black-and-white photographs depicting circus freaks during their "off hours" and men wearing women's hair curlers was particularly interesting. The morning came and went. The afternoon came and went. And Mrs. Mallomar never left her room.

Around dinnertime, Buster threw two steaks on the grill and heated a can of beans. Very gently, he rapped on Mrs. Mallomar's door to announce that her supper was ready, but she didn't answer. So, he left the tray by her door. Returning to his own dinner downstairs, he casually looked out the window to the corral and saw Stinker. With all the fluster of Mallomar's leaving, Buster had forgotten to unsaddle him. Buster looked up to Mrs. Mallomar's door. She was still sleeping. Very quietly, he got up and ran outside. It took him no longer than four minutes to unsaddle his horse, comb him out, put some fresh alfalfa down for him, and run back inside. He was just re-tucking his napkin inside his shirt collar before cutting into his steak, when he noticed the cabinet door under the kitchen sink was ajar. He knew that he hadn't opened it.

Buster put his knife and fork down and climbed the stairs, three at a time, to Mrs. Mallomar's bedroom. Her steak and beans were still on the tray outside the room, untouched. He heard a low moan coming through the door, and knocked again.

"Mrs. Mallomar…ya'll right in there?"

There was no answer. He tried the door handle. It was locked. He banged on the door, loud enough to wake up a sleeping person.

"Mrs. Mallomar, ah gotta know if yor all right. Would ya'll answer me, please?" There was still no response.

"Ma'am, if ya'll don't open this door, ah'm gonna have to break it down. The mister ain't gonna be too happy with that." He waited. Again, nothing. "Welp, you gimme no choice, now, ma'am! Ah'm comin' in!" Buster was about to put his shoulder to the door, but at the last minute, thought better of it and kicked the door handle with his boot.

Mrs. Mallomar was lying on the floor. Beside her, was an empty sixteen-ounce bottle of lemon-scented furniture polish. Buster placed an ear on her chest and listened for a heartbeat. She had one, but it was faint. He carefully picked her up—taking care not to touch her any place it wouldn't be allowed had she been conscious—and placed her back on the bed.

"Mrs. Mallomar?" He gently tapped the side of her cheek with a thick finger. Her jaw hung loose, her eyes rolled half-way back in their sockets, her breath, not surprisingly, smelled nicely of lemons. Buster agonized over what to do. He thought about calling Mallomar, but that wouldn't solve the immediate crisis. He considered calling Jimmy, but he hadn't spoken to her in months—what could she do, anyway?

Buster decided to call Doc Solitcz. There was no phone in Doc and Ned's cabin, and he was forced to dial the Stumplehorsts' main house. Mrs. Stumplehorst answered the phone. As anxious as Buster was to talk to Doc Solitcz, being terse and to the point would only draw suspicion from the old harridan. He had to be cagey about this. He traded pleasantries with her about Vanadium's chances for precipitation. He commiserated with her about the going prices at the Kansas City packing houses. Finally, just before he was just about to jump out of his skin, he broached the subject of his original intent.

"Uh, is Doc around?"

"Yes, I believe he is. It's not an emergency, I hope?"

"No, ma'am. No, thank goodness fer that. It ain't no ee-mergency. Jes wanna ax him a veterinary question."

"Well, hold the line, Buster," she said. "I'll go fetch him."

It seemed like years before Doc came to the phone. By now, all Buster could manage to pass through his tightened larynx was, "Doc, ah need you up here, raht quick."

When Doc arrived, he took a look at Mrs. Mallomar. Felt her pulse. Put a stethoscope to her chest. He told Buster to bring him two raw eggs and then wait downstairs. It was quiet up in Mrs. Mallomar's room for the longest time. Unable to eat, Buster gave his dinner to the dogs. Mallomar might not be too upset if Mrs. Mallomar died, but Sheriff Dudival, not to mention the rest of Vanadium, would definitely have something to say about his presence at yet another death. Finally, Doc Solitcz emerged and stood at the railing overlooking the great room.

"I need you to make a big pot of oatmeal for me."

"There's another steak, if yor hungry..."

"The oatmeal is for Mrs. Mallomar, Buster." With all the latest talk about Buster's success as a rancher, the Doc had almost forgotten how slow on the uptake he could be. "We need to soak up the poison in the lady's stomach that hasn't already been regurgitated."

"Ah'll git right on it!" Buster was grateful for something useful to do as well as the Doc's implication that Mrs. Mallomar was still alive.

Three bowls of oatmeal later, Doc emerged from the room and came downstairs. Buster had retrieved a drink for him from the chicken coop.

"She's not a very nice person, is she?" Doc quickly swallowed the glass of bourbon and handed Buster the empty glass.

"Why...what'd she say to ya?"

"It's not important."

"Ah a-pprec-i-ate you comin' out here t'night, Doc."

"And I'd appreciate you not telling her who I am."

"Shor 'nuff." The Doc headed to the door.

"You don't have to run off right away, do ya, Doc?"

"Well, actually I really ought to be getting back..."

Buster didn't relish the thought of being left alone in the house with Mrs. Mallomar again.

"How 'bout me burnin' a steak for ya? We got a thousand of 'em."

"Sounds tempting, but I already ate Mrs. Stumplehorst's grilled chicken-on-the-cross."

"We got a real movie thee-ay-ter here. Seats thirty people."

"I don't doubt it."

"C'mon Doc, why don't you stick around a piece?" Buster almost begged. "Mr. Mallomar's got himself the en-tire Hopalong Cassidy Collection."

Doc smiled and shook his head. "I gotta get back, kid."

"Sure, sure...ah unnerstan." Morosely, Buster followed him to the door. Doc turned around to take it in one last time.

"I gotta say, Buster, this is a helluva situation you got yourself in here." Buster wasn't sure if the situation he was referring to was good or bad. The fact was, he no longer knew himself.

"Yeah, it's a booger, ain't it?"

The Doc didn't smile.

"It's a booger, all right."

Up until then, Buster had been sleeping in the prefab office that had been used by Mallomar's architect. Under these new circumstances, he thought it wise to sleep in the main house until he knew that Mrs. Mallomar was going to be all right. Buster opened the different doors around the kitchen looking for the maid's quarters until he found it. When Mallomar built the forty-thousand-square-foot house, it somehow slipped his attention to provide space for the live-in staff that he would certainly need. At the eleventh hour, he and his architect were able to carve off space for a seven by nine foot room with a small sink and shower. Buster took his boots off and stretched out. His feet protruded a foot and a half past the end of the bed. After several attempts to get comfortable, he decided to take the pillow and blankets and sleep on the living room floor. At least, this way, he could keep an ear out for Mrs. Mallomar in case she needed something.

Buster dozed off as a weather front moved in from the west and began to gently buffet the big picture windows. He wrapped himself in a dream about Destiny Stumplehorst. That night, he saved her from a dangerous rock slide. His heroics, however, were not rewarded with what Buster yearned for most—to bring her back to his prefab and make love like they had done in the Stumplehorst barn. Lately, all of Buster's "I'll Save You!" dreams were confounded by Destiny having to get back to her "boyfriend."

A lightning strike hit a tree one hundred yards from the house. For a split second the living room lit up so brightly that Buster could see the bones in his hand. Thunder was booming now with unsettling regularity—sounding like someone was dragging furniture across the wooden floor upstairs. Buster sat up and cocked an ear. *Was* someone dragging furniture across the second floor?

Up the stairs Buster bounded once again. The door to Mrs. Mallomar's room was open. She wasn't there. He quickly looked around the horseshoe-shaped second floor landing. There was another pop of lightning, and then he saw her. Mrs. Mallomar was hanging by her neck from one of the roof's steel support rods, under her feet, a tipped-over chair.

"Mrs. Mallomar!"

He ran to her and attempted to get her weight off the rope—with one arm cradled under her buttocks lifting, while his free hand fumbling in his pants for a pocket knife. When Mrs. Mallomar fortunately regained consciousness, her first cognizant observation was that Buster's nose was firmly parked in her crotch as he struggled to reach above her head to cut the rope.

"Oh my god!"

"Sorry, ma'am. Jes tryin' to get you down!" Buster mumbled, her nightgown sticking to his mouth like a plastic dry cleaning bag. Incensed, she began to beat him furiously about the ears. Buster had to endure this until the rope was finally cut. Flustered, he placed her gently on the floor. She stood there, small and scowling at him, and then burst out crying.

"You fucking idiot! Why can't you let me die?"

Angrily she marched back to her room and locked the door. In the morning, Buster got up early and scrambled half a dozen eggs and toasted bread. By now, he had figured out how to work the stove, the microwave and the dishwasher, but the German coffee maker, with all its switches and dials, offered the biggest challenge. Still, he even managed to get that going. He jiggered some hot sauce on the eggs, sat down at the granite counter and stared out at the meadow waving with deep green new grass and wildflowers replenished by the rain.

"Who said you could stay in this house?"

Buster had been dreading this moment. Mrs. Mallomar was standing behind him, still wearing the nightgown from last night. There was a purple and yellow brushstroke of broken capillaries around the right side of her neck.

"Your husband wanted me to stay in the house whilst he were gone."

"'Whilst he were gone,'" she mimicked. "Why? Was he afraid I was going to *cap* myself?"

"Well, didn't you, uh…try to, ma'am?"

She cocked her head sideways and looked at him like he was crazy.

"What are you talking about?"

"Last night, ma'am. You had yourself a snoot fulla some furniture polish, then you kinda…hung yorself."

"I what?" She obviously didn't remember anything or was playing dumb—as Mallomar sometimes did.

"Nevermind, ma'am. Fergit ah said anythin'."

"That's right, nevermind! And God help you if you ever mention a word of that to my husband!"

"Ah woont have no need to, ma'am."

"Oh no? You and fatso seem pretty chummy if you ask me. One might even say *intimate.* I mean, that's the only way to explain why he has someone like you around."

Buster got the drift of what she was implying, but kept himself in check. He'd sat ringside when Mary Boyle would egg her husband on—hoping he'd slug her so she could get him arrested on a domestic. Buster wasn't going to fall for that.

"Can ah get you some eggs?" he said sweetly.

Mrs. Mallomar harrumphed. "Where'd he hide it?"

"Beggin' your pardon, ma'am?"

"Where'd he hide the vodka?"

Buster just sat there mute.

"Don't you speak *inglés*? Where…is…the…booze?"

"Ma'am…ah ain't at liberty to say." This was the first time Buster had employed Mallomar's favorite expression, and he liked the ring of it.

"You ain't, huh?" She reached across Buster's face to an overhead cabinet to get a coffee cup. Her robe parted, exposing her breasts, but she did nothing to correct the situation. Buster turned away and stared off in the distance at Little Cone and Lone Cone.

"Okay, so where's the coffee, Clem?"

Buster gestured proudly to the coffee maker. She looked deadpan into the top of it. The tank that held the water was filled to the top with coffee grounds.

"Who's the idiot who poured coffee grounds in here?"

For Buster, it had been a coin toss as to whether the water was supposed to go in the top or in the slide-out compartment.

"'Sorry, ma'am, never used anythin' but an ol' percolator. Almost had it figgered out."

"Uh huh." As she walked past him, she sniffed the air with a screwed-up face. "Why don't you *figger* out how to use the shower *whilst* you're at it?"

She may have been right about Buster's body odor. It had always been his habit to only change his clothes once a week. This too, he let slide.

"Ah'm ridin out to the Dander Ranch this afternoon to look at some cattle they got for sale. If you're innerested, ah'll saddle you up a pony."

"I *said*, you stink."

"We've looked at the stock from eight different ranches," he said unwavering, "We got it narrowed down to two."

"Why don't you check out the Rockin' Bidet Brand while you're at it?"

"Beg pardon, ma'am?"

"I was just taking another angle on the stink question." A bidet. Mallomar had three of those delivered to the house. Now he got it. Buster just took a sip of coffee and nodded appreciatively. He refused to be bucked off.

"You're sort of like having FiestaWare, you know that? Can't even give the stuff away once you're tired of it."

"Ma'am, my orders are not to leave you in this here house by yorself. Now, if you ain't carin' for breakfast, ah thought maybe yood wanna put on some britches and go fer a ride. Might make ya feel bedder once you got some fresh air in ya."

"Fuck you."

It was beginning to dawn on Buster that Mallomar had not been entirely forthcoming regarding his wife's ease of maintenance. Buster had one last trump card to play.

"Mr. Mallomar give me this note for you to read." Buster took a doubled up envelope from his pocket and handed it to her. "Dana," it read, "…your current state of freedom is a matter of my discretion. If you give this poor schmuck any trouble while I'm away, so help me God, I'll have you committed to a fucking insane asylum. Don't make me do something we'll both regret. Marvin." Mrs. Mallomar ripped the letter in half, then ripped it in half again and again and again and then maniacally tossed the pieces in the air. Buster maintained a straight-face.

"I'll jes go now and saddle up a horse for ya."

Mrs. Mallomar had little choice but to accompany Buster on horseback to the Dander Ranch. Buster could care less about the cattle, but considered the four mile journey with the missus a task akin to airing out an old sleeping bag. He put Mrs. Mallomar on Hilary, a gentle mare with a wide back and slow gait that rode like a '64 Eldorado. Dressed in black pajamas, a big floppy hat, and large black over-sized sunglasses, Mrs. Mallomar looked a bit like Audrey Hepburn in *Breakfast at Tiffany's* by way of *Apocalypse Now*. Together they clomped along in silence, Buster in the lead. He took a quick look back at her. He couldn't get over what a sour expression she had on her face. It almost made him laugh. Aside from Cookie Dominguez, Buster had never met such tempestuous people as the Mallomars. Anybody around here would have been tickled to have a speck of their money. There would be barbeques and parties. People would be howling at the moon and setting tires on fire. But not the Mallomars. Why did they make everything seem so complicated?

They'd ridden for a mile in silence when Mrs. Mallomar finally spoke.

"What do you say we take a break, Clem?"

Buster reined Stinker over and found a level place for them to rest. Trained from his days with Jimmy Bayles Morgan's outfit, he had brought a blanket to sit on as well as a nice lunch. Mrs. Mallomar had lost so much weight in rehab that her rear end, which in its heyday had been something of a masterpiece, was now flat and bony as a bluegill.

Buster served Mrs. Mallomar a sliced steak sandwich with grilled onions and Swiss cheese on spelt bread that had had its crust removed. She took the sandwich in silence.

"I'm allergic to wheat. This wasn't made with wheat, was it?"

"No, ma'am."

"What've you got to drink?"

Buster got up from the blanket and pulled a shaker out of his saddlebag that was packed with ice. He poured it into a large plastic cup. She looked at it suspiciously.

"What's this?"

"A strawberry milkshake."

Maybe Buster didn't know how to work the coffee machine, but he knew how to work the Hamilton milkshake machine that Mallomar insisted on having. According to Mallomar, not only couldn't he get a proper hamburger in Vanadium, but a decent milkshake either.

"No kidding," she said, slightly impressed.

Mrs. Mallomar ate all of her sandwich and drank her milkshake, then watched Buster carefully unwrap a candy bar as he gazed out at the mountains.

"What's that?"

"Lone Cone Mountain," Buster replied.

"No, what's that in your hand?"

"It's a Payday."

"Well, that's appropriate."

"Beg yor pardon, ma'am?"

"Meeting my husband has certainly been a payday for you."

Buster just looked at her and sadly rewrapped the candy bar, losing his appetite for it. When she saw the look on Buster's face she immediately regretted saying what she'd said."I'm sorry," she said. "I couldn't resist hitting a nice, fat meatball thrown down the middle of the plate."

"That's okay," he said quietly.

"Do you have another...Payday?"

"Sorry, ah don't."

Buster took the candy bar and handed it over to her. Most people would have politely turned down an offer to eat another man's candy bar, but not Mrs. Mallomar.

"My husband made me into this."

That was all she said for the rest of the day. Mrs. Mallomar's inflamed coccyx forced a premature retreat to the ranch.

Once ensconced back at home, she watched from a double cushioned deck chair as Buster unsaddled the horses in the corral. A profound sense of loss swept over her, for this would have been a wonderful moment for a vodka and tonic or a Tom Collins. Or, for that matter, a spicy Bloody Mary with a couple stalks of fresh celery planted in a glass dusted with seasoned salt. Or a nice, cold Chenin Blanc. Christ, she'd even take an Old Milwaukee right now. Did they still make that beer? If she hadn't already gotten off to such a lousy start with Buster, she could have yelled out, "Hey, Clem, what do you say we drive into town and I'll buy you a beer?" But the yokel was under her husband's thumb so there was no use trying that one. Frustrated and angry with herself, she picked up her cell phone and speed dialed her operatives in New York.

CHAPTER TWENTY

Tradecraft

MALLOMAR WAS PICKED UP at Avjet and taken straight to a late night conference in Manhattan with his lawyers. He used three separate firms, so no one knew the complete profile of his holdings, his business methods, or his personal life. The downside was Mallomar's legal triangulation created jealousy and suspicion. For example, the decision as to which firm would host this meeting took five days of haggling. It was only when they received a call from Mallomar informing them that he was "wheels down" that they quickly decided to have the meeting on neutral ground at the Sherry Netherlands. They rented a suite, brought in some vintage wine, and passed around Cuban cigars.

"Marvin, everybody in this room knows the insider trading allegation is absurd." This was coming from his friend, Sidney of Glasker, O'Reilly, Ng, and Erlichmann.

"I'm sure it will be resolved in two seconds tomorrow when you meet with the SEC."

"Have you been thinking about what I should tell them?"

"You simply say that your decision to sell drlivingstonipresume.com was based upon a unique trading method that you've been using throughout your entire trading career."

"I sold drlivingston at the time I did to raise capital for another idea."

"And what was that?"

He lit a cigar and took a sip of whiskey. Mallomar had always been a man of mystery when it came to business, and everyone at the table leaned in expectantly to hear the secrets of the organism.

"I'm not at liberty to say."

"But…we're your lawyers."

"Sorry."

Mallomar saw the looks on their faces and took a large swallow of whiskey. "So, obviously, I have to come up with something else, right?"

"What's so wrong with just telling the truth?" a young attorney's assistant seated against the wall was bold enough to ask.

Mallomar smiled.

"What's his name?" Mallomar inquired of his boss and not him.

"Jeremy Greenberg."

"He's fired."

Jeremy looked to his boss, who remained silent. He swallowed, closed his attaché case and left the room without saying another word. Mallomar addressed the crowd.

"Gentlemen, here's what we know so far. One: everyone in this room is on an exorbitant retainer. Two: I'm not going to jail. Three: you better fucking think of something!"

Outside the Sherry Netherlands, the callow Jeremy Greenberg was waiting in line for a cab. Under the hotel's marquee lights, he looked like a wax version of himself—as if he were about to faint.

"Hey, Greenberg…"

Greenberg turned in shock to see Mallomar. He held out a business card for him.

"This is the number for Albert Kohner of Kohner, Walsh and Anastasia. I called him on my way down the elevator. I told him you're a bright kid and to hire you. You start tomorrow." Before the dumbfounded Greenberg could say anything, Mallomar held up his hand to hail his car and walked out into the street.

His driver wheeled the car to the front curb. It was a bullet-proofed, black Mercedes S65 AMG that was capable of doing over a 205 mph. Mallomar climbed into the back seat and collected himself for a moment as a pulse of adrenaline coursed through his veins. When he was wired like this, there were only two things, besides medication, that could cool him off: food and/or sex.

"Where to, Mr. M?"

"Let's go to Brooklyn and grab something."

The driver turned the car into traffic and headed downtown for the Brooklyn Bridge. On the way there, Mallomar made him stop several times, first at a hot dog stand, then for a gyro truck, and once again for a taco. He could see the driver in the rear view mirror watching him eat.

"Why don't you get something?" Mallomar said.

"I'll eat after I drop you off."

"Get a taco for the ride. I'm in no hurry."

The second the driver got out of the car, Mallomar lunged over the seat to grab his cell phone—which he could see resting in the console. Quickly, he clicked menu>recent calls>received. Up came Dana's private phone number under the code name, WRANGLER.

This was just what Mallomar had suspected. Dana had been paying his driver to spy on him. He could have fired him on the spot, but didn't. It was better to know what was going on and then tailor the information that got back to Colorado. Mallomar returned the phone to its original position just before he got back in the car.

"Should I call Peter Luger's and tell them you're comin'?"

"Naw, I changed my mind. I feel like fish. Let's go to Lure."

The driver called in the reservation and made sure they knew who Mallomar was. He looked up in the rear view mirror to tell Mallomar that he was booked, but Mallomar was on his phone using exasperated gesticulations—indicating it must be a business call he was on. Mallomar knew that he was being watched, and of course, was not on a business call at all. A few minutes later he was delivered to the front door of the restaurant.

"I got you a private booth in the back, Mr. M."

"I'll call you when I'm finished." The driver watched Mallomar go inside and was promptly yelled at by a cop to keep moving. The moment Mallomar saw his driver pull away, he came right back out the door and crossed the street to the Mercer Hotel. There, a room was already waiting for him. He took the key from the front desk with greased efficiency and went upstairs where dinner from Nobu had been cabbed over from Hudson Street—along with two young Asian girls. One of them had been instructed to wear a USC cheerleader's outfit, the other, UCLA. Mallomar, a City College boy himself, had always taken a keen interest in the California schools' rivalry. When he had finished his order of sea urchin tempura, squid pasta, and chi ra shi, he slipped back across the street and called his driver. They stopped at Rice to Riches on Spring Street for some chocolate hazelnut rice pudding and then drove home—Mrs. Mallomar none the wiser.

Mrs. Mallomar called the driver the next day while he waited for Mr. M outside the Securities and Exchange Commission. From a small spiral notebook, he recited the boring details of Mallomar's previous night. The driver's per diem for this kind of work was a thousand dollars. The next call she made was to the doorman of their Fifth Avenue apartment building. The doorman received a $2,500 bounty for any information regarding her husband's misbehavior with guests who looked like hookers. She had the same arrangement with a young female maitre'd at Balthazar where Mallomar was known to have dinner on the way back from the financial district. But Mrs. Mallomar's most important contact in New York was his long-suffering secretary. Mrs. Mallomar had "turned" her many years ago by planting in the secretary's mind the nagging fear that Mallomar could not be relied upon to provide her pension or medical care. Mrs. Mallomar offered her a form of "Co-Pay" in return for clandestine HUMINT. Satisfied from her morning briefing that her husband was too busy trying to save his ass than getting any, she shut down WRANGLER INTEL for the day and decided to take her first sober look around her husband's dream house.

Mallomar, no slouch in the black arts of surveillance himself, had the best security firm in DC make the house "video and audio ready" before it was sheet-rocked. Cameras were integrated into the lighting fixtures in every room, every hallway, the exterior of the house and the outbuildings. Mallomar had his own secret website, and from anywhere in the country—anywhere in the world for that matter—he could, in real time, peer into his house from the privacy of his own laptop. That was exactly what he did the previous night when he came home with his rice pudding. The cameras, positioned on the house's exterior, showed another beautiful Colorado sunset with high cumulus nimbus clouds moving slowly west to east. Mrs. Mallomar was in her room reading the label of, what looked to be, a bottle of furniture polish. Loyal Buster was sleeping on a bed roll on the living room floor. Mallomar switched to a porno site for a few minutes, then called it a night.

The first stop on Mrs. Mallomar's tour of the house was the six-car garage where she hit the first clinker note. The phone box contained eight separate telephone lines. There was a dedicated circuit to the home security system. But it was neither of these that raised her eyebrows as much as did the unlabeled line that was connected to its own auxiliary power source. This could only mean one thing. Off she went to hunt for the video cameras which she was now sure her husband had installed to surveille her. Half an hour later, she was able to locate thirty-five in the interior of the house. To the lens of each, she applied a thin coat of clear nail polish. The thought of her husband spending half his day yelling himself red-in-the-face at his security company, didn't quite bring a smile to Mrs. Mallomar's face, but it did help take her mind off having a drink for the moment.

CHAPTER TWENTY-ONE

Short Reining

THE WATER IN THE newly completed Big Dog reservoir was cold enough to be used as anesthesia, but Buster waded in, nonetheless. Why he didn't bathe in the house was anyone's guess, but pride and not wanting Mrs. Mallomar to know her insults were getting to him, had something to do with it. Within seconds of entering the water, he had lost sensation in his feet and knees. He splashed a little water under his arms and lathered the antibacterial soap that Mallomar used Lady Macbeth-like several times a day to rid himself of filth accumulated under his fingernails. Armpits done, he looked down to his testicles quickly ascending, as if having the good sense of their own to retreat to the warmth and safety of his body cavity. This was the general area—if one were to take everything Mrs. Mallomar said to heart—that needed the most prioritizing. Buster got to work quickly, for although it was only six in the morning, Mrs. Mallomar was a wild card and could not be trusted to sleep late, or do anything for that matter, in a predictable way. Buster held his breath and lowered himself to his neck and scrubbed furiously.

Mrs. Mallomar did not sleep well during the night. Without her prescription sleeping aids, she felt as if she were lashed to a tossing and turning bed of self-loathing and regret. Why was she trying to kill herself? That's exactly what Marvin probably wanted her to do. She needed to take a step back and think this through. Her attempt at a unilateral withdrawal from the battlefield only highlighted her real problem. Lack of self-esteem had "flamed out" her starboard engine and put her in this steep dive. To pull out, she needed a plan—something her husband had obviously implemented for himself. He had brought her out here in the middle of nowhere and cut her off from drugs and alcohol. This, he hoped, would cause her to wig out in a very public way. She had to vitiate his gambit. Unfortunately, she had already dug herself a pretty deep public relations hole by alienating the hired hand, attempting suicide, and exposing the inner workings of the House of Mallomar to a doctor that she had never before laid eyes upon. All of this could be used against her in divorce proceedings. Therefore, things needed, as they say at Langley, to be "cleaned up." Tomorrow would be the first day of her charm offensive starting with the foreman.

Buster figured the two or three minutes he'd spent washing his testicles and cleaning his rectum was good enough. He found that if he kept moving slightly he could escape the filth and scum that was floating to the surface and wanting to buddy back up with him. A rubdown with crumbled sagebrush and he would be ready for the opera. Now as Buster began to wade out of the water, something caught his eye. It was the yardstick that he'd installed alongside the levee to measure the reservoir's water level. To his surprise, it was down slightly. How could that be? It had rained a good inch and a half the night before. Could the reservoir be leaking? Suddenly he was struck with uncontrollable shivers and needed to do the rest of his thinking on dry land. He scrambled up the bank to where Stinker was waiting patiently and dried off with a kitchen towel. Just as he was removing his clean clothes from his saddlebag, he heard a splash behind him. Odd, the reservoir had not yet been stocked with fish. He scanned the shoreline for telltale splash rings. Nothing. The surface was smooth. Then, as he turned back to his horse, he heard another splash. Buster spun around just in time to see the tail of the culprit dive back under the water. It was a muskrat. Muskrats are diminutive versions of beavers and, while they are cute and playful to watch, they're a reservoir's worst enemy. They dig their homes in levees. They start above the water line and go down—creating a honeycomb of tunnels that eventually flood, causing the integrity of the structure to be jeopardized. Buster hurried around the other side of the horse to his rifle scabbard. A one-hundred-yard shot was not out of the question with his 30-40 Krag. Still naked, he tried to stop shivering while he slid back the bolt to chamber a round. Almost imperceptibly, a little black nose broke the surface. He put the bead slightly under the water line and led it a couple of inches as the critter swam on its back. Slowly, he squeezed the trigger.

"What the hell are you doing?"

The muskrat quickly dove back beneath the surface. Buster stood up, forgetting that he had no clothes on. It was Mrs. Mallomar, wearing jeans and one of her husband's cowboy shirts.

"Ma'am, I…"

"Jesus Christ," she said covering her mouth in shock. Having already learned that most people were not like the Svendergards, Buster quickly scrambled around to the other side of Stinker and quickly threw on his jeans.

"Ma'am, lemme 'splain to you about these here muskrats…"

"You don't have to explain anything. There will be no killing on this ranch!"

"But with all due respect, ma'am..." Buster was hopping on one leg trying to get his boot on a wet, numb foot.

"Did you hear what I fucking said? I don't want you fucking shooting anything around here!"

"Yes, ma'am." This, of course, was not how Mrs. Mallomar had wanted things to go today. She softened her tone.

"I don't mean to be a...it's just that..." Now her eyes welled with tears. "Isn't there enough fucking cruelty in this world without you going off and shooting little animals for the hell of it?"

"Ah wern't doin' it for the hell of it, ma'am, ah..."

"Look, I don't care to talk about it anymore. If you need to shoot something, shoot a tin can or that moldy piece of cheese in the refrigerator."

"Tin cans don't tunnel under..." She glowered at him again. "Yes, ma'am, whatever you say."

"You weren't bathing in there were you?"

"Yes, ma'am."

A horrible thought occurred to her.

"Is that the water we drink at the house?"

"No ma'am. Is jes fer irrgayshun." That relaxed her a little.

"Why didn't you use the shower in the maid's quarters?"

"Ah cain't fit inside it, ma'am."

"You can use the guest room facilities if you like." It killed her to say that, but she was struggling to come up with something that would slightly humanize her.

"Much obliged, ma'am, but ah'd druther not make a mess."

"It's a ranch," she said with a winning smile. "Aren't we *supposed* to make a mess?" She wanted to add "...you dumbfuck," but didn't. "Let me ask you something, Clem. When my husband's at the ranch, what does he actually *do* here?" Buster wasn't quite sure what she was referring to, hopefully not Mr. Mallomar's assignations with Mary Boyle.

"Lil' of this...lil' a that," he said noncommittally.

"Well, I want to do a lil' of everything he does."

"Sure yor up to it, ma'am?"

"Just give me something to do. I'll let you be the judge of whether I'm up to it, or not," she said with a defiance that was almost laughable considering her pitiful physical condition.

The first job Buster gave Mrs. Mallomar was to clean out the stalls in the barn. From seven until nine o'clock, she shoveled manure and pitchforked fresh shavings. The cleaning of the Augean stables it was not, but Mrs. Mallomar did get a little wobbly at the end. Buster brought her a glass of ice tea and made her sit down, but she insisted on another job. Buster had her get the horses out in pasture and lead them back to the barn. After that, she spent the rest of the morning mucking the irrigation ditches. Clump pulling would have been back breaking for the strongest of men, but "downward dog" held her in good stead—her only complaint being that she could taste lemon furniture cleaner in her mouth every once in a while when she bent over.

Buster cast a suspicious eye on Mrs. Mallomar's relish for field labor. Even the women who grew up in Vanadium didn't go for clearing irrigation ditches. Buster figured this new wrinkle probably had something to do with her chronic mental troubles that Mallomar so ungallantly revealed to him. After all, there was no other way to explain her compulsion to fraternize with the hung-over field hands, tell dirty jokes or her insistance on riding the tractor cutting alfalfa in the hot sun.

By six o'clock that evening, Mrs. Mallomar was sunburned and filthy, but sober.

"Hey, could we go for a drive in your truck?" Buster made the mistake of letting her get behind the wheel. She was a much better driver than her husband. She drove for two hours due west toward Utah—fast—as if she were trying to escape Mountain Standard Cocktail Time. As they drove through Redvale, a truck with halogen headlights and an LED light bar on the roof came up behind them and followed on their bumper. There was no place to pass on this winding road and Buster, finally unnerved by it, had Mrs. Mallomar pull over to the shoulder and let it pass. There was not one blacked-out Suburban, but four. They accelerated in unison and headed off into the night toward Egnar.

"What the hell was that?" Mrs. Mallomar asked.

Of course, she had no way of knowing that the black ops caravan had been ordered by her husband—a DEA team on their way to Cookie Dominguez's compound. And they weren't the only ones who had taken note. Across the road in the darkness, a Harley was kicked started. A Busy Bee scout made a call from his cell phone and then tailed the intruders. Unfortunately for Buster, it appeared to the lookout that Buster had led the DEA men there.

It was past nine o'clock when Buster and Mrs. Mallomar returned to Vanadium.

"Is there any place to grab a bite around here?" Mrs. Mallomar asked.

"There's a coupla places in town still open, ah guess. There's the Bo-ho Coffee Shop and the, uh, High Grade."

"The High Grade. Isn't that the place my husband goes?"

"Yes, ma'am. He's partial to it, but ah really don't think yood like it ver much."

"Why's that?"

"Don't mean to be rude, ma'am, but they serve alcohol in there." Mrs. Mallomar flashed indignant, but seemed to realize she had relinquished the moral high ground when she drank furniture polish.

"All right, I've been fair warned. Where is it?"

Mrs. Mallomar gunned the engine and tore the two blocks down Main Street then made a hard right on two wheels into the High Grade's parking lot. With balls as big as any man's on Lame Horse Mesa, she parked in the handicap spot five feet from the front door—immediately drawing fire from the locals' faces sitting in the window booth.

The High Grade, under the constabulary of Sheriff Dudival, was the only restaurant in Colorado where cigarette smoking had not followed the statewide ban. Buster led Mrs. Mallomar through a blue mist atomized with Marlboro red smoke and French fry grease to a vacant booth. Buster felt the eyes of every patron on him. So did Mrs. Mallomar, who had already affixed a phony smile to her face. Buster stopped to say hello to Sheriff Dudival and Jimmy Bayles Morgan, who sneered, as if Buster had just waved Limburger cheese under her nose. She seemed like she'd lost weight, but maybe it was because Buster had spent so much time with Marvin Mallomar that everyone looked thin by comparison. The sheriff asked how the truck was running and if he'd seen a Mexican camped up in the tree line that had stabbed a chiropractor in Telluride. Buster said that he hadn't and quickly caught up with Mrs. Mallomar to make sure she didn't order a double Grey Goose with pickled onions before he got there. This was the first time that anyone in town, besides Doc Solitcz, had laid eyes on Mrs. Mallomar. They'd heard rumors about her, of course, but no one was quite ready for the way she looked—which was as disheveled as Howard Hughes at the Desert Inn.

Two tables away, Destiny Stumplehorst and her sisters were having dinner with their mother and father. Mrs. Mallomar caught Buster sneaking looks at them.

"Who's that?"

"The Stumplehorsts. They were my folks for a while."

"You were an orphan?"

"Yes, ma'am."

"Lucky fuckin' you. What about Heidi over there—with the ponytail braids?"

"She was sorta my girlfriend."

"What happened?"

"Her folks thought she could do better'n me."

"My, I find *that* very hard to believe!" Then, when she saw the way Buster's face fell quickly said, "I'm *kid-ding*." She caught Destiny scoping her and Buster again, immediately identifying the dynamic. "So, where's the can?"

Buster gestured to the narrow corridor in the back. Mrs. Mallomar sauntered to the back, along the way pausing to study everyone's food.

Mrs. Mallomar was only gone in the bathroom for ten minutes. In the meantime, Buster, knowing that everybody was looking at him, scrutinized his knife and fork and performed some preemptive cleaning of Mrs. M's silverware so she wouldn't complain and draw further attention. In the corner of his eye, he was watching to see if Destiny Stumplehorst was watching him. She wasn't. She was watching the woman who had just emerged from the bathroom.

Mrs. Mallomar had, to Buster's astonishment, given herself a complete makeover—using what little that was available to her in the grimy bathroom. She had dusted herself off. She had washed her face with the pink liquid soap from the gummed-up dispenser. She had fixed her hair with a twenty-five cent comb she bought from the machine—next to the one that advertised a fifty-cent product called *Hard Charger*—tied it back with her blue bandana and used a lipstick for her lips as well as impromptu rouge. She had also removed her brassiere and unbuttoned her blouse to a V-neck. There was not a man in the place whose jaw was not unhinged at the sight of what was easily the most beautiful woman they had ever seen. She kept her eyes fixed on Buster as she walked slowly, hips swaying, back to the table. Buster fiddled with his cigarette makings and shot a quick nervous glance at Destiny Stumplehorst. Destiny was looking gaga at the two of them, her strawberry blush above her collarbone, once again, giving her position away.

Mrs. Mallomar slid daintily into the booth and took the cigarette Buster was rolling out of his hands and stuck it in her mouth. When Buster reached across the table with a shaky hand to light it, she gave him a little, naughty wink that was downstage to Destiny. After an eight-count, Destiny excused herself from her parents' table and hurried outside, her sisters following. Mrs. Mallomar snorted softly, took a deep drag on her cigarette and turned her attention to the sticky laminated menu—front and back—then tossed it down.

"What does my husband have here?" She was staring at him in such a way that it shook Buster's confidence to deliver the obvious answer.

"Uh…" She cocked her head at him.

"You said he eats here…"

"Yes, ma'am."

"So, what does he *have*? Is that such a difficult question?"

"Chicken-fried steak," Buster said with a thick tongue.

Up her arm went—with a light snapping of the fingers—to flag down the waitress. To Buster's chagrin, their waitress was Mary Boyle. Mary, as well as Buster, looked as if she was about to walk a plank.

"Hey there, Buster."

"Hey there, Mary. Mary, this here's Mrs. Mallomar."

The two women assessed each other.

"Hello," they both said.

"Uh, Mrs. Mallomar, Mary here was my adopted mother fer a piece."

"I thought you said Old Sourpuss over there was your mother."

"Mary was my mother b'fore Mrs. Stumplehorst was my mother."

"Buster's had four mothers. Didn't he tell you that?" said Mary.

Mrs. Mallomar studied Mary for a moment.

"Do you know how to make an Arnold Palmer?" said Mrs. Mallomar.

"Sure," Mary said, in a poisonous tone. "What would you like for your entrée?" *Entrée.* That was a good one in a place like this, but Mrs. Mallomar let it go.

"Chicken-fried steak. My husband can't say enough about it."

"Yes, he likes his chicken-fried steak."

"I bet he does."

Mary held steady. She had dropped "flinching" from her personal menu the moment Bob had his sweetbreads shish-kabobbed on Highway 145. Mary turned to Buster.

"What'll you have, hon?"

Buster was staring off at the Coors beer sign—which featured a snow-capped peak and a clear mountain stream tumbling over boulders in the foreground. Buster wished he were there right now.

"Buster?" Mary asked again.

"Oh, uh…double burger, fries."

"Drink?"

He wanted a beer but checked his swing, remembering Mrs. Mallomar's condition. "Root beer."

"Okay, it'll be right up." Mary turned to go. Buster almost exhaled with relief.

"Oh, Mary…"

Mary stopped and turned around.

"Yes, Mrs. Mallomar?"

"I was just admiring your necklace. May I see it?"

Mary blinked. Slowly she came back to the table and with a shaky hand opened the top of her blouse to reveal a thin gold strand of tiny ivy leaves dotted with small diamonds.

"Is that a Cheryl Rydmark?"

"I…I really couldn't say."

"It's very pretty."

"Thank you."

They smiled at each other and Mary left again.

"Hey, Clem, I don't know if I can eat right now. Mind if you get something to eat back at the house?"

"No, ma'am."

They got up and walked out. Buster took care of the bill at the register. When he got out to the parking lot, Mrs. Mallomar was already in the passenger seat.

"Doncha wanna drive, ma'am?" Buster said timidly.

"Is she the reason why you wanted me to eat at the coffee house?"

"Ah don't know what yor talkin' about, ma'am."

"I think you do." Mrs. Mallomar took Buster's hand and placed something in it. Under the sodium parking light he could see it was a gold necklace, the same one Mary was wearing.

"Why don't you give this to your girlfriend?"

"Ma'am, I…"

Mrs. Mallomar almost laughed at his befuddlement, but what Buster saw, for just a moment, was a fighter who had taken a punch, but still didn't know yet that she was going down for the count.

"Don't say anything, okay? It'll only come out stupid."

"Yes, ma'am."

Buster put the truck in gear and drove down Main Street to the Lame Horse Mesa road and took a right. Mrs. Mallomar had her face turned to her window, but he could tell she was crying. He had an impulse to put a comforting hand on her shoulder, but stopped himself.

Meanwhile, twenty miles away in Egnar, neighboring ranchers thought they heard the *pop pop pop* of fireworks from Cookie Dominguez's compound—after all, they *did* sell fireworks. But it was automatic gunfire they were hearing. The DEA had rammed the chain link fence and taken the place with shock and awe—unfortunately unaware that they were already too late. Cookie's scout had called to say that they had company. Cookie had shrewdly placed the mobile home meth lab directly over the septic tank. There was a hatch in the floor that allowed them to dump incriminating evidence directly into a place that not even law enforcement would dare to tread. Cookie endured some grief about the equipment on hand, but the Feds had nothing substantial on which to hang a righteous indictment and left with egg on their faces. Cookie lost close to a hundred thousand dollars in product—his adopted brother, Buster, fingered as the rat.

Oblivious to the new trouble that soon awaited him, Buster headed his truck up the driveway to the house. He wanted the evening to end as soon as possible, but the uphill slog through the crushed gravel driveway to the front door slowed down Mrs. Mallomar excruciatingly as if she was trapped on a runaway truck ramp. He waited for her at the front door.

"G'night, ma'am."

"Aren't you going to have something to eat?"

"Ah ain't really hungry, ma'am."

"That's not fair. I didn't let you have your dinner."

"That's all right, ma'am. You must be pretty tuckered out. Why don't we all jes turn in?"

"You're probably right." Mrs. Mallomar walked up the stairs and stopped at the balcony, looking down at Buster laying out his bed roll on the living room floor.

"Was she a good mother to you?"

"Beg pardon, ma'am?"

"Was…Mary…good to you?"

Buster tried to think of the right answer under the circumstances, but couldn't, so he went with the truth.

"Yes, ma'am."

Mrs. Mallomar immediately put her face in her hands and ran into her room. Buster sat downstairs and listened to her cry for almost three and half hours—staccato whimpers, followed by outright baby-bawling. When it had finally stopped, he tiptoed up to her room and put his ear to the door. He could hear her snoring softly. Relieved, he went to the refrigerator, got himself a glass of milk, and went to sleep next to the Citizen Kane–sized fireplace.

Buster dreamed that Destiny was hopping mad with jealousy and demanded to know what was going on between him and Mrs. Mallomar. Buster started to explain that nothing was going on—but his experiences with the Mallomars told him to hold his cards close to the vest. "Why don't we start with you and that thar real 'state agint?"

"There's nothing goin' on. I don't know why people are always jawin' about that!" Buster McCaffrey, having seen it with his own eyes, knew that to be false. Then, as if in dreamlike punishment for her gall, a grease fire broke out in the kitchen. Mary ran out of the kitchen and stood in front of him, arms akimbo, ablaze. In the center of her chest, Buster could see her tortured, beating heart. Buster leaped from the booth and threw his body on top of hers, hugging her tightly and smothering the flames. When it was extinguished, Mary looked demurely to the side. Buster took this as a signal that laying on top of her was not right—she having been his mother for six weeks. No sooner did this thought transmit than Buster heard Destiny Stumplehorst scream with alarm behind him. She had burst into flames as well. Buster quickly got off Mary Boyle—who was smoldering, but safely extinguished, and leaped on top of his one true love. He hugged her, smothered her, so hard he could hear the air wheeze from her lungs.

"Buster," she said. "You always save me. Am I worth it?"

"Yes," Buster said and kissed her. And then for the first time since he began dreaming about her, she didn't prevent him from making love to her. Mary had retreated discreetly to the kitchen to continue dredging chicken legs and breasts in her patented chicken-fried steak flour. Buster and Destiny shed their clothes and made love on the gritty linoleum floor with much pent-up energy that reached its denouement with Destiny on top—riding Buster like a horse. They cantered, loped, then galloped to a climax.

Buster woke up from his dream covered in perspiration to find Mrs. Mallomar on top of him. She was sitting upright, her eyes closed tightly in ecstasy.

"Mrs. Mallomar!"

She opened her eyes wide.

"Jesus, you've got a big dick!"

"Jiminy Christmas, what've ah done did?"

"You've done good, Clem. You've done good."

She dismounted him and walked a little wobbly to the chair where he had thrown his clothes.

"Mind if I roll myself a cigarette?"

"Mrs. Mallomar, jes what were you thinkin'?"

"Payback," she said calmly as she licked two Zig-Zags together. "Isn't that the name of your favorite candy bar?"

"Payday."

"Payday, Payback…"

Buster put his head in his hands.

"Mr. Mallomar's my friend…"

"He's nobody's friend. It's about time someone broke that to you."

Buster and Mrs. Mallomar tried to pretend that nothing had happened. Nobody was fooling anybody, but that's the way they played it. Around ten every night, Mrs. Mallomar would tiptoe downstairs where Buster slept on his bedroll by the fireplace. She would arouse him, but he would pretend not to be awakened. She would then mount him, grind away to a climax then hurry back to her room before the first nocturnal snap of the mousetrap could be heard under the three-thousand-dollar stainless steel sink. Buster never betrayed their conceit by laying a hand on her. Only later would Buster experiment with dreamlike verisimilitude—mumbling as if talking in his sleep, or sometimes giving a little snore—as if this could somehow absolve him of guilt. In the morning, they would return to business as usual—Mrs. Mallomar, thorny and sarcastic with regard to Buster's misuse of the English language and his lack of worldly experience; Buster going about his chores on the ranch. If there was any good news to be extracted from their liaison, it was that Mrs. Mallomar no longer spent her days craving alcohol or narcotics. The bad news was that she had transferred her addiction to the innocent Buster. Mrs. Mallomar only thought of one thing while performing her arduous chores during the day—it was not as much Buster, but Buster's johnson. Her appetite for food came back with a vengeance. She gained twelve pounds—her bosoms and rear end refilled to their former head-turning capacities. And she found herself, for the first time in years, happy.

Buster, on the other hand, was miserable. His great beacon of manners and morality, *Miss Humphrey's*, would certainly have not approved of his actions. Rumors were starting to spread through town. Even worse, his heart belonged to Destiny Stumplehorst and this betrayal—even though she had abandoned him for Cord Travesty—was too much for him to bear. He wanted to cut things off with Mrs. Mallomar. He really did. He just didn't do it.

ᘓ

FIVE DAYS OF TESTIMONY and Mallomar was finally finished with the SEC. He returned to his apartment and after lightening his spirits with a Ukrainian call girl, he decided to go online and gaze at his ranch through the miracle of the Big Dog Ranch webcam. The interior cameras were still on the fritz, but he was pleased to see the exterior cameras were working fine. The grass was coming in nicely. He switched to another monitor. There were cattle at the edge of the reservoir drinking contentedly. He was sorry he had missed the branding. The cattle looked healthy enough, but he was a little miffed that Buster had not followed up on his aesthetic notion of hosing off the caked-on shit from their hindquarters.

Before turning in for the night, he remembered that he'd placed a lipstick camera surreptitiously in the ceiling of Buster's trailer. He clicked on the TrailerCam. The image was almost infrared, the trailer being lit by moonlight as it was. There was Buster asleep. He dialed the phone number and was already starting to chuckle when he saw another figure in the lower right side of the frame. It was a woman. She was on top of Buster. Her back was to the camera. She was bouncing up and down on his lap in a very familiar way that he couldn't quite place for a moment—until it dawned on him that that was the way he'd seen Dana ride her horse up to Hope Lake the fateful day they all met.

CHAPTER TWENTY-TWO

The Lightning Strike

IT WAS COMPLETELY BY accident that Jimmy Bayles Morgan had run into Lily and Lolly Longfeather at St. Mary's Hospital in Grand Junction. The girls had driven all the way in the thunderstorm from the res in Cortez to bring their grandfather his favorite meal—which was a "McRibwich," along with taco-flavored Doritos, homemade fry bread smothered with refried beans, farmers' cheese, habanero salsa, and Twizzlers. He had to eat it before 6:00 p.m. The anesthesiologist would not allow any food after that because the old Ute was scheduled to have both of his legs amputated the next morning—the reason, advanced diabetes. Jimmy was genuinely saddened to hear this news.

Old Longfeather had done some tracking for her grandfather back in the day, and had sent three of his young braves to Vietnam. For Jimmy, that put him on the righteous side of the anti-communist ledger. Longfeather was also a shaman and was said to have great powers. Longfeather was very much against modern medicine, but was forced to rethink his position when his toes turned black and the poison traveled all the way up to his knees.

"How's the old coyote's spirits?" Jimmy asked.

"Oh, he's fine," said Lilly.

"He ain't broke up 'bout losin' his wheels?"

"He says good riddance," Lolly chirped.

"'Good riddance,' eh?" Jimmy said with a head scratch. "Mighty bold. Has he thought 'bout what he's gonna do once they's gone?"

"He's gonna grow new ones."

"Them Jew doctors tell'm that…that he'd grow new ones?" asked Jimmy.

"No, no. It came to him in a vision…in sweat lodge."

The girls went on to tell Jimmy about the shaman's dream that had come to him six months prior. "The Great Spirit is returning to Our Mother. There will be a Great Storm, and he will be Reborn in the form of the first Red Man. The Great Spirit will seek out grandfather because he will need a shaman to interpret the ancient language, which our people have forgotten how to speak. As his reward, the Great Spirit will give grandfather new legs—much better than the old ones."

"Sounds like a damn good deal to me," was all Jimmy could cough up. This kind of talk about faith and spirituality made Jimmy's skin crawl, but she didn't want to rain dance on the old shaman's parade. She steered the conversation over to gossip. White people, in general, treated the Indian girls as if they were deaf or couldn't understand English. As a result, Lily and Lolly overheard all the town's gossip. This was how Jimmy learned that Buster had won the no-talking bet with Mallomar and how Mrs. Mallomar at first tried to get rid of Buster, but was now was having sex with him while Mallomar was out of town.

"Now wait a minute. Don't be passin' that around. Buster McCaffrey ain't havin' sex with that damn scarecrow!"

"Yes, he is. It's true."

"Did you see it with your own *eyes*?"

"No, we didn't see it with our own eyes, but we know."

"How's that?"

The girls looked at each other.

"Hey, we're from a family of *trackers,*" Lilly giggled. "We do the *laundry*." The rain poured off Jimmy's hat extinguishing her cigarette. She may have blinked, but she didn't give anything away.

"Well, whaddaya think of that?" she said.

Jimmy again wished their grandfather good luck and sloshed back in the rain to her truck. Her blood was pounding in her ears so loudly she couldn't hear her own yelling and cursing. Leaving the parking lot, Jimmy tossed her nasal canula aside and floored it—proceeding to sideswipe four cars—three of them on purpose—the fourth while attempting to light a cigarette.

That Jimmy had just learned that her lung cancer had advanced to her brain and that she had two weeks, maybe three, to live was inconsequential. She had kept her mouth shut when Mallomar bought the ranch. She held her fire when he bought all of the buildings in her town and transformed them for his own convenience—because it provided jobs for people who didn't have one, but now this. Buster McCaffrey had been *Mallomarized.* This, she could not abide.

ꟸ

IT TOOK THE BETTER part of the day and thirteen loads with a twenty-four-foot trailer to bring Mallomar's newly purchased Belted Galloways to the Big Dog Ranch. Thinking they might be stressed from the ride, Buster and Stinker led them up to the reservoir to water. They were beautiful cattle all right. Buster watched as one particular steer drank the water, ate grass, shit. He had been on a ranch in Utah this morning and now he was here. Did he just accept that some unknown force drove his life? Did he have any idea that he would end up on a plate by the fall of next year? Had he ever betrayed a friendship? Buster didn't want to go back to the house, but he knew that he had to. He mounted up.

As Buster rode back to the barn, one of the Blue Heelers sprinted to him, banjo-eyed, whining from fear. Buster dismounted and slid his carbine out of the scabbard. Mountain lion? He chambered a round and approached softly on the balls of his feet. As he rounded the corner to the corrals, he saw the source of the poor dog's panic.

Jimmy Bayles Morgan was in the corral swinging one of the Blue Heelers by his back legs. Buster raised his rifle in the air and discharged a round. Jimmy let go of the dog and he went flying.

"What the hell're ya doin' shootin' that fuckin' thing?"

"What the hell're ya doin' with my dog?"

"Ah was jes tryin' to git him to shut the fuck up and he fuckin' bit me."

Jimmy held up her hand for Buster to see. She was bleeding from a couple of punctures on the drumstick of her left thumb. Buster looked to his dog, cowering away from her.

"Best you go."

"Now hold on there, Cisco. Ah come up here fer a powwow."

"You and me got nothin' to say to each other."

"Still aggrieved 'bout them damn letters, are ya?"

"That's raht."

"What'f ah said ah were sorry? Would that make it better fer ya?"

"Well ah 'ccept, then."

"Ah didn't say ah 'pologized. Ah jes said, what *if*. But, since yor bein' big about it, ah'll tender my 'pology in full and 'ccept yor forgiveness."

"Why, if you ain't somethin'..."

"Ah'll have a cold beer if yor offerin'."

Buster led Jimmy away from the house into the barn—more luxurious than her own house. She kept nodding her head with approval in a way that seemed mocking to Buster. He sat her down on a hay bale in his tack room where Mallomar had installed a refrigerator. He sat opposite.

"It's got that new barn smell, don't it?" she said as she popped the top of a Colorado Fat Tire.

"Why'd you come up here?"

"Well, ah heard somethin' 'bout you today… kinda tickled me."

"Oh yeah? What?"

"That yor carryin' on with this here Mal-lee-mar woman." Buster's face fell. "Ah knew it was horseshit. Cause yor stupid, but ah know you ain't *that* stupid." Buster didn't say anything. His eyes filled with tears. Jimmy had bushwhacked him. "Why you fuckin' idiot. Ah oughta smash this bottle over yor head!"

"Do ya think…Destiny knows 'bout this?"

"Oh, who the fuck cares what she thinks? She'd suck hairy balls for a sniff a cocaine."

"Ah toldja, ah don't like it when you talk 'bout her like that."

"Now lissen ta me and lissen good. Ah may be the only real fren you got and what ah'm sayin' is you gotta quit this job and git outta here, right now! A coupla fuckin' vampires is what these people is!"

"Ah don't work for you no more. You ain't my dang boss."

Jimmy leaned in.

"Don't crowd me, mister. Ah got a mind to kick yor ass." Buster put his face in his hands and started to blubber.

"Ah made a mess a ever'thing."

"Well…ah ain't above tellin' ya ah tole you so." Jimmy took off her nasal canula and lit a cigarette. "Lookie here, ah come with a li'l propa-zishun."

"What?"

“How much Mallomar pay you still got?”

“Almost all a it. Thirty-two thousand four hundred and twenty-three cents.”

“All right. Tell ya what ah’m gonna do. Ah’m gonna let you buy inta my ranch fifty-fifty and pay the rest off ov’r tahm.”

“What? Why in tarnation you doin’ that?”

Jimmy took a beat before answering.

“Cause ah seen what you did up here for Mal-lee-mar, and ah figger if’n you do the same for me, we’ll both make out like bandits.”

“No, thanks.”

Jimmy was shot that her largesse was so quickly dismissed.

“Why you mo-ron! Why the hell not?”

“Ah’m too ‘shamed to live here no more. Ah’m gittin’ out.”

“The hell you say.”

“Ah mean it. Ah’m packin’ up t’night.”

“Ah’ll be damned! Ah allus thought you was a man.”

“Yeah, well ah could say the same ’bout you!”

Before he could get his hands up, Jimmy slammed a right cross into Buster’s jaw knocking him off his hay bale, unconscious. She casually finished her beer, slung her oxygen over her shoulder and left, but first stopping to examine a new bridle she saw hanging on the wall. After fingering its quality, Jimmy decided to help herself to it. When she got into her truck, she considered going back inside the barn to see if Buster was all right, but then shrugged it off.

“Fuck it.”

She threw her truck into reverse and immediately smacked into something hard behind her.

“What the hell now!”

She turned to see that she had backed into Shep Dudival’s police cruiser. He was walking up to her window.

“What’re you doin’ lurkin back there for?”

"That's not what you say when you back into someone..." Dudival said. "Especially if it's the sheriff."

"Looks like ah'm gonna be spendin' the rest of my fuckin' life apologizin'!"

"You and Buster have a meeting of the minds?"

"Inna manner a speakin'."

"Good. Glad to hear it. Is he in there?"

"He is, but he's unconshuns."

"Oh, for Christsake..."

"Sonofabitch smart...mouthed...me." Jimmy barely got the words out before she started coughing so violently that she keeled over. Dudival opened the door and pulled her upright.

"What can I get you?"

"My tank's behind the seat," she gasped.

Dudival rummaged behind the seat, clipped the canula onto her nose and opened the oxygen valve. Jimmy took a couple of deep snorts then pushed him away.

"What'd you want to say to him that was so damn emportant?"

"I got one of Cookie Dominguez's guys in jail on a eighteen-three-four-o-two. He tried to plea out with some information. Did you know that Mr. Mallomar asked for the DEA to come in here without my authority?"

"He can't do that."

"Well, he did it. They tried to bust Cookie."

"They git'm?"

"No. They didn't. And Cookie thinks Buster informed on him."

"Does Buster know this?"

"That's why I came up here. Cookie put a contract out on him. Twenty-five thousand."

"What 'xactly you gonna do 'bout it?"

"I'm going to have a talk with him."

"He wants to kill that boy and yor gonna have a *talk* with him?"

"I can't arrest him on hearsay."

"Partner, you are a dizgrace ta the badge my Grampie wore."

"Sorry you feel that way."

"Yeah, now move that fuckin' vee-hackle!"

"Hold on! You're in no condition to drive. You should be in the hospital."

"Git outta my way, damn coward!"

Jimmy put her truck back into reverse and hit the gas, pushing Dudival's squad car about twenty feet. She then wheeled around, spraying gravel on him as she tore away. This was not the first time time that Shep Dudival had disappointed the Morgans.

CHAPTER TWENTY-THREE

The Past Has a Half-Life

TWENTY-FIVE YEARS AGO, AFTER his aborted attempt to seduce Jimmy at the County Fair, the young Dudival returned to the sheriff's office to change out of his wet clothes. He ran into Sheriff Morgan who was dragging a drunken cowboy through booking. He had already beaten the crap out of him and was taking the subject's limp hand, pressing the fingers on the inkpad for fingerprinting.

"I heard you and Jimmy had a bit of a romp down at the river."

"We just went for a walk."

"That's not the way Jimmy tells it."

"Then why ask if you already know?"

Sheriff Morgan was not used to his deputy talking to him that way and reacted as if he had just been brushed back by a high inside pitch.

"She was confused by you," he said as he put his boot in the small of the cowboy's back and pushed him into a cell. "I told you that was going to happen."

"That's not the way I behave around women," Shep Dudival said and turned his back on him and walked out.

"No, it evidently is not," Sheriff Morgan said.

From that moment on, the sheriff wondered whether his trust in the new deputy had been misplaced. His suspicions were confirmed later that week. There was a union rally scheduled at the International Order of Odd Fellows Hall. Snitches had told Morgan that Ned Gigglehorn was going to introduce two visiting officials from the AFL in Michigan. Outside agitators were going to try to convince the uranium miners to go out on a wildcat strike—and stay out until the company agreed to guarantee a health and pension fund. Sheriff Morgan could not abide that and set into motion a plan to intercept Gigglehorn and the union officials before they ever got to the hall.

Word had gotten back to Sheriff Morgan that Gigglehorn had taken the union men the Suit Yourself Bar. They had chosen the back table in case they needed to make a quick exit if the goon squad arrived through the front. The two union boys were big, fleshy-nosed brawlers who demonstrated a great capacity for boilermakers. These men were used to traveling in hostile environments like Vanadium and were heeled.

At this point in time, there was no bathroom in the Suit Yourself bar. One had to go outside to the four-seater that was built over a lime pit. That's where the sheriff, Deputy Dudival, and Deputy Grizzard waited in the dark for the beer to do its work. The first man to relieve himself was O'Neill. As soon he unzipped, they jumped him and yanked his suit coat over his head, binding his arms so he couldn't grab for his revolver. He put up a pretty good fight—his urine spraying hither and yon on each officer. Finally, they hit him on the head with the toilet seat and he crumpled. He was quickly cuffed and dragged into the bushes where Deputy Grizzard gave him one last kick in the ribs for despoiling his clean uniform.

Inside, Gigglehorn and Polaski started to wonder what had happened to their colleague. Cautiously, they stepped outside in the dark.

"O'Neill?"

There was no answer. Polaski stepped up to the shithouse door. "You all right, Timmy?" Still no answer. Polaski pulled a little .32 Colt automatic from his waistband and opened the door. He was immediately rendered unconscious by Sheriff Morgan—who was waiting for him with a Vanadium Bank deposit bag filled with steel washers. With two down, the goons descended upon Ned Gigglehorn with their batons. Gigglehorn fell to the ground, his eyes rolling back in their sockets. Sheriff Morgan stood over him.

"Goddamn you, Gigglehorn. What have I got to do to shut that yap of yours?" Gigglehorn answered by grabbing the sheriff's balls and trying with his last bit of strength to twist them off. Sheriff Morgan, in excruciating pain, fired his gun, sending a load of graphite and steel shavings into Ned's face.

"My eyes!" Gigglehorn screamed in agony.

After the Vietnam War, the doctors at the VA hospital had assured Shep Dudival's mother that one day her son would snap out of whatever nightmare he had been living. Dudival looked down at Ned Gigglehorn, 'coon-faced. And he woke up.

"I threw her out the helicopter," Dudival said quietly.

Sheriff Morgan, in a crouched position trying to restore order to his scrotum, gathered himself and faced Deputy Dudival. There was no question that he had a weak link in his midst.

"What the hell was that about?" Deputy Dudival had his eyes glued to Gigglehorn writhing on the ground.

"Nothing," Dudival replied dully. Sheriff Morgan lifted Dudival's Smith & Wesson out of his service holster and clapped it in his hand.

"Then shoot that communist sonofabitch!" Dudival slowly raised his eyes from Gigglehorn to his boss. He looked at him in a way that Sheriff Morgan did not like. Then Dudival raised the gun. The barrel started to come Sheriff Morgan's way—prompting him to quickly lay his hand on the butt of his own pistol. Behind Dudival's back, Deputy Grizzard was posed to sap him, but Dudival reholstered his weapon and bent down to Gigglehorn.

"What's gotten into you, man?"

Dudival didn't answer. To Morgan's utter astonishment, he lifted Gigglehorn to his feet, threw him over his shoulder and carried him out to his cruiser. If he took Gigglehorn to the miner's clinic, they would probably kill him. Instead, he drove to Dr. Solitcz's still extant house. Gigglehorn, as it turned out, would lose only partial sight in his left eye, but his face would be blackened for life. Only prostitutes, from then on, would ever call him "handsome."

Sheriff Morgan and Deputy Grizzard smuggled the two union organizers onto a freight train in Grand Junction. Authorities found the dead men the next afternoon in Chicago. The bartender at the Suit Yourself was frightened enough of Morgan to testify to the Colorado Bureau of Investigation that the union men had been drinking in his bar then left out the back entrance. That was all he knew. There was no one to connect Morgan to the murders except his deputies.

Two weeks later, Grizzard was found in his skivvies floating face down in Svendergard's quarry. He had apparently been drinking—this according to Sheriff Morgan who wrote the coroner's report himself. Dudival did not need to be paranoid to believe that Morgan was "tidying things up." What had been keeping him alive so far was Morgan's hope that Dudival could somehow change Jimmy's sexuality. But that bit of matchmaking had come a cropper and Dudival knew he was now—like the late Deputy Grizzard—a liability.

The miner's union, in the meantime, did not take the murder of their comrades well. They, like everybody else, knew who was responsible and implemented their vendetta. Hubris, as is so often the case, ended up being Sheriff Morgan's undoing. His assumption that he was at the top of the Vanadian food chain caused him to violate the cardinal rule for any man who carries a gun for a living: never be a creature of habit, and never let your guard down. Morgan arose everyday at the same time. Had coffee at the same café at the same time. Had his lunch at the High Grade at the same time and took his nap in the alley next to the Geiger Motel at the same time. People who do things the same way all the time are a joy to assassins—in this case, two large men from the union who came to town dressed like lumberjacks and checked into the Victorian Vanadium Hotel. They claimed they were in town looking for work. This information was passed on, in the style of the Romanian Secret Police, from informant to informant to Sheriff Morgan. He saw them once or twice walking around town in heavy woolen trousers and plaid shirts and swallowed their cover story.

The special at the High Grade on Fridays featured an open-faced turkey sandwich on a slice of white bread, covered in giblet gravy with mashed potatoes and a side of cranberry sauce for $3.99. Sheriff Morgan polished off his lunch with a glass of milk and a piece of rhubarb pie. He left a small tip, but didn't pay. He never paid for anything in Vanadium. Such was the fear he inspired in everyone. Grabbing a peppermint from the bowl at the register, he walked across the street to the liquor store. He didn't go inside, but around to the back where he examined the lock on the door. He opened a set of picks in a leather wallet and proceeded to select the correct combination that would allow him to open the door in the wee hours of the morning, setting off the burglar alarm and bringing Deputy Dudival to the call. After going through several picks, Morgan found the two that worked and wrapped them with scotch tape so he could identify them in the dark. When Dudival came through the door that night, he would then shoot him with an old twelve-gauge goose gun he kept for such purposes, loaded with untraceable blue whistlers. The plan implemented, Sheriff Morgan warbled a little bird whistle as he walked back across the street to his cruiser and pulled it into the alley beside the Geiger Motel. It was shady there and was his favorite place to nap, or "coop" in policeman's parlance. In no time at all he was snoring up a storm, oblivious to the lumbermen who crossed the street behind him carrying a two-man saw. Very deliberately, they set to work on the telephone pole behind the sheriff's car—timing each saw stroke with the sheriff's own adenoidal wood cutting. It took them eight exchanges of the saw and a gentle push to send the telephone pole crashing down on top of the cruiser—flattening the sheriff's skull with such force that his brains extruded out his ears like Frosty Freeze.

Deputy Dudival watched this rendition of a classic Tex Avery cartoon through the Venetian blinds of his dentist's office. Pericoronitis had demanded the removal of both his third upper molars. The righteous police officer in Dudival was telling him to get up from the dentist's chair and do something about this, but the mask of laughing gas over his mouth and nose was telling him to sit back down and enjoy the show. And so, he took a deep, deep breath of gas and watched as the men dropped their saw, their gloves, walked calmly to a dark sedan and drove away.

When it came time to make the arrangements for the funeral, Deputy Dudival was at Jimmy's side handling everything. He chose the coffin, a mahogany laminated "Plainsman." A guest list was comprised befitting a man of the sheriff's stature, included the Mine's top brass, the mayor, fellow sheriffs from neighboring counties and the Vanadium High School band. They played "Requiem" on Jews' harps—

for this was years before Buster, with Mr. Mallomar's checkbook, had supplied the high school with real musical instruments. On the day, more than three hundred people showed up at Lone Pine Cemetery—some, admittedly, were there to make sure the sheriff's demise was not just another Vanadium rumor. The President of the Vanadium Rotary, in lieu of a padre, spoke a few words over the Colorado-flagged coffin—for Sheriff Morgan was not a religious man. Jimmy didn't cry or in any way betray her real emotions—one of them a nonspecific feeling that Dudival could have done more to protect her grandfather. After the funeral, Dudival considered turning in his badge, but didn't. Jimmy was exposed without her grandfather. Whether she realized it or not, she needed him. And, of course, he loved her.

CHAPTER TWENTY-FOUR

Blood

On the way home from the Big Dog Ranch, Jimmy stopped to see the only person who knew how handle a situation that had gotten out of control. Driving right into the walkway of Lone Pine Cemetery, she parked her truck and then staggered from headstone to headstone—at one point, resting at Buster's mother's grave before moving on to her own kin. Sheriff Morgan had a simple headstone with an engraved sheriff's star and the word *Order*. Jimmy thought the engravers had made a mistake by not having it read *Law and Order,* but Deputy Dudival, the one who bought the headstone, felt the bastard didn't deserve to be memorialized with the word *Law*.

Jimmy eased herself down onto the grass and filed her report. Then she listened for a good forty-five minutes. When her instructions had been completely issued, she arose painfully to her feet and placed a .455 Colt cartridge casing on Morgan's headstone next to the many others. She felt better already. There was much to do. Fixing Buster's love life had not been a high priority, but woe onto Cord Travesty who just happened to pull up to Jimmy at the town's only stoplight and catch her jaundiced eye.

ᘓ

DESTINY STUMPLEHORST WAS ASLEEP that night in Cord Travesty's bed when the phone rang. Since Cord was never sure if another girl was calling, he answered it.

"Hello?" There was silence. "Who is this?" Click. He angrily slammed down the phone and crawled back into bed. "It was a hang up," he said.

About fifteen seconds later the phone rang again.

"Fuck," Travesty said rolling over and opening his eyes. "This is getting old."

"You want me to answer it?" asked Destiny.

"No, that's okay." Travesty picked up the phone. "Hello?" Again, silence. "You assholes!" He slammed the phone down again. "Godammit. I'm gonna have to take an Ambien to get back to sleep. You want one?"

"Sure," said Destiny, at this point in her life loathe to turning down anything in the drug department. They each took a sleeping pill and then tried to get back to sleep. About two minutes later the phone rang once again.

"Are you sure you don't want me to get it?"

"Get it," said Travesty at wit's end.

"Hello?" said Destiny. But then she heard something on the phone that made her eyes widen. She put the phone down. "I think I heard Maple."

"Who the fuck is Maple?"

"Maple's my horse."

"Your *horse* called you?"

"I could hear her in the background."

Travesty sat up in bed.

"Hey, look, I've been meaning to say something to you. You're doing too much coke. It's supposed to be for recreation and you've been making it your fucking life's work."

"I know what my own horse sounds like. I heard my horse."

"Okay, never mind. Let's just go to sleep and hope she's used up her calling card minutes." Travesty rolled over once again and put the pillow over his head. As irrational as this was, the phone call worried her. She turned toward the window and was trying to get back to sleep when she heard a horse whinny in the field beside the house. Destiny pulled back the curtains and saw a horse, about fifty yards away, standing in the rain.

"Maple!" she yelled out the window. Travesty sat upright again.

"You have got to be fucking kidding me! What the hell is going on here?"

"I don't know, but that's Maple! She must've gotten out of the barn."

"And what…she called to tell you she was coming over?"

Destiny was already putting her clothes on. Travesty looked nervously out the window.

"Something's really fucked up about this."

"Hey, Cord, I've been meaning to say something to you. You're doing too much coke. It's supposed to be for recreation."

"What are doing?"

"I'm gonna go out there and ride her home."

"Don't. Don't go out there," he suddenly said, paranoid.

"Go back to sleep. I'll call you in the morning."

Destiny went downstairs, not seeing Jimmy sitting on the sofa in the dark, a bundle of dynamite on the glass cocktail table covered in the faint contrails of a white powder next to a gold-plated razor blade.

As soon as Destiny went outside, Jimmy turned on the gas in the oven. She closed the windows in the kitchen and sealed it up by placing a couple of wet towels along the bottom of the door. Jimmy slipped on her oxygen mask and waited for the gas to accumulate. When she figured she had reached a threshold amount for a good blow, she laid some fuse out the back door, lit it, and got back on her horse.

A mile away Destiny heard the explosion. She thought it was thunder. Days later, people were still finding dozens of *For Sale—Contact Cord Travesty* signs that Travesty had stored in the attic, scattered around town.

Jimmy rode back to her ranch and laid down for a little rest. When the Big Ben wind-up alarm clock went off an hour later, she tried to sit up but first leaned over to hawk up a glob of sputum into a paper bag she kept by the side of the bed. Her vision was going downhill and she had a headache to beat the band. Laboriously, she slung her legs over the side of the bed and forced down a 400ml Dilaudid with the backwash from a can of beer. It took her the next fifteen minutes just to pull on her boots. Once on her feet, she steadied herself against the workbench and pulled down an old canvas rucksack. She monkey-barred her way over to the Kelvinator and opened the freezer door to remove a three-pound tri-tip that she'd carved off a steer that she alien-mutilated a couple of months ago. She perused her old dynamite collection and selected four sticks that seemed to sweat the least nitroglycerine.

It took her four exhausting attempts to throw a saddle over Nicker. By the time she was done, she had to walk him over to a fence to use it to mount up—like she had taught a thousand undersized children. She pulled a rain slicker over her oxygen tank and took off on a lope toward Egnar, home to the Busy Bees.

Cookie Dominguez's headquarters was an old farmhouse attached to a dilapidated 1950s Desert Breeze trailer. Fifty years ago, a farmer had lived there with the dream of getting rich growing Echinacea for homeopathic drugstores. Today, the staunch traditions of western free enterprise and entrepreneurship continued with Cookie's production of ten pounds of crank a week.

Cookie's gang all lived in the farmhouse. The trailer was filled with their equipment and the toxic chemicals for producing methamphetamine. Since the attempted bust by the DEA, Cookie had acquired two scarred-up Rottweilers from the dog pound. As soon as the dogs smelled Jimmy, they bolted out the pet door into the dark like torpedoes from an aluminum submarine in a redneck navy. Jimmy could have just shot them, but she had nothing against a couple of dogs that didn't know any better. She calmly reached into her rucksack and cut the tri-tip in half with her grandfather's sheepfoot folding knife and tossed a piece to each dog. They immediately stopped their snarling and ran off coveting their meat.

With the rain and thunder making so much noise, she also didn't feel it necessary to dismount and sneak up on the place Injun-style. She simply rode up to the house and walked in as if she'd been invited for Sunday dinner. There was a flickering blue light coming from the living room. Ironically, Benito Sandoval, one of the gang members, had decided to stay in this night to see who was going to be eliminated on *American Idol.* It must have taken Benito a ten count to realize he wasn't alone. He slowly turned and was startled to find Jimmy—wrapped in a green army slicker head to foot, an oxygen mask over her mouth, dripping water all over the floor. He kind of laughed at the absurdity of her.

"Who…the…fuck…are…you?"

Jimmy, who never liked it when people didn't recognize her, promptly shot him in the head. Then she took a moment to have a look around. She had to chortle at the condition of the place. This was definitely the interior decorating style of a gang on methamphetamines.

Tweakers always have to be doing something with their hands. The microwave had been taken apart, as had the washer and drier. The stereo had been disassembled. Pieces of the dishwasher were arranged across the faded linoleum floor like a Rauschenberg. The parts of a vacuum cleaner were laid out the way cats take a chipmunk apart. There were posters of Hiram Graythwaite, the avuncular-looking leader of the Aryan Leaders of Tomorrow—a group quartered in Idaho—a Millet bullet press, at least ten thousand rounds of .223 ammunition, boxes of institutional peanut butter, and hundreds of cans of Spaghetti-Os. Cookie was obviously readying himself for his own apocalypse. The gang also seemed to have a predilection for 500–piece jigsaw puzzles. Jimmy looked at her pocket watch. It was 1:30, closing time at the High Grade. She thought she better finish up.

ഊ

SOON, COOKIE DOMINGUEZ ARRIVED home with his posse in the pouring rain. He didn't go inside right away. He was just as cautious about entering his own home as Sheriff Dudival was. He stood in the rain and called his dogs. They barked: "all clear." Cookie entered his house followed by the others, but pulled up short when he saw Benito in his BarcaLounger—the dogs sitting obediently by each armrest.

"Hey, fucker. Whadaya think you're doin' sittin' in my chair?"

The other gang members clucked at Benito's insubordination. *He must really be drunk*, they thought. Cookie slapped him on the side of his head, and his hand came away covered with blood.

"What the fuck," Cookie whispered and tiptoed to his bookcase pulling out a loaded Walther 9mm pistol from behind his first editions of Hiram Graythwaite's neo-Nazi literature. Silently, he signaled to the others to get behind him while he ventured into the lab. Very carefully, he stepped through the hole that had been chainsawed in the wall that led to the trailer. Cookie strained to hear a sign of the intruder, but was frustrated by the volume of the television. A new contestant on *American Idol* was gratingly singing—in the ersatz operatic style currently popular—about how this was the moment that she would not mess up this time. Cookie turned and hissed to his colleagues.

"Hey, one of you assholes turn that fuckin' thing off!"

One of gang hurried back to the living room and yanked the clicker out of the dead man's hand. He pushed the button and—in that split second—realized that it wasn't a TV clicker at all, but a garage door opener. When pushed, it sent an electronic signal to the garage door receiver. The receiver light turned red, and sent an electric current to the blasting caps Jimmy had wired to dynamite all around the lab. The blast ignited the multiple tanks of anhydrous ammonia used to convert the ephedrine from pounds of generic Sam's Club Sudafeds into snortable methamphetamine. Jimmy didn't bother to look back as the buildings, motorcycles, nails, bone, flesh, glass, and thousands of .223 rounds combined and shrieked through the night air. One more stop and she could go back to bed.

ꟈ

MALLOMAR'S GULFSTREAM LANDED IN the Montrose airport seconds before the full force of the storm hit. In the attaché case he carried were divorce papers—still warm and chemically fragrant from his lawyers' Xerox machine. Jaw-clenched, he climbed into his Mercedes AMG and shot off on the seventy-five-mile drive to the ranch, blowing through through every single traffic light.

Buster had spent the entire night driving, thinking about what he was going to do with Mrs. Mallomar. He dreaded facing Mrs. Mallomar but knew he had to do it. Almost out of gas, he pulled the '61 Apache up to the Big Dog corral. Rain was blowing sideways, lightning and thunder were letting loose on El Diente, making the horses froggy. Always cognizant of his duties, Buster put the animals in the barn then trudged into the house.

All the lights in the house were off—a flickering candelabra on the dining table the only source of illumination. The French doors leading to the patio were open, and the wind blew the drapes like ghosts in a silent movie. The table had been laid with a black tablecloth, two little red plates, and enameled chopsticks.

"Where've you been, Clem?"

Buster startled, as she appeared seemingly from nowhere, wearing her little black NVA pajama bottoms with her gauzy blouse.

Buster quickly averted his eyes from Mrs. Mallomar's chest, so as not to distract from what he had come to say. He, instead, looked to the coffee table where he found a curious white lump residing in the middle of it.

"Ain't that one of our salt licks?"

"Interesting look, isn't it?"

"Think it should be on that table, ma'am? Cows been lickin' at it."

Buster had, in fact, placed a dozen salt licks around the pasture. The cows could not resist them, and the salt made them want to drink water. The extra water weight translated to higher unit price at slaughter time.

"I think it's beautiful. Have you ever seen Henry Moore's, *Seated Woman: Thin Neck?*" she said, turning its tongue-sanded modern aspects in the candlelight.

"Don't know as ah've had. Jes think Mr. Mallomar may not like that bein' here."

"And…what would he think about *you* being here?" She laughed when Buster's face dropped. There was something unsettlingly buoyant about Mrs. Mallomar tonight. What was it? "Appetizer?" She held up a lacquered plate containing four spring rolls that she had hand-rolled with translucent rice paper to a suggestive length of eight inches. "It's Japanese night, in case you didn't catch that." Uncharacteristically, Buster did not take the food.

"That's a first."

"There's somethin' preyin' on me, ma'am ah gotta talk to you 'bout."

"Oh, please. Can we not have a conversation like *that*, tonight?"

Suddenly a gust of wind came up and pushed in the big Great Room's windows, then sucked them out with such force that the roof groaned like a dying man.

"Wow! Where in God's name did that come from?"

"Ma'am, you and me caint be havin' ree-lay-shuns no more."

A clap of thunder rolled out across the mesa.

"If this will ease your mind, we're not having relations. We're just screwing."

"Well, ah don't think we should be doin' that there neither."

"Why not?"

"It ain't raht."

"It's been right by me. Surprisingly so."

Buster turned and walked out the French doors. "Now where're you going?"

Buster had said what he had to say. In the barn, he once again began to pack his tack. His plan was to wait there until Mr. Mallomar returned. He was even hoping Mr. Mallomar would punch him in the nose. Buster backed his truck through the paddock doors and started to load up. Already, he was starting to feel loose in his joints again, the promise of returning to an uncomplicated life.

"Don't leave."

Mrs. Mallomar was standing in the doorway, wringing wet.

"Ah'm sorry, ma'am. Ah have to."

"My husband will want to know why you left. What am I going to tell him?"

"Don't you worry 'bout that, ma'am. Ah'll be tellin' him."

The thought of that did little to calm her.

"What do you mean? What are you going to tell him?"

"The truth."

"Okay. I understand how you're feeling right now. But could you come inside for a moment? There's something I need to tell you before you ride off on your fucking high horse." Reluctantly, Buster let her take his hand and lead him back to the house.

Mallomar was hoping to catch them in the act when he got home. He fumbled around in the glove compartment until he found what he was looking for—the instructions for his phone. Specifically, what he wanted to know was how its eight-megapixel camera worked. He'd get a nice snapshot of them to staple to the divorce papers. But when he walked in the front door, he got the shock of his life.

"What in hell's going on here?"

The living room was filled, wall-to-wall, with cattle. They had followed the scent of the salt lick from the pasture and had come through the French doors. Once out of the rain, they decided to stay. There was a great deal of bellowing and jostling going on. One steer was pushing his brisket against one of the hollow wooden pillars that hid the steel weight-bearing supports holding up the second floor. The resultant noise from the cracking wood cast doubt on whether or not the brackets that attached to it were made to take a lateral six hundred pound body slam. Mallomar pushed his way through the stubborn animals to the stairway, trying not to look at what they had done to his one-hundred-thousand-dollar Persian rug.

Inside the house, Mallomar climbed to his wife's room and dramatically flung the door open. Finding no one there, he stepped back on the balcony and looked down just in time to see Buster and his wife come through the French doors, hand in hand. The smartphone that he was holding suddenly didn't seem enough. He went to find the gun that he had purchased at his own hardware store.

CHAPTER TWENTY-FIVE

One Last Ride

JIMMY HAD RIDDEN THE mesa many times in the rain and lightning. It was one of her favorite things—even though a person on horseback is the highest object above the flat ground and subject to a better-than-average chance of being electrocuted. No matter. She loved—if one were so bold as to identify hers as a feminine attribute—the way the rain released the fragrance of the dry sagebrush and the way it mingled with leather and wet horse. She would miss that. And when there was a nearby hit of lightning, it excited her—the stream of maverick electrons seemingly passing through her navel and tingling all the way to her groin. She would miss that, too. But no use getting sentimental when there was still work to do.

The rain on the Lame Horse Mesa road had turned the finely grained dirt as slick and slippery as the woman's wrestling match that Jimmy had once attended with a bunch of cowboys in Laramie, Wyoming. Nicker was having a hard time of it as he worked his way up the mile and a half road to the Mallomar house, his hooves clumped with mud. Jimmy rode, slumped forward holding the pommel for dear life. She was feverish and twice had to lean over the saddle to throw up. Up ahead, she could see a halo through the rain.

"Thar it is, Nicker. We'll show'm who's the Big Dog around here!" She gave her horse one last gentle nudge in the ribs, but the horse just stood in the road, frozen like a statue. "C'mon, boy," she urged with another poke of her spurs. "Just a couple more and we can both go back to bed." But the horse stood still and took uneven shuddering breaths. "Not used to the action anymore, huh?" She clucked, scolding good-naturedly. "Giddyap." Nicker knelt down on both front legs. "You want me to get off, is that it? Don't have the gumption for it anymore? Well, that's some gratitude for ya, after all these years! Lemme walk a mile in the cold rain?" Breathlessly, Jimmy swung her leg over the saddle and jumped off. "All right then, dammit! Why don't you go the hell home and read the goddamn newspaper?" The horse gave one long sigh and keeled over onto his side. The evening's excitement had been apparently been too much for the heart of the twenty-six year-old horse.

"Damn you to hell!" Jimmy was screaming over the pouring rain. "Get up!" The horse's breathing grew faint. Jimmy suddenly became scared and fell to her knees. "Oh, no! You ain't gonna die on me, are ya? Please don't!" Jimmy took off her hat, shielding the horse's face from the rain. She gently caressed his muzzle. "You're the best damn horse ah ever had. There, ah said it. Satisfied? Now, come on now… Git up!"

The horse's breath grew even shallower. Jimmy lay down in the mud beside him. "Nicker, ah done a terrible thing! A terrible thing! Ah was allus meant to tell ya…" she began with a lump in her throat. "Yor real name was Ranger." She waited for a grateful acknowledgement, but Ranger would ride to the sound of Jimmy's dynamite no more. Jimmy just sat there for a moment in disbelief. Finally, she cleared her throat and struggled to her feet. "Ah 'spect ah'll be joinin' ya shortly. Lissen fer ma whistle." Then Jimmy pulled her hat back down on her head and started slogging up the road—for the first time in her life, on foot.

Up at the reservoir, the water level had risen two feet. The levee would have been safe for another three feet if it hadn't been infested with muskrats—the result of Mrs. Mallomar's orders. By one-thirty that morning, the rising water began to pour into the tunnels that they had honeycombed across the width and length of the levee. By two o'clock, a tiny hole, no larger than a fist, had broken through, jeopardizing the levee's structural integrity. By 2:30, large portions of the levee had collapsed. It was set to go. The muskrats climbed out of the levee and scampered off to save their own skins.

In a cedar chest under the stairs, beneath a pile of antique Pendleton blankets—that he had bragged to everybody that they were better than the new ones that they make—Mallomar had stashed his loaded pistol—the same gun the police would later find after a more thorough search of the demolished house. Mallomar, gun in hand, crept down the stairs. Buster and Dana, the cattle herd between them, waited for him to say something.

"I guess nobody took the cattle out for a walk," he finally said.

The last fifty yards of road to the front door of the Big Dog Lodge had been steeply graded to allow drainage. If that wasn't enough of an obstacle, the situation was exacerbated by a new development for Jimmy. Her tank had just run out of oxygen. Incredulous, she ripped the mask from her mouth and gulped for air like a landed catfish. The front door was just there, but she couldn't get her legs to obey. Lack of oxygen was shutting down her whole system. Soporifically, she stared down at her blue fingers, her numb and useless toes. Red, muddy water was pushing against her shins. Something must have happened to the reservoir up above. Was *anything* going to go her way tonight? Using every last bit of her strength, she pulled herself up on a boulder to get out of the way of the water. Then she heard a gunshot. There was a horrendous crashing sound, and a wall of mud and rocks came crashing through the house. The roof fell like someone kicking the legs out from under a chair.

From her safe perch on the boulder, Jimmy's figured out her escape plan and prepared her alibis. Her ranch was a good mile away. Walking was out of the question. Jimmy had no choice but to crawl like the wounded animal she was. Slowly, excruciatingly, she eased herself down from the rock and onto her stomach. She grabbed one tuft of grass at a time, pulling herself along. But now providence stepped in to deal a joker in the form of a cud chewing, wide-eyed steer that had escaped the house before the roof came down. It was following her along—not wanting to be alone after what it had just been through.

"What're you starin' at, you stupid sonofabitch?" Jimmy hissed. Then she got an idea. "Come over here, sweetheart," she said in a kindly voice that even surprised *her.* The steer played coy for another fifteen feet until it found a clump of cheatgrass to rip out. Jimmy took the opportunity to drag herself over and grip its shit-covered tail. After that massive oxygen-expending effort, she took a moment to rest and pant. Then she reached into her holster for one of the Colts and fired off a single round singeing the steer's rump. With a terrified bellow, the steer took off on a flight-for-life, dragging Jimmy over the mesa in a random zigzag pattern that ten cartridges later, brought her within ten feet of her front door.

PART THREE

CHAPTER TWENTY-SIX

Back to the Morning Of

Mrs. Poult had been knocking on Sheriff Dudival's door and getting no answer. Quietly, she opened the door to find him asleep at his desk. He was holding a tin pie plate that Buster had tapped out for him when he was a boy living with the Dominguez family. Buster had created a square-jawed profile of the sheriff with Vanadium's Main Street as the backdrop. She smiled and cocked her head sweetly, "Darling…I mean, Sheriff Dudival…" She rolled her eyes at herself. The sheriff stirred and gave a start seeing her there.

"What is it?"

Mrs. Poult winced at his brusqueness then recovered to make her report. Due to the Lame Horse Mesa's power outage last night, dispatch had only moments ago received reports of two massive explosions. One was called in by a neighbor of Cord Travesty's. The other was from a client of Cookie Dominguez's who, seeing firsthand the aftermath of the munitions and chemicals detonating at the meth trailer, clawed at his own face in horror a la the Münch painting. According to the First Responders, all of the residents were either dead or missing. Sheriff Dudival, hearing this news, wearily got up from his desk, went over to the office sink and washed his face and brushed his teeth. No use rushing. He seemed to know that, most likely, they were all dead.

"Careful when you go out the door," warned Mrs. Poult.

"Why?"

The sheriff opened the jail's door to the momentary blinding sunlight. At least fifty people from the media were waiting for him, microphones shoved in his face.

"Sheriff Dudival!"

"Have they found the body?"

"Was sex the motive?"

"Were they running away together?"

Sheriff Dudival fumbled for his sunglasses. He wasn't used to this.

"I have nothing to say to you people."

ꟹ

ARRIVING AT THE CORPORATE headquarters of Busy Bee America, Inc., Sheriff Dudival was able to determine a simple explanation for what was, to any trained criminologist, a murder scene. Cookie's death was the result of an occupational hazard—meth labs were notorious for their combustible instability. A lightning strike could have easily triggered the explosion in evidence before him. Sheriff Dudival motioned for an impromptu crew of orange-suited prisoners that had been waiting for his arrival to assemble. Each was equipped with rubber gloves and a black plastic highway department litterbag. County Health dictated that coroners make "best efforts" to gather body parts; in this case, the Busy Bees were scattered as far as two hundred yards from their notorious crank hive.

"Don't bother with any piece smaller than this." Sheriff Dudival leaned over to harvest a severed hand with three fingers that was nestled in nearby sagebrush. He knew whom it belonged to, and he also knew who had blown off the missing digits. In the past, that kind of thing had been jocular coffee conversation between him and Jimmy. Dudival then had the men stretch crime scene tape around the perimeter and placed a deputy there to keep anybody out who might get it in their head to drop by for a leftover snort.

Dudival's next stop on the mesa was the Cord Travesty property. Travesty's board-and-batten house was laid out in a perfect daisy pattern emanating from Cord's antique brass bed. It was here that Destiny Stumplehorst gave Sheriff Dudival her surreal deposition. Unlike the Dominguez explosion, the Travesty crime scene was harder to explain. The purported phone call carrying the sound of Destiny's mare being the reason for her leaving the house before the explosion—the very large horsefly in the ointment. There seemed to be foul play.

"Do you think you could be mistaken about your horse?"

"No, Sheriff. I'm sure it was her." Sheriff Dudival accepted her adamancy then slowly walked around the bed. He couldn't help himself from tucking in the corners of the bedcover, military-style.

"Destiny, if I were to take you down to the clinic for a blood draw right now...would there possibly be any traces of something that might—how should I put this—*color* your testimony that you heard your horse whinny to you on a cell phone?" He already knew the answer to that one. "Cord is gone. We can't change that. But you gotta live here. You understand what I'm saying, hon?"

"You want me to drop that part of my testimony."

"I'm not asking you to do anything. That would be conspiracy."

"Right." She looked into Sheriff Dudival's eyes and finally understood what he meant. Dudival had deftly steered the debutante onto the dance floor of her first crime cotillion and had managed not to step on her feet.

"Well, I do recall something…now that I'm thinkin' back on it."

"What's that?"

"Well, somethin' in the middle of the night woke me up."

"Some thunder or lightning, perhaps?"

"Yeah, and I just happened to look out the window, and I saw my horse. So I put on my clothes and went and got her."

"And when you took her home, did you see anyone around the house or anything suspicious in nature?"

"No, sir." Dudival scribbled all of that in his little notebook then flipped the cover closed.

Sheriff Dudival patted her shoulder comfortingly and then turned to get into his cruiser. As he opened the door, his eyes fell on a footprint in the mud—the shape of a small cowboy boot. Sheriff Dudival looked over his shoulder at Destiny. She was wearing flip-flops.

"Somethin' else I can do you for ya, Sheriff?"

"No, just wondering if you or Cord ever had trouble with that old gas stove of his?"

"It could be finicky at times," she said, stitching a little embroidery of her own into the narrative.

"Sounds to me like an unfortunate confluence of events," the sheriff said with a slight smile. "I'm just going to have one more look around before I go—if you don't mind." Dudival then turned and walked back to his police cruiser to get some plaster of Paris.

"If Buster did this, then it's my fault."

"I can't comment on that."

လ

Up at Jimmy Bayles Morgan's place, the thumping bass of her home oxygen compressor, combined with the buzzing of hundreds of bottle flies that circled her like buzzards, created the semblance of Senagalese dance music. Jimmy was laying in her crusty bed, dozing and sanguine after a night gorging on murder. If her pillow was slightly tear-stained, it was not out of fear of her impending death, but thoughts of her dearly departed Ranger.

Sheriff Dudival arrived in the Authentic Western Experience parking lot with a bag of groceries. He headed for the opened front door, but stopped short before walking in when he heard the faint double-click of a revolver hammer cocking.

"Hello there, Jimmy Bayles. It's Shep."

"Come in," said a weak voice.

He waited until he heard the hammer safely release then stepped inside. He had to mask his surprise at the sight of her. She had lost an alarming amount of weight. And she was filthy. She hadn't changed her long johns in days and the bedsheets were smeared with mud.

"I didn't see you in town for our regular coffee, so I thought the mountain might as well come to Mohammed."

Jimmy's brow furrowed. "Who the hell you talkin' 'bout?"

"It's just an expression."

Dudival took the coffee, eggs, and bread out of the bag and placed them on the counter of her camp-style kitchen noticing the array of heavy-duty prescriptions she was taking.

"So what did the doctors say in Junction?"

"Oh, them damn doctors. They jes wanna keep checkin' for this and that so's they can run up a nice, fat bill. Ah blame the Medicare! Take away Medicare and those sonsofbitches would jes feel your pulse then send your ass home! But ah diserppointed them, see, cause ah'm all right. False alarm. Jes need a lil rest, cuppa Mormon tea, and ah'm good to go!" She finished that diatribe with a coughing fit.

"Glad to hear it." Dudival opened a cabinet and found a clean set of sheets and another set of underwear—probably her grandfather's. He went over to her bed and lifted her up and set her down in her only chair. The groceries weighed more than she did.

"Now what the hell're ya doin?"

"I'm just going to make you a little more comfortable."

"Ah was comfortable before you come up here botherin' me!"

Dudival ripped the soiled sheets off her bed and changed them. Then he got a pan from the sink, filled it with soapy water and grabbed a sponge.

"What you plannin' to do with that?"

"You'll see. Stand up." Wobbily, she got to her feet and steadied herself on the back of the chair. Without any warning or permission, Dudival walked over and pulled her long johns down to her ankles.

"What the fuckin' hell! Shep Dudival, have you lost yor cotton pickin'...?"

"I'm washing you before I put you in these clean clothes."

"Ah can wash myself, thank you very much."

"All right then. Go ahead." He handed her the sponge and stepped back. The moment Jimmy let go of the back of the chair, she crumpled. She shook her head in dismay.

Dudival began to sponge her body matter-of-factly, the dirty run-off disappearing down the cracks of the floorboards. Dudival washed her hair, her face then her back. Naked, without the macho deception of her cowboy mufti, she looked like a scrawny, featherless baby bird. Her tan ended at her collarbone. All points south were like a US Interstate map, blue-veined against a white background—never having seen the sun in an entire lifetime.

"Ah caint fuckin' believe this," she grumbled.

"Shut up," he said softly. Dudival rinsed out the sponge and then washed under her arms and her chest. Her breasts, bound with Ace bandages since puberty, had finally achieved the flatness, thanks to the cancer's cannibalization, that she had so long desired. Her buttocks had shriveled into two wrinkled pouches no larger than the bags under an accountant's eyes. He washed her blistered ass and worked up her legs to her frizzy gray-bearded genitalia, her pubis bearing an uncanny resemblance to the poet Ezra Pound.

"Happy? You finally espied my cooter."

"I can scratch that off my bucket list. Next stop, Mt. Rushmore." Now he pulled the clean underwear over her head, buttoned it, carefully tucked her back in bed and propped her up with a pillow.

"How's that?"

Jimmy's cruel mouth began to form a wisecrack, but she aborted the launch.

"Better. Much better. Sheppie, ah'm right sorry ah said sech things to you the other day….'bout you bein' a coward and all."

"I knew you didn't mean it."

Jimmy reattached her nasal canula and saw that Dudival was just standing there looking at her. "You okay there, pard?"

"I'd like a drink." Dudival went into her kitchen and found a bottle of Crazy Crow under the sink. It was next to a ten-pin frame of bottled poisons. Dudival stopped for a moment and tried to remember which dead Vanadian citizens in the recent past had been diagnosed with intestinal or renal failure.

"Ah serpose you do need a drink after seein' what you jes seen," she croaked from the other room. He poured a stiff belt into a Quarter Horse Association coffee cup and casually looked around. There was evidence all over the place: On the work bench—blasting caps and Vulcan dynamite—the same brand he found eleven years ago at the Dominguez place—electrical wiring and a soldering gun from the Cookie job, a cell phone, which he was sure would give up Cord Travesty's number on the "recently called" list, and muddy boots that were probably a match with the mud from the reservoir. There was one pistol in plain sight next to a bottle of Hoppes gun cleaning solvent, which meant the other revolver, that he had heard earlier, was within her reach—probably under the bed. Either she hadn't had the energy to clean up after herself, or she was daring him to do something about it.

"Drinkin' on duty…thar's a new one fer ya."

"Jimmy, I'm up to my ass in alligators."

"Sorry to hear it. There some kinda…*trouble* in town?" she rasped disingenuinely.

Dudival reappeared at her bedside.

"We had a mudslide last night that took out half of Main Street. I'm not sure yet whether it was natural or man made."

"Ah recall we had a mudslide back in nineteen…fifty-eight. That's when we put in the town's storm drains. But you weren't here then, were you?" Jimmy would never miss an opportunity to point out to Dudival, that even though he had lived here since 1969, he was still a greenhorn.

"There were nine homicides last night."

Jimmy propped herself up on a boney elbow and feigned surprise.

"Whoa, Nellie! Nine ho-mo-cides!"

"Cord Travesty, Cookie Dominguez, six of his gang and…Mr. Mallomar." The news of Mallomar's demise momentarily threw her for a loop."Mall-ee-mar? You don't say. How'd he get it?"

"I don't know yet. We're excavating the house to recover the body."

"Folks in town must be hailin' the killer of all them bastards a goddamn hero!" Jimmy said.

"Not really," Dudival said, not giving it to her.

"Well, they should, godammit! Ever'one of them sonsabitches had it comin'!"

"You feel pretty strongly about it?" Dudival took and sip of whiskey and smiled. Jimmy froze for a moment then threw her head back and laughed and laughed.

"Ah wisht ah could have done it myself. Ah surely wisht ah could. But as this chamber pot here'll testify…" she said as she bent over and sloshed the chamber pot around. "Ah cain't hardly get m'self outta bed to take a whizzer." Dudival held off her invitation to corroborate. "Be a pal, wouldja, and fire me up a Commander?" She yanked the canula out of her nose and waited for him. "Ah suppose you already have yor person or persons of inneress."

"We're holding Buster."

"What! What the hell're you doin' that for?"

"He was with Mrs. Mallomar in the house the night of Mallomar's disappearance. And he was having an affair with Mrs. Mallomar." Dudival took some amount of sadistic pleasure watching the creaky wheels turning in her mind.

"That's just bullshit. He aint cap'ble of all that. He's a damn harmless crybaby." She took a drag on her cigarette. "So there was three people up there in that house. Since one of 'ems dead, it just leaves her word against Buster's. The only witness."

"That's right."

"Uh…where's she now?" Jimmy asked innocently. She and her grandfather were not shrinking violets when it came to eliminating a troublesome witness.

"She's in protective custody someplace in New York."

"Well, shit. That's too bad…maybe a stretch down in Canon City'll toughen ol' Buster up."

"If he's convicted, they're going to ask for the death penalty." The slightest flicker of pain registered on Jimmy's face, and then hardened.

"What does the big doofus say 'bout all this?"

"He won't talk. He thinks it's in violation of the gentlemen's code in Miss Humphrey's *Manners For Men.*"

"That damn book Grampie done give ya?" He didn't say anything. "Well, that's where all that gennelman stuff gets ya!" This made Jimmy laugh for real this time.

"I'm glad you're taking it so well."

"Ah tole that kid not to get mixed up with them people. He dint lissen to me. Now, I'm wipin' my hands of the en-tahr af-fair."

"So…you don't think that there's something *you* could do that might help straighten this thing out?"

"Like what?" She looked at him blankly. To Dudival, her instinct for self-preservation, even at this point, was nauseating.

"You tell me."

"Yor talkin' stupid. Now, ah think you should skedaddle. I'm tahred." Duival stood, but wasn't ready to leave. "What's he done?"

"What the hell's that suppose to mean?"

"Something's changed between you and Buster. I know how you operate. Buster's done something you don't *abide*. What is it?"

"It's b'tween me and him."

Dudival waited.

"We had words. Ah done a lot for that boy and now… he's crost off my list."

She flipped the cigarette out the door and replaced her cannula. "Now, like ah tole ya, ah'm tahred." And with that, she turned her face away from him. Dudival just stood there for a moment glowering over her, then walked out with one of his grocery bags.

Back in his police cruiser, he had a shooting pain in his left arm that radiated all the way up to his jaw. His hands were shaking so badly he had trouble putting the key into the ignition. He tried to relax, took some deep breaths then lit a cigarette—his eyes fixated on Jimmy's doorway. When the pain subsided, Dudival looked inside his grocery bag and retrieved the items that he had collected when he was in the kitchen out of her sightline. Dudival had the cell phone and the bomb-making detritus that he was sure would match the pieces that he had recovered at Cookie Dominguez's meth lab, the dynamite, and her cowboy boots. He had also helped himself to a crusty bottle of arsenic.

CHAPTER TWENTY-SEVEN

The Arraignment

Two weeks later, Jimmy was still alive, but to Sheriff Dudival's mounting frustration, she still showed no intention of turning herself in. That Tuesday morning, the corrections officer removed Buster and four other prisoners from their cells. Each man was strapped with a wide leather harness around the waist—each had a steel loop in the front for a chain to run from their handcuffs to their leg irons. Wearing orange county uniforms that said *JAIL* on their backs, the five inmates were helped into the rear of a county transport truck that had two benches facing each other. A restraining bar—not unlike the kind used on roller coasters at amusement parks—was lowered, locking them in place. They began the ride to the Lame Horse County courthouse in silence. The men, except for Buster who had made the effort to wash and shave, fell easily between the goal post uprights of depravity and decrepitude.

As is typical on these trips, one of the more seasoned prisoners, usually a two-time loser, presents himself to the uninitiated as something of a legal expert. Today it was an old geezer who was the most courtroom-savvy among them. His rheumy gaze—when falling upon the down-in-the-mouth expressions of his fellow travelers—caused him to burst out laughing and shake his head with the *commedia dell'arte* of it all. This, of course was meant to capture everyone's attention, which it did. Turning to the first person on the bench opposite him was a disheveled Japanese man in his thirties. His eyes were puffy from crying. Until last night, he had been a sushi chef at a Japanese restaurant in Telluride.

"What're you in for, Ching-Chong?"

"I get drunk. Chase girfriend with sushi knife."

"Kill her?" the geezer inquired nonchalantly.

"No, kirr. Just chase."

"Ever been arrested before?"

"No, no."

"Pretend you can't speak English." He smacked his fist, gavel-like, to his thigh. "Probation!"

The Old Geezer turned to Buster who was sitting quietly looking at his handcuffs.

"How 'bout you, pard?"

Buster remained silent. One of the other prisoners, a man accused of having sex with a dog, spoke for him.

"He killed Mr. Mallomar."

"So you're the one who was doin' the rich man's wife? Oh boy." The Geezer just shook his head. "Lethal injection!"

ꙮ

Judge Dora Englelander scrutinized the ragtag group as they shuffled single-file into the courtroom through the eyes of a gaudy Mardis Gras mask. She had just returned from Bangkok for some bargain basement plastic surgery followed by a restorative trip to a spa at Angkor Wat. Still looking a little black and blue from her wattle tuck and eye work, but she was loath to relinquish her bench. This was surely going to be Lame Horse County's most famous trial, and she wouldn't want to miss it for the world. She wasn't prepared, however, for the hundreds of people who packed the courtroom this day—as well as reporters from every major newspaper, network, cable news, and Court TV. Junior members of Mallomar's law offices sat with pens poised over yellow legal pads. Judge Englelander banged the gavel for quiet.

"Lame Horse Mesa County Court will now come to session this day of August fifteenth, two thousand eight." She looked over at the bench of orange-clad losers.

"I sent a fax to the jail outlining your constitutional rights. Did any of you read it?" They shook their heads in the negative—even though they all had. No one was in a hurry to get back to jail. Besides, today seemed like it could be interesting.

"I'm sorry to hear that. Now I'll have to read each of you your rights individually."

She then called upon the first man to approach the bench. Judge Englelander went on to recite chapter and verse—that the prisoner was not on trial yet, that the prisoner should make no incriminating remarks about his case, and that if he or she (even though there were not any *she's* there) could not afford a lawyer, one would be appointed by the court. She spieled out this Bill of Rights boilerplate in the kind of irritating, singsong voice a mother would use talking to a child that was nagging in a grocery store.

"Buster McCaffrey?" Judge Englelander asked, looking up from her roster.

"Present," Buster said and tried to raise his handcuffed hand.

"Would you approach the bench, please?"

Buster got up from his seat, jangled his shackles to the end of the aisle and then bent down as he approached the bench—as if he were in a theatre returning to his seat with popcorn in the middle of the movie and didn't want to block anyone's view. Sadly, the weight of his harness pulled down the orange county jail pants exposing the crack of his ass, which provoked big laughs from the courtroom. The people from out of town had heard he was quite a character, and Buster didn't disappoint. Sheriff Dudival, who had driven down to support Buster, was mortified on his behalf.

"You understand, Mr. McCaffrey, that this proceeding is merely an *arraignment*. You are not required to make a plea of innocent or guilty until you have consulted with a lawyer."

"Yes, ma'am, ah unnerstan. Can ah jes say somethin?"

"Yes, go right ahead."

"Ah'm innocent."

"Mr. McCaffrey, didn't I just tell you not to say that?"

"Sorry, ma'am."

"Do you have a lawyer, Mr. McCaffrey?"

"No, yor honor, ah plumb don't."

"Would you like the court to appoint one for you?"

"Thank you, kindly, ma'am."

"That's your right."

"Well, aint that somethin'? God Bless America," Buster said, smiling at her with all of his horse teeth.

"Uh, you can sit down now, Mr. McCaffrey."

Buster gave her a little salute with his index finger and turned to rejoin the other prisoners.

"Dint kill nobody," he stopped to say.

"SIT...DOWN."

CHAPTER TWENTY-EIGHT

Visiting Days

LUNCH, AT THE LAME Horse County jail, was prepared by the inmates—as Marvin Mallomar himself had once suggested as a cost-cutting tip to Sheriff Dudival. The cook was chosen on a round robin basis. Today was Buster's turn. He wasn't feeling like doing much of anything lately. Real depression was setting in—an emotion he'd formerly thought reserved for the Mallomars. He had to be ordered off his cot. He half-heartedly prepared a salad Nicoise in honor of Mrs. Mallomar. The inmates, meanwhile, had hoped for chili and gave Buster enormous grief all through the afternoon about his "pussy" menu choice, but they couldn't dish it out like Mrs. Mallomar. Over his many days in jail, Buster would often think of her and not in a sexual way. He wondered how she was. He wondered if she was wondering how he was. And he wondered whether she had told anybody.

"McCaffrey!" barked the corrections officer. "You got a visitor."

Destiny Stumplehorst, two weeks after the untimely departure of Cord Travesty and his cocaine supply, was beginning to regain some color in her cheeks—although her nose still dripped like a gas station restroom faucet. She sat primly in a steel chair across the table from him in the ten-by-ten visiting room. She was wearing jeans, boots, and a fringe jacket. Buster took her wardrobe as a possible embrace of the good old days.

"Hello, Buster."

"'Lo, Destiny. How are you?"

"Fine. How are you?"

"Fine," he said. "Nice jacket."

"Got it at the This 'n' That shop before they made it into the Cineplex."

"Raht," Buster said, the *they* being Mallomar, of course. "Can ah fetch you a cuppa coffee or a cold non-alcoholrik bevridge?"

"No thanks, I'm fine."

There was a long silence.

"Destiny, ah 'ppreciate ya'll comin down here ta see me today. Ah know the last time we met, we dint 'xactly leave thangs tip-top."

"I guess we didn't." Destiny tried to shift the weight off the buttock she'd been favoring. "You're a big hero with Ma now."

"Now why, in heaven's name's, that?"

"'The harvest is the end of the age, and the harvesters are angels.' Matthew thirteen-thirty-nine. Ma thinks you were my harvestin' angel."

"Beg pardon…?"

"You…" Her lips began to quiver, "…killed Cord Travesty and set me free from drugs."

"Oh." The smile dropped from Buster's face. He tried to push himself back from the table, but his chair was bolted to the floor. "Uh,

Destiny, lissen here. Ah'm real glad yor mom has a favribull o-pinyin of me an all that, but ah dint kill Cord Travesty."

"I'm sorry," Destiny said, quickly looking around the room. "It's probably ain't safe to talk here, is it?"

"It's per-fekly safe. Ah jes…did…not…kill…nobody. Why's it so hard fer folks t'believe me?"

"Okay, okay," she whispered. "Sorry. That was stupid of me."

"People 'round here thank ah did a lot of thangs ah never did. That's been goin' on my en-tahr life."

"But you *did* sleep with Mrs. Mallomar. That's somethin' you *did* do, right?"

Buster took a deep breath. She was dragging that up again.

"Destiny," he answered patiently, "Ah'll tell you true, if ah could take back one dang thang in my life, that'd be the booger…but we *all* prolly have a thang er two we ree-gret doin', now don't we?"

She hung her head and nodded. "Buster, why did this happen to us?"

"You know, ah've had a lot of tahm sittin' here thinkin' 'bout that very same ishoo. What'd we do to have the whole world come crashin' down 'round our ears? Ah rahtly don't know. Alls we did was try to em-prove ourselves a bit. Is it a sin for folks lahk us to do that? Ah don't think so. Ah reckon, the mistake we made was em-provin' a mite too fast."

The corrections officer opened the door and came in—signaling their time together was up.

"Is there anything I can do for you?"

"Ah'd be much o-bliged if you stopped in to see me once and agin."

"I will," Destiny said in a broken voice.

Destiny got up to make a quick retreat before she fell to pieces. Buster, obeying the dictates of Ms. Humphrey's *Manners for Men* jumped to his feet to see her out.

"Take care now," he winked good-naturedly. Destiny burst into tears and just shook her head with the heartache of it all. After all this emotion, Buster was actually looking forward to going back to his cell.

CHAPTER TWENTY-NINE

The Defense Rests

THE NEXT DAY THE sheriff dropped in to say hello. He brought, for Buster, the children's illustrated version of *The Scarlet Pimpernel.*

"Much o-bliged, Sheriff."

"What's this I hear about you not wanting to speak to your public attorney?"

"Oh, that ain't true. Ah speak to him aplenty."

"But he says you won't tell him what he needs to know to defend you properly."

Buster interlocked his fingers and stared down at the floor.

"Sheriff, he wants to make this out as some kinda war between the Mallomars and the folks here."

"He's just trying to get you out of this. See, people around here are under the impression that you're trying to protect Mrs. Mallomar. Some people might even be thinking that *she* might have had something to do with Mr. Mallomar's demise. What do you make of all that?"

Buster took a deep breath. "Ah aint at liberty to say."

Dudival just looked at him blankly.

"I'm going to ask you one last question. That night, did you happen to see Jimmy Bayles Morgan?"

"Ah woont see her if she were the last man on earth!"

"I mean, did you see her around the house that night?"

"Heck no. Anyways, ain't she too sick to go nowhere?"

Dudival felt as though the two people in the world that he cared about most were strangling him.

Buster remained obdurate in his refusal to implicate Mrs. Mallomar. Jimmy, it seemed, wasn't going to die soon enough to allow the dignity of a post-mortem examination of her assassin's career, so Sheriff Dudival drove back up to Lame Horse Mesa to the Big Dog Ranch to effect justice the only way he had left to him.

At the reservoir, he brought two crutches from his cruiser and placed Jimmy's cowboy boots inside them. He slipped out of his shoes and put on his bedroom slippers. Then he walked around the reservoir placing Jimmy's footprints as well as fragments from the dynamite he had purloined from Jimmy's workbench. He had covered for her and her grandfather his entire career, but would not do so at the expense of Buster's life. When he got back home, Sheriff Dudival took off his slippers and unlocked his closet to retrieve an evidence box marked "JBM." In it was the meticulously documented, twenty-three-year cover-up of Jimmy's career as a serial killer. He proceeded to unload his pistol and lock it in the safe with his other weapons. He put on a clean shirt, swatted his trousers with a clothes brush. He poured himself a glass of water, then looked around the room for anything he'd forgotten. In the top drawer of his desk was a document the size of a novella, and a pen. He opened it to the last page and signed, *This is my confession, Shepard Dudival.* He placed the document and Jimmy's file prominently on the desk so no one would have trouble finding it. He unscrewed the cap on the bottle of arsenic that he had fiddled from Jimmy's place and poured half of it into the glass of water. Dudival sat on the bed, raised the glass to his lips and opened his mouth. Then, his black dial phone rang. He lowered the glass and looked at it. It rang the irritating old-fashioned way. Exasperrated, he answered it.

"Hello?"

"Sheriff Dudival?"

"Yes, Mrs. Poult."

"What are you doing?"

"I'm…having my lunch."

"Aren't you going to the court house?"

"I was thinking of skipping that today." There was a pause.

"Are you okay?"

"Yes."

"Buster called upstairs. He specifically asked that you be there today." Dudival did not speak. "He's intending to be his own lawyer and thinks you're going to be proud of him." Dudival looked at the metallic grey water in the glass.

"All right," he said as he carefully covered the glass with a High Grade coaster. It would keep. He picked up the evidence box, put it in his cruiser and drove to town. Buster had been reluctantly approved by the court to act as his own attorney. The only meat left on the bone of this bizarre trial was Buster's rambling and inarticulate closing argument about why he was innocent, how he originally met the Mallomars, and what happened that night sans the blue material. It was a story with so many backtracks, dead ends, and side trails—that after four and a half hours both the judge and the county prosecutor felt like their brains had been dragged through wild rose bushes and beaten with a Sears Roebuck crowbar. Buster, although admitting to the jury that it looked bad, asked them to believe that he loved Mr. Mallomar, who was in many ways the father that he never had—even though Buster had officially had five. Some of the jury were visibly moved by what Buster had to say and even willing to forgive him for taking such a long time to say it.

It was the State of Colorado's turn. The county prosecutor, in his summation, lost no time in painting Buster as a homicidal opportunist who had planned from the beginning to get his hands on land by hook or by crook. Buster's seduction of Mrs. Mallomar, he said, was merely one cynical means to an end. Once he had won Mr. Mallomar's trust, Buster proceeded to woo Mrs. Mallomar, to replace her un-attentive husband so that the two of them could live at the Big Dog Ranch happily ever after. Destiny Stumplehorst was in court that day, but stormed tearfully out the back door at this accusation.

The jury was sent out to decide Buster's fate, but not before Judge Englelander took the time to pedantically instruct them in the legal nuances of "reasonable doubt" and the weight of "circumstantial evidence." They asked no further questions, nor did they request to see any of the evidence to review in their sequestered chambers. Even Court TV was surprised that, by the next day—Friday morning—they had reached a verdict. Outsiders had no way of knowing that Saturday was the start of Vanadium's 4H Ranchers of Tomorrow Days, and everyone was eager to get back home to spruce up their animals.

ੴ

"HAS THE JURY REACHED a verdict?" Judge Englelander said, when the jury had returned.

"Yes, your honor," the jury foreman replied.

"How do you find the defendant, Buster McCaffrey?"

"On the charge of first degree murder, we the jury find the defendant…not guilty!" croaked a phlegmy voice. Everyone turned around to see who dared interrupt at this sensitive legal juncture—and there was Jimmy Bayles Morgan, gaunt and hollow-eyed, standing at the back of the courtroom wheeling a small tank of oxygen behind her.

"Mr. Whoever You Are…" Everyone in the courthouse from Vanadium hee-hawed at the Judge's ignorance of Jimmy's gender.

"You're out of order. If you say another word, I'm holding you in contempt of this court," said Judge Englelander.

"Ah kilt him."

There was a gasp from the gallery.

"No, she dint!" Buster objected.

"Shud up, you mo-ron. Ah'm bustin' you outta here," Jimmy said out of the side of her mouth.

"I'll have to warn you…" said the Judge.

"No, ah'm warnin' you, lady. Ya'll about to pur-tissi-pate in a miscarriage a justice. Ah killed that sonofabitch Mallomar as sure as ah'm standin' here b'fore ya!" Judge Englelander banged the gavel to get everybody to quiet down.

"Identify yourself."

"Ah'm Jimmy…Bayles…Morgan."

It was at this moment that Judge Englelander regretted not having attended law school. She'd earned her judge's robes simply winning a local election by four votes. What was she to do? Everyone was waiting for her to say something. Her left eye, which was still a bit puffy from the surgery, started to twitch uncontrollably as if a grasshopper was trapped under her skin. She tried to suppress it with her index finger, but to no avail. Finally, she cleared her throat.

"Mr. Morgan, why did you take so long to come forward with this information?"

"Ah was feelin' under the weather after ah'd done it—the murder that is—and taken to my bed."

"I see. Do you know the defendant?"

"Yes, ma'am, ah most certly do."

"And what, sir, is exactly your relationship to the defendant?"

Jimmy turned around and looked directly at Buster and managed only the faintest of smiles.

"Ah'm his mother."

CHAPTER THIRTY

Jiminy

At first, Buster wasn't sure that he heard that right, nor did anyone else, for that matter. But as it set in, the pandemonium in the courtroom was so raucous that the soundmen from the media had to yank their headsets before their eardrums exploded. Jimmy turned around to face the courtroom, more specifically her old friend, Sheriff Dudival, who sat with Jimmy's incriminating evidence box at his feet. She slowly wheeled her squeaking oxygen tank to stand beside him and said, "'Gennelness and morill strength com-bined must be the sa-li-ent carakerstics of the gennelman'…Missuz Hump-freez *Manners For Men*." Dudival put his head in his hands and cried. Jimmy placed a weather-beaten hand on his shoulder and patted him as if she were comforting Ranger.

"Didja really think ah'd let anythin' happen to him, ol' soldier?"

The next logical question that occurred to everyone was this: if Jimmy was the mother then who was the father? Slowly, everyone pivoted around in his or her chair to gaze upon Sheriff Dudival, whose eyes were still moist from Jimmy's declaration. Twenty-five years of derision would now come to an end as he sat up proudly and looked with affection upon his old inamorata. Judge Englelander banged her gavel.

"Order in the court!"

Of course, none of the Vanadians took heed of her request. She considered her options for a moment then banged the gavel for the second time.

"This court is in recess!" Judge Englelander said standing. "Mr... Ms. Morgan, Mr. District Attorney...come to my chambers now!"

The corrections officer re-handcuffed Buster and began to lead him out. Buster looked incredulously at Jimmy, her skin waxy and yellow as a Yukon potato.

"Don't worry, son," she said and winked with typical bravado. "No one knows the law better than a Morgan—and Grampie give me the playbook on this one."

Buster, more confused than ever, was led out to the alley where the transport was waiting surrounded by the media and reporters. Jimmy was pushed, somewhat roughly, into the judge's chambers.

"This better not be bullshit!" Judge Englelander said, encouraged by the outlandish events to use profanity. Jimmy turned off her oxygen and started to fire up a Commander. "What do you think you're doing? You can't smoke in here! This is a government building!"

Jimmy smiled and, uncharacteristically of her, obeyed. She tossed the still-lit cigarette out the window. "All right, then." Judge Englelander was flummoxed. She had no idea as to how to proceed.

"Ah'm willin' to waiver my rights to self-incrimination," Jimmy offered, trying to move things along. The judge decided to take a page from the sheriff's book—as the highest ranking elected state official present—and improvise.

"Ms. Morgan, would you be willing to place your right hand on a Bible and say that everything you are about to say is the whole truth and nothing but the truth?"

"Hell, yeah," said Jimmy.

Now the sheriff entered the room, standing against the wall.

"Perhaps now you can tell me what exactly happened to Mr. Mallomar."

"Well, here's what happened. Ah had a powerful hate for that man. He came here for an 'Authentic Western Experience' and then whaddaya know? The sonofabitch goes and changes ever' damn thang! So I set a charge a dynamite to that there rezee-vor they got up there above the house. The resultin' mudslide swept the fat-assed bastard away. And the rest, as they say, is history." The judge looked to Sheriff Dudival.

"Is what she asserts possible, Sheriff?"

Jimmy looked sangfroid at her old co-conspirator. With Jimmy willing to stand tall on the Mallomar murder and Buster steered clear of the Dominguez and Cord Travesty homicides, a patch of sunshine was now shining over Lame Horse Mesa. "I would say, yes, that is entirely possible."

Of course, in Jimmy's tale, the only murder she owned up to was one murder never committed. She had cagily excised the part of the evening that dealt with Cookie Dominguez and Cord Travesty. The way she saw it, there was no use confessing to something that Buster wasn't on the hook for—thanks to Sheriff Dudival. But the judge still remained skeptical.

"Ms. Morgan, it's obvious that you're gravely ill..."

"Come down with cancer," Jimmy said, instinctively reaching for a cigarette but then putting it back.

"How can the court know that, having received a death sentence yourself, you're not attempting to take the blame for your son?"

Jimmy laughed so hard she had to spit a glob of expectorate into the waste basket. "Do ah haveta tell ever'body how to do their fuckin' job 'round here? Examine the damn crime scene, search my domo-cile!"

She looked over at Sheriff Dudival and winked.

"I'm not quite sure I understand your motivation in committing this crime."

"Ya don't need no motivation when yor carryin' out orders."

"And whose orders were those?"

"The kinda orders a body don't lightly agnore."

"By whose orders, exactly, did you kill Mr. Mallomar?"

Even Sheriff Dudival was anxious to hear where she was going with this one. A sly smile crept across the old cowboy's face as she slowly extended her cadaverous hand to the Holy Bible sitting on the table and tapped its cover with a nicotine-stained fingernail.

"His'n," she merely said, implementing Grampie's playbook.

Sheriff Dudival cocked his head slightly. How could she make this stick? Everyone knew her as the most profane, blaspheming person in the county. She was obviously having some fun on her way out.

"God ordered you. How?"

"He speaks to me."

"Is he speaking to you right now?"

"No, ma'am. He only speaks to me in one place and one place only."

"And where is that?"

"The Hail Mary."

Judge Englelander looked to Sheriff Dudival for the local information.

"It's an abandoned silver mine on Lame Horse Mesa."

Jimmy was remanded into Sheriff Dudival's custody. In the cruiser on the way back to Vanadium, Jimmy was finally able to fire up a smoke.

"Ah saw what you did up there…at the rezee-vor."

"Oh yeah? What did I do?"

"Ah am-bell-ished it a might. Go up and see fer yersef."

"I just might do that."

"Didja see how everbody looked at ya in the courtroom?" She cough-laughed and shook her head. "They think yor the daddy." Dudival smiled, liking that deceit. "Ah think it'd be better fer all concerned if'n ya jes let'm go on thinkin' long them lines."

"All right." It kind of cheered him to think of himself as Buster's father. After all, he had taken a proprietary interest in the boy from the day he was born—a guardian angel yes, but not, in fact, Buster's father.

After Sheriff Morgan's untimely death, Jimmy became the sole beneficiary of the Morgan's insurance policy that provided double indemnity in the case of his dying in the line of duty—a sum of fifty thousand dollars. There was also the deed to the dried-up Hail Mary silver mine that Atomic Mines had given their bought dog "in trade" for making a certain state mining inspector disappear. There were some books, clothing, weapons and an oil painting of a local prostitute named Hog-Nosed Fanny that Morgan had evidently commissioned. Jimmy used her inheritance to buy a vacant piece of land on Lame Horse Mesa that came with a sheepherder's wagon. Deputy Dudival, who won election as the new sheriff, was not in favor of her living up there alone and unprotected. He worried that there were too many people who hated her grandfather's guts and might want to take it out on her. But Jimmy felt she could take care of herself and that was that.

Just a few weeks later, she opened her eyes to find three men standing over her bed wearing potato sacks over their heads. It was around two-thirty in the morning. They were drunk, but not drunk enough for her to push them out the door. Jimmy's first gambit was to cajole them into having another drink with her. She got out of bed and went to the shelf where she kept a bottle of Highland Fling—

mainly for use as an antiseptic on horses. Behind the glasses was one of her grandfather's loaded pistols. Jimmy made a lunge for her gun, but they grabbed her before she could get her hands on it. The three of them beat her up badly then raped her—Jimmy, all the while coolly taking note of the kinds of boots they were wearing, their clothes, identifying tattoos, jewelry, wristwatches, etc. When it was over, they left. Jimmy washed herself in the horse trough. She didn't cry. She poured herself a drink and had a cigarette. She was about to get in her truck and drive to Sheriff Dudival's house but decided against it, feeling ashamed.

It was Jimmy, and not the poor Mormon girl, who struggled across that snowy mesa that New Year's night with Buster dangling between her legs. A few months after being raped, she started to feel changes in her body that scared and confused her. When she actually started to look pregnant, she retreated in horror to her sheepherder's wagon and stayed there. No one had laid eyes on her the whole time including Shep. When he drove out there to see her, she wouldn't let him in. Shep convinced himself she was acting this way because he had not found her grandfather's killers.

Finally, on the night that Buster came into the world, Jimmy realized that she could keep him a secret no longer. She needed help, and the only person she trusted was Shep Dudival. The snow on her dirt road was too deep for her truck to drive. With brass and determination, she made it the sheriff's office and gave birth to the baby on the floor of the men's restroom. She finally admitted what had happened to her, and Shep swore to find the men responsible and make them pay. She told him, with an odd look on her face, that that would not be necessary. Clearly, she'd already taken care of them. What she asked for, instead, was his cooperation in a cover story about the baby. She didn't want anyone to know that it was hers.

Whatever her motives, Jimmy and Dudival entered into a pact that would haunt them for the rest of their lives—she regretting having given up the baby and he regretting that he looked the other way for three of her first murders. Little would he know, when taking his first step on that slippery slope, that he would become her unwitting accomplice. Jimmy slyly concocted a phony person, the McCaffrey girl. Dudival produced a phony death certificate. There were only a few people still around in Vanadium who would ever stop to wonder who was actually in that grave in the cemetery—if it wasn't the poor Mormon girl. An exhumation would have revealed a pine box containing a ninety-five pound sack of rocks.

ꕤ

Sheriff Dudival had Mrs. Poult fix up a cell for Jimmy with a real mattress and other lady-like comforts, but Jimmy, taking one look at it, demanded a regular cell. As instructed by Judge Englelander, Dudival went through the motions of corroborating Jimmy's story. Once again, he returned to the ruins of the Mallomar residence. Crews were still hoping to find the Mallomar at the bottom of the Cracker Jack box. Dudival hiked up the hill behind the house to what was left of the reservoir and found not only the Jimmy boot prints that he made there—but entirely new evidence in place; Kleenex which contained Jimmy's bloody sputum, some of her cigarette butts and an empty bottle of Crazy Crow embossed with too many fingerprints to count. Jimmy had evidently been back to salt the "crime scene." As he placed these items in an evidence bag, Dudival couldn't help smiling to himself. That's why he loved her.

At Jimmy's cabin back at the pony ranch, Dudival found pictures of Marvin Mallomar clipped out of the local newspaper taped to her work board. She had taken a pencil and drawn a noose around his neck in one, horns and fangs on another. Dudival also discovered a hastily written "diary"—in the drawer next to a carton of Phillip Morris Commanders and a rolled up tube of Preparation H. The diary spoke of God's plan for Jimmy with Noah-like instructions as to how He wanted the reservoir blown and why it was necessary "to send Mr. Mallomar ass-under." Dudival had never realized that Jimmy had such a creative flare. When he submitted his written findings to the court, Jimmy, despite her terminal illness, was formally booked on pre-meditated murder.

The jury was reconvened and, once again, a public defender represented the indigent client. Jimmy threw herself upon the mercy of the court and asked for only one thing—that the jury be given the chance to hear the Word of God themselves. The public defender contacted Jimmy's doctor in Grand Junction and discussed whether it was neurologically possible that her illness was responsible for the heavenly voices she was hearing. The doctor confirmed that the position of her brain tumors were likely to create auditory hallucinations. Armed with this information, he gently warned Jimmy against pushing for the jury to discover what he already knew—that the voice of God had, in her case, a scientific causality.

Jimmy insisted, however, and gave specific instructions as to how and when the jury was to be taken to the Hail Mary mine. It had to be on a night with a streaky orange and purple sky, no earlier than six o'clock in the evening. Folding gallery chairs had to be placed in juxtaposition to the mine's entrance according to a drawing that Jimmy had crudely sketched on the back of an In-N-Out Burger bag (Jimmy was not a fan of Mary's catered food). And so, with everything carried out exactly as she had dictated, the jury was taken to the mine the next evening on a borrowed Vanadium school bus.

CHAPTER THIRTY-ONE

The Rapture

That evening, the Vanadium sky cooperated with Jimmy's production of what Cecil B. DeMille might have called an Authentic Ten Commandment Experience. Alizarin-washed cumulus nimbus framed a deep cadmium yellow egg yolk descending in the west. The folding chairs faced the boarded-up Hail Mary Mine's entrance at an oblique thirty-degree angle as Jimmy had specified. The jury, as well as the Stumplehorsts, Edita Dominguez, Mary Boyle, and almost everybody in town who owned a camp chair, sat with unbridled anticipation. Was Jimmy Bayles Morgan's claim possible? Did God, as some already believed, favor their town? Did His spirit reside here in the aptly named Hail Mary Mine? Six-thirty passed with only the solitary lowing of a cow in the distance. Seven o'clock came with some fidgeting and praying. The judge whispered something to the bailiff and he nodded in agreement. Jimmy had the feeling that they were about to call her game on account of darkness. She got up from her chair and, using a cane, staggered before them.

"Iffin ah could jes have yer 'ttention fer a moment… See a lotta fermilyar faces in the crowd—which is unnerstandabull since ah know alls you. See Kyle Andersen there mutterin' over that Bible a his… Hey there, Kyle. Remember 'bout ten years ago you was moaning to somebody in the café 'bout how yer neighbor wouldn't sell you that hundred and twenty acres so you could grow alfalfa cause he was fixin' to chop them up inta forty-acre ranchettes? You recall that? Didja pray that he'd change his mind? Cause lo and beholt, a week later, *somebody* forced him off the road into the canyon and he was kilt. Then what happened, Kyle?"

Kyle Andersen looked up numbly. "His widow sold it to me."

"That's right, she did, dint she?" Jimmy shaded her eyes from the setting sun and peered into the crowd. "And there's Edita Dominguez. Once your daddy and yer uncle were laid to rest, there was no controllin' yor husband, was there, darlin'? You thought he was molestin' yor boys and you went and taddled on'm to Social Services. Ain't that right? But they dint do nothin' 'bout it, did they—cause, well…yor jes a Messican. Then one summer night, what happened? *Somebody* locked him in that kiln a his and blew his ass to kingdom come."

Edita Dominguez put a handkerchief to her mouth. "*¡Madre de Dios!*"

"And Skylar…remember the time you were cryin' to some drunk at the Odd Fellows 'bout how you wisht you had a son? Well, it took some doin', but *somebody* cleared the brush fer it that ta happen. *Somebody* had ta kill that pink-assed land defiler Svendergard and then *somebody* had to send ol' Bob Boyle on up to Rodeo Heaven. Then you got your son, Buster McCaffrey, one of the best all 'round cowboys we ever seen in this county. And what'd you do? You fired him jes b'cause he gave yer daughter a poke! Tell you what, Skylar…

somebody dint 'prreciate that. *Somebody* was even thinkin' of settin a stick a dynamite in that outhouse you jerk off in. But then..." Jimmy looked over to where Destiny Stumplehorst was standing. "... *somebody* had a change of heart—thinkin' how unfair it'erd be to leave ol' Buster without a future father-in-law ta balance out that crack-less pee-stachio of a wife a yors." Jimmy looked at Calvina Stumplehorst, hocked up a goober, and spit. "Have you guessed who that *somebody* is, people? It ain't God, neighbors and frens, who's been answerin' the prayers of this fersaken land for over sixty years. And lemme tell ya somethin' else, ah don't work in mizsteeryus ways like some. My work is direk. My work sticks."

Here she paused for a dramatic sigh and looked out over her sheep.

"But alas, dear frens, my life is now comin' to an end. No use kiddin' mahself. And ah'm a powerful worried cause once ah'm a gone, who's gonna take care a this place that ah've so dearly loved? Ah'm leavin' a son, but he's a turn-the-other-cheek sorta feller. So ah'm puttin' y'all on notice. You try to take the easy money and sell this here town out and ah'll be payin' ya a visit—in one form or 'nother...and you ain't gonna like it ah uh-shoor you!"

Jimmy looked over the crowd and made fierce eye contact with as many as she could, conjured up a mighty goober, then spit. As the sun slipped below the horizon and cool air exchanged with warm from the canyon below, she raised her arms akimbo as an unmistakable moan emanated from the mine behind her. It started low and suffering-like then rose to an unsettling howl. Jimmy kept a straight face and just nodded her head as if she and she alone understood the tongue with which it spoke. This had the desired effect on the ad hoc congregation who, if they weren't fundamentally religious, were at least susceptible to seeing the face of Jesus in a burnt piece of Wonderbread toast.

Some of them dropped to their knees and started to cry. Others prayed. Others ran to their cars to get the hell out of there. The judge had had enough and instructed the bailiff to handcuff Jimmy and take back her into custody.

"You heard me! Ah'll be payin ya'll a visit!!!"

ᘐ

THE CORRECTIONS OFFICER CAME to collect Buster from his cell the next morning. He was taken downstairs to sign some papers and collect his personal possessions. His jeans seemed big on him now, and his White's Packers seemed stiff like they belonged to someone else. The clerk handed Buster his money and his wallet. He was asked to check and make sure that everything was there. He didn't care about the money—actually three dollars was missing to help pay for a pizza a couple weeks ago. There was only one thing that he cared about, and it was still preserved between the folds of an unpaid parking ticket.

Some men go out and get drunk the first thing out of jail. Some go and settle old scores. Some men go and have themselves two porterhouse steaks, mashed potatoes, and a gallon of pecan ice cream. Some go to a whorehouse and have the equivalent. Buster paid twenty-five cents for a shower and then rode out to Lame Horse Mesa where he gave Destiny Stumplehorst his buttercup and asked for her hand in marriage. She didn't bother with her parents' permission this time.

The two were married on horseback just as it was in Buster's dream. The bride wore a white rodeo queen outfit caped with a long white-fringed leather jacket. And just as in his dream, all of Buster's past mothers were there to tearfully see him off into Holy Matrimony—all paying deference of course to Jimmy Bayles Morgan, his biological mother. She was brought in on a tame old milk horse, the reins of which were held by Sheriff Dudival, Buster's best man. Jimmy, bald and weighing no more than a ventriloquist's dummy, was defiantly dressed as a man.

Jimmy let the newlyweds move onto her property. She gave them the old sheepherder's wagon that had been Buster's refuge as an exile. Sheriff Dudival moved out of his trailer and into his one true love's cabin. Since sex was no longer an issue with either of them, they slept comfortably in the same bed with each other. Doc Solitcz came regularly to make sure Jimmy was comfortable until she died a month later. Buster was at her side when she passed and held his murdering mother's hand.

"Son…ah did the best ah could."

"Ah know, ah know. Calm yorsef."

"And ah said a lot a terr-bull thangs 'bout people…ah dint mean half of 'em."

"Ah never figgered you did…Mommy."

Jimmy reached under her pillow and handed Buster an envelope.

"A li'l present fer yor birthday. Guess ah'm gonna be missin' it." Buster opened it. Inside was the $300 she had Martin Flowers cough up before he, too, joined the league of those Jimmy Bayles Morgan could not abide.

Sheriff Dudival, looking on, was pleased that Jimmy had been given this one moment of peace. Around these parts, love had been the true taproot of crime.

Buster, the sheriff, Doc, Ned Gigglehorn, and Destiny Stumplehorst made a little service for Jimmy and buried her next to Ranger. She had requested, despite her newly acquired reputation as a modern-day Savonarola, that no mention of the Creator be made over her remains. What little she had in her estate went to Buster. She left him her land, some horses, tack, her guns, and the Hail Mary mine.

The mine, which had not produced a dime in thirty years, turned out to yield a mother lode much richer than gold or silver. Word of Jimmy's performance at the mine had gotten out. At first, people said that this was the place where the devil speaks. A few months after that, the religious folks appropriated the miracle and soon pilgrims started showing up to hear the Word of God for themselves.

It wasn't exactly Buster's métier to market the Hail Mary mine. That was left to Destiny who knew how to do these things from her stint in the properties game. She secured a loan from the bank for an asphalt road and small turnabout for tour coaches. What came later was a gift shop/museum, bookstore, and T-shirt and coffee mug shop with the official literature about The Miracle. The first year, the mine took in seven million dollars from the merchandising and a movie deal financed by a Christian group called "Families at the Crossroads." Buster used some of that money to purchase five hundred acres from the Stumplehorsts—which the missus considered her Christian obligation to sell at ten thousand per. Most of the Hail Mary windfall went to rebuild the school, construct a new library, and endow the Jimmy Bayles Morgan Home for Unwed Mothers. The Vanadium High School Baseball team changed its name from the Vanadium Atomics to "The Rangers."

Sheriff Dudival, even knowing Jimmy all these years, had never been taken to the mine—let alone, heard the Miracle of the Spirit. One night, when the last of the holy pilgrims' buses had left, he drove out there to take a look around. He pried off the creosote slats that barred entry and went inside with a torch and climbing rope. The wind had come up with the sunset, and the "whispering" that people interpreted as the Word of God began. From inside the mine, Dudival could feel the wind at his neck as he followed the sound. With his flashlight, he illuminated the vent tunnel above him that traveled upwards one hundred yards to an opening at the top of the mesa. There was just enough room for a man to climb. Slowly, he made his way up until something blocked his path. He made sure he had a secure footing before shining his light on the obstruction. In front of him were the bullet-ventilated skulls of three men. Dudival could only assume that they were the rapists whom Jimmy had dispatched some twenty-five years ago. When the wind came into the mine at sunset, it traveled up the air shaft and through these skulls—stacked one on top of another like dried peas in a child's whistle—sending out the "Word." Sheriff Dudival clambered back down and, in honor of Jimmy's memory, took her last secret to the grave beside her, two days later.

Lame Horse Mesa's much-publicized rondo of violence had a deleterious effect on the real estate market. Vanadium found itself characterized as the most likely place to die of a homicide on a short list after Chicago and Mogadishu. As a result of this disaffection, the Svendergard golf course project was put on hold, and its attendant condominium and townhouse development evaporated. The Stumplehorsts and the other ranchers, who had prematurely set their sights for early retirement on Kiowa Island, had to reconcile with the fact that they would probably be spending the rest of their lives getting up at four in the morning to shovel shit out of cow stalls. Many of them, witnessing Buster's success on the Big Dog Ranch, grumpily followed his lead and returned native grasses to their land.

Buster continued to care for the Mallomar herd even though it was never asked of him. He figured it was the least he could do to honor Mr. Mallomar's memory. If Mrs. Mallomar ever got out of the hospital, she would have a nice little business and a healthy place to raise their child. Buster had already explained the situation to Destiny Stumplehorst. She was, of course, jealous. Having a child with another woman, however, failed to stack up against her losing her Buttercup to the gas chamber, and eventually she let it go. If she had learned one thing from the Thessalonians Home Study Course of Oxford, Mississippi, it was that the most enduring lessons from the Bible were always the ones attached to the most violent or lustful stories. And that was probably why the people who lived in Vanadium would not soon forget what had happened here. Did that mean they would go back to the way things were before Mr. M appeared on the scene? There was probably no going back—even if some of the old ranchers felt a smug moment of victory over progress with a question mark. Someone would surely be arriving any day, emboldened by undervalued land prices, to risk his neck for development. Would they allow the newcomer to once again tilt the delicate balance of the Vanadian ecology—that had been so carefully tended to by Jimmy Bayles Morgan and Shep Dudival? Who would be the one to do what needed to be done? That, of course, remained to be seen.

CHAPTER THIRTY-TWO

Cha-pol-loc, the Ute

FROM THE TIME SHE had arrived at the secret clinic in Park Slope, Brooklyn, Mrs. Mallomar had remained incommunicado and under heavy sedation. It was not her doctor's judgment that required this particular treatment, but her late husband's consigliore, Sidney Glasker. Trazadone was administered partly to block her anguish over what had happened the night of her husband's death and partly to block subpoenas for her testifying at the tabloid free-for-all which was Buster's trial. To make sure that the doctor was on the same page, Glasker had approved an endowment of five million dollars to the clinic on behalf of the Marvin Mallomar Trust.

While on this chemical vacation, Dana's health was strictly monitored and it could be said that she, while unconscious, was in the best shape of her life. To the attendants on duty, she seemed to have an active dream life and she often vocalized, but her mumblings were not allowed on her chart. Sometimes she called out for her husband.

Sometimes she would yell for "Buster"—who the nurses assumed was her pet dog.

Glasker would make a point to come visit her every other day. He would bring his lunch and sit with her. He liked Dana, and it wasn't for sinister reasons that he kept her on ice, but rather what he felt to be his ongoing responsibility to protect the Mallomar family. Typically, he would find her in a fetal position—with an almost transcendental expression of beatitude. And he would think, *why did Marvin have such a difficult time with this lovely creature?* When he heard from the public defender that the defense was now about to make its closing statement and Dana Mallomar's testimony was now moot, Glasker instructed the doctors to remove her from the sedative. However, Dana did not seem, at first, interested in regaining consciousness. The place that she happened to be was too warm and comfy, so filled with love that her mind refused to be taken from it.

This love mantra, if you will, played out in a series of simple images. The first was that she was standing in her Colorado house wearing Vietnamese-style clothing. She had gone to some trouble making a special dinner, despite the fact that she didn't cook. She was excited about something. Then her guest arrived. It wasn't Marvin. It was the cowboy who worked for them. She opened some champagne to tell him this incredible news. She was pregnant. Every fertility doctor in New York had told her it was impossible, but there it was. She was pregnant. And the cowboy was the father. The cowboy even offered to marry her. What an incredibly kind thing to say, she said. But she told him it wasn't necessary. She wept, not because she was sad, but because the cowboy was so kind, despite the fact that she had been so mean to him. She put her arms around him. She felt the cowboy stiffen. Someone else was in the house. She turned to find her husband. He had surreptitiously entered the house and had heard their conversation. He was standing on the staircase holding a gun.

He said that he had come home to shoot them. Then, just when they thought they were going to die, he said he had just had an epiphany. He was not the victim in this, he said—rather Dana. He said that a great injustice had been done to her—that all these years, she had been made to feel inadequate for not being able to conceive—when the inadequate one had been him, Marvin Mallomar. Then, her husband broke down and cried. He said the two people who he loved most in the world were standing in front of him. Dana Mallomar said, *You mean, you're not going to leave me?* And he said, *That's how some schmuck from Bensonhurst would act, not Marvin Mallomar. I love you, darling,* he said. *I've always loved you.* She said, *Marvin, I love you*. The cowboy started to cry. Mallomar said, *It's okay. It's okay.* Mrs. Mallomar started to walk to her husband. She wanted to put her arms around him, when suddenly a wall of mud came crashing through the living room wall and wiped the staircase and her husband from frame. The gun went off. She tried to go after him, but the roof collapsed on her and the cowboy.

Mrs. Mallomar played this dream over and over. Her private room was on the second floor of the clinic overlooking the playground of a children's school. Their laughter and chatter created the ambient noise of the dream, prompting her to wonder—"Did I have the baby?" And there was one other thing. For some reason unknown to her, there was a herd of cattle in the living room.

ꝏ

Sidney Glasker was just grabbing a cigar to take to lunch and was almost out the door when he received a phone call from the Securities and Exchange Commission. They were dropping the insider trading case against Marvin Mallomar.

"I'm sure he'd be very happy to hear about this, except he's dead."

"Yes, we know," they said.

"Not that I'm looking a gift horse in the mouth, but why are you doing this now?"

"We're not at liberty to say. We're just dropping it."

"You just had to make his last moments on earth a living hell, didn't you, you miserable shits?"

Glasker hung up the phone and sat sadly back down in his Eames chair. He forgot he was indoor and lit his cigar with a platinum lighter that bore the inscription, *I'M NOT AT LIBERTY TO SAY*. It had been a gift from the mysterious Marvin Mallomar on his sixtieth birthday. Sidney had never been allowed to tell anyone that he had known Marvin all of his life. They grew up together in the Bronx, both coming from working class families. Marvin had ambitions that required him to shed his skin several times. He started with a new name. His given name was Danny Dingle. His parents were from the Dingle Peninsula, County Kerry. Marvin knew a person with a name like Danny Dingle would never be taken seriously, so he changed his first name to Marvin after Marvin Miller, the actor who played Michael Anthony in the fifties TV show *The Millionaire*. He was the guy who delivered the million-dollar checks to deserving people from the eponymous millionaire, J. Beresford Tipton. For his surname, he chose "Mallomar" after his favorite cookie. Marvin Mallomar and Sidney stayed close for the rest of Mallomar's life. It was Sidney, unbeknownst to all the other lawyers, who actually knew everything.

"Marvin, you crazy sonofabitch, you beat it," he said to the lighter. "I don't know how you beat it, but you beat it." Sidney put the lighter back in his pocket, swallowed the lump in his throat and walked out through the reception area. He was having lunch with a group of downtown landowners opposing the building of a mosque at the site of the World Trade Towers. As he passed the receptionist, she tried to get his attention.

"Uh, Mr. Glasker..." she whispered. She made a funny face and wiggled her eyebrows in the direction of the seating area.

"There's a man over there who wants to speak to you, but I...I mean, he didn't look right...so I've already called security. You may want to wait until they take him out of here."

Sidney looked in the direction the receptionist was gesturing. There was a man sitting on the floor, cross-legged with his back to him. Glasker slowly approached. The man wasn't wearing any shoes. The bottoms of his feet were black with the grime of New York sidewalks. He was wearing tan Levis and a gaudy cowboy shirt, rolled up at the sleeves—his hands and arms red, the color of a Navajo. Glasker walked around the man, and feeling charitable from the SEC's decision, decided to talk to him.

"How may I help you, sir?"

The red man, about sixty years old, wearing a large turquoise amulet around his neck, bald on top with long strands of grey hair that fell to his shoulders, looked up at him with amused sparkling blue eyes.

"Hello, Sidney."

"Oh my god!" Sidney gasped, and fell to the man's knees, sobbing. Marvin Mallomar chuckled softly and patted his old friend's back while he waited for him to get over the shock before he told his story.

ຍ

THE NIGHT OF THE mudslide, Mallomar had in fact, gone to the house consumed with anger. He was so out of his mind that he considered killing Buster and his wife, and then himself—if he still had the stomach for it. Miraculously, the mudslide interceded and he was swept crime-free from the house. He tried to ride it out, but the tide was too strong for him. It tore at him, ripped out all of his hair and abraded his skin so badly that it absorbed the color of the red mud like a tattoo. He finally stopped trying to fight the power of it and gave in. Unconscious, he was carried down from his ranch all the way to Main Street where a dumpster behind Einstein's Book Store shielded his body from further abuse. When he came to, he managed to get to his feet and stagger naked into the street. A double amputee, named Shaman Longfeather, had his driver stop his truck for him. Mallomar was, of course, delirious at the time. His mouth, nose, and ears were filled with mud. Shaman Longfeather rolled down his passenger window and asked the man to identify himself. All Mallomar could get out of his mud-choked mouth were the sounds, CHA…POL…LOC. To Shaman Longfeather, the prophecy that he had received in sweat lodge had come true. The Great Spirit had sent his Messenger, Cha-pol-loc, borne of Mother Earth to save the tribe. There was little conversation after that realization. Mallomar was hurried into the truck and driven deep inside the reservation. No one was allowed to see him. Only the tribe's chief was permitted to gaze directly at his face and only after eating peyote—the fear being that looking soberly into the Messenger's face without preparation could drive a man crazy. The Utes believed that Mallomar's trauma was due to his difficult rebirth from the Mother and further complicated by being put in the presence of Man so quickly. Hundreds, perhaps thousands of the faithful, stood outside his teepee and waited as Shaman Longfeather—strapped into a wheel chair—chanted over him. Blindfolded women gave him the nourishment of a human being, but none of them were allowed to touch his sexual organs or watch him defecate—out of sensitivity to Cha-pol-loc's new encumbrance with both of these human complications.

When Mallomar finally regained some of his strength, he had no knowledge of the murder trial or anything else. His vocal cords had been so damaged by the mud and debris that he wasn't sure he could still speak. The Elders immediately put his body on a stretcher and drove him to the very top of Sleeping Ute Mountain—the holiest of holy places for the Utes. There, with seven pots of sagebrush burning, the tribe finally put it to him.

"Our people are tired and hungry—our youth, disenchanted with the Old Ways and we are poor. Cha-pol-loc, he who has been sent to us from the Great Spirit, guide us and tell us what should we do!"

Mallomar blinked his eyes and swallowed. He licked his lips and worked up a little saliva and beckoned for his tribesmen to come closer.

"Build…a…casino," he said.

ꙮ

GLASKER WAS INCREDULOUS. THIS was all too much.

"I came here to secure the financing…and straighten up a few other things," Cha-pol-loc said, helping himself to a cigar from the inlaid box on Sidney's desk.

"Marvin, I don't know what to say."

"I'm not Marvin anymore, Sidney. I'm Cha-pol-loc." Sidney searched Mallomar's face for a trace of a kibitzing twinkle, but there was none.

"Did anybody tell you what happened after your…disappearance?"

"I heard they tried the kid for murder, but he got off," Cha-pol-loc said, with an easy cast of his hand.

"You seem kind of blasé about it, Mar…Cha-pol-loc."

"I knew it was never going to stick."

"How could you be so sure?"

Cha-pol-loc just shrugged.

"The same way I knew the Mallomar Man was going to get off on the insider trading charge."

"You already know the SEC dropped the case against you?"

Cha-pol-loc smiled.

"All right." Glasker said and then decided to test Cha-pol-loc's sanguinity. "Dana's in a mental hospital…and pregnant."

"I'm aware of that also."

"This is your opportunity to divorce her in a way that protects your core assets."

Cha-pol-loc did not betray an opinion about that one way or another.

"It's not your child, Cha-pol-loc. You know that, too…right?"

"Cha-pol-loc has many powers. Procreating with a human being is not one of them."

"What's that supposed to mean?"

Once again, Cha-pol-loc smiled enigmatically.

"Sidney, I will need you to get copies of the Mallomar Man's identification and credit cards."

"You mean, you're walking around New York without identification or money?"

"That's right."

"Then how did you get here?"

"My tribe brought me here across the land of the Apache, Sioux, and Cherokee."

"Uh huh. When I get your…his things, how will I find you?"

"My teepee and my men are hidden behind the reservoir in Central Park. But I will know when you have what I have asked for and will find you." Cha-pol-loc rose from his seat.

"A casino, Sidney. Quickly."

The meeting was over.

Four days later, Mallomar's identification in hand, Cha-pol-loc and his braves broke camp for Brooklyn and the research laboratory of Dr. Howard Simes. He fitted Shaman Longfeather with the T-1000 titanium leg prostheses—complete with the cutting edged "Chandler

Socket." By moonrise, the Shaman was walking without a cane and, playful prankster that he was, tripping some of the braves when they tried to look cool strutting down Atlantic Avenue.

"May I help you?" said the night orderly at Mrs. Mallomar's clinic, somewhat nervously. The portico of the institution was filled with thirty Ute braves dressed for a healing ceremony wearing coyote skins over their heads.

"I have come for the Mallomar woman," Cha-pol-loc said simply.

The orderly considered calling the police, but there was a racial profiling lawsuit to consider. He decided to act like he was playing it out one more step and pulled Mrs. Mallomar's file.

"I'm sorry, sir, but Mrs. Mallomar cannot be released without the authorization of her doctor or her husband," he said, reading the cover Post-it note.

Cha-pol-loc calmly retrieved Mallomar's driver's license from his elk skin medicine bag and handed it to the orderly along with a one-thousand-dollar bill folded into the size of a piece of Wrigley's chewing gum.

Mrs. Mallomar was asleep in her room when Cha pol-loc, dressed in a full eagle feather headdress, gently slid his arms under her and lifted her off the bed. He looked at her belly, which bore a cantaloupe-sized protrusion. Mrs. Mallomar awoke, and stared blurry-eyed into the face of her rescuer.

"Marvin?" She didn't so much recognize his face as she did his breath—which was still not very good.

"Forgive me," the mighty Cha-loc-poc said, and kissed her.

"Am I dreaming?" she asked as he carried her out of the room.

"We are all dreaming."

POSTSCRIPT

Till We Meet Again

It was round-up time. Buster and Stinker were down a little draw looking for strays. Buster found a yearling hiding near the place that Mr. Dominguez had, once upon a time, dropped him off to collect sheep dung. Gently, Buster rousted him out and over the top of the rim when he saw a three riders approaching. They looked like Utes, and had grim expressions on their faces. He shamefully found himself fighting off the Vanadian prejudice that dictated that if you saw an Indian on your property, he's probably there to steal something. Stinker snorted. He could feel Buster's jangled nerves conducting through the reins.

"Easy, old feller."

The men came closer. They had rifles in their scabbards. The two Indians on the flank stopped. The rider in the middle got off his horse. He must have been the big cheese. Slowly, he walked toward him and didn't stop until his nose was almost touching Buster's. The Indian didn't say anything, but handed Buster an official-looking envelope. Then he got back on his horse, and with his braves, road away. Opening the envelope, Buster discovered that it was the deed to the Mallomar ranch.

Cha-pol-lac returned to the reservation with his wife, Shaman Longfeather, Lilly, Lolly, and a menagerie of crippled animals that he intended to cure, time allowing. His people provided him with a double-wide trailer. The Elders, as well as the pit bosses and croupiers from the new Ute Casino, came to bless it. Sage was burnt. A six-hundred-pound steer was slaughtered—its brain offered to Cha-pol-loc. He humbly demurred and passed it on to the Great Spirit as an offering. If he hadn't, his fellow tribesmen would have known he was a fraud and possibly assassinated him. Everyday was a new tightrope that Cha-pol-loc, the Messenger, had to walk, but then again, he had survived Wall Street and the SEC.

ꕤ

DANA WENT INTO LABOR. Before this, Dana could never have imagined having the slightest thing in common with Jimmy Bayles Morgan. Thirty-six hours of labor trying to bring a giant baby into the world taught her otherwise. She screamed for a cesarean. She begged for an epidural. She whimpered for an episiotomy. But Shaman Longfeather would not allow any of it, believing that the god-awful pain of childbirth would finally focus Dana's psychic energy away from her poisoning ennui and into the meat and potatoes of life. And so it was. After Muatagoci—or Moon as she was called in English—was born, Dana never took another drink. She never took another pill. She no longer needed medicine. She had Heap Big Medicine now.

People in Vanadium wondered what was going to happen to Buster, now that Marvin Mallomar was no longer on the scene in the form of a cash-dispensing white man. Outwardly, Buster appeared to be the same loose-jointed cowboy. He and Destiny had a successful enterprise. The ranch was doing well. That being said, inwardly, Buster was in turmoil. The implications of his true provenance—being a Morgan—weighed heavily upon him. Living in Jimmy's cabin with his new wife did not help. They could have afforded a nice place of their own, but Buster felt that since Jimmy had given it to him—and she was his real mother—he had no choice but to accept what had been bequeathed to him.

And there was something else, something darker. Even though most everybody in town thought of him as kind and caring galoot—secretly, Buster harbored the fear that the Morgan in him would someday show itself. Destiny noticed the change in him, but Buster refused to talk about it. He became quiet and withdrawn. Destiny suggested that he spend some time alone at the sheepherder's wagon to mull things over.

Buster decided to take her up on that. He packed a few days' supplies. Riding up to the old sheepherder's wagon with Stinker and a packhorse, he came upon the resident elk herd. He hadn't yet filled his tag, so he shot a young five-by-five. The rest of the day was spent gutting, skinning, and hanging the quarters in game bags a bear's distance from camp. He kept the elk's heart and roasted it in the same fire pit that he had built, once upon a time, when he sought sanctuary.

It was very quiet as sat looking down the canyon below Lame Horse Mesa. He ate his supper. Elk heart wasn't necessarily the best tasting part of an elk, but the Indians believed that by eating it, the hunter took in the best qualities of the animal that gave up life for him. And that's just what Buster was contemplating when a curious thing happened. The dead fir tree, fifty yards from his field of vision, which for years had been leaning on its young progeny, suddenly went cracking and crashing to the ground. Buster witnessed this and for reasons unknown to him, broke down and cried.

In the morning, he felt a strong desire to go home. He packed up his supplies, hung the elk quarters on panniers and headed down the mountain. As he came out of the woods, he was momentarily discombobulated. Jimmy's cabin, his usual reference point from the ridgeline, was nowhere to be seen. Destiny, determining that they already had quite enough baggage between them, used Buster's absence to burn the rotting place down. He found her with some high school kids calmly stacking planks of salvaged wood to the side. These, she informed her flabbergasted husband, would be used as paneling in the kids' playroom when they built their new house.

Destiny McCaffrey was born for champion barrel racing, real estate, and childbirth. In the six years that followed, she gave Buster four children—Shepard, Morgan, Bayles, and Joe. Of the four, the latter was the apple of Buster's eye. Joe was the winner of the Vanadium Cattle Roping competition five years running. Tall and strong like Buster, she could hit a muskrat at three hundred yards with a Krag .30-.40 iron-sighted rifle. At least, that was what folks in Vanadium said.

Telluride, Colorado
September 11, 2014